I, BRAX
A Battle Divine

A DRAGON ASSASSIN ADVENTURE

I, BRAX

1: A BATTLE DIVINE

A DRAGON ASSASSIN ADVENTURE

ARTHUR SLADE

I, BRAX: A BATTLE DIVINE
A Dragon Assassin Adventure
By Arthur Slade

Shadowpaw Press
Regina, Saskatchewan, Canada
www.shadowpawpress.com

Trade Paperback ISBN: 978-1-998273-26-3

Shadowpaw Press is grateful for
the financial support of Creative Saskatchewan.

For Ryan, Reece and Richelle.
And anyone who likes goats.

CONTENTS

CHAPTER I

AN ILLOGICAL DISCUSSION

My little pet of an assassin was going to get me killed. And it would all be the fault of her idealistic ways.

On the sandy land below us, a scene was presenting itself that I, Brax, dragon extraordinaire, knew would be messy and ugly to fly into.

Carmen looked at that same scene and came to a different conclusion.

The problem with mortals is that they have very tiny brainpans and very tiny brains that fit loosely inside those brainpans. That's why, with my sensitive dragon ears, I hear a rattle whenever they shake their heads. How they put two thoughts together is beyond the understanding of even my massive intellect.

The aggravating young woman standing in front of me was shaking her head, making that teeny rattling as she struggled to put together a half-formed thought.

"No, Brax," Carmen said. "You are wrong."

I ignored the fact she'd said I was wrong because one

must forgive creatures with tiny brains. She was still wearing her assassin cloak even though a long time had passed since she'd worked as an assassin. Her sword was out, and her spine set straight as if she were the most powerful creature in the world. Her dark hair had one strip of grey in it, though Carmen was still somewhere around seventeen summers. The grey did not indicate wisdom. "We must save them," she added.

The "them" she mentioned were circled below us. It was a wagon train of the stocky, grunting onion farmers common to this area of the Akkad Empire. Thick necks. Thick arms. Thick legs and thick brainpans. Yes, I'm stuck on brainpans today. My apologies. These farmers, fleeing a beastly drought, had tied their livestock to their two-wheeled wagons, stuffed their beds with farming implements and bags of food, and set off across a ragged patch of desert in search of what they hoped would be a land of milk and honey and gold pieces.

Instead, they found only death.

For, surrounding them and edging closer, jaws glistening with slobber, were a congregation of ammits. "Congregation" was a stupid word for these monsters, but that's what humans called a group of ammits. Yes, ammit sounds like a neutered swearword—and perhaps it is because they are the children of some long-lost Akkadian goddess whose name was likely being used in vain. An ammit had the head of a crocodile, the front legs of a leopard, and the hindquarters of a hippopotamus, which gave them an ugly appearance. Very, very, very ugly. These ammits were slowly making smaller and smaller circles around the farmers. The creatures did like to feast on flesh, and with the continued creaking and cracking and breaking up of the Akkad

Empire, the soldiers who used to patrol the roads and rid the land of these beasts were now too busy fighting on the borderlands.

"We must save them," Carmen repeated. I wouldn't describe it as a pleading tone. It was more of a petulant insistence. Yes, perhaps we have been travelling together for too long. We had been flying high above this scene, on our way to the city of Akkadium to deliver tidings from my sister, the queen of dragons, when Carmen had spotted this scene below us. She'd insisted that I land, which meant coming out of the high-speed air current, and slowing down from that great speed was a tiring process.

"I'm too hungry to save anyone today," I announced.

"Brax," Carmen said. She had a very aggravating way of saying my name like it was a profanity only used when one discovers a squished stink beetle on the bottom of one's foot.

"I *am* hungry," I said. The powerful timbre of my voice squeaked a little. It was something my father's royal vocal trainer would have rewarded with several lashes. "I have only had one goat since sunrise. That's not enough food to fight ammits."

"You are purposely aggravating me because of what I said." She waved her sword around to accent her words. That sword was named Lilith and had once belonged to the greatest of all assassins, Banderius. I didn't like it pointing in my direction. Partly because it had several spell runes etched into its blade. Also because I believe it to be evil. And finally, because I had killed Banderius, so a part of my mind believed the sword wanted revenge.

"I am not that petty," I replied. The truth is that while I may be a prince of Drachia, I am the king of pettiness.

"I only made that comment out of concern," she said.

"Your scales look only a pinch more translucent, and I know how sensitive —"

"Dragons are never sensitive!" A tiny torch of flame burst out of my nostrils. It's hard to contain the awesome power that exists inside my body.

" —and how reactive you are to any question about your appearance. But lately, there hasn't been the same lustre to your scales. I worry you are not getting enough seed oil. Or fruits."

"Fruits?" I coughed out the word like it was poison. "When have you seen me eat fruits?"

"Well, rarely enough." She now put her sword away, which meant she was content to stab me with words. "Put my observation down as the concern of a friend. A best friend. That is all." She might as well have added "only friend."

"My scales are perfect," I said. "Why are we talking about them again?"

"Would it help if I said they look better today?"

"No. That doesn't help. You should not have brought it up. And besides —" I lifted a talon to slice the air and illustrate my point " —you have so many things to apologize for. This *observation* is the least of your trespasses."

My left eye, that is, my mortal eye, was tearing up a little. Whether it was the dryness of the air or some emotion, I had no desire to find out. It is a long story about how I got a human eye, but the basic part of it is that this meek-looking mortal beside me one day plucked out my left eye, put it in her own head (she was already missing an eye, otherwise that move would have been squishy) and, over time, a mortal eye grew in mine.

Anyway, I don't like to dwell on that minor episode. Instead, I squinted and, with my dragon eye, noticed that the ammits were getting dangerously close to the mortals. I'd once tangled with these horrid creatures, and I knew they could move that bulk and ugliness with surprising speed. These ones were cleverly getting their prey within striking distance before unleashing that speed. There weren't any hired guards with this collection of mortals, only one large farmer with a spear and a loud, shouting voice. He'd be the first to die.

Even from this distance, I spotted a space between the ammits where the onion farmers could race their wagons and be free of danger. Most of the mortals would make it out alive if they charged through this opening. They could leave the grandpas, grandmas, and some livestock behind to occupy the ammits. But, as I mentioned earlier, mortals do not have very large brainpans.

I decided my observation deserved to be shared. "They could abandon the old mortals and old cows and flee. It's a logical sacrifice."

"Brax! That isn't funny!" she hissed.

This was genuine anger because normally, she would have a big, long, blistering complaint about my lack of humanity (I'm a dragon!). She would look down her nose at me (even though she was looking up) and go on and on and on. Instead, my name was used like a knife.

"Dragons would leave their old ones. And the old ones would be honoured to go out fighting."

"Brax!" she repeated.

I sighed and unfurled my wings. They had far too many scars in them, and most had been sliced or poked or burned there after I'd met her. I, Braxas Andorium, Prince of Drachia, was taking orders from a mortal. A mere, insufferable mortal.

Brax!

This time, she spoke inside my head. Oh, how I longed for the days when I had the inside of my skull to myself. But ever since she'd stolen my eye, I'd been stuck with her voice in my head, too. My name echoed around several times. Then I sighed and lowered my legs only slightly because I didn't want to make her ascension onto my back too easy. She ran the few feet between us, jumped, and landed behind the spike that she preferred to grip.

"This is going to stink." I spread my wings, dug in my talons for that extra little burst of speed, and leaped into the air.

"What do you mean?" Carmen asked. And I will admit to feeling a sense of relish at the horrid experience she was about to have. My little assassin had never faced ammits before. They were on my list of beasties to avoid for several reasons, but one sticky one in particular.

"Oh, you'll discover the meaning of my warning," I said, working my wings harder. "Think about the worst thing camels do, and then you'll know."

"Why are you bringing up camels?"

"Hold on!" I said. For I had perhaps played this game with her too long, and the ammits were about to pounce on the mortals.

I snapped my wings even faster but kept myself centred. I did not want her to fall off because I don't know what would happen then.

Oh, parts of her would break—mortals are like little

porcelain dolls. But what would seeing a broken Carmen do to me?

Anyway, such deep thoughts were pushed aside as we rushed toward what was soon to be our battlefield.

It really, really was going to stink.

CHAPTER 2

THE MOST EGREGIOUSLY HORRIBLE PART

We closed the distance to the onion farmers in a few heartbeats. Even though I am a Scythian dragon—the best type of all dragons—my smooth, impressive speed still sometimes surprises me. It also surprised the mortals, who, until that point, were concentrating on the ammits. In fact, one particularly pudgy spear-wielding man let out a shriek that would not have been considered manly in his culture.

I am used to mortals fearing dragons. We are rather awesome and awe-inspiring, and the sight of us has led to many mortals taking their pantaloons to be laundered. But his shriek was not helpful at all. To accent it, he pointed with his thick fingers and released a second high-pitched cry of fear. This gave the ammits ample warning of my approach.

Ammits are slow-witted when lying around in the sun, but once in the heat of the hunt, they become as clever as crocodiles and quick as jaguars. So, as I slashed downward, intending to strip open the back of the unsuspecting ammit with my talons, it turned and, using those cat-fast legs, jumped to one side.

And spat.

That was the horrible part.

The acidic projectile, a brownish, lumpy substance about the size of a mortal head, flew with speed, hitting above my eye and splooshing down my scaly cheek. A portion of the projectile splashed into Carmen's face.

"By Belaz, goddess of assassins, what is this?" she shouted. "It burns and . . . and it stinks!"

"I warned you this would be stinky," I said, holding back my laughter to prevent ingesting the spittle. "And it's only going to get worse."

The globule had blocked my mortal eye, which was fine since it was my weakest eye. I breathed through my mouth. I had caught only a tiny sniff of the odour, and the stink was enough to curl my nostrils inside out.

But Carmen, who was unprepared, was smacked full force with the most powerfully disgusting smell in all the worlds. Imagine a cesspool fed from a thousand cities and squished down to the size of that ammit spit. That is what hit us. And the reek was literally eye-watering.

"How do you feel now?" I said. The relish in my voice was tempered by the fact I couldn't completely block out the stench. I'd had the pleasure of smelling it twice before and had learned to keep a distance from these monsters. It was best not to think of what processes were failing inside their stomachs to create such a stench. There was one more property about this spit that I feared but couldn't remember what it was.

My dragon eye began watering, making the world a little blurry. I lost track of the ammits and the mortals and felt like if I stopped flapping my wings, I'd stay floating forever.

"It's so horrible," Carmen said. "Once again, you are right, Brax, and you are the most brilliant of all dragons in all the lands. I will never, ever doubt you. Your intellect is only matched by your undeniable handsomeness and the natural shine of your scales."

"You are so right to say that, Carmen," I replied, blinking my eyes several times. "And don't forget to mention how incredible I am at chess and marbles. And checkers. Right? Right?"

Several moments of silence passed.

"What on Ellos are you talking about?" Carmen said. "Chess! Checkers? You sound crazy."

A mental bubble popped in my brain. And I remembered the aspect of this horrid liquid projectile I had forgotten about.

"Oh," I said. "The ammit spit is also hallucinogenic. If you see things or say things that are . . . well, more weird and stupid than usual, you'll know."

"I'll keep that in mind," she replied.

I shook my head to clear my thoughts and my vision. The ammits were still chasing their prey, and the mortals were still fleeing. It had been a rather good hallucinogenic dream.

Was enduring this stink worth saving a few mortals?

In answer to that unspoken question, Carmen drew her dagger. I was uncertain what she would do with it from that height, but mortals are sometimes very good at posing.

Instead of posing, she threw it at the nearest ammit, striking him in the skull, and he fell, rolled over several times, and was dead.

I will admit, rare as a purple moon, she surprises me with her skill. She can be a useful partner to have. That blow meant that three ammits remained with their three sewer-spitting mouths. All we had to do was avoid their grotesque globules and their claws—getting a scratch or a bite by an ammit would lead to a horrendous infection and green limb loss. That was not its official name, but described what the wound would look like—green with an endless amount of pus. Then your limb falls off.

Something struck my wing and stuck into it. A spear! I glanced down to see that the falsetto farmer had a rather effective throwing arm. He had hit me as we flew over the shrieking, useless mortals. And, by the luckiest of throws, struck me right in a tiny space between scales. It stung and stayed in place.

"You idiot!" I shouted. "We're on your side!"

My eyes had cleared enough to turn back toward our four-legged enemies. An ammit launched another glob of stinkery, but I dodged it. Perhaps if the winged gods were kind, the spit would land on that man. But I hadn't turned sharply enough to strike the ammit. Ugh, I'd have to fly around again.

Without a word of warning, Carmen reached out and yanked the spear from my wing.

"OW!" I shouted. "That hurt!"

She didn't hear my glorious cry of pain because she had already jumped from my back at full speed, straight at the creature, spear held out with both hands. She does that sometimes: leaps from a secure, safe position where I can watch over her and becomes all stabby and brave. It's the tiny brainpan again, paired with the dragon strength that burns in her veins. My dragon strength, I should add. It often causes her to take on more than she can chew (an old dragon saying). Or should I say more than she can stab? And then I must flap in and save her.

It's eternally frustrating.

Then I saw what had caused her mortal heart to flutter and jump. The ammit was now pursuing a tiny mortal—a girl who looked to be only eight summers old. That was another thing about Carmen. She was always thinking about the little people. The downtrodden. The about-to-be-eaten. If she's not saving a slave, she's helping an old man kill an emperor. She's like that. But her being off my back meant I was lighter and could turn a pinch faster, avoiding yet another of the bilious projectiles sent my way by the nearest ammit.

I dashed down, grabbed that ammit by the hide, and lifted it into the air. They are not light—as I said, they are part hippopotamus—and the weight nearly made my wings rip off, but I flapped higher and higher, the stenchy creature hissing and twisting, trying to snap my legs in its crocodile mouth.

After a few moments of this struggle, my endlessly powerful muscles tired, and I realized that perhaps carrying something of such size was not the best idea I'd had. In fact, in a few moments, I would likely crash, and the next thing I knew, the ammit would be on me, tearing, biting, and spitting.

It's the spitting I feared most.

But then the winged fates shone favour on me. For I came across a rather steep incline and, with a massive effort, tossed the ammit over the edge of what used to be a river-bank but was now a deep, dried-out valley. The creature rolled and hissed and spat until it hit a stone and another stone and another until it eventually lay still. Dead on a long-dead riverbed.

That left two ammits.

One, I corrected myself, for when I turned back to the fray, I saw Carmen had used the spear expertly. She never paid attention to me but paid attention to the instructions of her maestrus, and they had taught her well how to stick pointy things into fleshy creatures. The ammit was dead. Alas, her maestrus hadn't instructed her on how to control her emotions, for she was supposed to continue dispatching our enemies, but instead took the little girl by the hand and led her to her parents.

"Kill all your enemies before you go for hugs," I shouted. The distance meant she turned her head, then put her hand to her ear. Clearly, my wit hadn't reached her. Once again, it was up to me to clean up this mess.

The last ammit, not the smartest of the group, had grabbed the spear-throwing mortal by his shoulder and was dragging him along, leaving a trail of dust behind. The ammits had a habit of carrying their food back to their dens and eating them over a fortnight. It was best not to become that food and best not to picture the misery of being surrounded by stink, losing your limbs one by one.

The ammit somehow believed it would make it to safety, even though it had recently observed one of its companions being destroyed by a creature perfectly designed by the fates for killing and eviscerating other creatures.

Me, that is.

I was about to race in the ammit's direction when I saw Carmen leave the girl with her parents, run several yards and leap toward the ammit, drawing her sword at the same time. I'm sure it felt like an impressive leap for a mortal. But since they have such short legs and no wings, it became obvious she was going to fall embarrassingly short. Being kind and caring and very dexterous, I snapped her up by the hood of her cloak and dropped her on the back of the creature.

The ammit released the man, who I was disappointed to see still had all of his parts, and turned its head to snap its jaws at Carmen.

My Carmen.

She gave it a poke with her sword, and that was enough for the beast; it bucked her off and fled, loping in a hippopotamus-wolf-leopardy kind of way, which, as anyone who has tried to describe their running style knows, is very hard to describe.

"Brax," Carmen said. "He's yours." It sounded like a command. Oh, these mortals, with their tiny breakable bones and their colossal egos.

"Yes, yes," I said, spreading my wings and picking up speed. "If he gets away, more of these horrible two-legged creatures who pollute the earth with their horrid poetry will die. I see that. I'll risk getting another shot of stink."

I swept after the ammit, impressed by the creature's speed. This one had found a deeper passion for living and was at the peak of its galloping hippopotoloping, occasionally looking back over its shoulder. The thing even crashed through a few dead bushes, making an impressive racket.

As I winged toward him, the beastie shot a spit of great disgust at me, and I dodged to the side. "Ha!" I shouted. "You have to be a better aim than that."

But the moment my words were out of my mouth, yet another spewing of this horrid stench globule hit me in the face. This time in my dragon eye. Which meant the ammit had been smart enough to send a warning shot and guess where I would be next.

My eye watered, my nostrils watered, my *soul* even watered at the smell, and it forced me to stare through my lesser eye, my mortal eye, the one I got from Carmen all those ages ago. How mortals even got around with eyes that see such a short distance was a mystery. But at least it was a beautiful shade of blue. I kept staring at the ammit. I even fought off the hallucinations, which included several luscious lambs floating through the sky on white wings. They were very hard to ignore.

He tried his same trick, and I double-dodged him, which meant I was right over the monster and, well, angry. And when I'm angry, my flames burn a little hotter. So, I set to with a blast that would bring down an armoured elephant. I won't describe the sight of hairy flesh melting or the crackly sound of his hide burning as if I had suddenly blanketed him in lava, but, well, it was all mixed in with the stench of a burning cesspool.

It takes skill to burn and fly, and when I was certain the beast was dead and gone, I landed beside what was now a pile of ashes in the form of an ammit. There were also several bits of grass and a brush that were burning.

I hoped that my powerful, flaming display would make those mortals give me a little more respect. One particularly overzealous farmer might even apologize for sticking me with a spear and offer me a goat in compensation. Or ten goats. I'd take ten. But none of the mortals were looking my way.

I turned back to the ashes because my clever mind had thought of a question. "I bet that was a hot experience," I said, disappointed that the ammit would never hear my wittiness. And never make a reply. Not that ammits could talk.

But I will admit that I, Brax, was surprised when the pile of ashes spoke.

"I have taken the measure of you," a woman's voice said. "And I will lacerate you from liver to limb for your transgressions."

CHAPTER 3
AN ASHY TALK

First off, I had never heard ashes speak before. And I hadn't noticed that this particular ammit was female, but it is hard to tell. They are so hippopotamy and leopardy and crocodily that it gets confusing.

"Uh, how is it you speak?" I looked down at the ash pile, which was still. The voice had been calm and powerful. And much to my chagrin, I had to give the ashes a compliment. "And using 'I'll lacerate you from liver to limb' as a threat—I really appreciate the creativity. The use of the 'l' sound in lacerate, liver, and limb adds a poetic sauciness to the taunt. Pair that with the image of a wound from there to here is perfectly frightening. I'll use that liver-to-limb threat in the future—actually, better yet, I'll do it and then say it! Thank you so very much!"

The ashes didn't move. Nor did they answer. A pawful of moments passed, so I wondered if I was being beguiled by the hallucinatory aspect of the stink spit. This was proven to be true when several purple mushrooms, each about a foot high, grew out of the ashes. Then they sprouted legs and scuttled away, whistling a jaunty tune.

I glanced over at Carmen, who continued to deal with the onion farmers while holding the little girl's hand. My partner had seen none of my impressively destructive display of murder or the purple mushrooms. Of course, they likely weren't there.

"Ah, so it *is* the ol' stink-spit hallucinations. Again." I said this aloud because sometimes, hearing my voice made me feel saner. There are philosophers who argue that self-talk isn't a good habit to get into, but it works for me. "No more mushrooms," I added. "Please. Especially ones with legs."

The pile of ammit ashes obeyed my request: it didn't move, speak, or do anything oddly surreal. I turned away, but a motion caught my attention. The ashes began swirling around. I fully expected more mushrooms to appear and dreaded that these might have eyes. I hated mushrooms with eyes. Fungi shouldn't be able to stare at you. "Please, stop," I said. "Please."

But the ashes didn't listen. First, they formed into an ancient symbol: the sun surrounded by a snake. Then they slowly rose higher and higher, like a contained whirlwind, and with that movement, my nostrils caught a scent that reminded me of flowering lotuses.

Not that I spend much time sniffing flowers.

But as I sniffed and watched, two rather thick, hairy but mortal-like legs appeared—it was grey hair—everything was ashen coloured. This was followed by a chain-mail skirt. Then the torso formed out of the swirling ash, a rather scaly and leathery torso, in that a leather vest covered it. And finally, a head appeared, high enough that we were eye to eye.

I glanced back to see if Carmen was watching because I knew this sudden rising out of the ashes would look very impressive from a distance. But simple, soft Carmen was down on one knee chatting with that tiny mortal girl. Ugh, she was missing this because of some horrid emotional moment.

"Carmen! Look! Look!" I shouted. But she didn't turn her head. Instead, she reached out to pull a bramble from the girl's hair. Double ugh! And the girl was handing her one of Carmen's daggers, which she might have yanked from a dead ammit. The sweetness of the scene was sickening.

Although the scene made me wonder if Carmen had been that cute when she was younger. That would explain her ability to survive assassin school.

Anyway, the face in the ashes was taking its time becoming a proper shape, but the mortal-like apparition now stood about twelve feet tall. Shorter than a giant by a lot and slightly shorter than a Zarek, which is a type of purple mage giant I never wanted to see again. There were leopard-like spots on the muscled-yet-feminine arms. An ashen-grey necklace of rubies hung on her throat.

Then the face formed: it was like a mortal's, except it stretched out with a reptilian snout populated by long, sharp teeth.

The blank ash eyes rolled toward me. I will admit to feeling a minute chill down my spine. And a tiny, tiny voice in the back of my head warned me I was in a terrible situation. Something about this scene reminded me of my time as a young dragon reading every book in the Royal Library of Dreki, for I had memorized the history of the dragons and the mortals and had taken a keen interest in the various gods, goddesses, and titans that the mortals had worshiped. This tall female creature had been illustrated in one of those books, but my perfect and mostly memorable mind couldn't recall exactly who she was.

Only that she was bad. That's what the tiny voice was screaming.

"You have angered me, winged creature," the ashen woman said. "You will tremble before my awesome power."

"Uh," I said, gesturing with one of my talons. "I have news for you. You are a floating pile of ashes. One good huff and this conversation is over." I puffed out some air, but the ashes didn't change shape—in fact, I worried that they were growing more solid. "And I'm not a simple winged creature. I am a dragon. Clearly, a paragon of winged creatures, and—"

"You have murdered my children," she said. "For that, you will be filleted, fried, and fed to fowls."

"I love your threats," I replied, truly meaning the compliment. I pointed at the dead ammits some distance away. "These are your children? If this is what you produce for offspring, you may want to look into being childless."

One ashy leopard-spotted arm raised up, and a long finger with a claw at the end pointed toward me. "The weak rely on their humour for bravery."

"I'm proof you can be brave and funny." The tingling in my spine was getting more, well, tingly. Why would my perfect mind not remember who she was?

"I will boil your intestines for soup and tear out your intellect piece by piece."

"You are very good at threatening. Really, you are. But you are still ashes and a dramatic voice. That part is not so impressive."

"I am above trading words with such an insignificant creature."

This was getting my gander up. Not dander, which happened in humans and dogs when they got angry. A gander was a male goose, and they were the most frightening of all winged creatures when angered. Every magnificent dragon has an inner gander. "Insignificant! I am a prince among dragons, a god to these mortals here, and you—"

"Still thy overused tongue!" Her voice didn't get any louder but somehow drowned me out. "You may have enough brainpower to pass on this news to the inhabitants of these lands: I am coming. You can tell the mortals and any other creatures. Herald them with the news that I am coming, and they will be dust and bones before me."

"I'm not a town crier," I said. "You tell them. Besides, I don't know your name."

"YOU COULD NOT CONTAIN MY NAME!" Then, with a speed I couldn't have counteracted, the ashes slashed toward me. The claws carved five deep lines in my snout.

"Ouch!" I reared back, put a paw to the bleeding tracks there. So much for her being a collection of ashes. She had briefly become a part of this world. I got the feeling she was reaching from another realm. Whether it was the land of the spirits or somewhere worse, I wasn't certain.

"Tell them, winged creature, that I will dance on the broken temples of their dead gods. I am coming, and all will fall before me."

"I'll tell you a thing or two," I started, but she raised her hand. This time, I could see the claws at the end of her fingers shining like metal.

"I will remove your head, stuff it, and place it in the pit of everlasting pain," she said. Another marvellous threat! And now that I was bleeding, I believed she could make that threat, and all the other creative threats, come true. That tingling fright in my spine was now ringing like a bell in my head.

"I shall assume," she said, "since you are silent, that your limited intellect has given you the power to understand my words and accept your doom. Do as I command, tiny creature. I am coming. First shall their leaders fall. Then everything will follow. Warn them. Do not fail at this task."

I opened my mouth, hoping that a witty reply would burst out, but at that moment, the ashes lost shape and fell to the dry ground.

"Joke's on you." I poked gingerly at the ashes. They didn't spring up again or lash out. "You didn't even tell me your name. Ha! Now I have to say 'what's-her-name' is coming! And no one will take me seriously. Ha. Ha. Ha!"

I stopped talking by actually biting down on my tongue. My blathering was taking over my mind, and blather suggested a minuscule amount of fear.

But I wasn't above taking revenge. I puffed out a huff of air from my excellent lungs, and the dust and ashes blew away, mixing with the sandy ground.

It was as if she had never been here.

I looked over to where the mortals and Carmen were standing. They were all listening to her, which suggested she was in the middle of a lecture. If so, it was probably about hygiene, ethics, or how she had tamed me by tearing out my eye. Not one mortal was looking my way, which meant no one had seen the powerful ash creature I had confronted and scared away.

No one would believe me.

As you can see, this day was turning out just perfect.

CHAPTER 4
NOT ABOUT YOU

You are probably wondering who *you* are or who it is that I keep referring to.

Don't worry, I won't do it too often, for it would be distracting.

Yes, I keep mentioning and talking to you as you read this. It's all because this is my diary, which I am etching on vellum in my spare time when Carmen isn't forcing me into situations where I get stabbed, poked, or burned by fireballs. Despite that pain or because of it, I believe that in the future, they will want to know why Prince Braxus Andorium, son of Xerx, brother of Kon who is now deceased, humbly stepped aside to let his recently revived sister Brenna become the queen of the great land of Drachia.

It was better for the world and for Brax's peace of mind.

I imagine that dragon historians and mortal historians and all historians of every time period and all realms, including those on other worlds, will read these scrolls. For it was Brax who brought down the Akkad Empire, fought the giants to a standstill, and even faced one of the First Ones, Deathwings. Yes, nearly every moment of my life—I mean Brax's life—has been something to write about. Mortals may quibble about whether they aided me in these endeavours (especially one particularly whiny assassin), but I am the lever who pried history into better, more pleasant directions.

Me. Brax. The mighty destroyer of goats.

I am certain there are those who are curious about how a dragon bonded with one of those humans and allowed that young mortal to sit upon his royal back. It's a little too embarrassing to write about. But maybe, by the fact that it happened, something of the bigness of Brax's heart will be revealed to you.

Those are a few of the heroic and wonderful things I've done in my life. But I am also a poet. I don't mean that I write anything as ridiculous as rhymes. No, I am a poet of thoughts—a philosophic creator of clever sayings. And I know that many of the sayings I come up with and phrases that I phrase will be spoken throughout the world and stamped in philosophy tomes or even on the signs of pubs for many ages to come.

I am being humble here, but my words will change the world, and they will usher in a brighter day, and a golden age called the Age of Brax's Wonderful Thoughts and Aren't We Lucky That He Existed.

My stomach is rumbling right now, so I'm losing interest in you. I'm just writing all this down because it entertains me. And if we aren't being entertained, we aren't living.

So, who are you?

I don't know. And I don't care. Figure that out on your

own. I hope for you the best life and that there are many goats in your future. And if reading my words gets you closer to those glorious experiences, then I have accomplished something.

CHAPTER 5
A TALE RETOLD

I walked back to the mortals instead of flying, as mortals get all wide-eyed and hidey when a dragon is in the air. A walking dragon is also threatening, but it at least isn't above them. Me lowering myself (literally) to their level and crawling along gave them the time to accept the fact that a creature of such amazing power was about to be amongst them.

Also, I was tired. The fight and, more importantly, the conversation with the monstrously large ash woman was stuck in my head. Usually, the only conversationalists who tired me out by talking were fans of the Cryden: The Soul Singer series of books, which were boring tales of a minstrel. Anyone who read them was also clearly boring.

Carmen finished the lecture she had been delivering to the mortals, and the group of them, as one, edged away when I stood beside her. That included the tiny-brainpan man who had pierced me with his spear. He had very wide eyes that reminded me of boiled eggs, except his eyes held less intelligence.

"You are safe with us, dear farmers," Carmen said. "Brax is a friend."

"I want to poke that one with a talon," I said, indicating the balding spear chucker. "Right through the shoulder. After all, he poked me. And you're all about things being fair, Carmen. Eye for an eye, right?"

The man paled, and his eyes continued to widen to the point they threatened to pop out. He glanced from me to her and back to me again. "Is . . . is your dragon being serious?"

"If his lips are flapping, he is not serious," Carmen said. "When he is serious, he's silent, and he acts."

"First," I said, now forced to give my own lecture to these lesser beings, "my lips don't flap. And second, since she didn't correct you, I will: I'm not *her* dragon. This is a very important point. Mortals always think they can possess everything, including creatures that are more sentient than them. I am NOT a possession. I allow her to ride on my back as a favour to all of mortalkind so that at least one of you meatbags can experience the majesty of dragon flight. Otherwise, your entire existence would be pointless. Understand?"

I'm afraid I was so engaged with the topic that a little spittle came out. The man nodded several times at great speed and dodged most of my outburst.

"Anyway," I continued. "You should gather in your wagons. The ammits are vanquished thanks to me and slightly thanks to her, and you are safe for the rest of your journey. A little tip, though: if you get in this situation again, sacrifice your elders."

"He doesn't mean that," Carmen said. "You and your elders should be safe until you reach your destination."

"You won't be coming with us?" the little girl asked. She

did have cute eyes and a button nose. I could hear the dripping of Carmen's heart melting.

"No, alas, sweet child, we won't," Carmen explained gently. "You have these adults to keep you safe."

The rabble gathered before us did not look like they could protect themselves from rabid rabbits, but I kept my glorious mouth shut.

"We need protection!" the spear-thrower whined. "There may be more ammits. And bandits. And other untold dangers."

"No," I replied. "You couldn't afford us. Your goats are too scrawny, and besides, we're not guardians. We are royal messengers, and we have more important things to do than keeping onion farmers alive. I don't even eat onions."

"What Brax is saying is that we know you'll be safe because you are travelling the path we just flew over, and we saw no enemies." She reached out and shook the spear-thrower's hand. "Good luck in your travels."

"Thank you," he said to her. He didn't thank me. Instead, he backed away as if expecting I would leap over and slice him into several pieces. Ungrateful two-legged creature!

We watched as they rounded up their wagons and belongings. Soon, they were on their way to a lifetime of planting, digging, eating and selling onions. The lives some people lived!

"Well, I hope you gave them a lasting lecture," I said. "Was it about how important dragons are to the limited intellectual literature of mortals?"

"They were coming from Omus, where the drought is," she said, clearly ignoring my cultural dig. "And hoping to travel to Daega." This was one of the two reborn countries that had popped up as the Akkad Empire fell apart. One can conquer a land but not conquer its spirit. The collapse of the empire happened because I, Carmen, and a collection of armies had leaned on the empire a little, and it had fallen over. So careless of us.

But I was reminded of how much the mortals of Ellos owed me. I assumed they'd soon be building Brax statues in every village and city square across all the realms.

"Well, I have news," I said. My eyes were still watering from the ammit spit. "I made a new friend."

"A new friend?" Carmen said. "What are you talking about?"

"Well, first I burned the final and strongest ammit to ashes, then, when I least expected it, a voice rose out of those selfsame ashes and . . ." I continued in a spellbinding manner, telling her about how those ashes had spoken to me. I skipped over the part about the walking mushrooms. But even as I told the tale, it sounded a little like madness. My stupid mortal eye continued to produce ammit-spit tears, and I wiped it with the back of my paw as I repeated everything the tall, ashy woman had said. "And then she told me to tell everyone that she was coming. But the jest is on her because she didn't give me her name. In fact, she said I couldn't contain it, whatever that means!"

Carmen, looking back at me with my own dragon eye (and her mortal one), waited patiently until I was finished before picking at my story like an assassin vulture picking at a beautiful corpse. "Are you sure it wasn't a hallucination?" she asked. "I saw some horrible things right after getting the spit in the face. Those imaginary phantasms seem to be gone now. That manure-spit was . . ." She shook her head as if trying to find a word to describe it—an impossible task.

"Anyway, it's a smell I never want to experience again. I saw my maestrus as crows cawing lessons at me at one point."

"That sounds completely normal. Maestrus are very bird-like."

"You joke," she said. "But you've never had to face an angry maestru. Only my dragon eye got me through the situation."

"Yes, and you're lucky to have that." I sniffed in through one nostril, which produced a whistling sound I know aggravates her. "Thanks again to me and my wonderful generosity. But I am certain—I mean mostly certain—that this scaly goddess was really there. And she seemed familiar. She did. Really."

Carmen raised one of her eyebrows. "A tall mortal-looking creature with hairy legs and leopard-spotted arms and an extended crocodile-like toothy maw was familiar to you?"

"Yes, well . . . umm . . . she looked a bit like the ammits, of course, which I realize sounds odd. But she was smarter. A lot smarter than them. Though not smart enough to laugh at my amazing wordplay."

"And where did you see her before?" Carmen asked. Was she believing me?

"That's the thing. It's something that I read a long time ago, so it isn't emblazoned in my memory. And before you go on about how important literature is, remember it is we dragons who invented words."

That last statement got her to cross her arms. "I'm not sure that theory of yours has been proven. But where will we find out who you were supposedly speaking to?"

"Back in the Royal Dreki library is a book that has her picture. I'm certain of it."

"You are suggesting we go all the way back to Dreki so you can read a book that may or may not be about an imaginary goddess woman who rose out of the ashes?" She said this gently, but the doubt in her voice was cutting.

I pointed at my snout. "That imaginary creature sliced through Scythian scales."

"That's not even a scratch," she said.

Now that I looked at the end of my snout, which unfortunately made me a little cross-eyed, I saw the claw marks weren't as deep as I'd thought. In fact, they were barely visible. They had certainly stung. Were they even real? "But, but . . . it was deeper before."

"You were fighting with an ammit, and it very well may have done that damage to you. They are strong despite their ridiculous appearances."

I crossed my forelegs but kept my talons pointing down. "I knew you wouldn't believe me. You're the only one allowed to see interesting visions."

Carmen put her hands on her hips. She liked to rest them right near her weapons. She thought it made her look more confident. "Your sister wants us to deliver a message of welcome to Emperor Lipit and his new heir. That is what we will do."

"Delivering a message to the emperor was something I was not in favour of, anyway," I said. "She could have sent one of her ravens."

"She saw we needed to stretch our wings," she said. "Your wings, I mean."

First, she takes my eye; next, she's eyeing my wings. That's the thing about mortals—they will thieve everything you have. It's in their nature.

"Yes, well, I did promise," I said. "And Queen Brenna,

my dearest sister, has an angry side. She's still not forgiven me for turning her to stone." I took a slow breath. "And the ashy goddess with hairy legs didn't say exactly when she was coming. Goddess-type creatures aren't good at telling time. It may be another thousand years."

"Nor did she say her name," Carmen added. "You would think a powerful entity that could make ashes take form and cut your wonderful snout so deeply would remember to give you her name."

"Yes, well, perhaps she was intimidated by my presence." I put a paw on my snout. "Hey, you said it's a wonderful snout. You noticed." She was only trying to get on my good side, but I accepted it. Carmen was right. Scythian dragon snouts are renowned around the lands. I bet mortals wished they had snouts such as ours.

"Then, is it agreed?" she said. She patted her belt where the message for Emperor Lipit sat. "We will finish our task and then return to Drachia, and at that point, we can visit the royal library to discover who this ashy visitor was."

"Agreed," I said. "In fact, I say we first deliver our message, then we return to my homelands."

She rolled her eyes. "That's what I said."

"You're right, it was my idea," I replied, then stretched out my wings, indicating with a head nod that she should get on my back.

She did so with grace. I will admit, for only two legs, she could be a dexterous creature. I decided not to mention that I had the tiniest bit of admiration for her.

"Maybe we'll get to save more onion farmers," she said.

I bit my tongue and headed for the sky.

Saving more mortals was the last thing I wanted to do today.

CHAPTER 6
A PLACE OF BAD MEMORIES

The flight to Akkadium, capital of the ever-shrinking Akkad empire, went well. By that, I mean there were no more helpless mortals to pluck from the path of disaster, and no piles of recently created ashes rose out of the ground to insult my soul and scratch my snout. One takes one's victories where one can.

As we neared the city, my mind dredged up rotten memories.

"Hey," I said, pointing down with my snout. "Aren't those the same geysers and cliff faces where we fought your brother and plucked out his eye?" I tried to make my tone light, but the answer I got back was very, very heavy.

"Yes. It. Is." Carmen said this through gritted teeth.

I guessed that not enough time had passed since that incident for her to accept a jest about the entire experience. Another sign that mortals are odd. My brother Kon and I would joke about our sibling fights halfway through the fight itself. We were hilarious! I guess Carmen didn't want to remember the horrid side of Corwin, her twin. He was a betrayer, a stabber, a poisoner, and a boaster—really, the perfect assassin. And perhaps she still felt some guilt for the gouging and binding punishment we'd meted out, which included robbing him of his memories. Then we tied him to a swan and sent him far, far away.

He came back as a much different, stranger man.

It already seemed like it had all happened a thousand years ago. He was a wizard and an assassin now and had changed his name and his personality several times in the process—finally, uncreatively, settling on Corwin again as his name. If it isn't all pretend, he is also a kinder and more empathetic young man.

I almost trusted him these days. Though I didn't like the sharp-beaked black swan that he rode. That beast had tried to poke out my eyes on several occasions.

We flew on silently for the next while. The terrible memories kept coming, especially when I glimpsed the distant walls and spires of Akkadium. First, there were the hours and hours I sucked in foul air in a nearby barn beside a manure pit—a very unfond memory. I'd also had a few hundred crossbow bolts loosed at me by the Immortals in an attempt to make me into a flying pin cushion. And finally, the emperor Sargon, who'd grown strong by eating the hearts of wizards, shot holes in my wings with fireballs. It truly was a treasure trove of bad times. I'd put this city on my list of places never to return to and had my sister to thank for sending me back.

The city itself was impressive despite being built by mortals. They had a habit of constructing walls around their cities, and since the Akkad empire had been the largest empire in the history of Ellos, it naturally had the largest walls. These reached out in a star shape to protect part of the port, where I recognized ships from several of the mortal kingdoms: Truskian, Wodenite, Punician, and Avenian. My great mind had learned to recognize these sails from a distance—I guess that happens when you spend too much time at war, either on the same side or against these countries. But the busyness of the port was a sign, too, that the empire was trading again with the other realms.

Calling it an empire was only done so the Akkadians didn't feel bad about losing so much of their power and land. Its leaders, of course, liked grandiose names as much as anything and still preferred to be called emperors. So far, the seven other realms were putting up with that.

It was my sister Brenna who was overseeing the treaties. They could have chosen the Zareks, who were mage giants and incredibly friendly, but Akkad had insisted on dragons, believing they would respect their empire. It turns out Queen Brenna was as fair and cutting as a talon. In fact, I liked to tell my sister she was the fairest of them all.

That's a little joke that only makes sense if you've read mortal books about princesses. You see, it's a play on how fair princesses were held hostage by ugly dragons . . . oh, it would take too long to explain.

"It is such a beautiful and ugly city," Carmen said.

"Yes," I replied. "It reflects the Akkadians perfectly."

Akkadium, which had never been captured, had lost some of its glow. Maybe it was all the reparations the empire was paying to the other realms. Despite that drain on its treasury, the city was the finest of all the mortal cities, though I'm certain the Avenians, with their marvellous libraries and myriad columns, would argue with that conclusion. Emperor Augillian—yes, I studied mortal history in royal school, if only to laugh at their tiny accomplishments—had levelled the original city and built this perfect shining jewel on the edge of the desert and the Ursa Sea. From a distance, the star-shaped walls, designed to keep any mortal armies at bay, were impressive, even though they wouldn't be all that great against armies of dragons. That said, they had magic wards to protect them from attacks from the air. For any mortal city to stand more than a thousand years was an accomplishment.

As we swept over the walls, I expected ballista bolts to be loosed upon us or magic wards to boom and warn the Akkadians of our presence. But all was quiet in terms of lethal responses. There were soldiers on the wall. Even from this height, I could see that their armour was duller and cheaper than the regiments I had faced. These soldiers clearly had been forewarned not to shoot at dragons. It was bad for business, considering Drachia also traded with Akkad, and if there was an attack on a royal dragon, a gigantic Quant dragon might be sent to roll around in the city until the palace and other buildings were reduced to dust.

"That place still frightens me," Carmen admitted. "So much death and power there."

I glanced back to see that Carmen was staring at one particular structure that was a major part of the Imperial Palace: the White Tower. It was where wizards had been sent to die by Emperor Sargon. Carmen had been inside that place of death, and it had nearly drained her into a physical and spiritual raisin. The tower still stood and glowed, the magic of the wizards' and witches' blood keeping it strong.

"Well, it is a rather evil creation," I finally said. "Thankfully, we don't have to go in there."

The palace itself had been built on the tallest hill and was surrounded by smooth marble walls. Naram-Sin, the Executioner, who was also called the Architect, designed it. I don't like to say this about mortal buildings because dragon-built buildings are so much larger and more impressive, but for creatures with such small brainpans and tiny, tiny hands they can create works of great wonder. Of course, it involves a lot of slavery on their part (then again, dragons were not immune to using a few slaves here and there in our history).

As we crossed over the walls of the palace, the Akkad soldiers kept their bows pointed at us. These guards were in shining armour, and their eyes shone with anger and a willingness to do damage. Nice.

I shuddered. Not at the malefic intent of the soldiers, but at another feeling of power testing me.

"Did you feel that?" I asked.

"No," she said. "I mean, I felt a little of something."

"It was a magic ward," I said. "It measured us and let us through, but it was a powerful one."

"The emperor knew we were coming," she said. "Why would they leave the wards up?"

"It suggests they are expecting, or should I say fearing, something else." I shivered again, then shook my back in case Carmen had noticed the shiver.

I spotted the *Welcome* symbol on top of the ambassador tower, winged over to it, and landed there. This particular tower was the safe place for dragons and other winged envoys to land—well, as safe as one could be in Akkadium. I wasn't blind: I noted that two of the nearest towers were taller. Which meant behind those slitted windows were guards with crossbows pointed at us.

There was a large door to our left, marked with the God Bear symbol of Akkad.

"Odd that no officials are here to greet us," Carmen said. Without my permission, she slipped off my back.

"Yes, odd," I said. "They would have seen us from a great distance. There should be at least twenty guards for me to terrorize with my presence. I will admit to being subtly disappointed." There weren't even royal trumpets, which I had grown to appreciate—well, only as I arrived at a destination. A trumpeter on a hillside was aggravating and might find himself falling from a great height.

There were a couple of thuds inside the room, which could be someone opening the interior door. Carmen had one hand on her sword hilt and the other hanging loosely a few inches behind her dagger. It was an old assassin trick; the enemy's eye was drawn to the hand on the sword. Meanwhile, the other would flick up the dagger and toss it in a heartbeat into a heart. And Carmen rarely missed: she could hit a mouse from twenty yards, not that she would hurt a mouse. She was too soft-hearted . . . or soft-headed. A dragon she'd definitely hurt because she'd stabbed a few. And mortals, too.

"Well, do we wait?" I said. "Or do we poke our noses in the door and see what happens? You poke your nose first; it's smaller, so it's harder to cut off."

Carmen, who had been pacing back and forth like she was on parade for her maestrus, stamped her feet. "I'll poke my nose in the door of the receiving room and see what's happening."

She went to the door, which was barely large enough for lithe dragons like me to fit through. They purposely made it harder for Crimson dragons to get into their palace. That breed of dragons was rather odious sometimes, so I agreed with their planning.

She pushed. The door didn't open.

"It's locked," I said. I had deigned to come a little closer. "It's almost like they don't want powerful dragons or sneaky assassins to creep into their palace."

"Shhh!" she said.

"Don't shush me—especially since I was done talking." I put a talon to my chest, doing my best impression of an affronted dragon. I should have chosen acting as a career. "Don't ever, ever shush me."

She raised a finger to her lips. I'm certain Maestru Beatrix, the librarian assassin, taught her that little move. "Dragons shouldn't be shushed," I continued. "Well, some should. In fact, I could make a list."

"Did you hear that?" she said.

I paused my interesting observations long enough to listen.

"*It's . . . it's you,*" a desperate male voice said from inside the room. "*How?*"

There was a noise, which could have been a grunt, and it was followed by a *thud*. Then came a sound that made my scaled hackles rise—the *schtick* of something being cut. And a gurgle quickly followed.

"Those are death rattles," I whispered. "I'm very familiar with them."

But before Carmen could respond, another noise came through the door:

"Help." It was a small voice. *"Help me."* Not much more than a raspy whisper.

"A child needs our help," Carmen said.

"Full points for being observant," I said. "I think our best course of action is to not do anything hasty."

"Smash open the door," she commanded. She stood back, expecting me to bash it with my head or a powerful paw the moment she asked.

"I'm not a battering ram. I'm a thinker. This situation feels like a trap."

"We are needed now," she said. "And you—"

I knew what was coming next. A long, sanctimonious lecture. So, I interrupted her by slamming a paw into the door.

It didn't budge. That made me angry. Mortal-built doors shouldn't stand in my way. I took two steps back and then threw my whole body into it—head first. That extra weight was enough that a thick wooden bolt on the other side snapped, and the door swung partway open.

Now, slamming your head, even one with a skull as wonderfully thick as my own, into a solid door tends to scramble the brains, so I stood there for a moment, gathering my wits and getting a bit of my blurred vision to clear. I raised a paw, intending to indicate to Carmen that she should wait until I was at my sharpest. But being an over-ambitious mortal, she slipped by me and into the receiving room.

"Oh," she said, the tone showing that she was embarrassed and had perhaps caught another mortal picking his or her nose. But there was a bit more of a negative feeling to it.

"What is it?" I asked, still shaking my head.

"Poke your nose in and see." She swung the door a little wider.

I poked my nose in, so to speak, and I saw what she had seen. "Oh," I uttered.

Several Golden Guards were dead.

Oh, and so was the emperor.

CHAPTER 7
THE MURDER ROOM

"I have a bright and clever suggestion," I said, looking at the collection of bodies. The coppery scent of blood was fresh. "Carefully pull your nose and the rest of you out of the door, get on my back, and we'll be gone. It will be as if we were never here."

"We can't do that," she said. I could have said her reply at the same time as her—she was that predictable. "They'll think it was us who did this massacre. We were seen by all the soldiers on our approach and several commoners. This will be interpreted as an attack by your sister, the queen of all Drachia."

"I know who Brenna is." My eye-roll was magnificent, but she missed it because she had stepped farther into that murder room. "The easiest solution is to kill every single mortal who has seen us. We'll start with the onion farmer who poked me with his spear." When I get a teensy bit nervous, my sense of humour sharpens. I'll admit it was not that funny of a suggestion, though ridding the world of that overeager spear-chucker would improve my mood.

"I know you're kidding." Her assassin training had kicked in because she was now giving the room a good perusal: staring up at the ceiling, into the corners, sniffing the whole time—all with blades out. "But we can't do that either." Since her mind was one big encyclopedic book of rules, she was likely going through them one by one: look for the killing weapon, footprints, signs of entry and escape. Though truth be told, assassins were taught more about being the killer than catching the killer. As much as I liked to jest about the brainpans and brains of mortals, Carmen hadn't let a lesson from her maestrus slip from her mind, and those maestrus were some of the smartest mortals in all the realms. I'd only met one—an assassin librarian—who had an impressive knowledge of books, but I could also judge by the lessons passed down to Carmen.

"You're right," I said. "It would be too messy and too time-consuming to kill everyone. But I know how this works. Mortals stumble across us, standing beside all these recently breathing bodies. They see the big, handsome dragon with impeccable talons and shout, 'He did it!' Then, they try to peel my incredibly valuable scales from my body. And pull my amazing teeth. And pluck my invaluable eyes." I let that last word hang in the air for a moment. "Anyway, that's why I think it's better if we go home. We'll fly back above that magical ward, higher than arrows and bolts can reach, and be in Dreki by nightfall. It might even be a Great Greensward goat special at the palace tonight. Yum!" I resisted rubbing my belly. Promises of food rarely swayed Carmen. It's one of her biggest faults.

"Again, we have to see what or who killed them," she said. "It's our moral duty."

"You're such a goody two-talons," I said. It was a dragon

saying: dragons had four talons, but dragons who were too kind would lose at least two talons when their good deeds eventually bit them on the paw. "I don't see it as our duty. Our duty was to deliver my sister's message to the emperor. If you want, I can drop the scroll beside his dead ear. The ear that's still on his head, that is." The smell of the blood continued to assault my nostrils. I should mention that the bodies were not in great shape. In fact, the more I looked at them, the less comfortable I felt. Maybe it was the stink from the manure spit of the ammits continuing to make me woozy. Emotions are not something I normally experience when gazing upon scenes of death. It's how my dragon culture raised me.

"Many of them have been torn and slashed apart," she said, her voice taking on the measured tone of a maestru.

"So, it's not a poisoning," I observed. "Case solved. Let's go."

If there is anything more aggravating than having a mortal ignore you, I don't know what it is. But she ignored me.

"We heard a noise and a voice earlier," she said. "And a cry for help." Instead of retreating, she took another step into the room and knelt down to put her finger in a puddle of blood. She lifted it and examined the stickiness.

"You must be fun at parties," I remarked.

"These murders are only minutes old," she said, still keeping one hand on her dagger.

"Of course, it just happened: we heard the death throes."

She ignored me again and wiped the blood on the trousers of a dead guard, which I thought was rather callous. Carmen would feel all the emotions later, but her mind was going into that problem-solving focus she'd had drilled into her since she was a child.

The guard wasn't an Immortal—the elite guards of the empire had been disbanded as a condition of peace reparations after the war with the Five Realms. But this man had similar armour and had the sigil of the Bear God on his chest. Another Akkadian mental quirk was they thought they were related to bears—they even worshipped one. Cute.

"That armour wasn't much help," I said, pointing with a talon. The metal plates had been torn in two like they were made of paper. I won't describe what that did to his flesh. His spear was broken into pieces. Even the metal tip had been shattered. "They look like claw marks to me."

"You're right." Carmen was now examining the wounds as if they were puzzles to be solved. Her training allowed her to shut off the side of her heart and mind that was breaking for the lives lost. I mean, she wasn't a dragon. We dragons grew up on this murderous stuff, and every second cousin of mine has died in blood battles. Though she had been raised in a somewhat violent culture, too, in her own way.

"I'd feel safer if you came farther into the room," she said. Her admitting fear was rare, and my chest puffed out a little. I took another step inside and continued to peruse. There wasn't anyone else alive in the room or lurking in the shadows. And I noticed one odd little detail.

"Both doors were locked," I said, indicating the bolt I'd snapped on the outside door, then gesturing to the other door, which I knew led to a set of stairs. That bolt had been dropped, and the door was thick enough that I'd have had difficulty knocking it down.

"Good eyes," she said, without a hint of regret. "Whoever did this didn't go out either door. In fact, they locked the doors before the killing."

"Locking the royal party in," I said.

She stood and arched her back, glancing around the windowless room. "Yes, it's very curious. It's the type of murder an assassin, say Banderius, would do to get people believing a violent spirit had been involved. He would use threads or magnets to lock the door."

"You assassins spend an excessive amount of time contemplating the delicate art of killing other mortals," I said. "But no mortals have claws for hands, so this havoc was caused by something else." These dead people had been given a messy ending. Even the Emperor Lipit, whom I'd met once before at a boring summit between Queen Brenna and the leaders of the now seven realms, was clearly dead. I'd found him odious and long-winded, especially when he began listing his long line of relatives that led him to become the emperor. Despite his tedious manner, I wouldn't wish this fate on the man.

Parts of a symbol made of ash remained on the floor—it could have been a sun-snake symbol. I ran a talon over it, and a layer scraped away. I was about to mention this to Carmen when a very odd thing happened.

"Are you here to rescue me?" the emperor said. His voice crackled with squeaky emotion. His one remaining arm wiggled a little.

Dead men or dragons tell no tales, nor do they speak when they've lost that much blood. I pointed at the emperor's body.

"Uh, did he say something?" I said. "I really hope I was hearing things."

Carmen crept closer, carefully bending down to be nose-to-nose with the emperor. I didn't need to move closer. He was dead. He shouldn't be able to speak. And if something was speaking through him, I had no desire to meet it.

Carmen put a hand on his neck to feel if his heart still beat. "He's dead," she said. "Maybe it was a last exhalation of air that sounded like speech."

"Are you here to rescue me?" he said again. His lips didn't move and his voice was so small it had to be coming from deep in the back of his throat. His arm flopped, and I thought it might come up and point at me for murdering his third cousin, two hundred times removed. These Akkadians held a grudge when you killed their emperors.

Then the arm fell to one side, and I saw that Emperor Lipit had an extra limb. A smaller limb with a foot at the end. The toes, still in a leather sandal, were small, too.

"He has an extra limb!" I said. "You'd think minstrels would sing about something as curious as that."

"The leg doesn't belong to him," Carmen said.

"Ugh." I imagined the worst. There were far too many unclaimed limbs in this room.

Carmen, without even a hint of being grotesqued-out, grabbed the emperor by his shoulder and rolled him to one side.

There was a young, very frightened boy hiding behind him.

"Are you here to rescue me?" he asked.

CHAPTER 8

A MOSTLY FRIENDLY DRAGON

The thin boy had the look of someone who'd witnessed a very, very horrible series of events. His eyes were wide, his mouth even wider, sucking in air, and his limbs trembled. He maybe had spent thirteen summers on this world. His robes were shining because he was wearing some of the finest silks in all of Ellos and his hair was pulled back in the style of the emperors. Blood stained his clothing, and there were handprints on his face—clearly he had been covering his eyes throughout the entire event.

"It's the nephew of Emperor Lipit," I said, though I couldn't think of his name.

"Come out, Nagar." She had obviously memorized the list of Akkad leaders and their successors, a habit she'd picked up in assassin school. Carmen reached for him. This was the boy we were supposed to be welcoming to the line of succession. Emperor Lipit had chosen Nagar as his heir in some convoluted way because the emperor had no children of his own, I remembered. "You are safe, Nagar. We're friends and allies. My name is Carmen, and this is Brax. You're safe."

He managed to lift a finger to point at my magnificent self. "That's a dragon." He didn't sound frightened by my awesomeness so much as stating a fact. That said, his hand shook. I guess hiding under the body of his uncle might make one a touch jumpy.

"I'm a wise, friendly dragon," I said in my wisest and friendliest voice. "I'm here to protect you." Carmen glanced at me, clearly expecting some sort of sarcasm to follow that statement, but I wasn't such a horrible monster that I would needlessly scare a young mortal. Especially one who had survived this disagreeable situation.

Nagar watched me for a few moments. Somewhere behind his eyes, his brain was trying to decide whether he should believe my statement and what he should do next. After a few heartbeats, he finally nodded. "Oh," he said. He glanced at his dead uncle, then immediately looked away and stared out the open door, towards the light.

Carmen hadn't let go of his hand, and she chose this moment to help him to his feet. "Why don't we go outside?" she suggested. "To warm up and chat. It's nicer out there. The air is fresh."

"Yes, and there are no pools of freshly spilled blood out there, either," I added, in a cheery manner. I'd meant the information to be encouraging, but Carmen still shot me a look.

It was like watching a calf struggle to its feet for the first time. Eventually, Nagar stopped slipping on the blood and found his footing. Carmen led him out into the warmth and brightness.

I took one more look around the room. I had been on a

great number of battlefields and seen a great number of horrible deaths, including that of my father and brother and... well, it was a long list. These soldiers, who were the best trained in all of Akkad, hadn't mounted a noticeable defense. Whatever had killed them had claws, and if it had claws, then it likely had scales or fur, but neither of those coverings was on the floor. In fact, the Golden Guards still had their weapons, except for a few shattered spears. It was as if they hadn't been able to lift a finger. Which meant this attack had all happened with blinding speed.

Dragons have a rather keen sense of smell, and, of course, I smelled the blood and the death, but there was something familiar that I couldn't place. It was a scent I'd scented before—the slightest lingering flowery perfume. Perhaps it was whatever oil the emperor's stylists had put in his hair. Also, floating in wisps in the corners of the room, was a purple smoke. Even as I looked at it, the vapor dissipated. I closed my mortal eye and gave the room a scan with my dragon eye. Sometimes the mortal eye saw more colors than my dragon eye and, I'd never admit this to Carmen, gave me a better appreciation of paintings and art. But it didn't see the other aspects of life. The dark and horrible things.

There were a few strands in the air, invisible to most eyes, barely even visible to mine. Magic. Like webbing left after a spider egg has burst.

Magic. Smoke. Sand dust. And it had all resulted in blood being spilled.

This was not a good sign—well, none of it was. Like an ancient dragon who can feel the coming bad weather in his bones, my bones ached, and I experienced fear. Really, it was only a thimbleful of fear, but it was enough to give me a chill.

I stepped out into sunlight, and the desert warmth soon took care of that chill. I never wanted to die in a locked room. Give me open spaces in which to fight. That horrific event had been a slaughter that one wouldn't even wish on the most horrible of enemies.

Carmen had seated Nagar on a small stone bench. He was looking around as if the sky and the few clouds were something he'd never seen. That is what horrible incidents did: they erased the world you knew and, if lucky, you'd blissfully forget the past. Sometimes, for mortals and the occasional dragon, events could be so horrible that they would forget everything. Even their names.

"Do you know your name?" I asked.

The boy turned his head slowly and looked right through me. "Yes," he said, finally, but with little strength. "I am Nagar."

"Good, good," I said. "Now, what happened in that room, Nagar?"

"Brax," Carmen whispered. "It's not wise to squeeze answers out of him so soon."

Nagar stared at Carmen as if he were seeing her for the first time. Maybe his mental state was even worse than I had first thought. "I can tell you what I saw," he said. "I think I can." His voice, like many mortals on the edge of manhood, crackled up a few warbly octaves. He cleared his throat. "I was with my uncle Lipit. Accompanying him to see you, the messengers from the greatest of all dragon royalty, Queen Brenna of Drachia."

"Well, greatest of all dragon royalty is a bit of an over-statement," I said. "But it's excellent that you still remember your protocols and your royal hierarchies. And respect for dragons. Good boy." I'm sure Carmen was impressed by my kind encouragement.

"My uncle believed it would be important for me to understand the protocols. And he wanted me to meet a dragon and not be afraid. Even a lesser dragon such as yourself would be a great test of my courage."

"Lesser dragon?" The two words slipped out as a snarl. I drew myself up a little higher.

"I… I meant no insult." Nagar's words were still laboured. "My lesser reference was to your royal line. I know you were once in line for the throne and stepped aside. A great, brave sacrifice. You see, I paid attention to my lessons. You are a formidable dragon who has, several times, changed the history of our world."

"Well, as long as you have the matter of my absolute importance straight," I said. "And I'm not sure you can ever truly be unafraid of dragons. But try to find a level between comfort and bed wetting fear. So, you came with seven Golden Guards?"

"Yes, seven," he answered. "It is a good number, a number the Bear God loves."

"I counted seven," Carmen said, as if it were a competition to identify bodies in that mess. But the number was important. Out of seven of them, they should have been able to protect their emperor. Or at least get one good stab into their attacker.

"And you knew them all?" I asked wondering if there were traitors.

Nagar nodded, with a flash of eagerness, almost like he was the type who preferred to please others. "Yes. Yes. They were the most trusted soldiers. The most strong. They had all once been Immortals, but were raised up to become members of the Golden Guards. Now, they are gone." He looked down. "All gone. Demetroy. Agus. Surgon. Mik —"

"You don't have to name them all," I said. Next he'd be listing off their wives and children.

Carmen put a hand on his shoulder and gave me a baleful glance. As I had received hundreds of baleful glances from her, this didn't even measure very high on the baleful glance list. "You don't have to tell us anything else," she said. "If it's too hard."

Nagar wiped at his eyes, but when he looked up, they were dry. It was as if he expected to cry but couldn't. "No. I... I can tell you more. I can tell you what I remember."

"And what is it you remember?" I asked.

"We went into the receiving room and before we crossed the floor, both doors slammed."

"Of their own accord?" I asked.

"What does 'accord' mean?" His voice broke again.

"On their own," Carmen explained, her voice gentle. "Did the doors close on their own, or did someone close them?"

"Or more than one someone," I added. That mess suggested several clawed enemies.

"They slammed on their own, as if pulled by invisible hands," he said. "Then there was a hissing like a snake."

"A snake closed the doors?" I leaned a little closer. He continued to rub at his eyes and now a tear was forming. But we needed to know things now. What if the danger was still there?

Sarcasm doesn't help, Carmen sent to me.

Clarity does, I sent back.

"No, a snake didn't close the doors," Nagar said. "But...

but there was the sound like an enormous snake: a hissing and rattling, then the doors closed."

"And what happened next?" I pressed. "Don't leave out any details."

Carmen kept her hand on his shoulder. "Again, Nagar, if it's too hard, we can wait until you are stronger."

"No. No." He put his hand on hers. "I need to remember. The torches on the wall went out. Then choking purple smoke filled the room, along with a swirling of sand followed by a horrid, unholy growling. The Golden Guards fell back into a circle around us, and my uncle said, 'It can't be you, dear gods of the desert and sea. It can't be you.'"

"So, he knew the attacker?" I asked.

Nagar nodded, though partly because it looked like he was about to cry. "I had lowered my gaze by then and something stopped me from lifting my head: the brightness."

"I thought it was dark in there," I said, perhaps a pinch too quizzically. Carmen gave me another one of her *if-my-eyes-were-spears* glances.

"It was dark," Nagar whispered. "But there was a brightness I couldn't look at inside that darkness." Oh, great, the boy was giving us mental puzzles. "Then came the hissing, the swishing, and the gurgling. Bodies fell, my uncle said those words, then he collapsed and I was trapped below him. I didn't move. I didn't dare. Not until you came and found me."

"You failed to see the creature or creatures or whatever did all the slashing and gouging?" I asked.

"Brax," Carmen said.

"I couldn't look upon them," Nagar said. "They were too bright. But I smelled them. They smelled."

"Was it a battlefield smell?" I asked. "I realize you may be too young and unbloodied to have smelled that scent."

"No." His voice broke again. "It smelled like flowers. Hundreds of flowers."

"Flowers?" I said, but I had smelled the vestige of something sweet in there, too.

"I caught that scent also," Carmen said. "A lotus perfume. Specifically, the blue desert lotus."

She was such a braggy peacock. She'd likely taken a class on smelling flowers at assassin school. And another on how to stab people with the stems. "Well, great," I said. "We all smelled something in there. But what was it that smelled like flowers and sweetly eviscerated seven Golden Guards and an emperor?" Even as I spoke it, my memory was reminding me of a recent encounter.

"I don't know that we figure that out right away," Carmen said. "But—"

Someone banged on the interior door to the chamber. Even out here, echoing from inside the reception room, it was loud. Then came the shouting of a gaggle of furious Akkadian soldiers. They were smashing at the door with battering rams, judging by the increase in volume.

"The cavalry has arrived," I said. "On foot." I pointed north towards Drachia. "There is still time for us to flee."

Carmen didn't remove her hand from Nagar, who had huddled himself against her. "Go let them in, Brax."

"You forgot to say please," I replied.

"Go let them in and don't kill any of them." She held my gaze for a few seconds. "Please."

CHAPTER 9
A MONSTROUS ACCUSATION

"Don't all come stumbling in at once," I commanded to the collection of grunting, angry voices on the other side of the blood-spattered door. "Do you hear me?" I shouted that last bit fiercely, and they stopped banging and fell silent like good little mortals. "And don't stab me. That's an order!"

I lifted the thick wooden bolt and pulled the door open a few inches, then stepped aside. An overly eager Golden Guard with enormous feet kicked the door, so it swung with speed, but stopped halfway when it hit a dead body. Seven guards, two servants and a vizier stumbled into the room waving weapons and a bear-headed staff. "Stop waving your pointy things around," I shouted. A flicker of flame came out my nostrils to show that I could back up my threats.

The soldiers took one glance at the carnage and turned pale, and two of the servants, in their clean white robes, ejected the contents of their delicate stomachs. The only calm faces were the rail-thin vizier in a grey robe decorated by lavish golden stripes and a tall woman with dark skin, dark eyes and red robes who walked calmly into the room a moment after all the charging, blustery men. She had snakes in her hair—snakes made of gold that stared at me with embedded gem eyes. Black makeup outlined her eyes, making them almost owl-like and piercing. Her robe had a cowl on it.

Immediately, the guards pointed their spears in my direction and began shouting in that way mortals shout at cattle. I puffed up my chest. I was not a cow. "I said don't stab anyone!" I blared.

The vizier ran a hand through his greased back hair, then gestured at me and said, "You murdered them, you monstrous beast."

"Yes, you murdered them, beast," the woman repeated, also pointing. "And we shall harm you as sure as the sun rises in the east." She was clearly a priestess, judging by her red robes and red hair. Something about the way she held herself made me expect lightning bolts to come out of her finger.

"If I had murdered them, they wouldn't be in so many pieces. I'm not that messy."

"Kill the dragon," the vizier commanded. "Kill him now."

I put up my paws. "Wait, wait, mortals. Do nothing you'll regret for the rest of your lives. Which would only last a few more painful moments."

Apparently, my open paws were seen as a sign of weakness, for one of the Golden Guards charged ahead with his spear clutched firmly in both hands, intending to pierce my heart. Bravery and stupidity often charge hand in hand. I intended to leave his entrails and all that other gucky stuff inside him all over the room, but a tiny voice in my head said: *Don't kill any of them. Please.* Funny thing is, I wasn't certain if Carmen had sent that message to me or it was an echo of her previous request.

So, I hit the guard with the back of my paw, snapping his spear and slamming him into the wall. He tried to stand, which was kind of impressive considering how much force I had used. Then he clattered down and moaned.

"Now!" I pointed at the group with a talon that was as sharp as my wit. "Let's make this very clear: no stabbing!"

"I command the rest of you guards to charge him," the vizier said after running his hand through his hair a second time. I wondered if greasy hair burned faster.

"Yes, charge the monstrous dragon here," the woman echoed. "Do not show him any fear."

Clearly, she had some sort of odd rhyming speech pattern, but I didn't have time to comment on it.

The soldiers were brave, I'll give them that. They raised their weapons, set their feet and their jaws, and, with a simultaneous yell, took the first two steps of their charge.

But before they got to me, a voice cut through the din in the room.

"By the name of my Uncle Lipit, Emperor of the Akkad Empire, I command you to halt!"

The voice was powerful and deep, and the soldiers stopped in their tracks and lowered their spears. I even stepped back a little, expecting to see a ten foot tall man behind me.

Nagar, the young boy who moments ago had been curled up like a baby in the sunlight, stood there. His back was straight, and, though that didn't make him an iota taller, he looked older and must have somehow forced his voice to become deeper. He gestured at me with an imperious index finger. "That dragon is Braxus Andorium, brother to the queen of Drachia, and not a scale on his hide is to be harmed. If it is, there will be executions. That includes your life, Vizier Arbaim and yours, Enheduanna, high priestess of Iktar, the ." That imperious finger now pointed at the vizier and the high priestess. The guards backed even further away to avoid the finger.

"I must say, I like this new version of you, Nagar," I said. He had respect for dragons, knew my name and position in the world, though he'd forgotten to mention all of my many accomplishments. Then again, I suppose there wasn't time. Maybe a minstrel would sing them later. With a trumpet introduction.

"Your royalness," Vizier Arbaim said. "Your uncle is the supreme commander of all worlds and the one who blesses us with holy commands."

Nagar, who was using his index finger incredibly well in this situation, pointed at his uncle's body. "My dear and immortal uncle is right there. He no longer breathes and is no longer immortal. And with his last breath, what happens?"

Vizier Arbaim fell to his knees with such force, bones cracked. The High Priestess hit her knees to the floor equally hard. They were in a kneeling competition! Then the Golden Guards all kneeled in unison.

Enheduanna opened her mouth to say something, but Arbaim spoke first: "Welcome to the world, Nagar the III, Emperor of Akkad and all worlds upon which you gaze."

"May the world fear your god sandaled feet and your god mind," the priestess said. "Welcome to the world you find!"

"Welcome to the world?" I said. "God mind? God strength? God sandals?" These mortals certainly thought a lot about themselves, especially the Akkadians. I shook my head, knowing that this was not the time to point out how tiny they were compared to dragons.

Carmen stood behind the newly "born" emperor, her face as surprised as my own. Well, dragons, with all the scales and snoutiness, don't show a lot of surprise, so she looked more surprised.

Once again, the new born emperor was using his index finger to point at me and Carmen. Was it a god finger?

"These messengers—" Nagar took a deep breath and trembled, but stayed standing. "These messengers from Queen Brenna arrived after the horrendous murderous deeds were over and delivered unto me comfort and aid. They are to be given—" And with that, his face twisted into a rictus and he collapsed to the floor.

"To be given a thousand fattened goats," I finished. But I see their slow minds did not fully appreciate my humor. Instead, the vizier and the high priestess and the guards rushed over to lift Nagar up. The boy, if he was dead, could be proud that he'd had the shortest reign of any emperor, not even a full half hour. History would forever remember him for that.

"It took all his strength to give those commands," Carmen said. She was also kneeling at his side, one hand on his temple. "But he is alive. His heartbeat is strong."

"So, no goats?" I asked.

The vizier motioned for another figure in robes who was outside the door to enter. His robes were decorated with an image of scissors. I assumed this meant he was a physician, not a tailor, though sometimes tailors were less harmful that physicians. On second look, I realized my eyes deceived me, for the physician was a woman, which was a rare occurrence in Akkad for that occupation. Her hair was not greasy, and she'd cut it short, either to look more like a man, or, judging by the seriousness of her face, she preferred not to have it block her eyes while she did her work.

She snipped away the robes, took a salve container from her belt, and began applying the lotion to the boy's chest. Nagar groaned and shook, his eyelids fluttering enough to show the whites. Then they closed tight. Well, the boy had witnessed the gory death of his uncle and seven guards, and on top of that, came face to face with a dragon of incredible calibre. It is no wonder his mind and body were shutting down.

"Take him to the royal healing room," the physician said. Two of the guards lifted the newly birthed emperor, and he made no further noises. They were careful, though, for he wasn't a sack of potatoes. The physician followed, attending to the boy as they walked. "And bring him, too," the physician said, pointing at the guard whom I'd introduced to the wall at great speed. A third guard helped my victim to his feet and guided the crumpled man towards the door.

Vizier Arbaim, now with only three guards and the high priestess beside him, looked us up and down. He opened his mouth to say something, perhaps even to utter a command, but I interrupted.

"Do you think your greasy hair would burn faster than non-greasy hair?" I asked.

His mouth shut with such speed it made a popping sound. He stepped back two steps. One guard let the smallest smile curl on his lip before returning to his professionally grim stare. The high priestess didn't hide her smile at all. She put a hand to her snake crown, as if her silent giggle might knock it off.

"Brax!" Carmen admonished in that way only Carmen could. "My apologies, Vizier Arbaim. He is overheated from the encounter and sometimes he gets an overheated sense of humor. You are safe."

"Oh," the vizier let out the fakest, shakiest laugh I'd ever heard. "Ha. Ha. Ha. Ha. Ha. I get it. I knew it was a jest all along." He leaned a little harder on his bear-headed sceptre.

"You were about to say something before I jested," I said.

"Yes, yes." He drew himself up and gave a well-practiced bow. "I want to invite you, at the behest of Nagar the Emperor of Akkad and all he gazes upon, to dine in the royal hall."

"Is that wise?" Enheduanna, the high priestess, asked. "I see a beast in his eyes." She was no longer smiling.

She worships Iktara, the Cowled Goddess. Carmen's annoying educational voice appeared in my head.

She needs a cowl, I sent back. *Maybe it will muffle her rhymes.*

Only their highest priestesses speak in rhymes.

It's very annoying, I replied, and nearly said it out loud.

"Does your goddess have hairy legs?" I asked her.

The priestess recoiled from the words. "No, our goddess does not have hairy legs, but she can have whatever legs she wants! This beast has insulted my religion, banish him to the dregs!"

The vizier ignored Enheduanna. Instead, he pointed around the chamber. "We would like you to be comfortable and calm while you detail what you know of the horrors that occurred here." Already other soldiers and servants had arrived and were moving the remains. "We also want to show you the generosity of Akkad and, through you, extend that generosity to your sister, the illustrious Queen Brenna.

Would you do us the honor great dragon and wise assassin courier?"

"We gladly accept," Carmen said, before I could open my mouth.

You were going to ask him about goats, she sent.

Guilty, I sent back. *You know me so well. We'll eat what they give us. As long as they give us goats.*

"Then follow me," the vizier said. He looked me up and down like he was sizing my head for a shelf. "You may have to hold your wings very close against yourself to fit our narrow doors." Then he went through the door without a glance at his old emperor.

"Mortal before magnificent being," I said, motioning for Carmen to go first. She laughed and we tread carefully through the room and into the stairwell.

The high priestess stayed behind. She was tracing the sun surrounding a snake symbol on the floor with her fingers, shaking her head, which made the snakes in her hair look alive.

A small cloud of dust rose from the symbol as if some magic remained.

Or as if it reacted to her touch.

CHAPTER 10

A HAPPY MAW

There was a goat, perfectly roasted and flavoured with enough of the famous Akkadian garlic and cumin to almost humble my taste buds. If such a delicious dish was their way of making me amenable to their charms, it was a culinary victory. Along with that goat came the famous Akkad purple turnips, which I ignored, but Carmen consumed. And grapes from Avenus, still fresh, clearly brought here on ice in a fast galley. They had laid out tuna on a round silver plate, but I ignored it—I wasn't a sea dragon.

"Well, this is scrumptious," I said to Carmen. We were the only ones at a white marble table that was long enough to seat at least fifty mortals. I stood at one side while Carmen sat on an ivory chair. She was eating in her own delicate manner, using the three-pronged fork and rounded knife in an equally delicate, reserved way—all the while pretending that she wasn't jealous of my ability to tear meat in half with my talons and then stuff it into my mouth.

Through the wide, opulent windows, we could look out

over the walls of the palace and down upon the lights of Akkadium. This was a view that any emperor would adore —a controlling, manipulative, ruthless shepherd gazing down upon his flock.

"I could be a royal messenger for life if this is the reward." I used both paws to scoop the contents of a plate of chicken toward my maw. Sadly, a few vegetables snuck in. My grandmother, Dillia the Destroyer, had once told me vegetables were good for you because they reminded one that the world holds significant moments of disappointment and disgust.

"Well," Carmen said, "we want to keep an eye out for them poisoning us."

"Oh, heavens, you are so suspicious," I responded. "If it was poisoned, my nose would tell me. Unless they hid it under the smell of garlic and cumin." I sniffed. "And oregano."

"None of this is poisoned," she said. "I checked."

She had started her meal by nibbling the tiniest of bites from each item on her plate. Her tongue was taught from an early age to detect poisons, and she had also, through limited exposure, been made immune to several of them. I hadn't seen her eat suspiciously for such a long time that I thought she was dining in her usual polite "I've got the appetite of a bird" way.

"You are certainly being suspicious."

"Trust no one. Not even your brother," she said. "That's what Maestru Alesius drilled into my head."

"In your case, it was entirely literal." I popped a whole game hen into my mouth and spoke over the sound of crunching bones. "Then again, with my brother, it was also almost entirely true."

"Well, no one has explained yet what happened in that room," she said, bringing a grotesque carrot to her mouth. I should point out that the carrot looked well-roasted and peppered, but it was grotesque by the very fact it was a carrot. "And since they can't explain Emperor Lipit's death to us, that means the event will be even harder to describe to their citizens and their enemies. It would be logical for them to pin the blame on us."

I raised a talon that still had a piece of mutton on it. "They might fatten us up for the kill," I said.

"You are taking this lightly," she replied. Thankfully, Carmen was done chewing the carrot, though a bit of orange was stuck between the tiny, cute gap in her front teeth. I might mention the carrot piece to her if it was still there a few weeks from now.

"Well, I, for one, think that as long as the boy emperor wakes up healthy and alive, we are safe," I said. "He took a real liking to me. Maybe he sees me as a scaly, powerful uncle figure. Though, remembering what happened to his uncle, that might not be a good thing. Besides, you worry too much: they would need a regiment of Golden Guards to hurt me. It's not like any of them can cast spells like Emperor Sargon did."

"But what or who did all the murdering in that room?" she asked.

"I have a suspicion," I replied. "But I worry you'll pick at it like a scab."

"That's a grotesque way to put it, but tell me." She daintily lifted another carrot, and my stomach churned.

"I think that goddess that rose out of the ashes did it," I said.

"The one you imagined when you were smacked with ammit spit? That one?"

"You're picking at the scab." I narrowed my eyes. "Are you going to listen or not?"

She gestured in a placating manner. "Please, go on."

"Well, there were ashes on the floor."

"I saw those."

"And they smelled like lotus flowers," I added with a hint of triumph. "The goddess also smelled like lotus flowers."

"There are lotus flowers everywhere in Akkad." The way she swung facts around like a dagger was very bothersome. "Do you have any other proof?"

"Well, someone summoned *something* in that room. There was enough magic remaining to suggest that. And what remained of the summoning symbol looked like a snake encircling the sun."

"I saw that, too," she said. "So, we can conclude that magic was involved. And someone called forth something. But it doesn't—"

The door opened, and Carmen fell silent. Vizier Arbaim did not so much walk into the room as floated across the floor. Not literally, for he wasn't a wizard, but some have politics stuffed so much up their posteriors that they walk without bending their knees. He had changed into purple robes, and he had plopped a squarish felt hat on his head. I wondered if my comments about his hair had made him cover it up. Was it a hat that was proof from fire?

"Dearest guest from Drachia and from the Red Keep," he said. It didn't matter how much time had passed since Carmen attended assassin school; she was a representative of the assassins' Red Keep, more so now that she sometimes taught there. I couldn't shed my scales, and she couldn't shed her past. "My apologies that you must dine alone without the blessing of Akkadian conversation."

"This grub is a thousand times better than any Akkadian conversation," I said.

Carmen kicked me under the table. She had a rather pointed boot and an uncanny ability to hit right in that space between scales. "What Brax means is that we appreciate this bounty you have provided humble servants of the Drachian crown."

The vizier stopped beside Carmen, keeping her between him and me. "I am pleased to hear the humble offerings are pleasing," he said. Most viziers lived in a world where flowery language overflowed like . . . well, like overgrown flowers.

"Enough about flowers," I said. They both gave me a confused glance. I guess they hadn't been reading my mind. I distracted them by stuffing a whole roasted pig into my mouth, legs, snout, and all. Then I chewed, spitting out my words between the pork. "Why are you here?"

"To thank you from the heart of Akkad. Your sister's message of support for the new emperor has been passed on to our trade contacts and has been received and accepted by Emperor Nagar the Third, greatest of all emperors." We had, as ambassadors, told them that Brenna would accept the little boy as emperor. It was the only logical course of action. And having dragons being the first to endorse him meant we would be on better terms with this shrinking empire.

The emperor must be awake if they spoke to him, Carmen sent.

Yes, that's good news, I replied inside her mind. She gave me a kind of funny glance I ignored. She had expected me to add some cutting comment.

That relief I felt was tempered by the fact Arbaim continued to speak. "The offer of this new trade treaty and the recognition of how important the Akkad Empire is to the land of Drachia honours us. Our doors of friendship and culture and finely crafted goods are always open to your illustrious land. You will forevermore be welcome in these hallowed halls."

"It sounds as if you are sending us home," I said. "We haven't even had dessert."

"No. No. No." Arbaim waved his bone-skinny hands. "You are welcome to stay here at the palace as royal guests for as many days, hours, or even minutes as you want. But I am certain you have thousands of wonders in your home-lands to explore or experience again. Such travellers as you two luminaries are needed at home, and not just for your inspirational stories of past victories."

When he spoke about victories, I knew he was thinking about how, with Carmen's help and that of a few other mortals, I brought down the Akkad Empire. Well, that's the way I tell the story. And the winners with the biggest mouths get to tell the tales. As proof of my political tact, I didn't speak any of those thoughts aloud.

"And we are certain that the queendom of Drachia would not glow so brightly without your visionary advice and heroic presence." I will admit he was hitting me right in the flattery liver, which was an old dragon saying.

"We are visionaries and advice givers," I said. "Why, I once, when visiting the woods of Byrn Haven, came across a red stag, the most royal of beasts, and tore it to—"

"May I ask about the health of the emperor?" Carmen

interrupted. Which was rude. Never interrupt a dragon telling an evisceration story. But I bit my tongue. One must constantly be forgiving these mortals.

"He is well," the vizier said, bowing his head slightly. "Nagar the Third, Emperor of Akkad and all its lands, is awake and awesome and fully invested with the god-like power of his title. He sends his well-wishes and thanks and hopes to see you again many moons from now when you return on future official business."

"We weren't questioning whether he was emperor," I said.

He only wants us to pass along to your sister that all is well in Akkad, Carmen sent. *Kingdoms do not want to show weakness to enemies or friends. Or dragons!*

Thanks for explaining basic politics to me, I sent back to her. I'm sure my words were glowing red with fake anger inside her head. *Besides, mortal kingdoms are always weak.*

Says the dragon, who has several scars from fighting those kingdoms.

That's your fault! I shot back mentally.

"Emperor Nagar the Third is fully invested with his powers," Vizier Arbaim repeated, looking back and forth between us. I guess we had been arguing in each other's heads for a few too many seconds. "He is strong, and he has the wisdom of ages on his brow."

"Wisdom of ages?" I said. "I'm not sure how much wisdom a wetling has, or did you age him with some potion?"

"What my companion means," Carmen said, patting my paw, "is that we are pleased he has those powers and that wisdom, both on his brow and at his side." For this compliment, the vizier awarded her with the very smallest of smiles, not a natural occurrence on his face. She was good at this. I guess those assassin classes, including *courteous compliments for second-class power movers and shakers*, had paid off. "We will report that the ascension was smooth, and the hand on the throne is steady, and that the Akkad Empire is as strong as the great walls of Akkadium."

Vizier Arbaim nodded until she was done speaking. "We appreciate this truthful report. You are truly a wonderful, wise, and observant ambassador." Then he cleared his throat and looked at me. "Ambassadors, I mean."

"Speaking of truth," I said. "Have you discovered what dismembered your guards and your previous emperor?"

This made him stand straighter, and his face, which had still held that smile, narrowed and grew stiff. "It is an internal matter. But our consuls and our royal mage have examined the room and reworked events and are certain you two were not involved. We thank you for being there to bring comfort to the emperor. Not that emperors need comfort, for they are impervious to the emotions and pains of mortal lives."

He clearly has forgotten that every other emperor has been "impervioused" to death, I sent.

Remember, we are ambassadors.

Remember, I mimicked her, *I am a dragon ambassador. And that is different.*

Sometimes, subtly works, she sent back.

"Queen Brenna, whom we represent in our capacity," Carmen said, "will want us to give official greetings in person to the emperor."

Good thinking! The vizier and the rhyming witch may have strangled and stuffed that poor boy and are running everything now.

Brenna will want to know that. No sense sending gifts to a stuffed emperor.

"I am sorry," the vizier said. "Emperor Nagar the Third was so close to his uncle and is in three weeks of mourning and will not be available to ambassadors and . . ." he glanced at me ". . . others."

"Why don't you want us to see him?" I asked. "And please give me a simple answer devoid of flowery language."

"My dearest dragon of the land of Drachia—"

"Don't 'dear' me!" I tapped a talon on the table, chipping the stone.

He paled, but only for a moment. He was an experienced vizier. "It is a sacred right when an emperor has passed on to the cavern of sombreness for his successor to mourn."

The Akkadians believe that when their people die, they go to a great cavern and live a sombre life of contemplation, Carmen sent to me. She enjoyed being a teacher.

What a horrible afterlife, I sent.

For people where the sun burns them every day, perhaps a cavern is glorious. And they get to eat endless grapes.

"Though we appreciate and respect the mourning period," Carmen said. "I am reminded of the story of Archon Demetre, from the land of Avenus, bringing her condolences to Emperor Shar-Kali-Sharri the Fifth and how that prevented a war." Score a point to Carmen for being so studious and memorizing every book in her endless need to impress her various maestrus. Being the teacher's pet paid off in this case. "We would like to follow that protocol."

"That will not be allowed this time," the vizier said. "Nagar the Third is in the very deepest of god-like mourning."

Now I'm sure they've stuffed him, I sent.

"We will have to report this to my sister," I said. "That we could not see the newly crowned or laureled emperor — whatever it is you do."

"They get the Great Bear God Amulet," Carmen explained in a way that made my teeth grate.

"Or amulet him," I added. "This will cast aspersion on our recognition of Akkad. It is best to start a god-like rule with no doubting allies."

The vizier had crossed his chicken-leg-thin arms. Then he looked down, realizing he was being unambassador-like, and put them at his sides. "There will be a time in the future when all the kings and queens of other lands will see our great and grand emperor —"

"Enough," a deep voice said. "Enough. They can see me now."

Then Emperor Nagar the Third entered the room.

CHAPTER II

READING KING CROKE

The boy was standing at the end of the table. No guards protected him; his back was straight, and he wore royal-purple pantaloons, a silk purple tunic, and the white bearskin cloak of the Akkad emperor. On his neck was an oversized golden bear's head amulet—well, everything looked oversized since he wasn't all that big. Nagar, thankfully, didn't remind me of another emperor whom I'd met and disliked immediately. Mostly because Sargon, the first emperor I'd faced, blasted a fireball through my wing as a greeting—the spot still hurt slightly whenever I thought of him. Oh, and he had caused a war that nearly destroyed the five realms and resulted in the death of thousands of mortals.

Emperors! Always so aggressive.

Vizier Arbaim fell to his knees with such speed I expected to hear his kneecaps shatter. He didn't even wince. He must have the thickest kneecaps in all of Ellos.

I bet he wears pads on his knees, I sent. *And practices falling on them for hours.*

Carmen struggled not to laugh. That's why I kept her around—she could be a wonderful audience.

"My great god, Emperor Nagar the Third, ruler of all Akkad, lord of all that is encompassed by your godly gaze, you have risen from your royal bed and have, uh, wisely and bravely broken from the traditional period of mourning."

"Yes," Nagar said. He looked around the room. "I am up. Awake. And the sleeping teas were not effective." It was not clear whether this was an accusation or a complaint. "And I am hungry." As if on cue, his stomach grumbled at an imperially loud volume. In an instant, I identified with this tiny collection of bones and flesh and a stomach. Who says dragons and mortals can't find common ground?

"'My kingdom for a good meal,'" I said. It was a quote from one of my favourite mortal novels, *King Croke*.

"'Then open the floodgates of food,'" Nagar replied, smiling widely.

He's read King Croke! Carmen and I sent to each other at the same time. It's very odd when someone else's voice appears in your head, saying the same thing you're thinking. But it is also wonderful.

Finally, an emperor I don't want to tear to pieces, I sent.

"My great emperor." Vizier Arbaim continued to kneel but dared to lift his head a couple of inches. "I shall have our chefs bring you a meal fit for an emperor. This is—" He gestured disdainfully at the table. "This is the ambassador-flavoured meal. Not fit for royal lips."

First off, the wording of his statement made me wonder if this meal had been flavoured *with* an ambassador, but that was more the type of meal dragons would serve. No! What the vizier had meant was that there was better food than this! Emperor food! I had the urge to grab the skinny vizier and shake him until he commanded those chefs to *cook, cook, cook*. But with grace, exceptional control, and immense humility, I held back.

"This will do," Emperor Nagar said. He reached his royal hand out and plucked a chunk of mutton from the carving plate with his royal fingers, then deposited it in his royal mouth. At least he knew goat was the best way to start a meal.

"Are you certain you don't want the emperor's feast?" I asked.

He looked at me, chewing thoughtfully. This youth of so few summers seemed to have an uncanny wisdom, which was shown when he pointed at me and said, "You would like to try an emperor's food." It was not a question.

I nodded my royal head (I was a prince, after all). "Yes, Nagar the Third, Emperor of Etcetera, I would." I ignored Carmen's protesting nudge. "Would I ever."

"Then rise, Vizier, and make it happen," Nagar replied, clapping his hands. The vizier rose to his feet and lifted his hand to his mouth to bark a message to some servant outside the door, but Nagar shook his head. "Arbaim, go to the chefs personally. Explain my needs and inspect their utensils and their stock to be certain they are using the very best of the very best ingredients, and only when every dish is ready will you escort the food back to me."

"My brave and wise emperor, the chefs are capable of—"

"Go, now!" Nagar exclaimed, sounding older. "Do as your emperor has commanded. And bring the food to the Empire Garden."

"With absolute servitude, I shall!" The vizier bowed with such fervour he nearly smashed his head on the table, then he float-walked out of the room at speed.

Once he was gone, Nagar helped himself to another piece of mutton. "Will you be kind enough to come with me to the garden? It is beautiful and open and reminds me of my mother's garden in Eladium, where I spent so many hours reading." Then he whispered the next line. "And it will be harder for any spying ears to listen in to our conversation."

I wanted to question whether ears could spy, but Carmen spoke first, "Yes, Your Majesty, it will be our pleasure."

With that, we followed the great but tiny emperor as he walked along his hallways in sandalled feet, his white bear cloak dragging on the floor. My talons clicked on the marble. Servants—well, those who didn't jump in fright at the sight of a dragon—would throw themselves against the wall, then bow as we passed. I could get used to being an emperor.

Eventually, we went down a wide set of stairs that opened into the Empire Garden.

I had only visited the gardens once during a treaty negotiation. It was an architecturally glorious collection of statues, greenery, and opulence: spraying fountains, waterfalls in each wall, benches of gold, statues of every emperor of the last thousand years reaching toward the sun as if they each wanted to grasp it. Surrounding all this finery were plants and trees and other green things brought from each corner of the empire. In a desert land, this kind of greenery was the purest display of wealth and power.

We passed one ugly thing—a black stone that someone had roughly carved into a large rectangle.

That's the Sacrificial Stone of Slaughtering Kings, Carmen sent.

Do the kings do the slaughtering? I sent back. The thing had several blood-draining channels chipped out of it.

No, she replied inside my head. *The Akkadians slew their first king there, then every king they've conquered since. And whomever else they deemed needed sacrificing.*

Soon, we were past it and onto a more comforting sight: a large stone table. I rubbed my forepaws together.

Nagar climbed up onto the largest stone chair. I didn't know the protocol—whether I should sit down in his presence—but Carmen sat across from him and didn't tell me not to stand.

"I wanted to talk to you two alone." The emperor's voice had gone up an octave or two.

"No one is nearby," Carmen said after glancing left and right.

Nagar collapsed into the emperor's chair—which was larger and more ornate than the others and made him look smaller so that he projected all the power and winsomeness of a youth of thirteen. "I am scared," he said, running a finger under the bear amulet. "And I—I am lost," he added. He lowered his head and stifled a sob.

Carmen and I exchanged a glance. A few minutes ago, he'd been flushed with imperial power. He had been puffing himself up whilst in the presence of his servants.

"A meal will strengthen your resolve," I said. "It always works for me."

"Your words are kind." Nagar looked my way. He was not weeping, which relieved me. Seeing and hearing mortals weep is like the noise of fingernails scratching on glass. "And they are wise words. I—I know I sounded like my uncle there for a moment. So . . . so imperialismistic."

"I think you mean imperialistic, Your Royal Highness," Carmen said.

"How dare you correct the emperor!" I loaded all the fake anger I could into the words.

This display got a laugh out of the young man. "Yes, yes, you are right, Carmen. You are a lover of words. And so is Brax. I've read the reports our spies have assembled about both of you."

I'm curious what they say, I sent. *I'm sure they're very impressed by me.*

But the emperor still had more to add. "My mother, bless her soul, encouraged me to read from a young age. I like words, too, as you surely have guessed. Much of my life has been lived inside books. But the word I think of when I look at you two right now is this: trust."

"Trust?" I said.

At that moment, an orange butterfly landed on my snout. How annoying! Normally, when any insect dares to land there, I fry it with flames from my nostrils. It's a fun game I played with my brother and sister in my youth—who could fry the most butterflies.

But the boy was staring at the butterfly like it was amazing. Mortals were so sentimental about these weak insects.

"A good omen," Nagar said. "You are someone I truly can trust." The butterfly, not knowing how close it was to death, flapped off. Nagar pointed south, toward the ambassador tower where the murders had happened. "That horrible and frightening event, it . . . it shocked me. Darkened me. It was so . . . final. And both of you protected me."

"We did what any caring mortals or dragons would do," Carmen said. I didn't point out that it was a really short list, dragons who cared about mortals.

"Comfort and protection were needed, so we provided it," I added. "That is what allies do."

Carmen gave me an *I can't believe you're talking like a caring creature* glance.

"You have good hearts," he said.

"I like to eat hearts," I replied. I guess it sounded flippant, but it was also the truth. "Not of mortals, though. To be clear. Too salty."

This got another kick from Carmen, but Nagar laughed. "That is what I mean. You are naturally humorous. But also truthful. Both of you. Ever since my uncle chose me as his heir at the behest of Enheduanna, the high priestess, I have felt surrounded by lies and mysteries and subterfuge. I am not a simple boy, but I grew up far away from the throne. My family lived in Eladium, on the coast, and were not concerned about life in the royal palace. It was in the shade of a Clyptus tree that I would read my books."

"We've visited Eladium," I said. It was a city where the rich Akkadians frolicked in their beach homes and compared their war scars received in realms they'd conquered. Someone called the Executioner had met us there and had entrusted us with the plans of this very palace and the task of assassinating an emperor. I didn't mention that part to Nagar. "Eladium is beautiful," I added.

"And far away from the throne, as you say," Carmen said.

"Yes, but I was plucked from my family and my books and thrust into this life only a few short months ago. My uncle, Emperor Lipit, had no children, though I'm sure you already know that. I was his closest living young relative, and I became his heir. He was neither kind nor cruel, and I spent little time with him. My greatest joy would have been to bring my mother to court, but she died last year. And my father, too." I could tell from his voice he had a lump in his throat. "Anyway, there were always whispers around me."

At that moment, the leaves on the Bunyan tree rustled. I glanced that way, but no sudden visitation happened.

"What sort of whispers?" Carmen asked. "About power struggles?"

"No, actual whispers." The boy emperor shivered. "While I lay awake in my room, I heard them."

Uh-oh, I sent. *He's mad as a village hatter. Royal bloodlines are often tainted. Mortal royal bloodlines, that is.*

"Were they a part of your dreams?" Carmen asked. She sounded like one of those dragons who studied nighttime phantasms.

"No, it was the sense that something else was out there beyond the palace," he said. "Something bad."

"Well," I said. "Clearly, you were not wrong. A very unfriendly something came to visit, and it clearly did more than whisper."

"Yes, it was horrible." He shook like a little doll. "The cracking and the tearing. It still haunts me."

That continued "haunting" was not surprising—it had only been a few hours since the eviscerations. My guess was that memories of those horrid minutes would slouch after him for the rest of his life.

"But did you see anything?" I asked. "What creature did the attacking? Tell us."

Carmen, for the tenth time that day, kicked me under the table. "What Brax means is, if you are comfortable speaking, then tell us."

Well, he wants us to aid him, I sent. *We need to know what it was.*

"I remember the doors slammed." He'd told us this part before. "And then a swirling of smoke and ash started above a symbol someone had drawn on the floor. And the voice said my name." This was new information.

"One of the guards?" Carmen asked. "Or your uncle?"

"No," Nagar said. "The voice came from inside the purple swirling smoke. And it was the voice of a woman. A goddess."

CHAPTER 12

THE CHOSEN ONE

"Please don't leave out a single detail," I whispered, worried that speaking loudly might make him crumple. I resisted the urge to grab Nagar by the shoulders and make him sit up straight. That might not go over very well —there were many open windows above us. Any of them could have Golden Guards aiming crossbows from the shadows. "What exactly did that goddess's voice say?"

"It said, 'Nagar of Eladium, child of Akkad, blood of emperors, you have been chosen.'"

"Well, that's pretty specific," I said. "Clearly, the murderous entity knew who you were."

"Yes, that's one of the more frightening things about those horrible minutes," he said.

"And it was a female voice?" Carmen asked.

"Yes. But it was . . . it was so powerful. A voice not meant for mortal ears."

I leaned against the table. My weight made it creak despite being solid stone. "And how did the guards and your uncle react?"

"My uncle commanded whoever was behind this trick to show themselves. He promised their families wouldn't be executed. In his mercy, he would only have them blinded and their fingernails pulled out."

"Well, that sort of threat would work with most mortals," I said. "But did the voice respond?"

The boy shivered for several seconds, tempting me to put a paw on his shoulder. Not in comfort, but to stop the shivering. It looked weak. Carmen, as if reading my mind, reached out to touch the emperor's royal shoulder. It was probably breaking some official protocol, but the boy became still.

"The voice said, 'Soon-to-be dead emperor, I shall lacerate you from liver to limb.'" Before I could mention that it was a very familiar taunt, the boy continued. "The voice then said to me the following: 'Nagar of Eladium. The way to the glorious future is through your heart.'"

"It's never good to have something go through your heart," I said.

"'And the way to the heavens is through your soul,'" he added. "She was very clear about that. The voice then said: 'You are the pillar upon which we build.'"

"It was a very talkative voice." Despite my flippancy, I was impressed that this murderous goddess would go on so long, without a whit of worry, in front of a room stuffed with the most well-trained soldiers in Akkad.

"And did your uncle continue to confront her?" Carmen asked.

"He commanded two of the Golden Guards to open the doors and the others to stab into the smoke and kill the intruder."

"And what happened next?" I asked.

"The purple smoke turned black, and the voice said to me. 'Cover your eyes, Nagar of Eladium.' And so I did."

That explained why his face hadn't been bloody. But the fact he didn't watch the proceedings wasn't helpful for us: it would be nice to know whether this thing had claws or talons or teeth or tentacles. Or even talons on the ends of tentacles. I realized it was likely good for the health of his mind not to see the bloodletting. Mortals are so weak.

"Did you hear anything else?" Carmen asked. Her hand remained on his shoulder, and he leaned toward her. "I understand the sounds you heard in that room would be . . . bothersome."

"The guards didn't yell out in surprise or anger." He had closed his eyes to relive the event but kept his voice steady. "But I heard a tearing sound, and there were gurgling exhalations. Seven thuds followed this when the seven guards fell to the floor."

In pieces, I thought, but didn't add that aloud. I should win points for kindness.

"And my uncle said, 'It's . . . it's you . . . how?'" We had arrived in time to hear that through the door. "And after several deep, frightened breaths, my uncle whispered, 'But I prayed every day of my life.' And then he fell."

We hadn't heard the whispered part. "That's a curiously religious thing to say," I said. "Was he a particularly worshipful emperor?"

"The emperor is the head of the God Bear church of Akkad, the Bear God who rules over all the worlds, including the underworld, and so all the rites are the emperor's to perform." Nagar touched his head as if he were realizing something for the first time. "I am now the font of the sacred gods."

Apparently, being a font didn't help the previous emperor much, I sent to Carmen. She didn't reply other than to say, "And what followed?"

"The voice told me to open my eyes. But what I looked upon was blinding. I think there were tentacles coming out of her back—"

"Were there talons at the end of the tentacles?" I asked.

"Uh. No," he said, and I hid my disappointment. It was a good guess. "But there were also leopard legs, with spots and—"

"It sounds hideous," I whispered. "And familiar." I gave Carmen a knowing glance.

"—I thought there was hair at the edges and spikes sticking out of her shoulder, but her eyes were so bright that I had to cover my own again. 'This is the first visitation,' she said to me. 'In all, there will be three.'"

The prince fell silent. He gave us a puppy-dog look. I loathed dogs, but I couldn't help but be moved by the begging sadness in his eyes. He clearly did not want to be in this situation.

"Well," Carmen said. "I hate to say this, but it sounds like there will be at least two more appearances of this . . . this . . ."

"Eviscerating monstrous-bright-eyed-smoky-leopard-legged-tentacled goddess," I filled in, being ever so helpful. I was rather proud of putting that sentence together. All I got from Carmen was an eye roll.

"Yes, this entity," she continued. "It clearly wasn't an assassin who performed these kills. There was magic. And . . . so much power involved."

"That is why I came to you," Nagar said. "I have told none of this to my vizier. Even Enheduanna, in her complete high-priestess garb, spoke with me to discover what I remembered. They were both so . . . hungry for the details."

"They may want to protect you," Carmen said. "After all, you are the emperor, and that is their function."

"Yes," he said, then he glanced around the Empire Garden suspiciously. I already knew we were alone since I would have smelled any nearby observers. "But I don't trust them. Normally, either the vizier or the priestess is with the emperor when he meets with delegates from other nations. Neither accompanied us. Now, this could be because meeting a courier is not that important." He looked at me. "Sorry."

"Totally understandable," I said. "I don't get out of bed to talk to couriers."

"In fact," Nagar raised a finger, showing he was proud he'd come to another conclusion, "in most cases, it would be the vizier who would greet you. Emperors sit on their thrones, and supplicants come crawling to them: that's how power works. But either the vizier or Enheduanna had convinced my uncle to take me to meet you the moment you landed."

"So, you think one of them knew this was going to happen?" Carmen asked.

He nodded. "I have already said I am suspicious."

"And yet, you come to a handsome dragon and a plain assassin from the land of your traditional enemies for help?" I said.

"I prefer to think of neither Drachia nor the seven realms as enemies," he said. "I am like Corkie of Nok."

This kid had read all the same books as me! Corkie of Nok was a chef who cooked food for every manner of mortal and monster. His food brought peace to Ellos in the book *Nok, Nok, Eat.* Every book should have a cook as the hero.

"You make a brilliant point about Corkie," Carmen said. She was the only other mortal I knew who had the same good taste in novels as I. Well, most mortals can't read or are too busy fighting each other to expand their brains with books. Discussing plot points was the reason I kept her around.

"Someone had to have drawn the summoning symbol on the floor," I added. "And it very well might have been either of them since I'd guess they both have some access to those arcane arts. To solve your problem, you could have them executed."

"Executed?" He spat out the word like it was poison.

"Yes, it's how most emperors begin their reigns. Once their heads are rolling, you'll pick a new vizier and new high priestess to work with whom you trust and who will, after seeing what happened to their predecessors, serve you properly. Done and done!"

He shuddered at my words, and I will say my estimation of him went down a smidgen. This kid seemed to have nothing but kindness in his heart. Coming from the soft life in the city next to a warm beach was likely not a good thing. "I cannot do that," he said.

"Harden your heart." I gave him this advice for free, another sign of my glowing kindness. "Or you will be a short-lived emperor."

"It is generous of you to disperse such royal knowledge," Carmen said to me in a tone that indicated I wasn't being generous. "What do you want us to do, Nagar? We are here with the limited protections afforded to couriers of Drachia. Even speaking to you alone is against all protocol."

"An emperor can make his own protocol," he said. He sounded like he'd grown a bit of backbone until he added, "Really, he can."

"Yes," Carmen agreed. She had removed her hand, perhaps now worried about protocol. "But it is not always received well by his servants."

"Forget protocol," I said. The kid read books. He was in a bad place. It reminded me of a certain assassin I'd met some time ago. Though she'd survived by swindling my eye from me. "What do you need from us?"

He reached into his pocket and came out with two coins, which he set on the table. The sun glinted off them. They were the largest golden coins in his realm and could have bought a small palace in the south. To my chagrin, they were stamped with Emperor Sargon's face. "I want to hire you." He whispered this so quietly it seemed he didn't want us to hear. "As assassins."

"I'm a dragon, not an assassin," I said. "And who would you have us kill? You seem to be refreshingly reticent about killing people."

"I don't know yet," he said. "This—this entity goddess? Or maybe whoever is behind summoning her and trying to kill me?"

"First off," Carmen said, "you survived, so the attempt wasn't on you. But it is worrisome that you have been chosen for some nefarious purpose by this entity."

"I still prefer eviscerating monstrous-bright-eyed-smoky-leopard-legged-tentacled goddess," I said.

She drew in an annoyed breath. "Second, Your Highness, we cannot become your assassins. As Brax said, he is a dragon and, despite his manners, a prince of Drachia. It would be very poor form if he started poking his snout into the affairs of the Akkad Empire. That could cause a war. And though I am a trained assassin, it is not a position I am pursuing these days. I am still searching for my place in this world."

Your place is on my back, is what I wanted to say. But that sounded sentimental. She'd get all mushy and start blubbering about her emotions.

"But you could protect me," he pleaded. "You could save me from . . ." He gestured around him. "All of this. And you could do it quietly. No one would know. I don't expect you to protect me every moment of every day."

"My dear emperor," Carmen said, then must have realized she wasn't being formal enough. "Honourable Lord and Emperor of Akkad, I, a humble servant of Drachia and the Red Keep, cannot accept this task."

I put my paw on her shoulder. She looked like she needed help to stand because I knew it was killing a tiny part of her kind soul to turn down this request. But I also knew she'd need support once I spoke my words.

"Honourable Lord and Emperor," I said. I took in a breath through my nostrils to add a bit of drama. "We will accept this sacred duty."

The emperor's eyes brightened with surprise. "You will?" he stood up and did a twirl that may have been the start of a dance. "You will? That's wonderful!"

My heart lifted a smidgen.

"What?" Carmen said. "I—I did not expect this, Brax. Why did you accept?"

"Because he reads books," I replied. "And if we don't keep an emperor who is wise enough to read books alive, then who should we keep alive?"

A look of shock clouded her face. Ha! She could speak

inside my head and look through my eye, listen to all my wisdom, and still, she didn't know me. Ha!

And, as if the fates were on our side, the door into the Empire Garden opened and the emperor-flavoured food arrived, held by several servants in white robes.

"He reads books," I repeated.

"Then that is reason enough," Carmen said.

CHAPTER 13
CHEFS OF GLORY

The fates have a funny sense of humour. Or should I say, a funny *taste* in humour? Seven plates of delicacies were brought into the garden by seven servants who lowered all seven at the same moment, backed away seven steps, and then returned to the inside of the palace. It was a glorious gastronomical dance.

The vizier floated past a few shrubs, a smile stuck on his face like it had been painted there. "My lord of lords, emperor of emperors, master of all you see, your meal has arrived. May this bounty feed your royal heart and royal soul." He gazed at the table, momentarily looking curious when he spotted the golden coins.

Carmen stood up and walked past each plate, taking a deep sniff. "This is amazing!" she said. "Amazing." She pointed with her left hand toward the sky. "It is a feast for the gods and goddesses." The gesture was so compelling that the vizier looked at the sky as if expecting the Bear God to materialize.

I, though, in that moment of distraction, saw her quickly

take a bite from each plate and slip it into her mouth. The cheat! She was getting to try the food first. But then my magnificent mind put it all together: she was testing for poison.

You can take the assassin out of assassin school, but you can't take the assassin out of the assassin, I sent.

Suspicious is as suspicious does, she sent back, which I assumed was another of the ten thousand maestru sayings she'd memorized. *The food is not poisoned.*

Emperor Nagar reached for the sliced meat of an unfamiliar roasted bird. He took a modest portion with his fingers, which got the vizier to raise his eyebrows. Even the vizier couldn't tell the emperor to use his utensils. Then, the kind, wise boy looked at me and offered the plate. "The first bite for any emperor is The Golden Turkey of Time, which will spread wings of hope and power over the empire."

"Sounds powerfully delicious," I replied, stabbing about twelve thick pieces with one talon and throwing them into my mouth.

The explosion of salt and heat made my eyes water, and it was all I could do to stop from spitting the meat out—the biggest sin a dragon could ever commit. Even through my watering eyes, I saw Nagar grinning.

The horrid emperor boy had played a trick on me!

"Yes," the vizier said, for his smile had widened enough to show his small, tight teeth. "The first bite is salted and infused with Great Hades pepper heat in order to remind our emperor god of the desert heat and the great salt flats from which the empire sprang."

I'll spring you into your next life, I thought, but in my wisdom, didn't say aloud. Instead, after swallowing the burning ball of salt, I said: "Interesting." Even Carmen was grinning. At least I was being entertaining.

"You should follow it with this." The emperor offered a golden goblet. I eyed it suspiciously but took the goblet with a gentleness that was impressive for a creature my size. The goblet was small and hard to clutch in my talons. If this was another joke, in order to save face, I'd have to slay everyone in the garden except Carmen, whom I'd give a good lecture. I tossed the contents of the goblet into my maw and nearly exploded.

With joy. For it was a honeyed melon sweetness and coolness that belied the size of the drink. I closed my eyes. It seemed as though I had been given a flavoured oasis amidst a burning desert.

When I opened my eyes, the emperor was holding a large plate spread with several meats and no vegetables.

"My lord of lords," Arbaim said, "I am uncertain one of your exalted heights should feed an honoured guest by hand. Especially one with such large teeth."

"Please leave," Nagar said. "You can teach me protocol in the future."

The vizier's face became stone—well, it was still flesh, but he could have been a morose statue. He turned away and floated out of the room. Even in that smooth motion, he expressed his haughtiness.

I took the offered selection of meats and threw three of them in my mouth. It was the most perfectly spiced, perfectly cooked food that had ever graced my taste buds.

"We could live here forever," I said to Carmen.

"No, we can't," she answered. She had helped herself to vegetables and fruit and some of the meat. She had wisely skipped the Golden Turkey of Burning Fire. "Though I understand why you feel that way. My emperor friend, the glory of your chefs should be sung across all of Ellos." And Nagar smiled at this compliment as if he had cooked the meal himself, but his smile faded as Carmen continued. "But we have to remember our duties. Despite agreeing to assist the emperor, we still have to return to Drachia and report to Queen Brenna."

"You cannot leave me," Nagar said. "I am not safe."

"Nor can we follow you into every officious meeting," I added, for I saw Carmen's point. "I'm too big for most of your tiny halls. Being a dragon, I cannot be seen even poking a talon, let alone a snout, into your business. Wars have been fought over such slights. And frankly, our impressive presence would frighten your enemies further underground. We need them to stick their necks out so we can chop off their heads."

Nadar looked unconvinced. "But, but you are my, my new friends. I trust you."

"First lesson is free," I said, grabbing the coins from the table and flicking them to Carmen. She caught them as if we'd practised that move. She'd likely give the money to orphans or a minstrel—which was kind of the same thing. "We are not your friends. And though you have rightly placed your trust in our good-heartedness and skills, you should be more guarded. I have some understanding of the amount of pure power it would have taken to summon a creature to kill your emperor. There is magic involved that we will need to understand much more deeply."

"Yes," Carmen said, excited by the prospect of there being reading to do. "We must research!"

"But I need to be safe," Nagar said. "I can't trust any of

these servants, the vizier—even the priestess. One of them killed my uncle."

"Being suspicious is the best protection," Carmen said. "And you will not be alone, though we are not here. I have other assassins who will watch over you."

"There are assassins in my palace?" Nadar stole a glance over his shoulder. Sometimes, mortals who spent their lives reading books were not always properly prepared for the real world.

Carmen nodded. "You do not have to fear. I have already communicated with this assassin."

What communication? I sent. *What assassin? When?*

Sometimes, all you see is the food before you.

"This assassin will report to us directly and is as much your friend as we are," Carmen added. "You will be safe. And you will be able to communicate with us at any time." Seeing him brighten, I'm sure she pictured a flock of the empire's ravens coming our way every minute with messages from a scared child. "Only when absolutely necessary, of course."

"Of course, of course." He stared at us for several moments, holding himself together, getting his emotions in check. Nagar swallowed and took a deep breath. "You are right," he said, and his voice was deep again, controlled. *The boy might be able to do this job,* I thought. He just might. "I will keep in contact, wait for your findings, and rule this land with a firm, ruthless hand."

"A firm, ruthless hand?" I asked.

"I was kidding, my friend," he said. His smile showed two dimples on his cheeks. "That is something I have always wanted to say, along with 'charge my great armies into the maw of victory!'"

It was another quote from *King Croke*.

Both Carmen and I laughed. "I hope you will have time to read," I said.

"I will read during every meeting," he replied. "You may leave my presence now. That is, if you have had enough to eat."

Carmen bowed, I took one more chomp of mutton, and then we went to an open space in the garden next to the Sacrificial Stone of Slaughtering Kings. Bad luck is not something I believe in, but as I took off, the tip of my left wing brushed that stone, and in that moment, I felt a deep, horrid magic there. Or maybe it was the screaming souls of all the kings who'd been sacrificed on that stone.

Once in the air, I took a moment to look down at our little emperor. He had pulled a book out of his robes and was reading while eating slices of meat. Maybe, just maybe, he'd survive being the most powerful person in Akkad.

CHAPTER 14

THINKING BEYOND GOATS AND THE BEST SEASONINGS FOR GOATS

"I have one stop I'd like to make before we leave," I said. We had just winged away from the palace, and the many tasks before us were crowding my thoughts. A part of me regretted we didn't depart the moment we heard the death rattles in that murder room. It's horridly messy when you get mixed up in mortal affairs.

"You have a stop?" Carmen replied. "You are usually quite eager to flee Akkadium."

"Flee is not a word you should ever use to describe how I exit a situation," I said. "Leaving in 'handsome haste' covers it. But yes, I have a very important building I'd like to visit."

"And you will not tell me which building?" She patted my back, or maybe she was punching me. I was too tough to tell for certain. "Is it a goat farm?"

I sighed, which is not a simple thing to do when one is flying. "I am disappointed that you see me as only having goats on my mind. That's insulting! I think of other things: sheep, cattle, overly plump rabbits." I listed them off one by one with my talons as I flew. "But you are right—this destination will be a delightful surprise for you."

We flew low over Akkadium, and even though the population had been spotting dragons more often since the trade between Drachia and the Akkad Empire had opened, people still looked up in fear at my dark outline in the sky. Instilling that fear brought me great joy. There were many scars and aching places where Akkadians had sliced or stabbed or fireballed my body. So, I didn't feel any guilt for giving a handful of them nightmares.

I expected to find my intended destination among all the great governmental buildings in Akkadium. But no luck. I did spot the Temple of the near the market. It was obvious because it was made of bright red stone in the form of the goddess's cowled head—the same colour as the priestess Enheduanna's robe. Sensing that Carmen would know I was flailing in my search, I sped up and widened my circle farther into the tougher parts of the city.

In time, I saw the rounded plain roof from high above, swooped down, and landed near the front steps. I should have guessed they would stick this important building in the seedy side of the city—it showed how unimportant learning was to the Akkadians.

"Ha!" Carmen said as she eagerly slid off my back. "I should have guessed. This is the one thing you like as much as goats."

The Imperial Library of Akkad stood before us, a plain building with grey, thick walls. A ragged bear waited out front, looking like it might maul anyone who left a book or document dog-eared. I should clarify that it was a real bear pacing and snuffling back and forth in a metal cage, not some statue. It had seen better, freer days and didn't show any fear when it saw me.

"Well, that's horrid," Carmen said. Again, she immediately identified with the downtrodden. "Both for the bear and for the readers. Who's going to be thinking this library is a quiet place to read when there's a ravenous bear outside?"

"Maybe any reader who is tardy returning books is fed to the bear." I said that as a clever jest, but there were a great number of bones in the cage, and the Akkadians were rather fond of hosting games where gladiators fought lions or bears or each other.

I pointed above the bear to a plaque on the library's wall that had a date and the name *Naram-Sin*.

"The Architect, who is also known as the Executioner, designed this place," Carmen said.

"I guess beheadings didn't take up all his time." Seeing the Executioner's name was another reminder of how intertwined my history was with Akkad. But that old, dead architect knew his architecture—it was an impressive building that spoke of strength, with clean lines that drew the eye toward the sky. Again, I must say, this was impressive for a *mortal*-built building. In Drachia, this would serve as a toilet-house or a dung gathering station.

"Why are we here?" Carmen asked.

"Because . . ." Stringing her along was one of the great pleasures in my life. Carmen was an aggravatingly clever mortal, so any time I had something over her, I made sure to make the whole experience prickly and painful. If I was in a particularly bad mood, I'd use puns. Yes, puns. "There was something the emperor boy child said that got me thinking."

"Nagar," she corrected. "We can call him Emperor

Nagar the Third, Lord of All He Sees and of All His Sandals Tread Upon."

"Yes, yes, Nagar." I waved away her correction with a paw. "But I see no point in remembering any mortal's name since none of you live long enough to be memorable. One comment he made got me thinking about a library. And of a particular author."

"Which author?" she asked.

"Tut, tut!" I waved what I hoped would be an aggravatingly clever talon in the air. Well, the talon itself wasn't clever, but it suggested my cleverness. "You see, Carmen of Little Mind, Nagar is a reader. And he described the entity monster goddess very particularly, giving her familiar attributes." I was working up to the big reveal. Her face showed her brainpan was exploding with questions, and yet there was no hint of her being incredibly impressed by me. I waved my clever talon a bit more. "The description was the same as the description of the great monster, The Beast of Parnel. Which is a very particular creature in the third book of Cor—"

"—Corum of Croth!" she finished. "You are right! Nagar had described it as having a leopard's spots. And tentacles. And I see where you're going with this, Brax; you think there's a connection between his reading habits and—"

"Yes, yes, you're so clever!" I barked, then took in a calming breath. "I forgot you've memorized every book ever written. Clearly, you should have spent more time on your murderous killing skills in assassin school." She really was good at wrecking my brilliant reveals. No wonder her brother had tried to stab her frequently. "Well, that description stuck in my mental craw, so I wanted to read it again and see if it helps us understand what happened in the murder room."

I folded my wings against my back and strode up the steps to the large doors, ignoring the stares of the Akkadians who were sitting on benches nearby. It was not every day they would see a dragon going into a library, so I was adding some grace to their lives. Opening the door with one paw, I let Carmen enter first, then followed, squeezing through an opening that was barely wide enough for me — the Architect could have made the doors a little bigger!

The most dangerous cornered beasts in all the worlds were inside the door: librarians. Three of them stood behind a thick, rounded wooden desk: two males who looked like they might have parchment paste in their hair and a grey-haired woman who was sharp-eyed and, well, extra sharp in the bloodletting department because she was pointing a rather heavy, loaded crossbow at me.

"Do not take another step," the librarian commanded with a voice that suggested she was used to being obeyed.

CHAPTER 15

THE JOY OF PERUSING

"What is your business here?" crossbow-librarian demanded.

The gnarled librarian either didn't know that the bolt would be harmless unless she hit me in the eye, or she knew that and was a superb shot. Judging by her unwavering aim, it was the second reason. Despite my obvious impressiveness, the other librarians showed no fear—in fact, they continued checking through a book-borrowing ledger as if I didn't exist. Banishing dragons wasn't part of their duties, and they left that chore to their companion.

"We have come to read one of your greatest manuscripts," I said, instilling my voice with the intelligence and gravitas I knew librarians would respect. "Which you had better have, or I will be fierly disappointed."

"I assume you meant to say fiercely," she said without lowering the crossbow or being impressed by my voice. She was pointing directly at my left eye—the mortal eye is my weakest. "These are very flammable collections, and never in all the history of the Imperial Library of Akkad have we

had a dragon amongst our books. We don't have any protocols concerning your monstrous visit. If we had, you would
not have made it through the door."

"I didn't see an army outside—how would you have
stopped me?" I asked.

"We would have stopped you," she said with a confidence that I will admit unnerved me. Librarians, whether
they be assassin librarians, dragon librarians, or Akkadian
ones, did often have knowledge that lesser mortals and other
creatures did not possess. They soaked it up from the
surrounding volumes. Carmen had put her hands beside her
weapons, but I wondered whether her respect for librarians
would delay how quickly she'd react. "Do you swear on the
blood of all dragons," the librarian said, loud enough that
everyone in the building would hear, "including that of your
mother, Bali Andorium of Drachia, to not harm a single
page, Braxus Andorium?"

The librarian knew my name and my ancestors, and
more importantly, she knew that if I swore on my mother's
name and memory, I wouldn't break my oath. Well,
Scythian dragons didn't break their oaths, anyway. This was
extra protection. This librarian certainly had a vast archive
in her grey matter to draw from. "Yes, I swear."

She lowered the crossbow and made a motion with her
hand, dismissing me. The other two librarians continued
ignoring us. I assumed they had developed that skill to deal
with annoying patrons.

"Would you be able to tell us where the Corum collection is?" Carmen asked. None of the librarians acknowl-
edged her question. "I'll go this way," she said to me,
pointing toward a narrow set of steps leading to the second
level.

I couldn't fit up the stairwell, which meant the main floor was where I would have to search—more proof that Naram-Sin hadn't designed the library with dragons in mind. Mortals were so two-legged-centric. I walked carefully, knowing that the Architect probably designed it that way, with spears ready to fly out of the wall if a bookshelf were bumped. At least there was enough room between the bookshelves for me to travel.

I did my second-most favourite activity in the world—I perused the shelves. The Imperial Library had a vast collection on desert plants, desert weather patterns, desert snakes, and desert maps, which looked incredibly boring. I wanted fiction. The Akkadians were not known for their love of fiction—not a single fiction writer from this land had become famous in the rest of Ellos. No, the Akkadians worshipped at the altar of conquering and destroying other realms and cultures, then planting buildings on top of the ruins and calling the land and remaining bits of culture their own. Thus, there were several books on how to rebuild aqueducts and toilets and city walls.

Patrons of the library got out of my way as they should. Well, most of them did. One bent-backed woman was so engrossed in a book that I was forced to step daintily around her—not a straightforward task for a dragon. I eyed the title that was engrossing her: *Poisons and Other Ways to Kill Avenians*. On the nearby shelves were books about Avenus, the city-state that the Akkadians most often dreamed about destroying. There was a whole series with the creative titles *How to Kill Avenians I* and *How to Kill Avenians II* and, well, it went on for the rest of the row. They looked worn and well-read. I was tempted to open one book but remembered that I actually liked Avenians. They were, paws down, the best mortals at writing fiction: their minds soared into imaginary worlds. In fact, it was an Avenian who had written the Corum book.

Aha! I thought to myself. This is exactly where the fiction books from Avenus would be. All I had to do was search for the smallest, dustiest shelf. I kept moving down the aisle. A few shelves later, I discovered the smallest, dustiest shelf in the entire library. Horrid dust, I should add —horrid because it showed no one had read any of these books in at least a decade. For all the impressive, thick-walled cities they'd built, along with some of the finest bathrooms, these Akkadians were barbarians!

A woman, face hidden behind a cowl and in a dark red robe, stepped by me. It was surprising that she had even come down the aisle, considering a dragon was standing there. I was very proud of myself for not asking if she was hiding her face because of shame for Akkad losing its latest war. Or not having enough novelists. Neither of those comments seemed clever enough, so I held my tongue.

I perused the shelves for a few more seconds before noting that the woman was circling an open space between the bookshelves. She glanced at me once, then walked faster. Maybe she was one of those readers with odd habits, like having to walk in circles before reading a book about circles. She did kick up a bit of dust. Guess dust wasn't only on the books! Then she glanced at me one more time and departed.

Well, I could spend my days wondering what was wrong with mortals. Or I could read a book that made them seem heroic and hilarious. So, I bent lower and discovered, sitting amongst the few novels, a plain copy of *Corum of Croth: The Beast Of Carnum*. I lifted it carefully from the shelf and flipped through the pages. I had long ago learned to have a deft touch and not poke holes in pages with my talons. A human librarian may seem dangerous, but a dragon librarian was Hades in a handbasket. Even a tongue-lashing scarred one for a lifetime.

"Yes! You found it!" Carmen hissed right into my ear.

I shuddered. When a dragon shudders, sometimes we lose control of our tails. Mine swept to one side and bumped into a small bookstand, making it tip. Only a quick grab with my hind paw stopped it from spilling several books onto the floor.

I glanced over my shoulder. The grey-haired librarian tapped the crossbow now resting on the desk, giving me a look that could have melted a building.

"You are a horrible sneak," I said to Carmen.

"No, I am a talented sneak," she corrected. She patted me on the shoulder, believing a sign of affection could placate me. Never! "You have a wonderful nose for books," she continued. Well, words like that would soon soothe my anger. "What does this love of mortal books say about you?"

"Allow me to correct your assumption," I said, tapping the page. "I read mortal books as a sign of pity. I honour your whole mortalkind by allowing my dragon eye to grace your prose." She laughed, indicating she thought differently. Since the first time she'd found me, I'd always had books within reach—in fact, I forced her to carry my favourites in her haversack. I couldn't help but respect any culture or creatures who wrote novels.

Poems, not so much. But novels, of course.

I flicked forward and quickly found the passage I was searching for, as it was practically imprinted on my memory. "Now, here's the scene where Corum meets the Kammit, the

Beast of Carnum." I read the piece aloud, using my most dramatic and impressive whispering voice, for I feared the shushes and crossbow bolts of the librarian. Also, any passing mortals would beg me to read more. "'Corum was surrounded by his enemies, their spears out to deal deadly damage to his earthly body. But before they could strike, he heard a sound of wetness and sliding, as if some great, monstrous entity were crossing the many worlds and arriving before his eyes. And his enemies' eyes! The Kaddians turned to face this new arrival: for there, in that holy sepulchre, on the nine-starred symbol of the goat, an unholy smoke arose. It was a half-god, half-man, with leopard legs and a mortal torso with clawed fingers and toothy tentacles twirling out of his back, swishing danger-ously above his crocodile-like head. The half-god spoke with words of power, 'Corum of Croth, you will be safe. For you have been chosen.'"

"But that's almost exactly what the emp—" Carmen began to say.

I raised a talon and continued reading: "The great god slew his captors in a heartbeat with powerful great eviscera-tions and grotesque slashings. All the Kaddians fell. It happened in two beats of Corum's heroic heart. 'Corum of Croth. The way to the future is through your soul,' the great voice said again. 'You are the pillar upon which we build. Look upon my glory.' Corum looked but was momentarily blinded, for a mortal cannot gaze upon a god. And then the god was gone, leaving the Kaddians all dead."

"First," Carmen said, "I can see why Akkadians don't read these books. The Kaddians are clearly meant to be Akkadians, and they die by the dozen. But second: that passage is very near what the emperor described. It is almost word for word. Except for his attacker being female."

"You should thank me for having such a wonderful brain."

Carmen chose not to thank me. Nor did she wax on about how wonderful my brain was. Instead, she asked, "But why was he lying to us?"

I raised a talon to my lips. "Not so loud. We are talking about the emperor of all the mortals in this room and beyond. Perhaps his mind retreated to this scene, his only way of making sense of what was happening around him. After all, there were real eviscerations in that room."

"Then what is the connection between that scene and what really happened?"

I tapped the book with the pad of my paw to avoid poking it with a talon. I did my best impression of a maestru's lecturing voice. "Well, in this book, Corum visits Kaddia, as I'm sure you remember. Often, he defeated Kaddians—the Avenians were obsessed with that, rightfully so." Out of politeness, I did not say this too loud. Maybe it's why the book hadn't been borrowed for decades. "And the author based his story on what he said were the real, true stories of Akkad and its gods and goddesses."

"So, you are saying that entity is real?"

"I am saying there must be another source. No author would stick his nose out of bed when he could research from the safety of his home. What we need is to find that source. That genuine source—it may be the book I read all those years ago in the Royal Library in Dreki. There is something else I can't quite put my talon on."

Before I could continue my thoughts, the floor, which was made of stone, shook slightly, and a book a few feet away fell to the floor. This ran a cold streak of fear through my heart. Who had dared to knock a book off a shelf? Neither Carmen nor I had moved, so it wasn't our fault. But I was certain we'd be blamed and punished for the deed. I expected to hear the whistling of a crossbow bolt and turned to catch it. Either with my body or my paw.

But instead, I caught the deepest words I had ever heard uttered.

"I will eat you from the inside out," a voice said. "And you will be delicious."

CHAPTER 16
AN INKLING ABOUT INKERTAIN

No one visible spoke the words.

With a sense of dread and a wonder at how many times this could happen in the space of a few hours, I noted that red smoke was rising from the floor. Not from a fire — that would be cause for *favourite-book-grabbing* alarm. No, it rose from a pattern on the floor between the bookshelves. The pattern appeared to have been created with coloured sand, forming a circle with several snake images inside — not a familiar symbol. Patrons were already bolting down other aisles toward the exit, books in hand. If they didn't stop to check them out, they might be bolted by a crossbow. Or fed to a bear.

"This is bad," Carmen said.

"Your ability to state the obvious is completely under-rated. Your maestrus must have been so proud of you." I raised my voice to an impressive volume. "Now, who is in that smoke who wants to eat me? Yes, I would be incredibly tasty because, judging by my way of winging through this world, I am tasteful. But I refuse to be food. Please come out where I can eviscerate you. I'll ask questions later."

As far as pre-battle taunts, it was a little too long and didn't flow properly. We dragons grew up prefacing battles with long, clever, stinging taunts before we tore our enemies apart. Our creativity thrived there, and we recorded some of the grandest battle taunts in *The Great Ledger of Battle Taunts*, which is kept in the Royal Library in Dreki. There was one famous dragon, Igrondul the Bearded, who made his taunt so long that his opponent died of old age.

Anyway, I had blessed the world with my battle taunt and in response the smoke thickened and grew high enough so that it reached the ceiling.

Something tall is in there, I sent to Carmen.

Should we flee? she asked inside my head.

I told you before that Braxus Andorium never flees.

Should we walk away with handsome speed? she sent. *Discretion is the better part of bravery, as Maestru Alesius used to say. Usually before trying a new hot-pepper dish.*

Before I could answer, the voice rumbled out of the smoke. "I will dissolve your bones and spread the broth across all of Inkertain." It was so raspy and deep that it was hard to tell whether it was a male or female speaking. What is it with so many creatures offering to destroy my bones lately? It hadn't yet mentioned Carmen, so perhaps its grudge was only against me. I could start making a list of my enemies in Akkad, but that would be nearly all of Akkad.

"Though it is kind of you to offer to turn me into broth," I said with an impressive amount of calm and aplomb, "I shall have to refuse. I like my bones in my body. And I demand you reveal yourself. Or are you too frightened?"

The voice used the word Inkertain, Carmen sent. *What's Inkertain?*

I glowed a little inside because I knew something she didn't! Reacting that way was a bad habit I should stamp out—otherwise, I'd be glowing all the time. *It's an old mortal word. Before Akkad, there was Inkertain.*

How can you know more than me about my world?

I let her mentally stew in that question. We now had the library to ourselves. Funny how smoke and evil voices clear a room. Even the librarians had vanished. So much for being fearless protectors of their collection—they'd obviously rather keep their skins on their backs than save the hides of their books. Of course, maybe they knew something I didn't.

No. Impossible.

"Fear. Fear is for flesh." The deepness of the voice made my own bones vibrate. "For bones. For those with hearts."

"Show yourself," I repeated. "And I'll show you what these bones can do."

A rounded snout emerged from the fog. I expected fangs or tentacles to come next. There were two nostrils at the end, and the skin was warty and dry as if the creature had spent the last few thousand years out in the sun. "Leave this hallowed empire; go back to your lands," the snout said.

"You leave," Carmen replied.

Two glowing eyes as orange as burning suns were visible now. And they glared at my little Carmen. "Go before you are turned to dust. Crushed. Poisoned. Broken. Destroyed."

If it is urging us to go, I sent, *then it fears us. Hold your ground!*

The snout emerged farther, and I got a better impression

of the creature's size. It wasn't as big as I had first thought —in fact, it was only about as tall as Carmen.

"If you're here to borrow a tome," I said, "they prefer you use the front door."

"All things fall," the snout said. "All things turn to desiccation and dust."

I am of the opinion that it doesn't really hear us, I sent.

Or it is so powerful it can ignore us, she replied.

The red smoke dissipated in a few heartbeats, and I couldn't help myself: I laughed.

"It's a frog," I said. "A great big frog!"

"No, it's a giant toad," Carmen corrected. She had visibly relaxed. She was right on both counts, for the toad had dry skin and was fifteen to twenty paws tall, so Carmen could look it eye-to-eye. I had no strong opinions on toads, mostly because they weren't that interesting to eat.

"You wanted to flee from this," I said. "Ha, some assassin you are."

"I was being circumspect."

The toad looked back and forth. "Leave this place, return to your lands," it said. "I will crush your innards." The voice still sounded impressively deep, but it was very hard to take it seriously since the threats were coming out of a toad.

"How about you shut your fly-catching gob hole," I said. I will admit to being rather proud of that one. "Before I stuff you full of ancient Timmerian texts. Or turn you into toad-legged soup."

"I will dissolve your bones," it said. "And make soup."

"It's repeating itself," Carmen said, again stating the obvious. "Whoever sent this toad wanted to frighten us."

"Well, don't get too close," I said. "It might lick you to death."

"Toads don't have long tongues." That was twice she'd corrected me in the last few moments. She could be incredibly aggravating. "We used the gall sacks behind their eyes for poison, so we dissected hundreds of them."

"Have a heart," I said. "Don't mention that in front of our guest."

"Well, it seems to be here to warn us. Who would go through all the trouble of sending a toad?"

"Your guts shall be cast across the lands," the toad said. "We'll make a banner of your hides."

"And the threats don't even make sense," I said.

"We might shoo it outside before it damages a book." Carmen raised her hands like she was about to chase a sheep out of a stable.

"Are you now a toad shepherd who—" I started to say.

The toad opened its mouth, and its tongue shot out and smacked Carmen's cheek, making a slapping sound that echoed across the room. She hadn't even had time to raise a blade. The tongue flicked back in the same eye-blink.

"Ha!" I laughed. "You were wrong. This toad has a long tongue. I bet that was grotesque and intellectually humiliating." She didn't echo my laughter. "Carmen? Carmen?" Her eyes were wide with something akin to fear, and she stood completely still. A purple bruise spread across her cheek.

"Oh, I guess they have poison," I said. I grabbed her by the cloak, lifted her bodily, and planted her behind me. Sadly, I hadn't used enough finesse, for she tumbled over like a statue made of flesh. "You may have surprised her," I said to the beastly toad, "but there's no way you have enough poison in your tongue to stop a full-grown Scythian dragon."

I drew in a breath. What this situation required was a very direct blast of pure flames that would melt the frog without burning the books behind it. A blast like that required incredible skill. Luckily, I had that skill. And that incredibleness.

I sucked in air through my nostrils, feeling the fire in my chest forming. This frog was about to become a dried-out memory. But before I could open my mouth, the toad's tongue shot through the air and smacked me right across the snout. There was a barb at the end of the tongue, and it stabbed perfectly between my scales, making me feel very much like I'd been stung by a large hornet. Then the toad's tongue snapped back.

"Ha," I said. "That didn't work on me at all." Then I laughed. "You are so, so dead."

Then I realized something. My lips hadn't moved while I spoke. How strange. In fact, the words I thought I'd spoken had only appeared in my head. *Oh, no,* I sent. *Are you trapped in your head, too?*

Carmen's voice appeared between my ears. *Yes, I am frozen.*

This is very, very bad.

Your ability to state the obvious is legendary, she sent. *At least you are not a rigid statue with your face to the floor. I can just move my eyes enough to watch the toad. And by the way, you said it had poison. That's incorrect. If you bite it and you die, it's poison, but if it bites or stings you and you die, that's venom. So, this is a venomous toad.*

If only you could be a silent statue, I sent.

The toad had stopped threatening us, at least. But it was

not quite ready to surrender. In fact, it looked to be bubbling.

By that, I mean the warts on the toad's back grew larger and larger, bulging all along either side of its spine. Something squirmed inside each one of those sacs, dripping a gooey mess.

Can you see that? I sent.

It's eggs, she said. *This situation is now a whole lot worse.*

That was an understatement. For there was a popping sound, and it wasn't tadpoles that squirmed out onto the floor. Instead, a tentacle rose out of a sac on the frog's back. More popping and more tentacles immediately followed this. Several of them swung out, arced down, and stuck to the floor.

Ha, I sent. *The frog couldn't tentacle the broad side of a pub.*

I think it has a reason for tentacling the floor, Carmen replied.

What good would sticking to the floor do?

Then, one of the largest tentacles slapped the top of my head and stuck like glue. Another hit my muscular chest, and two more stuck to either broad shoulder. The toad pulled me, using the tentacles on the floor as a grip.

Oh, I see. I'm a little worried about where this is all leading.

Even as I sent that thought to her, the toad's endgame became clear. It unhinged its jaw and its mouth opened wider and wider so that it was like staring into a green, fleshy cavern with a roiling tongue as a floor.

I am about to become toad food, I sent. *This is not the heroic death I had envisioned for myself.*

What would it be like to be consumed by a toad? I assumed it would be a slow, acidic experience. Would I quickly suffocate or get to enjoy every moment of its digestion? Its tongue grabbed me around the snout, giving me one more dose of its freezing poison.

It's the source ingredient for the paralysis tincture Corwin used on me once, Carmen sent. *To prevent me from going to graduation.*

That's incredibly interesting, I replied. *But I'm looking at a toad's tonsils.* The mouth also had its share of saliva. For a creature that was so dry outside, the inside looked like a slimy mess. This was ignoble on so many levels.

Oh, Carmen sent. *I can wiggle my toes now. I am partly immune to this venom. Keep doing what you're doing.*

I'm being consumed! That's what I'm doing! At this speed, it will be about three hours before I'm devoured.

Then the toad shook and let out a grunt. It opened even wider, but just as I was about to be yanked inside, its mouth snapped shut an inch from my face. It began shrinking, allowing me to see the toad's eyes again. There was a crossbow bolt in one eye and another in its side. A tentacle lashed out to my left toward another target.

The librarian, eyes narrowed like she'd watched a book burning, was standing there, calmly slipping a third bolt into her crossbow. With a nimble move that belied her age, she jumped to the side, and the tentacle slapped a bookshelf. It then latched onto a book, and, without making much of a fuss, the librarian snapped out a kick, and the book fell to the floor. She sent another crossbow bolt into the toad, hitting its chest. Clearly, this toad didn't have a heart. It slammed another tentacle madly on the floor and was rewarded with another bolt.

Five tentacles came unstuck from me and flew toward the librarian. Following them closely was the toad's tongue. The librarian didn't move, and I assumed she was about to be venomed. Instead, at the moment before those appendages arrived, she loosed a bolt. It hit somewhere in the toad's open mouth. And clearly, the librarian knew toad anatomy, for behind that softness was its brain.

It let out a surprised croak and fell over, the tentacles sludding—I just cleverly invented that word, a combination of slamming and thudding—on the floor. They squirmed around, then grew still.

Red smoke came up from underneath it, and the toad itself folded into what looked like a hole in the floor. All that remained was a slimy puddle and a frozen dragon and assassin.

"I knew it was wrong to allow you entry to my library," the librarian said. "Now look at this mess."

CHAPTER 17
A TOADY METAPHOR

I wanted to say something of great wisdom to this librarian or at least tell her it wasn't my fault the toad had appeared. Instead, I stood completely still. My spine was tingling as I blinked my clever reply. Then I felt something at my side. A pat. Well, at least I was feeling things. Carmen came around to the front of me, her gait lopsided. Her face was also lopsided, and I truly hoped that would fix itself.

"My thanks, Imperial Librarian of Akkad, guardian of books and great wisdom," she said. "You arrived at exactly the right time."

"I had to get my *summoned creature* bolts," she explained, "and take the antidote so as not to experience any of the toad venom side effects."

"You are a kind and wise saviour," Carmen said. "Would you reward me with the gift of sharing your name?"

The librarian's eyes showed a slight reduction in severity at this display of civility and contrition. "My name is Anandi

Endarka. And you don't need to introduce yourself, for you are Carmen of the Red Assassin Keep."

"You know of me?" Carmen put a hand to her chest, either feigning modesty or truly modest. It was hard to tell with her.

"We have an enviable selection of books about Red Assassins that include accounts of their services to the empire of Akkad and their strikes against our empire. Several of those entries have been recently updated."

"Well, it is an honour to be in a tome in your legendary library," Carmen said. She was beaming with pride.

Just because they put you in a book, it doesn't make you great, I sent to her. *I'm in hundreds of books.*

Villains get the most mentions, she sent back to me, viper-quick. If I'd had control of my limbs, I would have tripped her.

Anandi gestured towards me with her crossbow. It was loaded, so I would have preferred she point a finger. "I see your scaly friend is not the worse for wear but now exists in a rather pleasant state of quiet stillness."

Carmen patted my shoulder again, though I felt only the slightest bit of pressure. "Yes, we should enjoy the quiet while we can. Quietude is important, especially in these hallowed halls."

Another degree of severity retreated from the librarian's eyes. Carmen had long ago learned that the best way to a librarian's heart was to speak highly of their library, their books, and their filing skills. They are rather simple to manipulate.

"Clearly, you have a partial immunity to the toad's venom," the librarian said. "The paralysis in your face is retreating."

Carmen touched her cheek. "Yes. It still tingles, though."

Anandi, the aggravating librarian, waved the crossbow at me again. "And your scaly friend didn't have immunity."

"He's only a dragon," she said. "Not an assassin." Now Carmen was trying to rile me. "What exactly was that creature?"

"A Gutian toad. It was grown in an inter-realm vat. It waits in that vat sometimes for centuries, its hunger growing each hour until it is finally released."

"But who opened the gate to that vat?" Carmen asked.

"Well," Anandi said, "clearly you have enemies here in Akkadium, which isn't a surprise judging by that one's mouth." She didn't even look at me, instead jabbing a thumb in my direction. That was mildly better than pointing her crossbow.

"Who in this city has enough power to do a summoning?" Carmen asked. "From my studies, which I'm sure are nowhere near as in-depth as yours, it takes great skill and knowledge."

"Emperor Sargon could have done so easily," she said. "But he's dead." I had helped to slay him, so wondered at her motives for mentioning that particular emperor. It was hard to tell if there was regret in her tone. "Our new emperor, the reader that he is, has none of that power. Now that the wizards and witches are no longer being hunted, the palace has hired a few—sometimes, residual magic drifts out of the gates. But we are uncertain who uses it. In the old days, if a magician got too powerful, the emperor would eat their heart." Ah, how I missed that emperor. He made dragons look gentle and kind. "Clearly, someone sees you as enough of a threat that they will attack you in public. In an Imperial library." Her hands tightened on her crossbow. I wished she'd put it down. "In *my* library."

The two other librarians came into view, buckets in hand, and began wiping up the dust that had been used to make the symbol on the floor. The gooey remains of the toad stained their mops green. A few braver patrons, perhaps having set down a novel before fleeing, were now coming back to see how it ended. They made a wide berth around us.

Does she know when this will wear off? I sent to Carmen.

"Was the toad attack symbolic?" Carmen asked. Her ability to ignore my voice inside her head was incredibly aggravating.

We're not looking for an essay on amphibian symbols, I sent.

The librarian rubbed her chin with the non-crossbow hand. "Do you mean if it had consumed you, which surely would have happened without my intervention, would the other powers in Akkad know who had done this and, therefore, been warned to stay in their places?"

"Exactly," Carmen said.

"Toads are respected here in Akkad. Some are even worshipped, for they can bury themselves in the desert and survive the heat until it rains again, coming to the surface. It is very much a metaphor for our empire. And our people."

I'm not sure comparing your entire race to toads is tasteful, I sent. *But ask her who specifically worships the toads.*

"The toad as a national inspiration is truly inspirational," Carmen said without a hint of sarcasm. Sadly, she said most things without sarcasm. "Which of your various religious groups worships toads the most deeply?"

"There's a sect in the Temple of the Cowled Goddess that worships them," the librarian replied. Though her face looked to be made of fleshy granite, she seemed to be showing a hint of disdain here.

"And are they a violent sect?" Carmen asked.

"All sects are violent when they don't get their own way," the librarian said. She glanced toward where the two other librarians were finishing up the cleaning. The sand had been swept up into a golden pail. They were handling it carefully—it was obviously important to them. It now looked as if the toad had never been here. Well, except for the fact that there was a frozen dragon standing in the middle of the library.

Ask her if that fancy antidote works on drag—

"I would place odds that your friend—" Librarian Anandi gestured with the crossbow again "—would like to be freed from his condition."

"I suppose it is the easiest way to get him out of the library," Carmen replied. "Though, with the help of a few elephants, you could drag him outside and mount him on a pedestal opposite the bear."

Oh, ha ha ha, I sent.

"That bear deserves better companionship than this scaly beast," the librarian said. Now, I'm not an expert in mortal voices—they are too tinny sometimes—but I was certain there was regret in her voice. She liked the bear! The librarian set down the crossbow and, from inside the folds of her plain brown robe, retrieved a small vial, which she handed to Carmen. "This should be enough for twinkle talons," she said.

Twinkle talons, Carmen said. *I love that.*

If you ever say it again, especially aloud, you will find my twinkle talons tickling your brain.

Carmen laughed with enough volume that the librarian gave her a *do I have to shush you?* look.

Still smiling, Carmen popped the cork off the vial and gave it a deep sniff, then, not happy with that, put a drop on her finger and tasted it. She was testing for poison. Despite her horrid laughter, she still cared about me. A very tiny sliver of my heart melted metaphorically.

"Oh, blueberry-flavoured," she said.

"I am not offended that you don't trust me," the librarian said. "Since your maestrus have trained you to trust no one."

"Better safe than dead," she said. "That was Maestru Alesius's favourite saying."

Some help that saying was . . . he's dead right now, I sent, then felt a stab of guilt. She had truly loved him. Sometimes, the snarky side of my brain was too fast for the wise side. *He shall be missed,* I added, but it was too late. Carmen stiffened and lifted the antidote high enough that she seemed to consider smashing it on the floor. She turned toward me, her smile as tight as a bowstring.

At least I hadn't made a joke about her long-haired Wodenite dying. I wasn't completely insane.

She had to pry my mouth open, and it took serious exertion. I was worried she would resort to using her sword as a pry bar—maybe taking out a few teeth at the same time. But with enough grunting, she eventually forced my jaw down, then moved my head so that my throat was at a good swallowing angle. If she'd wanted to, she could have posed me in many ridiculous poses. Or, worse, dropped vegetables straight into my gullet.

But Carmen's kindness won over whatever vengeance rested in her heart. She emptied the vial, and a burning pain spread across my tongue. Within a heartbeat or two, my mouth worked, and I swallowed. The burning sensation continued down my incredibly long and elegant throat and into my guts. The heat then spread outward through the rest of my body.

I flexed my chest muscles, then moved one leg and nearly fell over, catching myself at the last moment. Better to stay still until the antidote worked its way through all of me.

"Well, that was horrible," I said.

"I thought you liked blueberry," Carmen said.

"It's a fruit," I replied. "But the horrible part was being frozen like that and not being able to retort to your conversation. Anyway . . ." I bowed slightly towards the librarian, who, I noted, continued holding her crossbow. I was very pleased that I didn't fall over. "My thanks and thanks from the glorious land of Drachia for your aid."

"You are welcome," she said. "If I hadn't already known you were a reader, you wouldn't be allowed in here. And I might not have been so kind."

"As it should be," I replied. "I have a question. You mentioned that sect in the Temple of the Cowled Goddess. Do they wear red robes?"

"Yes," she said. "They do."

It was Enheduanna of the who set the toad upon us, I sent. Best not to say it aloud, as I didn't know where the librarian's loyalties lay.

How do you know? Carmen replied.

I saw a minion stamp the pattern on the floor. I thought she was another confused mortal.

The librarian was looking back and forth between us. "Well, now that the books are safe, if it is not too much trouble, will both of you depart my library?"

"Dearest Librarian of the Imperial Library of Akkad," Carmen began. "We are in your debt, and if—"

"Begone," the librarian said. "Enough with the niceties. My filing awaits." She pointed the crossbow at the front door, and we got the hint.

I turned to walk. It wasn't easy yet, and I bumped one of the book stacks, but it didn't fall over, so I counted that as a victory. A glance showed that Anandi was ready to murder me with her eyes.

Carmen held the door open and I squeezed through without snapping the frame and took the stone steps slowly. I somehow travelled at an angle down the stairs and ended up beside the bear. He gave me a look that he might have learned from the librarian.

"Well," I said, "let's never come back to this library." My voice slurred somewhat.

I glanced again at the bear, and it reminded me of the time when I had been chained in a cave: weeks of starving, the torture of only having a few books to read, and finally, Carmen coming in to release me. In her mind, it was a rescue. Of course, not that many rescued prisoners must trade an eye to get out. "I understand," I said to the bear. He now gave me a look that I interpreted as commiseration. He'd spent his life being bothered by Akkadians. Even being this close to a library wasn't a help for him. "I really understand you, my hairy friend."

"Hairy! What?" Carmen spat the words out. "Are vestiges of the venom affecting you? Are you of sound mind?"

"I'm completely sound." I closed my eyes, then opened them to discover the entire world had shifted at an angle. "Is this the end times?"

"Brax, I'm getting worried." She reached high to put a hand on my forehead.

It wasn't the end of times. I was leaning to one side because the muscles in that leg weren't yet working properly. Even the bear had a worried expression. "You are a good friend," I said, though I wasn't certain if I was talking to Carmen or to the bear.

"Yes, yes, and so are you." Her hand was pleasantly cool.

"I need you to get on my back," I said. "For I know what we have to do."

"Brax? I'm uncertain that it is safe for you to fly in this condition."

I unfurled my wings and flapped them a few times, causing dust to swirl from the steps. It got the attention of several Akkadians approaching the library. They turned away as if they suddenly remembered they'd left their books at home.

"I am feeling as strong as a . . . well, as a dragon," I said. "It's perfectly safe. Trust me." My thoughts were getting clearer.

"I will trust you," she said, though her voice was hesitant. "But only because I've seen you fly with several holes in you."

Holes that she likely somehow caused, but I didn't say that out loud. Carmen jumped into her place and grabbed the horn on my back. I took off, going straight up so that we rose above the library.

Looking down, the bear was much smaller. The steps, too. Even the library. Everything was small if you flew high enough.

I took a deep breath of the somewhat fresh air and,

without warning my rider, dived straight down. Carmen let out a little shriek that I'm sure would have caused the assassin maestrus shame. The bear let out a roar of surprise, too, because I was plummeting straight for him. He tried to lurch out of my way, but I am a hunter.

I grabbed the bear by the shoulders, careful not to cut him with my talons. He let out another roar.

"Brax!" Carmen shouted. "You've lost your mind!"

"No, I haven't," I slurred as I lifted the bear out of his cage.

He was heavier than I'd expected, and I wasn't a Quant dragon. We Scythians were not all brawn. Maybe if I'd dropped Carmen off, it would have been easier to lift this weight. But with a mighty flapping of my wings, we were in the air. The bear missed hitting the top of the library by a few inches.

"What in the seven Hades are you doing?" Carmen asked.

"The right thing," I answered as we flew across the city, a confused bear dangling below us.

CHAPTER 18
A TERRIBLE TINY AGGRAVATION ARRIVES

There were several people who pointed upward at our awesome outlines, including guards. But Carmen wisely was quiet, perhaps seeing that it took all my strength to carry the three of us over Akkadium. I imagine she came to this conclusion when I bumped the bear into a bronze bear statue sitting atop the church of The Great Bear. I am certain that years from now, that accidental bumping will be remembered as a religious event. Neither the bear nor the statue fell, but the accidental bump left one slightly askew. After that, I squeezed a bit more height out of my wings and cleared the city walls with several inches to spare. We flew over a series of flat wheat fields until I saw, in the distance, a group of low hills covered with spotty clumps of grass. I immediately named them the Bald Maestru Hills.

I chuckled at my cleverness.

"What are you laughing at?" Carmen asked.

"Nothing, nothing," I said, knowing she was sensitive about maestru jokes. "Hold tight."

As we approached the hills, I glided down and expertly

used all my strength and skill to lower the bear. I wanted him to have the softest landing possible, so I worked hard at flapping in place before releasing him. He only rolled over once, so I was a little off the mark on that. I'm no fool—I winged a suitable distance away, landing on the baldest spot on top of the hill, out of paw and teeth range, and thunked down. Then I turned so we were facing our former passenger.

The bear glanced to the left and the right, perhaps looking for the bars of his cage. He then began whipping his head back and forth with more and more speed until foam lathered his lips. It seemed like he might go mad—a bad thing for a bear and any creature that encountered him. I knew dragons who were released after being locked away in prison for years, sometimes crouched under arches, afraid of the open sky. The head shaking became even more fervent, so the gathering lather on his lips flew off. He was going to shake until his brains came out of his ears.

Then, in the space of a heartbeat, he stopped. He sniffed the air, stared directly at me, and let out a loud roar. Then, and this is where I think my mind might be a little overtired, he uttered two lines.

"Ursus in thanks, Ursus in need. Ursus is here for you when you bleed. Just say the name of Ursus, and he will heed."

It was a powerful name. Maybe it was his own. The three lines stuck in my head, and I had the sense that he was very thankful and perhaps all the bears who had ever lived, even the Bear God, were thankful, too.

"Did you hear that?" I asked.

"Hear what?" she replied.

Clearly, the bear had spoken only to me. Or the ammit spit or toad venom was still poisoning my blood.

The bear let out one more roar that I interpreted as, "You are a mighty and wise dragon with shiny scales; we are brothers forever, and I will name my children after you." And then he rushed down the hill, up the next one and out of sight. It was one of the most beautiful, heart-stirring things I'd seen in the last few months, not counting the fried goat we'd had in the palace.

"Do you want to tell me what that little escapade was all about?" Carmen asked.

"It would take too long," I replied, though I will admit I was working hard to hide my smile.

"Well, he looked happier."

"Truthfully, that was the point."

"I have this feeling my sunshiny personality is rubbing off on you." She patted my neck.

Just like her to claim the glory for something I did. Mortals!

"Don't insult me, Princess," I replied. Being a commoner and proud of it, she abhorred any suggestion she was royalty. As far as I could tell, mortals who grow up in an assassin keep dream only of killing princesses and other royal types. Seeking some respite, I tucked myself into a ball beyond the hill, away from the city's view. "If you could scrounge up a goat and several waterskins of boisonberry-flavoured water, I'd very much appreciate it. I may need to lie here for a decade before I tell you what our next move will be."

I closed my eyes. The sun was warm, my body was tired, and I felt safe enough because Carmen could see in almost every direction. Sun on scales is one of the glorious joys of being a dragon. Each scale heats, and the energy of the sun goes right into our bodies. Some of our great dragon thinkers believe that sunlight powers the flames inside us. I, though, have seen a dragon imprisoned in a cave who could still make flames. Well, that dragon was me. So, I preferred to think of the source of our flames as a wonderful mystery.

Speaking of thinking, I stopped doing that and slept. I didn't even hear when Carmen left.

When I next noticed the outside world, it was because my nostrils were wrinkling on their own. A sudden consternation swept over me. Were my nostrils being controlled by some powerful magical force? If so, soon the rest of my body would be under a spell, and I would become a dragon of destruction for a mighty wizard. No, I decided a moment later. My nostrils were moving for a reason.

For a smell.

A very good, wonderfully perfect smell.

It was obvious that the toad venom remained in my insides, for it took what felt to be two and a half millennia for my eyes to open. But what a sight I beheld, for something red, pink, and beautiful was dangling in front of my nose. A honey-roasted ham. And holding it on a sharpened stick was Carmen, who displayed a proud, mischievous smile. "I thought that might wake you. I also thought it best to not put my hands in harm's way."

She flipped the ham into the air, and I caught it in my jaws. It took three chews to tear it into many glorious chunks of tastiness. It was coated with garlic and honey mustard seasoning! I had a sudden urge to hug my beautiful mortal friend but didn't want anyone watching from the walls of Akkadium to see that I had a soft side. That would sully my reputation.

"Carmen, I hereby forgive you for all your trespasses and your inequities," I said. "You are marvellous."

There is a special glow she gets when a superior gives her a compliment.

"I know I'm marvellous," Carmen replied.

"Wow, you sounded on the edge of being conceited. A little like your brother." Corwin, her twin, was like someone had pulled her reflection out of a mirror, made it male, and added a trunkful of conceit and anger. Or, at least, he was that way in several of the versions of him I'd met so far. The latest version was a little friendlier and kinder and not so puffed up with ego.

"I got the ham from a nearby farmer," she explained. "I traded a dragon's tooth for it."

"That's not funny," I said.

"Well, two coins. And, because I know you'll ask, not the ones Nagar gave us." She raised a finger. "And speaking of Corwin, my dear wizardly brother, I sent him a message. In fact, this might be the reply."

With that, one of the most aggravating, tiniest, ugliest, and completely unnecessary creatures came popping out of the sky at full speed and hovered in front of us: a spellbird. They are slightly larger than a sparrow but with the personalities of a vulture and an emperor combined. These spellbirds were created by wizards centuries ago and instilled with all the conceit and self-importance of the very worst humans.

"Are you Carmen Dore of the Red Assassins?" the spellbird asked. This one was female, which didn't mean she would be any less horrid to deal with.

"I've always wondered," I interrupted. "Why do you call yourself the Red Assassins? You only wear black cloaks."

"Because we wear red cloaks on graduation night," she replied.

"You name your group after a piece of clothing you only wear once?"

"Making other people bleed red is also part of our history," she said with no regret.

"Will you two stop talking?" The spellbird's voice cut right into my eardrums. "I have a message. Are you or are you not Carmen Dore of the Red Assassins?"

"Yes, I am Carmen Dore of the Red Assassins," Carmen replied.

"Well, aren't I lucky to have found you?" The tone suggested it was the same luck one experienced when landing in cow dung. "I have a message for your ears. Is your mind intelligent enough to receive it?"

"I will struggle to understand your eloquently delivered words," Carmen said, clearly not taking offence. I believe that somewhere in her mixed-up mind, she thought of these creatures as being cute. And she also knew compliments were the only way to make them act somewhat civilized. I would never stoop that low. "Please deliver the message, my fine feathered friend," she added.

The bird landed on her hand. I stifled the need to scream, "Watch out for droppings!" The bird first preened a few feathers and then sucked in a deep breath like a thespian preparing for an important soliloquy.

"Carmen Dore of the Red Assassins," the bird said, except this time, it was not the bird's voice. They had the evil ability to mimic any voice they heard. This voice was that of a female, with a raspiness that suggested the speaker had been gargling glass and eating lit torches. A little prickle ran down my scales, for I was familiar with the speaker. "It is I, Blacktooth of the Witches' and Wizards' Council of Azadiq." The woman paused, letting her name sink in, for she was a witch who had tried to murder us with a murder of crows some time ago. Hearing her horrid voice was not good news at all.

It was even worse news than I had expected. "I am certain that you remember me. Well, it gives me no joy or pleasure to announce this, but I have grave news: your brother Corwin is dead."

CHAPTER 19

A Tale Horrendously Told

Carmen sucked in her breath but didn't reply, partly because there was no point in replying to a message from a spellbird but also because the spellbird, after a dramatic pause, spoke again in that evil witch's voice. And as she spoke, I pictured Blacktooth standing in her grey robe that matched her long grey hair, with her face that was magically altered to look young and her wonderful collection of sharpened black teeth.

"As I said, there is no joy in these words."

"Ha," I spat. "I bet! You're loving every bit of this moment, you—you murderous murderer of a witch."

"Shush!" Carmen said. I gave her a glare, but she was concentrating on the bird like it might explode.

The witch continued: "I have grown to enjoy the work I did on the council with Corwin, and there was one case where he came up with a solution that was nearly passable. I wished him no ill will or harm."

"But what happened to him?" Carmen hissed.

The bird, being a pompous spellbird, ignored her and continued mimicking Blacktooth's voice. "I am sure you are curious about his death, and I can only say that it was horrible. Or it must have been horrible, for there were no witnesses to the horrendous battle he had, other than his black swan. And, as you know, they cannot speak. They only honk. Unlike ravens, who, if trained properly and encouraged with the proper spells, are superior winged creatures. The most superior of all winged creatures, I should add." A dig at me! I counted a hundred ways to get revenge. Even the spellbird seemed upset.

"But I know you don't want a lesson on how ravens were taught to speak or a similar lesson about the order of importance of winged creatures."

We have no interest at all! I was tempted to shout, but I bravely held my impatience in. Well, for a heartbeat and a half, because I could suddenly no longer restrain my anger. "Out with it!" I shouted. The bird clearly fed on my anger, for it somehow made a grin appear on its beak. Yes, physically, that's impossible, for beaks are beaks. But he was grinning. And Blacktooth likely imagined my outburst, which would only widen her black-toothed grin.

"So, to get to the point," the witch continued. "This is what happened: we received a message from your brother, delivered by a crow, no less. Not a raven! And it was not one of these spellbirds, like the one you are listening to right now that you sent to your brother." She cleared her throat, a throat packed with a thousand years of phlegm. Even I, who have a stomach of steel, was contorted by disgust. She had once spat at us a bile that burned the grass at our feet. It was particularly horrid phlegm. It was frighteningly amazing how the spellbird could replicate the horking sound to perfection. "Sorry about that. There was a frog in my throat."

"I bet literally," I said.

"I imagine Brax has said something clever in reply to that admission," the spellbird version of Blacktooth continued. "Like any small-brained creature, he is patting himself on the back for an insult only a child would consider funny. I sent the spellbird to you because I prefer my ravens to stay closer to home, and I save them for very important messages." She let this last line sink in. "Corwin's meagre crow arrived at the council and told us in its crow voice—they don't do that same trick as the spellbirds, where they can copy the timber and tone of a voice—it's really kind of a ragged sound. But this desperate crow asked us—well, ask is the wrong word. What's the right word? Oh, yes, it begged. It begged on behalf of Corwin for us to immediately aid him at his home in Algaria. As you know, he inherited the fief from his master, Goran, a much better wizard whose only fault was choosing bad apprentices and bad, off-island friends. I am certain you remember Goran, as it was your sister who killed him, Carmen. With a spear, no less! Well, that's not something that a sibling would readily forget, right? No matter what guilt or lack of guilt one felt."

"Tell us about Corwin now!" I shouted loud enough that the spellbird's feathers were blown back. It glared at me, and if it could spit poison, it would have done so at that moment. "Can we not skip ahead to the important part? She's delaying and throat-clearing on purpose."

"Brax," Carmen whispered. "Let the bird speak. Please."

The bird hadn't stopped speaking, but I understood Carmen's meaning and took a deep breath, both to calm myself and to remember that she was ten times more on edge about any events that involved Corwin.

"So," the witch continued. "We left the council, three of us, and travelled by our own separate means. My lovely murder of ravens carried me, if you must know, and Ob took giant step—steps that he had borrowed from a giant— and finally, Oma used a broom. I know, I know, a stereo-type, but she had been using it to wipe cosmic cobwebs from the obelisks at the Gorzed Circle. With a snap of her fingers, it became her transportation. We travelled with all speed toward Algaria, hoping to save him. But when we arrived at his fief, it was in a rather poor state: the fence for his live-stock had been broken, and the sheep were wandering around free. His black swan, Camden? Callda? I can't remember her name, but she was honking at us in an admonishing and slightly aggravating tone. Her wing was clearly cracked, and her beak bloodied. Behind her, his house was in flames. House? Well, I would call it a hut— you're welcome to call his ramshackle dwelling whatever you want. Ob cast a water spell while Oma and I burst into his home; I was first, in case you doubt my motivation, and not because I was hoping to find him in a horrid state, but that is exactly how we found him—in a wretched, horrid state. He was on the floor, his face pale, and he was not breathing. His clothing had been shredded by claws. Corwin had clearly put up—well, I won't call it a valiant struggle, perhaps a desperately thrashing struggle, to judge by the state of his home. There was a star-snake symbol on the floor, and its lines had been broken, which meant he had sent back whatever he had been struggling against." She breathed deeply in, the rattle in her lungs making me want to purge the contents of my stomach. "We dragged him out of the half-destroyed hut and into the sunlight. To our surprise, we discovered he was still alive, though on the very edge of leaving this world. First, he rolled his bloodshot eyes toward me, and then he spoke, using his last few breaths. His rambling sentence was this: 'Blacktooth, I admire you, and please forgive me for being a difficult fraud of a wizard and not worthy of your attention.'"

Corwin didn't talk like that, and he would never compliment her, but I didn't say it out loud. Instead, I tried to sift for the truth in this tale.

"I replied, with all magnanimity, 'I forgive you, child. You strove beyond your meagre abilities. But at least you strove.' And he closed his eyes, and I nearly turned away, believing my forgiveness was the last thing he needed to hear before passing. But he opened his wizard eye—well, it's really Boqin's eye if you want to be specific—why your brother was allowed to have another wizard's eye, I will never understand. He was spoiled. Spoiled!"

The spellbird drew in another breath. I don't know if this meant that Blacktooth had drawn in a breath or the bird did not have big enough lungs to talk as long as the witch could talk. "Your spoiled brother spat out a few more words: 'I—I was attacked by two adversaries, which you could have easily beaten, but they were far too strong for my meagre skills. One was a toad, and the other a woman with hair on her legs, I mean thick hairs, like a hide.' He really talked about the hair on her legs for too long, but I guess he spent most of his time on the floor, so that's what he saw. Hair on a woman's legs is not something to dwell on, and to be clear, it's perfectly natural, and there's nothing wrong with it. Nothing at all. 'But there wasn't just hair on her legs,' Corwin said to me. 'She also had claws on her long-fingered hands and the snout of a crocodile.' I will say, for someone who was dying, he went on for an interminably long time about his opponent's appearance. He always was vacuous. 'The toad stuck me with venom, and she attacked me with her claws and mean, mean words. My valiant swan tried to intervene but was smacked aside. And thus, I have I been delivered these deadly death-dealing wounds.'" The bird took yet another breath. "And there were many wounds, let me tell you: small ones, big ones, deep ones, long ones. A smorgasbord of slices. Mostly claw wounds. But there were burn marks too. You can probably picture them, so I don't need to go into any more detail. Please imagine the worst, and you will be almost close to what he looked like. Though, I would be remiss if I didn't mention the big purple sore on his forehead where the toad's tongue stung him."

The bird took another deep breath. This time, I was certain it couldn't talk as long as Blacktooth—perhaps its lungs were expanded by special spells. And, for the very tiniest moment, I felt a thimbleful of empathy for this creature.

"But your brother still wasn't dead. I'm surprised he didn't talk about the hair on Ob's legs, who was standing next to us. His monk's robe is always cut a little high, in my opinion. Wizards and witches shouldn't show their legs. Anyway, your brother, finally at the end of his time, rambled and coughed out words I will only pass on to you when I have the great pleasure of seeing you in person because I am certain you will come here to bury him, burn him to ashes, or turn him into a vial of poison—whatever it is you assassins do to your dead. But rest assured, he breathed his last breath and shuddered unpleasantly. Ob put an ice spell upon his body to preserve it. So, you'll get to see him in all his gory glory. Ob even froze him with an unhappy look on his face."

The spellbird took a crackling breath in and finished with, "We expect you to come to settle the affairs of your dead brother. Despite your past transgressions, you and the dragon are welcome here on Azadiq. We have lifted the ban on assassins, which was only logical because most of you are dead. Ironic, isn't it? Your kind hunted us, and now we no longer fear you. As you likely guessed, I drew the shortest straw and so was forced to tell you this tale. My sincere and most sad condolences on the death of Crowin—I mean Corwin. Safest of travels." The spellbird cleared its sparrow throat as if imitating Blacktooth had scarred it forever. It spat a tiny bit of spit.

"Well, that was unpleasant," the bird said. "Though not as unpleasant as being face to face with her."

"You have my sincere condolences for that experience," I said. "She once sent a flock of dead ravens to capture us and then spat her spittle toward our—"

"I don't care about your tedious travails," the spellbird interrupted. "If I have to listen to one more self-important dragon regurgitate their thoughts, I shall wish for a quick death."

"I'll grant that wish," I hissed and swiped at the bird. With a blurring flick of her wings, she flew up, avoiding the blow. And she avoided the next and the next. Her laughter had a tinkling sound that reminded me of breaking wine glasses. I wanted to hear breaking bird bones.

"You little son of a winged excrement." I will admit my insult didn't quite make sense. The bird was getting under my scales! But there was no way this creature could avoid my flames. I drew in a breath, intending to send the spell-bird to whatever annoying afterlife it had waiting.

"Brax," Carmen said softly. "Brax, stop. Please." She put her hand on my snout.

I let the breath out. "Fine. But one day, I will destroy every spellbird in existence to be sure this one is gone."

The bird landed on her hand and winked at me. "Ha, ha, ha," she said in Blacktooth's voice. Was the witch speaking again? "I see your confusion," the spellbird said in its normal voice. "I can keep whatever voice I've learned in my head. Sadly, all of yours. Even hers." She pointed a wing at Carmen. "As I have delivered a message for her in the past."

"Which one?" she asked.

"To someone named Thord, you said the following words—" And without missing a wingbeat, she spoke in Carmen's voice: "'Right now, I am safe. And far away from the war. And from Ellos. And I hope you and Megan can stay safe, too. I miss . . . uh . . . I miss you, um . . . two. Hope to talk someday soon. Brax says hi. Um, goodbye.'"

The bird stopped. Carmen was shaking, and I fully expected her to burst into tears. To hear of her brother's death and to be reminded of her lost friend was too much. But she managed a few words. "You are the very first spell-bird that was sent to me."

"I am," the bird said. "One and the same."

"Well, that was an impressive memory trick," I said. "Some other time, we might want to hear all your messages—especially secret ones. If we plucked your feathers off one by one, we could pry them out of you."

"That wouldn't work," she said.

"Well, I'd like to try it."

"No, I could only repeat her message because it

belonged to her," the spellbird said. "When they created wonderful me and my winged brethren, the wizards thought of everything."

"Except humbleness," I said.

The bird rolled her eyes and then turned back to Carmen. "Anyway, I am not done. Is there something I can do for you? Do you have a reply?" Then she paused. "I'm not supposed to say this, but I'd prefer never, ever to see that black-toothed witch again. She's the absolute depth of horridness."

Carmen stared at the spell bird for several moments, long enough that I worried her mental strength had broken like a glass goblet, and she couldn't even find the will to speak. "There is nothing else for you to do, my brave, tiny hero," she said, surprising me with the clarity in her voice. "You may leave us."

The bird didn't even make another peep. Instead, she winged so quickly away from us it was as if she had disappeared.

Carmen looked at me. "Brax, it is time for you and me to visit my dead brother."

CHAPTER 20

A DRIBBLE OF DRAGON DOUBT

"We have responsibilities here," I said. The world felt different. Bad news could do that—it could completely alter everything around you. We were standing in the same place with the same city of Akkadium behind us, looking exactly as it had only a few minutes before. But the world had shifted. "We can't up and leave. There is the young emperor to think of."

"I have eyes on him, which will report to me," she said.

"Eyes," I replied. "What eyes? I know you told him about a protective assassin, but I assumed that was only to comfort the boy. How could you have organized that in the short time we've been here?"

"Our mutual friend, Megan, is here in Akkad on other business, so I asked her to keep him in her sight."

Megan was yet another assassin Carmen had gone to school with—a young woman with fiery red hair and a fiery personality. She was one of the few assassins I had respected from the moment I met her. She always looked me directly in the eye and spoke the truth. Plus, she'd never stabbed me or caused me to be stabbed, so I appreciated that. Sometimes, the little things really matter.

"When did you have time to contact her?" I asked.

"One of the staff who served us the emperor-flavoured meal was Megan herself," she said.

"That's not possible." I hadn't been able to hide the incredulity in my voice.

"She had a mask on," Carmen explained a little too slowly, like she was speaking to someone with a not-so-quick brain. "Looking exactly like a servant."

"I would have smelled Megan," I said. "Like all of you, she carries the almond stink of the Red Keep."

"Assassins can cover their scent."

There was no point in continuing the argument. I had missed one of her little friends hanging around right under my nose.

"Impressive," I said. And though I was rarely impressed by these tiny bags of meat and bones, hiding your scent from a dragon was a wonderfully developed skill.

"We communicated by blinks," Carmen said. "Megan will keep us informed. And protect Emperor Nagar to the best of her ability. She is there on behalf of another country, whom she wouldn't name, but it clearly has a great interest in Akkad."

"Avenus, then. You certainly can share a lot of information through blinks." I sighed. "Well, her presence is good news. I wouldn't want an emperor who can read books harmed. One with empathy is even rarer. But I have two comments about everything we've learned from the spell-bird. Three, actually, now that I'm counting."

"What are they?" There was a frosty tone to her voice, indicating she would barely brook this interruption.

"The first is you have gone into a *control everything* mindset so that you don't have to deal with your emotions."

"You think so?" The reply was pure ice.

"I know so. And secondly: I am sorry." I kept my voice solemn. "This news about your brother must be very difficult to hear, especially to have the tidings shared by Blacktooth herself. I—I am here if you, um . . . if you need anything." I put my paw on her shoulder. It was an awkward movement since I was not raised to express sympathy. Or sadness or any of those soft and stupid emotions. My mortal eye, traitor that it was, formed the smallest tear in existence. I turned my head so she wouldn't see it.

The moment was made even more awkward by her shrugging her shoulder enough to make my paw slip off. So, this is what being slighted feels like!

This wasn't like her. But Carmen had such a look of fierce concentration in her eyes. I'd seen that look several times since I'd met her, and it was bad news for anyone who stood in her way. Also, bad news for me, since that look often resulted in me somehow getting puncture wounds in my flesh.

"You had a third thing to say." Her voice was steady. "Out with it."

"Fine. The third thing is that I don't believe he's dead." I didn't want to create any false hope, but this was a conclusion that came straight from my dragon guts.

"Blacktooth, horrid as she is, has no reason to lie," Carmen said. She had her hands on her dagger's hilt. "We are no longer enemies. And we are not a threat to her."

"I know, I know, but your brother has a terrible habit of not staying dead. It's frustrating."

"I doubt he could fool a witch," she replied. "Let alone another wizard and witch from the Grand Council of Azadiq. He is extraordinarily clever, but not that clever."

"See my statement as a sign of my respect for him. He is a chameleon, and chameleons are hard to kill because they change their colours."

"Thank you for sharing your opinions." It was clear she had moved along because she was already patting the secret pockets in her cloak, where she kept poisons and other unpleasant powders. She then began moving her blades in and out of their scabbards to be sure they were properly loose. "But I can tell you have more to say. Spit it out."

"Now don't get testy," I said.

"We are delaying. We need to leave now."

"We will, but it is clear to me that Corwin was killed—attacked, I mean—by something that sounded very similar to the snout-faced-woman goddess thing that visited me. And a toad attacked him, too—just like in the library. It is insulting that these enemies sent two things after him and only one after us." I paused to let her comment on this grievous affront to our skills.

"Keep going!" she snapped.

I restrained myself from snapping back, which was a sign of great maturity that I'm certain the universe noticed. "And, anyway, the emperor was also attacked by something that appeared out of a sun snake symbol on the ground. So, these visitations are connected, someone is going after me and . . . you . . . and your brother and the emperor."

"You still believe that the first encounter wasn't a dream?" she said. There was a hint of something that never occurred in her voice: derision.

"It happened. I have the scratch to prove it." I touched

my nose, but the cut, like so many of my wounds, had healed without a sign that anything untoward had occurred. "It happened."

"Is that the end of the more than three things you wanted to say?" she asked.

"Yes, and you don't have to sound so excited that I am done."

"I am sorry, Brax." She let out her breath, and I got the sense that if she kept breathing out, she might collapse. But she drew in more air. "There is so much to understand. I don't know what this attack on Corwin means. And his . . . his death. My family is so small now."

I am your family, I thought, but didn't say aloud. She did not need to hear that. She knew it.

She must.

But Carmen wasn't done talking. "I need to focus, Brax. To burn my thoughts down to the essential actions."

"That sounds like something your maestru would say."

"It was," she said, and she got that *I still miss Maestru Alesius* look. I wish I'd met the man. At times, a green jealousy rose in my heart when I thought of the sway he had over her. He must have really been something. "We fly now," she said.

"Is that a command? Because I don't do commands. You know that."

"No," she said, and for the first time, her stone face broke a little. "It is a request. You are my friend. My protector. My rock. Will you take me?"

"You don't have to beg," I said, hoping she would laugh at this.

"Will you take me?" she repeated.

I nodded, seeing there was no point in anything but

honourable capitulation. She wasn't even considering that we had completed the long flight from Drekki to Akkadium, pausing to save some onion farmers, then eaten a meal with the emperor before rushing to the library to fight off a toad and carry a bear almost a league through the air. So much in one day and only a short nap to gather strength! Exhaustion made my muscles and bones heavy, taking me to the brink of collapse. But the look in her eyes decided it for me.

"Yes, Carmen, my friend," I said. I lowered myself so she could climb onto my back. When she was in position and had grabbed on, I unfurled my wings. "But I warn you, I will not be a silent partner. There is something deeper going on, and if we don't examine it, it could bite us in the tail."

She gave no reply, so I took to the air. Then, at a sharp angle, I flew toward the highest heights as she whispered "*aerea,*" the magic word that cast the spell that covered both her head and my own with air sacs.

I hunted down the airstream that would lead us directly to Azadiq, the land of wizards and witches.

I hoped she wouldn't be silent the whole way.

CHAPTER 21

ANOTHER MURKY MURDER OF RAVENS

A hard time we had of it. And by "we," I mean I, Brax, was having a hard time since Carmen's only task while flying along the speedy airstreams between land masses was to hang on. That's it. That's all she had to do. For me, I had to hold my wings steady, fighting with winds at least twenty times faster than those I faced in the regular realms of the air. And this was a nasty airstream. It was a struggle of concentration and a battle against exhaustion, and I nodded off several times. These tunnels of wind reduced a trip that would normally take days to hours.

A dragon mage named Vecterix had discovered these streams and made us dragons aware that they existed, and it had changed communication and trade among the dragon, mortal, wizard, witch, and giant realms. On our trip to Akkadium, we had chosen a slower and lower route because we wanted to have an easy outing. But here and now, travelling at great speed toward Azadiq, the winds wore at me, and if we were to be tossed out, I felt I might tumble tail over tooth. Such was the speed that we would burn up on the way down and crash into the ocean. An incredible sight from a distance, but I didn't want to be inside that fireball.

The spellbirds spent most of their lives in these airways. Impressive little aggravating tiny beasts that they were.

How goes it? I sent to Carmen. She answered with a big, black silence. And I mean that literally. When we speak mind to mind, we can sense each other's presence, thoughts, and even moods. But it was as if she wasn't there. After developing this mental bond between us, we eventually learned, when we needed a break, how to shut off the part of our minds that responded. She had certainly heard my inquiry but was so deep in her own brooding that my words were echoing somewhere in a backroom of her mind.

Hey, did you ever wonder why dragons are so amazing at music? I sent. *Because they really know their scales.* I waited for a reaction—a laugh or derisive interior chuckle or a dagger stab because it was such a bad joke, but all I got back was another big, fat nothing. It might as well be a lump of mortal-sized dung on my back. *Fine,* I sent. *I'll entertain myself.*

Perhaps I should have been more caring about why she was so upset. But it wasn't like her to be this angry. She had fought against her brother for years and developed what I would call a twisted, messy, mind-altering relationship. Hey, I'm a dragon and I know what it's like to always be fighting with siblings. But their interactions had changed over time, and Carmen had more recently fought beside her brother. And though she had another brother and nephews in some small town near the Red Keep, Corwin was the member of her family she was closest to. Assassins perhaps only understand each other. It is hard to talk to commoners who live regular lives of gathering grain in sacks and raising goats and sleeping in the same bed every night, and not killing or being attacked nearly every day. Corwin had become, over time, the brother she needed.

Carmen had especially needed him after losing her Wodenite—Corwin had reached out on several occasions in the last few months to check in on Carmen. No wonder she was deeply worried now.

I left her alone in her brooding broodiness. I didn't have any extra strength for her, anyway. Better to keep my eyes, mind, and exhausted but incredible wings on the task of staying aloft.

We were above the Gorgon Sea—it was a blur of blue below me that seemed like it would never end. But, in time, a blurry green patch came toward us—the land of Azadiq. I blinked a few times to be certain I was correct. Yes, it stayed green and stayed Azadiq.

I changed the angle of my wings and flew out of the airstream, suddenly slipping into currents that weren't pushing me forward like the hand of a god. The change in speed and pressure tore at my wings so that we jerked left, then right, and I flipped over once—which was a bad thing for me but always worse for the rider. When I looked back, Carmen was still there, that steely, determined look in her eyes.

Our air-sacs spell popped, and I said, "Are you well? That was a bit of a rough entrance into the normal skies."

She responded by lifting her free hand, pointing toward the eastern sky, and saying one word: "Ravens."

I snapped my head to the front in time to see the green land and blue ocean blotted out by a cloud of black. Hundreds, if not thousands, of spell ravens poured like a cawing, feathery stew out of a maw-like hole in the air a few hundred feet in front of us. And before I could turn and dodge, we were surrounded with their cawing and clawing and the stink of death—they were mostly bones and feathers and dried guts. How long these ravens had been dead was any dragon's guess, but they smelled like they had endured a thousand years of deterioration. The offal stayed aloft without properly working wings through insanely intricate spells created by one of the most powerful witches in Azadiq.

They were Blacktooth's ravens, of course.

I made the mistake of delicately sniffing. The stink made my eyes water and my soul shrivel. So, I took in a breath through my mouth, trying to avoid any of their moulting and mouldy feathers. These bony-winged beasts, if so commanded, could peck us to pieces. Instead, they flew close enough to block our sight.

"It's impressive that they found us so quickly," I said.

"Yes," Carmen replied. Oh, so she *was* still alive. "My guess is Blacktooth has a portal spell that activates whenever someone emerges from the airstreams. No one will surprise the wizards and witches of Azadiq."

"Yes, yes, I had already come to that conclusion," I said. I hadn't, though I could blame my lack of conclusions on being so very, very tired.

The birds edged nearer to me, making me edge away, which in turn guided us down, down, down. For all I knew, they could be aiming us at a cliff wall. But I had to trust that Blacktooth didn't want us dead. Well, she likely wanted us dead, but not today.

Then, as suddenly as they had appeared, the ravens all shot straight into the air. There was green directly below us and blue above, and bright sunlight stabbed into my eyes.

We were heading at full speed toward the ground! I snapped my wings wider, gave a few quick flaps that slowed us, and tumbled into the earth, landing awkwardly but not spilling right over or losing my rider. It was as graceful as I could make it.

We had found a perch on green grass. There were sheep on the opposite hill, and my stomach began grumbling. Alas, directly in front of us, those black teeth glistening as she grinned, clearly enjoying our troubled landing, was Blacktooth, the witch. Her grey robe continued to match her long grey hair. Her olive face continued to look too young for the rest of her. My guess is she was at least a hundred years old.

She waved her long, intricately carved staff at the skies as if she owned them.

"Welcome to my humble fief of Sartoria," she said. "And, especially, welcome to the ever-free island of Azadiq. It is a great pleasure and honour to greet you." Her sharpened teeth were as black as molasses. Maybe it was age that had changed them.

"Take me to my brother," Carmen said. "Now."

"Ah, yes, rudely and forthrightly straight to the point," Blacktooth said, her grin widening. I really wanted to wipe the look of relish off her face with my talons. But the cloud of ravens was hovering several feet above us. And, well, it's best not to attack witches on their own soil. "Then I will set aside the welcoming rituals, the warming teas, and take you straight to your brother. I am certain you are up for another journey. Don't fall apart."

The ravens swooped down and grabbed Blacktooth from every side, lifting her into the air. With impressive speed, she began flying away toward the east.

I stretched my wings. It felt as if they had turned into hardened clay.

"Brax," Carmen whispered as Blacktooth became a black spot in the distance. "Follow."

"Just a moment, princess." I mentally swore at my wings several times, shook off the tiredness, eventually spread them out even though my incredible muscles were aching, and found enough strength to take to the air.

We followed the black cloud of ravens, avoiding the trail of rotten feathers they left floating in the air.

CHAPTER 22

HIS FINAL GURGLING WORDS

We, of course, had to cross the full length of Azadiq. This suggested to me that Corwin's mentor and my friend, Goran, had chosen a domain as far away from Blacktooth as possible when the magic-using mortals divided up this island. More proof that he had been a wise man. I don't know why the wizards and witches didn't gather to make her whole portion of Azadiq slide into the sea.

She didn't slow down, nor did she look back, but I knew she was watching me through the dead eyes of her ravens. And smiling.

We followed silently for hours. She had guided us into a faster stream of air, but it tore at my wings as if it were angry at us for using it.

At least she's not actively trying to kill us, I sent to Carmen.

No. She isn't.

Well, wonderful. My bubbly companion, who would bend my ears with words until they nearly fell off, continued to be in a sour mood about the whole dead-brother situation. Well, clearly, she needed her spirits improved.

Do you ever wonder if she brushes her teeth? I asked.

No answer.

Maybe she brushed them with coal dust. Or arsenic. Or molasses. Or burnt black bugs. Or—

I don't need cheer, Brax, she sent. *Though I appreciate what you are doing. I truly do, my friend. But I don't know why I am so . . . dark right now.*

It worries me, I said. *My mother used to always say, "When the world throws mud at you, don't help by spreading it all over yourself."*

I appreciate that advice, Brax. I felt the slightest tap on my side. Which was a miracle. I mean, she tapped me all the time, but right now, my body was not exactly capable of feeling anything but a sluggish tiredness. She'd had enough loss in her life. Her parents—who gave her up to be trained as an assassin, then died of a sickness; her brother, two or three times now; her sister; her maestrus, especially Maestru Alesius; and, perhaps the sharpest of all, that Wodenite with the fair hair. I knew how losses could gather in your heart until you eventually fell from the height of self-pity into the deepest pools of depression.

And I understand, finally, why you—

I stopped sending her that thought when we came over a clearing that revealed a familiar orange-bricked round home. In front of the hut was a small pasture with a thick wooden fence that held back several sheep and other edible farm animals. There were several plump chickens and a rooster, and one brown cow next to the barn. The shadow next to the orange hut moved, and I groaned. For lurking in a featherly manner against Corwin's home was a horrible creature: the black swan, Carnda.

Blacktooth landed near the hut, and her ravens

vanished, leaving only feathers behind. The witch didn't look as if a grey hair was out of place, although I now wondered if her teeth were black from hitting clouds of bugs in the air. I chose a place to land halfway between the home and the barn's fence but again misjudged, catching the fence with one of my paws and falling forward, nearly throwing Carmen into the ground. But she was strong and quick and jumped off, landing on both feet. I heroically stopped the tumble with one powerful leg, gritting my teeth the whole way.

Blacktooth gave us a familiar, black-toothed grin. Her eyes gleamed with joy. "Welcome to the fief of Goran, recently inherited by Corwin," she said. "It is with great—"

"Where is my brother's body?" Carmen spat. She had already begun marching toward the hut. I wondered if she were about to stab the witch, for she had her hand on her sword.

"He is in the hut, under Om's care, and I suggest, before entering, you gird yourself. "

Carmen, sadly, didn't stab the witch. Instead, she strode by her. I gathered up my strength and my tired body and also marched past. "We will call you if we need you," I said.

To this, Blacktooth only laughed. "Enjoy your visit with the corpse."

Carmen was already twenty steps ahead of me. The swan, Carnda, watched us with her devilish eyes—a look that suggested she was ready and willing to eviscerate anyone with her sharp, mean, poking beak. I did, for a moment, think that perhaps I should work harder on not making enemies of everything that existed. But who needs a swan in their life? My grudge against her had nothing to do with the fact that Carmen had ridden that swan for some time.

Truly, it didn't.

Carmen paused in front of Carnda. The swan lowered her head, and Carmen stroked it. One of these witches or wizards had been brave enough to bandage the beast's wing. I respected that. Carmen said something too quiet for me to hear, and then she pushed open the door.

"Hello, Carnda," I said. "Friends?"

The swan, stupid creature that it was, couldn't talk, but she watched me warily and nodded her head. I saw the pain in her eyes from the loss of someone she had carried so many great distances. Without meaning to, without even knowing I was going to do it, I reached out my paw to touch her healthy wing and rested it there for a moment. "You have been a brave companion for him," I said.

She held my gaze and nodded again. I must be getting old, but at least I didn't have to wipe any tears from my eyes. Well, that's partly because the one tear from my mortal eye fell directly to the ground with no mortals noticing.

Then I poked my head into the door, going only as far as my shoulders since the frame was not wide enough for my magnificence. Corwin's recently inherited home was as chilly as a deep mountain cave. He had been wrapped in white linen and placed on his bed in the corner, near the bookshelves, with only his face exposed. They hadn't left every wound for us to see, as Blacktooth had taunted. Frost spread out from his body halfway across the room. The wizard Om was seated beside him, a rotund man with dark skin and a balding head and a heavy cloak. His eyes were closed, which meant he was sleeping or communing with the spirits. The freezing spell had preserved Corwin well, for he looked as if he might still be alive despite his paleness. I wondered if they had, for some sorcerous purpose, drained his blood.

His eyelids were closed, though. The scar I'd given him around his left eye was still visible. Behind that lid was the eye of Boqin, the eye the wizard had given him. It didn't shine with any brightness.

Carmen stopped the moment she hit the threshold of the frost and drew in her breath, perhaps gathering strength to get nearer. I reached out to comfort her, but she was too far inside the room. As if given an invisible push, she struggled forward and stood beside Corwin's bed.

And seeing her that close, seeing the life in her, the brightness compared with the death in him, it became clear to me that Corwin really was dead this time. The realization hit me hard, not that I had any great emotion—I would have pushed him off a cliff if it was needed—but the pain that Carmen was feeling, the hollowness of her sadness, spread into my soul. She didn't deserve this. And he—he had been improving as a mortal; he didn't deserve this either.

Carmen touched Corwin's shoulder, and at that moment, I expected his eyes to open.

They didn't. But others did.

Om snapped open his eyes, clearly startled, looking at us with surprise. "Oh, oh," he said. "You are here."

"Were you communing with him?" I asked.

He shook his head. "He is far beyond the earthly realm." I couldn't remember if I had met this Om or tried to kill him. He didn't exude the same ego as Blacktooth, so I felt like I might be able to endure his presence. "Corwin is beyond all of us."

Carmen put a hand on Corwin's cheek. I didn't want to

imagine what it felt like for her to feel the coldness of her brother. "And what is your purpose here?" I asked.

"To preserve him," Om replied. "Until you arrived to prepare him for the funeral rites."

"And to care for his belongings." This came from Blacktooth, who startled me. I was blocking the door, and somehow, she was inside the home. Did she have that much power that she could appear where she wanted? Then I saw a side door had been left open. I was clearly tired and inattentive.

"What are the words of his you wanted to share in person?" Carmen asked without looking away from her brother.

"Yes, his final, gurgling words were that he was leaving this home and fief to you. That includes all the animals, the fence, the barn, and the land up to the ocean. All of it is for you. Oh, and to be clear . . ." Blacktooth motioned with a finger a little to my left. "That property includes the swan outside the door."

"And what does the council say about Carmen not being a witch?" I asked. "Can she remain on Azadiq?"

It was Om who answered. "We have ruled that she, for the space of five years, will own this fief, and in that time, she must settle her brother's affairs. And then we will vote again over whether she can continue being the owner of this fief."

"And my brother?" she asked. "Did he express any wishes for his remains?"

"No," Blacktooth said. "Guess he ran out of air." Om gave Blacktooth a look that set her back a step. Then she continued. "There are traditions among wizards and witches and assassins about funerals and disposing of corpses. It will be up to you to decide which ones to follow."

Carmen touched Corwin's face again. I shuddered because he looked so similar to her—it was as if she were touching her own face. "He shall be cremated," she said. "With his assassin robe, his wizard staff, and his assassin weapons. This shall happen tomorrow at sunrise, sending him off to the afterworlds."

Well, that was fast, I thought. *Very fast.* "Uh, don't you want to think about this for a bit?" I asked. "Others might want to come to, uh, to say goodbye. You know, do all the mourning stuff you mortals do. People like . . ." I couldn't think of anyone who might care about Corwin. He had made enemies as an assassin, and when he became a strange wizard who loved solitude, he didn't make any friends. Plus, he had killed most of the maestrus who'd trained him. "What about your family?"

"No, it is time to get it done," she said with a finality that suggested the argument was over. Well, he was *her* brother. I would not stand in the way of that. "Tomorrow, as the sun rises, so shall he rise to the other worlds."

"We can arrange a pyre," Om said. "Correct, Blacktooth?"

"Yes, yes, we will."

I wondered at the dynamic between them—maybe he was more powerful than he looked.

"I shall have my ravens bring the best wood, only the best for Corwin. And a fire that will be sure to burn him to a crisp. I mean, to reduce him to proper ashes."

"Yes," Carmen said. "To ashes he must go. To ashes, my dear brother."

I breathed in, for even as someone who, to put it bluntly,

had burned quite a few people and other dragons and, well, whoever got in my way, to ashes, this was moving with too much speed.

"Then ashes, he will be," Blacktooth said. She really did seem to be enjoying herself. "To ashes he will go."

The unsettled part of my mind grew even more unsettled when a voice suddenly said to me: *Don't let them burn my body.*

CHAPTER 23

A NAGGINGLY ANNOYING SPEAKER

I t was a voice I knew far too well.

My front leg gave out in surprise, and I slammed into the doorframe, making the wood crack and frightening the mortals. The door frame continued to creak and crack because it took me a few moments to find my balance, for my leg had gone all tingly. "What?" I spat the word out. "What?"

"We will reduce him to ashes," Blacktooth said. "It is a noble thing to do with a body. I believe your dragon may be so tired from his journey that he has lost both his physical and mental balance, and he doesn't understand this simple concept. Do you want me to give him a seven-year sleeping balm?"

I didn't argue with the "your dragon" part, even though no one possessed me. If anything, Carmen was *my* rider. Nor did I take the bait on the sleeping balm offer. But in my mind, I continued to stagger.

Do not let them burn me to ashes, Corwin said again inside my head. He didn't sound desperate. It was a direct statement. *It is not my time. I am not gone.*

"He doesn't want you to burn him to ashes," I said. "He's not gone."

"He is dead," Blacktooth explained as if she were talking to a very, very simple child. "He doesn't get a choice. His spirit is long gone. Believe me, I know about long-gone spirits, having sent many to the shades."

"I agree with my companion," Om added. "Corwin no longer exists in the mortal realm. I know these things, for other than Corwin, I am the most skilled at travelling the planes beyond life and death. And Boquin, whose eye Corwin looked through, is also completely gone."

"Corwin spoke in my head." I tapped my skull with a talon, unfortunately with enough desperation that I stabbed my flesh. Blood trickled into my human eye, forcing me to blink. And blink. And blink. "He spoke. Really, he did. Believe me."

"I thought it would be the girl who would break," Blacktooth said. She had dampened the glee in her voice only the teeniest bit. "But instead, it is the dragon. Interesting. Very, very interesting. But not inconceivable."

"He spoke. He spoke. He spoke." I hadn't meant to repeat it three times. Nor had I intended to jab myself three more times, producing another three little spouts of blood. I lowered my offending talon when I realized I was acting like a madman. I hadn't quite moved up to acting like a mad dragon.

"Brax," Carmen said, her voice on the edge of anger. "What is going on with you?"

I leaned against the opposite side of the door, and the

whole cottage creaked again. Why hadn't Goran built a bigger door? Mortals never planned properly for visiting dragons—they were such inconsiderate creatures, only concerned about beings of a certain size. I wiped at the wounds above my eye. "Corwin's voice was in my head," I said. "I heard it. He clearly said, 'Do not let them burn me to ashes.'"

"Brax," Carmen hissed. "This is an unwelcome jest."

"It is not a jest!" I said. "Corwin added that, 'It is not my time. I am not gone.'"

"My friend," Carmen said, almost sadly. "You are being cruel now. If he would speak to anyone, it would be me."

I waved my front paws around like I was shooing invisible birds. "Prove it to them, Corwin." I snapped my head left and right, goggling around the room for the slightest hint of his presence. A shade. Or a glowing eye. Even a glowing skin flake. Anything! "Come out and talk to all of them. Tell them you are here, in my head. Say something. Say it now. Appear, Corwin!"

I realized I hadn't been exactly giving him space to speak, so I fell silent.

And so did my mind. I couldn't sense him. Nothing. I waited another moment. Nothing. "Oh, for crying out loud, speak," I said. "Say something, you sneak. Say anything!"

"Brax has not been the same since being struck by the spit of an ammit," Carmen said. "And later, he was stung by a Gutian toad."

"That explains it," Om said. "Both the spittle and the venom are powerful and remain in the blood for many weeks. I have seen some mortals who have spent years babbling because of these poisons."

"He's done some odd things, too," Carmen added as if she were listing my sins in front of a jury. "He saved a bear."

"That wasn't odd," I said. "That bear was trapped. Trapped like I was once trapped in a cave with only a few books to read. And you approved of me saving him. In your heart, you did. And he really talked to me."

"The bear talked to you?" Om gripped his staff a little tighter. "This is worse than I thought!"

Blacktooth let out a raucous chuckle.

"Yes, the bear talked to me," I hissed. "But that's not important. Today, it was Corwin who squeaked inside my head." I pointed at his frozen body, which looked very, very dead. "He really did. He did!" Exhaustion was making me repeat things.

"It is a great tragedy when a mind fails." Blacktooth leaned on her staff. Though she wasn't grinning, she showed her teeth on the edge of a smile. Somehow, their ebony darkness, wet with her spittle, caught the light. "It depends how much of a mind one has to begin with, of course. But a tragedy nonetheless when this degradation happens."

"Carmen, ignore these nuts, nuts, nuts." I slipped, slamming into the other side of the frame, shaking the cabin again. Dust floated down from the rafters. Well, maybe there was something more than exhaustion in my head. "I heard your brother, Carmen. No lie. I heard him. In. My. Head."

"Brax," she said calmly, "if he were alive, I would know. I would feel it." She drew in a breath as if she were about to deliver a blow. "He is my twin."

Having never had a twin, I couldn't pretend to understand their connection. Maybe she truly could sense him. Corwin's voice could be my imagination. I shook my skull.

Nothing rattled, so I accepted that I was not insane. "He is alive," I could only get these words out in a hoarse whisper. "He is there. Trust me. Tell them, Corwin. Stop playing this as a joke."

Silence ruled for several long moments. And in my mind, in that place where he had been, there was still nothing. He wasn't there. He wasn't in his body.

"You are tired," Carmen said. She took a step closer. "I am tired. And this decision on his funeral does not have to be made this very moment." She put a hand on my shoulder. "We will sleep on it." Her suggestion sounded very logical and like the most wonderful thing to do. "In the morning, we will decide what should be done with my . . . with my brother. How does that sound, Brax? Rest. Then, when our minds are awake, we will continue this discussion."

"That sounds heavenly," I said. The warmth from her hand was reaching into me, making my muscles go soft. My brain, too.

"Then go sleep, my friend," she said. "And dream healing dreams. You deserve them."

As if her words were an incantation, I backed out of the hut and turned away from the three of them. Well, the four of them, if I counted Corwin. The swan made a soft, inquiring honk, but I was too tired to communicate with a swan.

Collapsing was very much a real possibility. I had some pride and knew that lying down in the middle of the path would be silly. So I kept my body upright as I crawled past the barn and the fence, even the delectable sheep, which I wouldn't eat since they were Carmen's now. Though I added asking her which ones I could eat to my list of things to do.

Then, I found a pile of clean straw. Straw is not always

the best for dragons to sleep on since some of us noble beasts shoot out a few sparks when we snore, but I would risk it.

I fell into the softness, and sleep fell on me.

CHAPTER 24

NO BLOTTING TODAY

There was no snoring produced by this magnificent dragon. I know that because the straw did not start on fire. And believe me, though I live with a fire inside me, when it is outside your body and heating your scales, it can be very unpleasant. My dreams were horrible and heavy—it felt like two Quant dragons had squatted on my mind, nearly suffocating my imagination.

The sun was rising in the east, warming my scales and turning the surrounding farm into a pastoral painting. We dragons love paintings of sheep and other farm animals. The entire scene was a little blurry, so I wiped a bit of crust from my eye sockets, which I thought was that typical sleep crust that seems to bother all creatures. But after examining the red flakes, I discovered it was blood. Then I remembered stabbing myself in the forehead while insisting Corwin was alive, then stabbing myself again. The crust was a symbol of how horribly odd yesterday was. Today would be a brighter, better day.

As I was clearing out my eye, a rooster let out a gods-awful noise. What was it called again? Crowing. Yes, a rooster crowed. No, that couldn't be right. My mind tried to understand that. Do they crow? Shouldn't a crow crow, but instead of that, they caw? Clearly, I was too sleepy and tired to get caught up in this semantic problem.

The rooster continued to crow in a proud and aggravating manner, as if it didn't care about the argument in my head or the aching in my brainpan. That's why they are called fowls. Their foul nature. I chuckled at that play on words. Ah, wordplay. My old friend. Even as a young dragon, I had loved it. I chuckled a bit more at the image of me in the Royal Library in Dreki Palace, laughing at a book of puns.

I wondered if young Nagar liked puns. Retelling this whole stream of puns would make him giggle. That idea made me chuckle even louder.

The chuckling stopped when I smelled smoke.

Both my eyes snapped wide open. Had my chuckling started a fire? It wouldn't do to burn down Corwin's genteel pastoral farm before Carmen could figure out what to do with it and the buildings, and especially the sheep—though since he could be alive, that shouldn't be any of her concern. I urged my sore muscles to make me stand, and after some complaints, they did so. The straw beneath me was not on fire. Smelling smoke was a figment of my imagination. The rooster gave one more horrid crow, and I glanced over at it, intending to kill it with an icy glare.

The evil, venomous creature stood proudly on the fence, staring toward the sun as if challenging it to a fight. "Hey, silly rooster," I taunted. "You will not win—"

That's hot, Corwin's said inside my head.

"What's hot?" I asked aloud, but he didn't reply. "The sun? Are you near the sun?"

My body may need help in the mortal realm, he continued.

"Help with what?" I asked.

He didn't answer, but the answer came to me. Beyond the rooster, a plume of smoke was rising. The barn blocked a view of the fire. I gathered my wits in an eyeblink and raced toward the smoke, not feeling strong enough to fly. Was the hut burning? I accidentally went through a fence, and the sheep streamed out behind me, but I paid them no mind. For what I saw was a very unpleasant scene.

A funeral pyre burned in front of the hut, and on that conflagration, swaddled in his black assassin robe, was Corwin. On one side stood Oma and Blacktooth, and with her back to me was Carmen, watching as the flames licked at what remained of a rather enormous pile of very combustible wood.

Well, so much for waiting to have a logical conversation about the voice I heard in my head! I stumbled ahead, building up speed as I raced toward the flames. I hit a stone well, smashing a few of the stones, and still carried on.

I tried to shout, but it came out as a whisper because my throat was so hoarse. The fire reached toward Corwin. "No," I yelled, and this time my words carried. I found the strength to take to the air. "No! No! No! We didn't have our logical conversation!"

This had to be stopped! Oma opened his eyes from his funeral meditation and looked, well, shocked to see a dragon haphazardly coming down from above. Carmen was turning toward me, but I couldn't see her face yet. And then the final one to see me was Blacktooth, who was smiling in her most aggravating way. Leave it to her to smile at a funeral. She raised her staff to swat me.

But it was too late. I was coming down with all my speed and power to snatch Corwin out of the pyre and lift him away from danger. Any moment, I expected to hear his voice screaming in pain inside my head.

I was coming down like vengeance. Like a saviour. Like a powerful god dragon.

A murder of ravens surrounded me in the next heart-beat, hundreds of them digging their little talons and beaks into my flesh so they could hold me in the air, stopping my dive. "Release me!" I shouted, anger making my voice wilder. I whipped my wings faster to clear the air, but the pure number of ravens out-muscled me, pulling me upward. I glimpsed Blacktooth through the cloud of feathers—she continued to laugh. "Release me!" But the ravens held on tight, and no matter how I fought, I couldn't escape them.

"His kin has decided this," Blacktooth said. "Leave the body be."

The flames reached Corwin's robe. Again, I expected to hear him scream. Instead, I screamed, "No."

I shot an angry glance through another break in the ravens at Carmen. "Carmen, this can't—"

Then I saw her eyes. She had messily spread dark makeup as if she had not looked in the mirror as she applied ash eyeshadow. There was so much anger and hopelessness in her gaze. Rarely had I seen those emotions in her eyes. She was the kind of mortal who always projected hope. "Carmen," I said softly.

She opened her mouth, and I thought words would come out, but she put her hands to either side of her skull and screamed in agony. An absolutely horrendous disgorging of despair that threatened to tear the very world asunder. All the pain of her life, all the losses, were coming out in that scream. Even Blacktooth took a step back, and Oma opened his eyes even wider.

But the scream did something to me. A reminder that she had literally pulled me to safety several times with her dragon strength. This hopelessness was not her. It was wrong. And with that realization came anger. Corwin could die, and she would feel an even greater pain. I drew in a breath, and pulling the flames from deep inside me, I sprayed my flesh. I am not impervious to my own flames, for they are meant to melt things—faces, metal, and even magical, already-dead ravens. It hurt, oh how it hurt, but I kept going until at least half of the birds were gone. Then, as the ravens were screeching and flying to pieces around me, I fell onto the pyre, smashing it to pieces.

I rose with Corwin clutched in my forelegs as ashes and burning raven pieces fell from me.

"This is wrong," I shouted, backing away, not wanting them to grab him. Blacktooth raised her staff again, but another blast of flame sent more of her ravens into ashes. And another blast after that sent the rest to Hades. But it was my third use of my fire in a row, which meant I would have to regenerate. "This is all wrong!"

Corwin was light and maybe had been half-burnt, but I kept backing away. I couldn't carry him into the hut; I wouldn't fit. But I didn't want to take my eyes off Blacktooth.

"Brax!" Carmen shrieked, glaring that ashy eyeshadow glare. "Release him. He is mine. My brother. Mine!"

"Yes, release him." Blacktooth swirled her staff, and a green, fiery cloud formed above her. It seemed to be from some other world—I glimpsed truly evil-looking ravens inside it. "Or I will blot you out."

"No blotting!" I said. "He is not dead."

"Brax," Carmen said. "I command you!"

"No one commands me!" I shouted. "You know that!"

"Release him!" Carmen drew Lilith, the sword that loved blood so much. "He is mine, mine!" I had stumbled into an upside-down shadow world where my truest friend would threaten to kill me.

"Did you taste the venom of the Gutian toad?" Om said softly.

"Yes," I said. "You know that. Why ask me now?"

Om raised a hand. "I am asking her."

Carmen glared at him. "What has that to do with anything?" The anger in her voice surprised me. She usually had more respect for older mortals.

"Did you?" He strode ahead, motioning Blacktooth to be still. And to my surprise, Blacktooth made her cloud disappear. I liked this Om. "Did the toad sting you?"

"Yes," Carmen shouted. "But I am immune. Immune. Let's finish this. Now give me my brother back."

"No," Om said. "You weren't immune. That's clear to me now."

And before she could move, he struck her with his staff.

CHAPTER 25
WORSHIP MY WORDS

To strike an assassin who has trained to avoid blows her whole life is impressive, especially from a somewhat pudgy and slow-looking older man. Carmen had brought up her sword to deflect the blow, so it wasn't like she had completely forgotten all her skills and let an elderly man hit her. That would have been very embarrassing. She would have succeeded in chopping his staff in two, but the staff turned ghostly blue, passed through her defence, and struck her right in her heart. In my experience, this was the point in a battle where a lot of red spurting happened. Instead, her eyes widened, and then she snarled, swiping at the offending stick twice. Her sword passed through it both times, so with a melodramatic growl, she swung at Om's head. I was relatively certain he couldn't do the same ghostly blue trick with his body.

"Begone, *bufonem venenum*!" he shouted.

Clearly, it was one of those magic phrases his kind had perfected, for she halted her swing and began jittering like a toad on a stick, which was a perfectly apt comparison if I do say so myself. It was made even more perfectly apt because a great number of toads jumped out of her. I mean, not out of her ears or nose, which would have been painful and grotesque, but little toad spirits leaped from her torso, her limbs, and her head. They arced in toadish delight through the air, then hopped across the green grass and promptly vanished with popping sounds.

Om pulled back his staff, and Carmen fell to the ground. Normally, I would have jumped forward to save her, but I was holding her recently toasted brother.

"Did she have a bunch of toads inside her?" I asked.

"She is not the only one," Om replied and, without asking permission, stuck the staff right in my chest, narrowly missing Corwin's head. A blazing fire burst in my heart, which I did not like, but I didn't start jittering or dancing. Instead, one green toadish demon jumped out of my chest, let out a croak, and then croaked. I suddenly felt stronger. Smarter. Less toad-like.

I shook my head. "What in the seven blazes was that?" I asked.

Carmen struggled to find her feet. Blacktooth stepped over to her. I fully expected the witch to smack my dear friend a couple of times with her own staff, but clearly, she either thought this was the wrong time and place to do that, or there was a smidgen of goodness staining her black, black heart. For she put out a crooked hand and helped Carmen to her feet.

"What happened?" Carmen said. "Why do I . . . feel lighter?"

"The Gutian toad venom had infected you," Om explained. "Though you were immune to its freezing effects, it does also enter your mind and picks the darkest impulses, the saddest thoughts, and makes them expand. I might have noticed sooner, but all Blacktooth told me was that you were aggravating, heroic people."

"She called us heroic?" I asked.

Blacktooth let out a low grunt and stepped away from Carmen, letting her stand on her own. "I am being misquoted." She spat a bit of spittle on the grass. The blades it touched died.

"Those were your exact words," Om said. "Perhaps you have had a touch of toad venom, too." He laughed at the look of anger that Blacktooth shot at him. Clearly, he didn't worry about her lashing out.

"And you . . . you dispelled the remaining toad venom from me?" Carmen said.

"Yes." Om shook his staff. "I sent it away. But your need to burn your brother was obsessive. I had mistaken it for mourning."

Carmen looked over at me. I was, of course, still holding Corwin, and he was still as cold as ice in my forelegs. The black assassin's cloak had protected him from turning into ashes, and that made me wonder why she'd let him wear it —perhaps some part of her mind knew she wasn't acting normally. "So, the venom made me expect the worst in life and also made me less likely to believe Brax."

"Yes, very much so," Om explained.

"That's horrible," she said.

"Yes, it is," I agreed. "My every word should be put upon an altar and worshiped. Along with my deeds, of course. And a multitude of images of me."

"That is not what I meant," she said. "I can't believe I wanted to have my brother's funeral without other family and friends."

"The venom is very powerful." Om leaned on his staff in a way that made me think he was about to give a lecture. "You will have to forgive yourself. And even your assassin's guild would not know all its dark spirit properties. I have spent a lifetime studying such things."

"Is my brother dead?" she asked, looking over at his pale and still ice-cold body. "Or should I believe that Brax is hearing his voice?"

"Every sign I can read tells me he is dead," Om said. "But he is also somehow talking in your dragon friend's head."

"And that wasn't the venom or the ammit spit that had twisted his brain?" Carmen asked.

"Oh, please," I said. "Even venom and ammit spit aren't so horrid as to make me hear his wheedling voice in my skull."

She took a few steps closer to me and placed her hand on Corwin's cheek. "Is it really his voice?" she whispered. "Is he still there?" Her own voice broke a little. It dawned on me that, like any conscientious mortal, she might be feeling a bit of guilt about the whole cremation-whilst-still-alive thing.

"Only Brax can tell us that," Om said.

I drew in a breath. I decided the best thing to start with was a history of the dragon mind and how powerful it was compared to all other creatures, even giants. And lead on into the philosophical annals of Vecterix—although his mind had shattered over time, so maybe I wouldn't bring those up. And then turn to . . .

I am here, Corwin said inside my head.

"Oh, great," I said. "He's back in my head now." I looked down at his body, but he was still a frozen turkey.

"But why? Why is he only talking to you?" Carmen asked.

"Because he wanted an intelligent conversation," I said, then felt momentary guilt when I saw the hurt in her face.

She was not open. I could choose only one to channel through. So, I chose Brax. My . . . friend.

I repeated those words but left off the "my friend" part. I didn't know what to think of that. Was he being sarcastic? I had never been friendly with Corwin. He might very well have been sarcastic.

"So, he's stuck talking to you?" Carmen said.

"It's not a horrible fate," I replied. "Some might even call it heavenly."

"Brax is correct," Om said. "I don't know about the fate part. But clearly, Corwin has only a thin line of communication from wherever he is and so they are entwined together."

"But the question is," Blacktooth said, "what does Corwin have to tell us about where he is and what he's doing?"

CHAPTER 26

THE WIZARD ASSASSIN TALKS AND TALKS AND...

"Well," I said, "I do not want to be his conduit. But I am getting a great sense of distance from his voice as if he is at the bottom of a well that has been dug at the back of a cave, and I'm listening from three continents away."

That was a wonderful comparison, he said inside my head.

I have a way with words, I sent back. *Now, you will explain to us how you ended up with a seemingly dead body and a disembodied voice inside my beautiful skull.*

Speak my words as they appear in your head. Please don't add any extra colour to them, my friend.

"Stop calling me your friend," I said aloud. Then, seeing the looks of curiosity and incredulity in the eyes of my companions, I added, "My apologies. He has an annoying way of speaking inside my head. I will relay his words as he puts them to me, so any grammatical errors or boring phrasings are on him. It is important to once again point out that I do not appreciate having to be his town crier." Again, for the very slightest moment, I felt sorry for spellbirds who spent their whole lives speaking the words of others. Obviously, I was getting soft.

Ready, Brax? he sent. *This is going to be fun, my friend.*

Now, he truly was being sarcastic. The playful manner of that was a good sign, meaning his spirit had enough strength to laugh.

"Here are his words as they appear in my head, mostly," I said. Then switched my tone to match his. "'Hello, my dearest sister. I forgive you for trying to cremate my mortal body and completely understand the conclusions that—'"

Please don't do my voice as a falsetto, he sent.

You can hear me? I replied.

Yes, your words echo in your head. Please, this is serious, and your theatrics will undermine the message.

I drew in a breath. *Fine, I guess I won't have any fun. Please continue, and I'll dutifully repeat your words.*

As I spoke, his ugly swan moved closer to us. I used a normal voice, though I pitched it slightly higher than my gloriously deep voice, convincing myself that this was not mocking him but was the best way for my audience to understand these were not my words. "'I want to thank my dear swan, Carnda, for doing her utmost to protect me. She is always close to my heart.'" The bird made what sounded like a pleasant honk. "'Also, may I, Corwin, add greetings and salutations to my fellow witches and wizards and companions of magic. My apologies for missing the last meeting of the council of Azadiq and for causing you consternation by allowing my corporal self to be attacked. For your information, I would have voted in the positive for the bylaw about banning the floating goats that travel to another fief for sustenance, but as for Bylaw 7 concerning golden eggs—'"

Holy toenails of the green evil giantess, I sent. It was something my mother would say whenever she was angry at me or my siblings. Or Dad. I heard it quite a few times. At that point in our lives, giants were the most frightening thing a dragon could be threatened with. *Make it short and snappy, Corwin. There is only so much air in the world.*

Your wish is my command, he sent. *My dear, brilliant friend.*

I don't know if that's sarcasm, but it wouldn't take much to send you from near death right over the edge.

"Corwin continues to say the following: 'My apologies; we will solve those council concerns later. I shall explain what happened to me. I was in my hut, having topped off a day of astral projection with a hearty and vigorous shovelling of manure from the goat pen. Nothing like farm work to remind you that you truly are in the corporal world. I will, of course, later use the manure for fertilizer on my crops of corn and wheat. Anyway, I sense another complaint bubbling up from my friend Brax, so I will get right into what happened to me. I had washed up and was at my table reading—'"

What were you reading? I sent.

What? Why does it matter?

It lets me judge your taste in books, I sent. *I am looking forward to looking down at you.*

"'Fine, Brax has asked what I was reading. It was *Vindor's Revenge*—'"

Oh, that's an excellent book! I couldn't help sending him that comment. *I love Tybor Ulfling's writing.*

Now who is interrupting? Corwin sent.

Blacktooth and Om were staring at me like I had grown three heads. Carmen was the only one with the slightest bit of patience, for she was also a fan of *Vindor's Revenge*. It was the greatest Wodenite novel ever written! Vindor, an axe-wielding draugr hunter, gets his revenge on a family of drau-grs, but eventually, after saving his village, is brought down by his own jealous kin. The Wodenites always had their hero die in the end. No happy endings for them! I enjoyed the dark sense of humour that coursed through Ulfling's work. I wondered if Nagar had read it and would ask him when next we met.

"'Anyway, as I, Corwin, was saying, I was reading when I felt a presence in my hut. I glanced up from my book, for the fire had swayed, and my candle went out. "Who is there?" I asked. But no answer was returned to me. A motion caught my eye—three small toads had appeared on my floor. They were chalky-bottomed because they circled around, dragging their chalk bellies and creating a pattern. I stood immediately, knowing they were drawing a summoning pattern that I soon recognized as the Zirkin Hydrex.'" He said this as if it was a pattern we all should recognize. I didn't, and neither did Carmen nor Blacktooth, but Om narrowed his eyes. "'It is a sun circled by a snake. I reached for my staff, which I had left at the door. It flew toward me, but in that same moment, the barrier between worlds was broken, purple smoke rose from the pattern, and out of that sulphury thickness came, like demons of old, two figures. The first was a man-sized toad. It swallowed my staff and then—'"

Hey, we fought a toad, too, I sent.

"' Yes, I know,'" I continued in his voice, which was becoming rather strained. "'With my staff gone, the second figure came clear. It was a woman with scales and—'"

Hey, I saw her, too, I sent. *She had hairy legs, right?*

"Brax," Carmen said. "I know you keep interrupting

Corwin, and though I appreciate your excitement, please let us know what happened to my brother. Then we will quiz him."

"Fine," I said, then continued in my version of Corwin's voice. "'The female figure was of such great power I will admit to trembling. She had strong, hairy legs and scaly arms and a crocodile snout. She gave me several grievous insults.'" I didn't interrupt him to say that I, too, had been verbally assaulted by her and was very impressed by her ability to sling insults. "'She told me she was here to erase me from all things and all places. Then she slashed my cheek. I threw a shield spell that broke as it deflected her next blow. Then she laughed, what I can only describe as a very aggravating laugh, for her blow had been a feint, and there was a sharp pain in my neck: the toad had tongue-poked me.'" Again, I didn't quibble about how he had phrased that, but I would have used something like "the toad had smacked me with his tongue" or "his tongue had twisted its torturous pinkness through my spell." Corwin continued: "'The venom from his stinger froze my body, and he pumped a large, killing amount of it into my neck. "Your sister, that dragon, and this world will fall because of a child," the woman said. Being frozen, I couldn't respond, not that I understood the reference to my sister and Brax. But in that last moment of consciousness, I let out a breath of sour smog, which distracted her, and I jumped out of my mortal shell with my spirit body and threw myself down the toad's throat.'"

A breath of sour smog, I sent. *There are mint-tree toothbrushes that would fix that.*

He ignored me and continued to speak through my mouth. "'I then used the interior of the toad as a portal to pursue my staff—for being a netherworld toad, it sent items it swallowed to other worlds to be sorted. And no, Brax, I would not be leaving through his nether regions, I can sense what you're thinking—the staff and I were taken to a distant realm through the toad. But whilst I hid my spirit inside this other realm, the toad and the nameless goddess believed their work was done. They vanished from my home and left me adrift. I am now very far away, following the trail of the toad so that I can find the name of this goddess.'"

"So, you're not dead," Blacktooth said. She sounded incredibly disappointed.

"No, he's not," I replied. "He's very much talking inside my head."

"And what does Corwin suggest we do to help him?" Om asked.

"'There is a book on my shelf of unknown things; open it,'" I commanded on Corwin's behalf.

I couldn't carry him in because of that narrow door, so Carmen came up to me and put out her arms, and I handed Corwin over. It was odd how light he seemed. If I didn't hear his voice, I, too, would assume he was dead. She lay him down on his bed and wiped ashes from his shoulder.

Om went to the bookshelf and, after a moment's searching, found a very slim volume. "It's *The Compendium of Monsters and Goddesses Who Have No Names.*"

"Open it to somewhere in the middle,'" I commanded again in Corwin's voice.

Om did so and recoiled a little at what he'd found. He showed it to Carmen and Blacktooth, who both wrinkled their noses as if an ammit-rich smell had risen from the book.

"Show me," I commanded.

Om crossed the room without seeming to move his feet, a nice trick that made me think of vizier Arbaim. He then held the book open. A woman with hairy legs and scaled skin, a snout, and horrid eyes glared back at me, looking like she might leap out of the page and lacerate me from liver to limb. "That's her," I said. "She's the one who attacked me on the plain." On top of that, it was the very image I had seen in the Royal Library all those years ago. A book of such rare value was sitting in a magician's hut! I was about to announce this but remembered that Corwin's teacher had always had a wonderful collection.

I skimmed the description below her. It said: *The Nameless Goddess is an Akkadian goddess of the old pantheon who is associated with snakes, Gutian toads, and ammits. She has not been worshipped for millennia. Her temples were taken over by Iktara, the*

"Well, that's not much of a description," I said. "Though she might be grumpy about the taking her spot in Akkad's religion."

Corwin then spoke. "'The Nameless Goddess is a daughter of one of the Old Ones. Her power comes from no one knowing her name.'"

"And what should we do?" I asked, even though it was very much sounding like I was talking to myself.

"Yes, what do you want from us, Corwin?" Carmen added. Clearly, she was feeling contrite about the whole almost killing him thing. Again.

Corwin gave another answer through me. "'I will continue to let the goddess believe I am dead while I clandestinely endeavour to find her secret den in the otherworlds. There, with luck and skill, I will discover where she has hidden her true name.'"

"Her name is the source of her power," Om added. "Knowing it will make her weaker."

"'Exactly, my dear friend,'" Corwin said through my mouth. "'Clearly, this is a goddess who is planning to ascend to our realm and sow complete destruction. We will have to find the way to stop her. As I search, I will send messages back when I am able.'"

"Ugh," I said. "I guess that means I'll continue to be his messenger. The fates are feeling unkind to me."

Yes, dear Brax, he sent me. *Often will my voice chime in your mind.*

The winged gods clearly have cursed me, I sent back.

"Then fight hard, my brother," Carmen said. "We will help from our end in any way we can."

"And I and the council will protect his body," Om promised. With a gesture, he wove a blanket in the air and placed it over Corwin. "His protection will be your most important consideration, Blacktooth."

Blacktooth had never looked happy anytime I'd seen her, but the angry glint in her eyes was the most unhappy I'd witnessed. It is with great pride I report I held myself back from laughing.

But to my utter and delicious surprise, she said something that was wonderful. "I'll protect him on one condition: that I can dress his body up in the garishly bright outfits of jesters. That's the only way I'll care for him."

No! Corwin said. *She somehow found out that I fear jesters!*

"You have my permission," I said.

"And what did my brother say about it?" Carmen asked.

"He said as long as the almighty Blacktooth keeps his body safe, that is completely fine."

No! Corwin shouted in my mind.

A small price to pay, I sent to him. *This is a bitter, soul-eating world. Let us have this one glorious bit of entertainment.*

"He's going to love the paintings I'll make of him in this garb," Blacktooth said. "I might even bring his dressed-up body to the council meetings."

My laughter drowned out Corwin's whining reply from the far, far ether.

CHAPTER 27

A HORRID LITERARY REALIZATION

You saved his life, Carmen sent.

We had decided to return to Akkadium because it was the last place the hairy-legged annoying goddess had shown up, and we were convinced she was more likely to appear there since that's where all the people who had worshipped her thousands of years ago had lived—deities do like their worshippers. And it was the only way to fulfill our pact with Nagar.

Corwin had said that if we discovered her true name, we would have some power over her. Because dragons were better scholars and had a better facility with language, and our histories were not as snivelling and over-the-top dramatic as mortal histories, I was tempted to go to Drachia and continue to study the Nameless Goddess. But that would take up too much time.

Don't you agree with me? Carmen sent.

She was talking in my skull because our heads were covered in air bubbles, and we were flying at bone-rattling speed through the airstream far above the surface. I had taken a full day to rest and eat goats. Well, two goats, since that's all I could stomach. Usually, my stomach can stomach much more than that, but Corwin, after I suggested I dine on his livestock, asked two of them if they were willing to sacrifice themselves for my hunger. They did, gladly, for they saw the importance of our cause. Then he introduced them to me, and I felt guilty eating goats whose names I knew: Tanngris and Tannjós. His only request was that I spit all their bones back into the pen.

The strangest thing is that they appeared in the pen the next day, perfectly regenerated. An endless supply of goats!

They didn't taste as good the second time I ate them, though.

Are you ignoring me? Carmen sent. *Because you also saved me.*

Fine, I sent back to her. *I saved him, and I'm not proud of it. And I didn't save you; just prevented you from doing something stupid, which seems to be a full-time livelihood for me. Though as I use that word livelihood, I am aware I don't earn gold pieces for putting out your fires.*

Well, Carmen sent, *I am thankful that you are always so dependable. You are my rock, Brax.*

Don't make me weep while I'm flying at such a great speed! We could end up in the ocean. Or smashing into a mountain.

She laughed inside my head, a tinkling sound I'd love to have echo for a lifetime. *I will keep my maudlinity to a minimum. Well then, let's review our intentions for when we arrive in Akkadium.*

Certainly! I sent back. *We visit our little emperor, and you can be his nursemaid while I go do the heavy work of hunting down that priestess and finding out how she sent a toad to the library to kill us and why she sent a toad and a goddess after Corwin. We were only worth one toad!*

It's not a competition, Carmen sent. *And Enheduanna is the priestess for Iktar, the Cowled Goddess, not the Nameless Goddess.*

I flapped my wings a few times, marvelling at mortals' inability to name their gods and goddesses in an interesting manner.

They are both stupid names for goddesses! I sent. *I mean, if you're a goddess, why not pick a name that instills fear, like Fire-ToothBurningStalkerKiller, one of our ancient, winged goddesses? Just saying her name frightens me. Iktar, the Cowled Goddess? It sounds like she's hiding a pimple problem. My coins are on Enheduanna being the source of all our problems. These goddess religions stick together.*

She would be an enemy of the Nameless Goddess, Carmen lectured. An image of her pointing at a classroom papyrus board appeared in my head. *Iktara replaced the Nameless Goddess.*

My money is still on Enheduanna! Her goddess likes Gutian toads, and so did the Nameless Goddess. I'll twist her arms, legs, and tongue until she leads us to this goddess with the hairy legs, and then we'll kill the goddess.

Do you think it'll be that easy? she asked. *Corwin is doing a much more subtle search.*

Nothing I ever do with you is easy. You are like a giant bad luck charm.

Charming of you to notice, she sent. *Though I will point out that the Nameless Goddess revealed herself to you first.*

She chose the most powerful creature she could find, I sent. *She fears me.*

I knew that last statement wasn't true. No dragon had killed a god or goddess in any of the histories that I had read.

I don't think there are any stories where mortals kill the gods, Carmen said.

It bothered me how closely our thoughts ran and yet it was also comforting. *We will find a way,* I sent. *It's what we do. Now, let me concentrate on getting there.*

We winged along, each in our own thoughts. Mine turned to Nagar, the recently ascended emperor. Why was I feeling an urgent need to return to the boy? Did I have some disgusting need to protect him? That wasn't logical. The basic law of dragons was that the weak were left to die. It must be Carmen's influence, or else it was this stupid mortal eye.

It dawned on me that I had helped Carmen long ago when she needed it. It's a character flaw! I nearly lifted my paw in surprise, which would have knocked us off course. A character flaw! The realization struck like lightning through my skull. Just like Egor the Brave, who always gave his heart—metaphorically—to women with red hair, or Baldur the Great, who couldn't stop gambling until he had gambled his own kingdom away, I had a character flaw! And my flaw was to help the weak.

Character flaws could be fixed, I decided. They never were in the stories I read, but I wouldn't succumb to the fate of being too nice. First, I'd save the young emperor, and then no more would I help the weak.

The blurry outline of the lights of Akkadium appeared, and I adjusted my angle, taking us out of the airstream and into the fresh, calm skies. I circled down slowly, mesmerized by the beauty of the city. That was another character flaw: admiring mortal buildings.

We landed on top of the ambassador tower. I will admit to getting the *heebily-jawjabs,* which is a condition that inflicted my mother right before something bad was about to happen: usually, an attack on our kingdom. Or my brother and I breaking one of her favourite crystals. Standing there, I was reminded of the horrid events in that room and finding that poor child in the midst of all that destruction. I had seen bloody scenes a thousand times. But it matters differently when you know someone who nearly died.

"Are you getting a chill?" Carmen asked.

"No," I replied because there was no point in letting her know I had any weaknesses. "Not even the slightest. Though I'm comfortable with you going into the murder room first."

"Master Alesius used to say chills were a sign you hadn't trained enough. Every action and reaction should be logical, precise, and calm."

For the hundredth time, I wished I'd met this maestru. He didn't sound like he had any character flaws. Other than being a mortal.

I reached for the door, but before I could push on it, it swung open.

Vizier Arbaim was standing there, hat on his head, bear-head staff in his hand, and a scowl on his face.

CHAPTER 28
A TOUCH OF MADNESS

"Greetings, Braxus Andorum and Carmen Dore," Arbaim said. He did that strange float walk into the sunlight, his hat nearly bumping my snout. I really wanted to lift the bottom of his robe to see if he was using his toes to perform that smooth movement. Or were his feet giant caterpillars? The image of him having caterpillars for feet infected my thoughts. Just one look. That wouldn't break any sort of protocol. Would it? "It is with immense pleasure and inarticulate joy I welcome you back to Akkadium, ruled by Nagar, the Great God Emperor of All He Sees." Despite his welcoming words, Arbaim's tone suggested he was not pleased to see us.

"Well, Vizier Arbaim, user of many words," I said, "we are also pleased to be here in your presence, and we are —"

"Send them home!" a woman's voice shouted from the darkness of the murder room. "Let them leave from here to roam!" Enheduanna, both her red robes and her mouth aflutter, came flapping out. "We do not need eyes from other lands to gaze upon our golden sands. Begone, meddlers!"

Vizier Arbaim turned his head slowly toward the red pythoness of a woman, and I, being someone who knows hate very well, saw that he clearly loathed her. *Oh, how lovely,* I thought. The blistering, festering hate that grows between members of a royal court is the very worst of all, wrapped up in jealousy, petty games, and pustulant personal repugnance. This hate was something we could play with.

And I so loved playing with hate.

"It is a pleasure to see you, Enheduanna of Iktar, the Cowled Goddess," Carmen said. "For we—"

"Want to take your head off," I finished. Carmen and I often had the same thoughts, and I'm certain that is how she was going to end her sentence. Vizier Arbaim, despite himself and years of protocol training, grinned.

"Brax!" Carmen said. Then, clearly wanting to show a front, she sent me this burning message: *BRAX! Stand back and watch my royal courtier skills. I was at the top of my class.*

"You want to remove my holy head?" Enheduanna met my eyes. Impressively, she did not display even the slightest bit of fright. Neither did the golden snakes sticking out of her hair. "It is you who will be dead. Never should a lowly messenger threaten the high priestess of the Cowled Goddess, for that will cause you deadly distress."

"First off," I said. "Your rhyming scheme is horrible, so you shouldn't be allowed into any poet pubs. Second, what do you know about toads? Specifically, large Gutian toads that are ugly and can be summoned from other dimensions to sting dragons and their helpers with their icky tongues?"

"You accuse the living voice of Iktara?" the priestess said. "I shall give you such a scare-ah."

I ignored her forced rhyme. Whenever mortals talked down to me, it got my dander up. I imagined taking her head off and then putting it back on and taking it off again and . . . well, let's say I pictured that happening many times.

"Listen En-DUH-hanaana . . . whatever your name is." I pointed a talon at her heart. "I am not a lowly messenger, and I will not—"

This time, it was not Carmen who interrupted me.

"Halt. Halt." Vizier Arbaim bravely float-walked between the two of us. "It does not matter what Enheduanna threatens or that you desire to behead her, as wonderful as that event would be. What does matter is that the emperor has spoken. He ordered me to bring these two directly to him and grace them with his powerful presence."

The high priestess opened her mouth, but before she could speak, Arbaim continued, saving us from another couplet. "I will guide them now. Come along, welcome guests. If you have any complaints, my dear Enheduanna, please make your petitions directly to the emperor's staff. I shall look into it personally."

With that, he turned, and Carmen, knowing it best not to have any more tension, followed him. I walked myself and my very wide smile past Enheduanna, giving her a dragon-eye glare.

She watched me with her two mortal eyes. They could have been made of fire.

"You will find the emperor much more healthy than when last you met him," Vizier Arbaim said when we reached the hallway. He appeared to be the slightest bit friendlier after that showdown with Enheduanna, and his joyful mood showed in the speed with which he floated ahead. When he came to the stairs, would he step or float down? I watched him descend and couldn't truly tell.

Do you think he has caterpillars for feet? I sent.

What? Carmen replied. *Caterpillar feet? Are you hallucinating again?*

You don't have to mentally snap at me. You should be happy I'm showing an interest in mortals. Especially their peculiar walking patterns.

You are *hallucinating. I'm going to get more of that antidote.*

We had reached the bottom of the stairs, and it was a squeezing move to turn a corner through the door, another reminder that these hallways were not built for dragons.

We made our way through several more halls. Staff stepped out of my way, looking like they wanted to flee. The image of caterpillar feet crawled into my mind again, and I nearly chuckled. At that moment, the vizier looked back at me. Maybe I *had* chuckled.

"Lead on," I said. "With your smooth gait and perfect style."

"I don't know what you're referencing," he said, "but we have reached the battle room."

Now, "battle room" could mean either a room where a battle was about to happen or—

He swung open the door and walked in.

The pimple-cursed emperor sat behind a table with an enormous map and several ivory pieces: a dragon, soldiers, boats, assassins, and other miniature battle paraphernalia. My first instinct was to go over and be certain he was whole and hadn't been harmed and even give him the gentlest of hugs—which, for a dragon, is a very horrible reaction to have. My second reaction was to realize that the boy was playing a game.

"This is a battle *planning* room," I said. "A vizier should be more careful with words."

"I did not intend to ruffle your feathers," he said.

Ruffling feathers was a very demeaning thing to say to a dragon! The suggestion that I, or any dragon, had ever had feathers was horrid. We were not birds. And the vizier would certainly have studied enough dragon protocol to know it was an insult. A fire, like a sudden burst of a forge, flamed up in my stomach, and I lifted my talon and opened my mouth to correct the vizier. "Listen, Arbaim—"

"Yes, listen," Carmen said loud enough to drown me out. She was using the Big Voice trick the maestrus had taught her. "Brax is much too powerful and mighty of a dragon to have even the slightest words cause slight."

"She is correct," I said, letting the fire in my belly fizzle. "I am unperturbable. I am a stickler for language, though. I should be since we dragons invented words."

The vizier looked as if he would like to correct me on that front but said instead, "Apologies to our kind allies."

That need to do the worst thing possible overtook me again as I approached the table—I still wanted to give the boy a hug. But he had not looked up. Instead, he was engrossed in moving the pieces around on the board and whispering to himself. At the moment, he clutched a dragon that looked very much like me, though it had a bit too large of a belly. In his other hand, he held a wizard. Maybe, in his game, I'd get to bite the wizard's head off.

"This, then that," he whispered. "Up, then down. In, then out. Fires all around."

The boy had clearly gone barking mad.

CHAPTER 29
A GUT STUFFER

"Uh," I said, not tactfully, for that was not my greatest gift. "He doesn't seem to be aware of our presence. Did you scramble his brains?"

Carmen elbowed me, which I barely felt, and the vizier narrowed his eyes. "It is the tongue of the gods," he said.

Well, that is an icky expression, I sent to Carmen.

"Explain," I said to the vizier.

"All the emperors have some of this gift. The gods allow them to block out all the world and speak directly to the gods themselves. To mere mortals, it sounds like nonsense."

Nagar flew little miniature me over beside a giant monster. My gut truly wasn't that big—I was always impressively fighting fit. I made a note to talk to the royal chess piece maker about proper proportional representations of princely Scythian dragons. The emperor then moved another multi-tentacled monster to the outskirts of the city of Akkadium. "Out of the sky, out of the dust," he said. "Into the darkness comes the thrust."

"At least he's a better poet than that priestess." I had

meant to send that observation to Carmen, but it came out of my mouth instead. The vizier stiffened.

"As I said, it is a gift of the desert gods," he whispered. "A sign of his connection with the other worlds."

Royalty and madness go hand in hand, I sent. *Believe me, I know.*

I'm sure you do. Personally.

As the sanest creature on Ellos, I ignored her grievous attack.

Nagar, holy font of the Bear God and a boy playing with toys, suddenly froze, took in a deep breath, and blinked repeatedly. "What is this?" he said.

"It's a miniature version of me," I replied. "Except the proportions are incorrect. I can eat as many goats as I want without my stomach growing in volume." My voice, mellifluously grand as it is, clearly made him shudder, and he looked my way with a fear that I hadn't expected to instill. He momentarily froze and stared at us like we were strangers. Finally, a youthful, energetic smile flashed over his face. "Brax!" he said. "You are here!"

He jumped up and ran over to me, nearly bumping the vizier, who got his caterpillars on full caterpillaring to shoot out of the way.

The emperor of Akkad then hugged me.

I will admit, and this is a horrid thing to admit, I melted a little.

Dragons shouldn't ever melt.

"Your Holy Highness." Vizier Arbaim held his head at such a severe angle it made it easier for him to look down his nose. "Your holy self should not be allowing your holy flesh to come in contact with mere messengers."

"Yes, yes," I said, gently pushing the emperor back.

"Vizier Arggh—I mean, Arbaim—is correct. What would the commoners think? Besides, Carmen here, who I know is second-best to me, will have her nose out of joint at this display."

"Carmen!" Nagar exclaimed, and this time, he didn't go in for a hug. Instead, he touched Carmen's commoner shoulder. "You came back, too!"

Ha! I got the hug! I sent to Carmen.

"Yes, I am here," Carmen replied to the boy, clearly ignoring me. "It is my pleasure to be in your presence again, Emperor Nagar."

"You are both so very welcome," he said, his voice hitting an un-emperor-like squeaky tone.

A servant poked her nose into the room and set food on the table, careful not to place it near the map. Then, after a quick glance around, she backed out, meeting no one's eyes.

I sniffed deeply, pretending it was the food I was smelling. There was no scent that suggested that the servant was Megan. If it was her, she had a genuine gift for masking her scent—usually, you can smell mortals from a league away.

Carmen went around the table and lifted the cover on the plate, meanwhile resting her other hand on the table, covering something. She also sniffed, checking for poison. At the same time, she placed something in one of her many cloak pockets.

"I ordered that for you, Brax," Nagar said. "As soon as my messenger reported seeing you crossing the borders of Akkad."

"My Lord!" Vizier Arbaim said. "Though you never make a mistake, one should not let outsiders know that we have sentinels tracking the high airstreams. Nor should we give them information about our efficient messaging system."

Nagar waved his hand. "These are friends."

"The vizier is correct," I said, though it pained me to say it. "Even friends should be given the least information possible. In case they get tortured. Though I saw your sentinels as I passed." I hadn't—in fact, we were travelling at such a speed that I couldn't spot anything but a blur and was curious how they had tracked us at that height. "It's best not to let your allies know everything."

"But you let us know you could spot us," Nagar said.

"Uh, yes," I said. "But was I telling the truth? That is the question to ask."

He gave me a measured stare, searching for a sign I was lying. Big mistake. Dragons have the gift of looking like emotionless stones. Which I did at once.

"Ha," Nagar said. "That is a good card face. I will remember this lesson in my mind that makes no mistakes." The kid might have learned sarcasm. "Now, my dear friend, come and eat."

He motioned. My nostrils were already in love with the scent, even though it wasn't goat's meat sitting on the silver plate. It was darker and, sadly, only a small piece. But he offered it to me. I glanced at Carmen, who nodded. Her well-trained nose detected no poison in it.

As daintily as possible, I lifted the meat and placed it in my mouth. Immediately, it grew, quadrupling in size and in flavour. Fearing it might fill my entire mouth and choke me, I took two quick bites and swallowed it. Then, I became worried that the food would continue to expand in my stomach until I filled out like an air bladder. I'd soon look like the toy version of me.

But the expansion stopped the moment I felt full—which does take a lot of food. The taste, which still rested on my tongue, was heavenly—a goat-like meat with a hint of auroch steak. "What was that?" I said. "It was delectable. Delectable! There was an oaky taste and a pinch of boisinberry with the perfect amount of garlic."

"My chefs have been working day and night to perfect it," he said with great pride. "I call it goatswan meat."

"Uh, does it have a swan in it?" Carmen asked.

"No, no," he said. "The swan in the title is to suggest the beauty of the meat. As you know, 'Beauty is in the eye of the beholder . . . unless you poke it out.'"

He had quoted from *Vindor's Revenge*! "You have brilliant taste in books." That was the very book I'd wanted to inquire of him if he'd read it. There was some hope for this empire.

"Thank you," he said. "We have magically altered the meat to expand. Our chefs are looking at ways to fill a soldier's stomach before battle. A fed soldier is a soldier who will conquer a thousand kingdoms, my uncle told me. It was his plan to have his soldiers march many hours on this goatswan meat."

Arbaim opened his mouth as if to speak, then closed it. Clearly, this was more information that he didn't want us to know.

My stomach was so full and satisfied that a nap threatened to overtake me. "Well, your uncle, the desert gods rest his soul, made a wise choice with this meat."

Vizier Arbaim cleared his throat. "And what, may I ask, is your reason for returning? More messages from Drachia?"

"No," Carmen said. "All is well in Drachia. We were passing through your wonderful empire."

Oh, right, we don't want to raise any suspicions, I sent. *Got that.*

"We cannot get enough of your lands," I said. "Your religions, too."

"If there is no official reason for your visit," the vizier began. "May I suggest—"

"You may leave us, Arbaim." Nagar made a motion as if he were shooing a rather large fly. "I promise I won't hug them again."

Arbaim bowed immediately. "Yes, my great and wonderful lord emperor," he said and floated toward the door.

When he was gone, Carmen closed the door. She took a quick tour around the room, perhaps searching for spy holes or listening crevices, then returned to us. "Dear friend Emperor Nagar," she said. "Please tell us how you have truly been."

"There was another appearance of that monstrous entity and more deaths," he said.

"Who died?" I asked. "And how?"

"Three servants were torn apart before my eyes," he said. "And one of them was someone you know."

CHAPTER 30
THROW A FEW MORE DEATHS ON THE PILE

"Who died?" Carmen asked. "Please tell us now."

"It is . . ." He faltered, and in that moment, it was clear he was still a child. So many things had happened, from being ripped from a quiet life of reading on the beaches near Eladium to being deposited beside an emperor in a palace stuffed with intrigue, only to witness a massacre that eviscerated that same emperor.

Go easy on him, I sent.

"It . . . it was three of my servants," Nagar whispered. "Yesterday, they were in the bathing chamber, drawing my bath. It is madness that I may not draw my own bath. I always did before I came here. I am not a child. But while waiting, I was reading—"

"What were you reading?" I asked.

"*Bartum's Revenge,*" the young emperor said.

"Oh, I love that one," I replied. "And Carmen here has read it, too. And—"

"We can discuss literature later," Carmen said in what I

could only call a maestru-like tone. "Please tell us about this horrible event."

Oh, yeah, I sent. *Some people died. Sorry. I forgot.*

"Well," Nagar continued, "a *thud* interrupted my reading. Then another *thud* and another *thud*. I had heard that kind of wet thudding before and set my book on the side table and gently called out to the servants. When an emperor calls, the reply is always immediate. No one answered. Then purple smoke began pouring out of the bathing chamber."

"Let me guess, you've seen that sort of smoke before," I said.

"Yes, I have . . ." He drew in another breath. "Gathering my bravery, I went to the door of the bathing chamber—a room that is five times as large as my bedroom at home—and the servants were . . . well, you remember how the others looked in the greeting room? They were like that." He shuddered. I resisted putting a paw on his shoulder.

"And did you see anything else?" Carmen asked. "Perhaps hear a voice or see tentacles or a Gutian toad?"

"A toad?" he asked. "No, and nor did I hear any voices. Only the slickening sound of death." Though he'd made up the word "slickening," it sounded perfect for this context. "I never want to hear it again. But whatever caused those sounds was gone."

Carmen continued to dig at the poor child with her questions. "And how did we know these servants?"

"I believe one of them was your friend," Nagar said. "There was a female servant who listened more closely to my conversations with Arbaim and others. I hope I'm wrong. There wasn't very much left of her. At least it happened in a bathing chamber. It . . . it was easier to clean up."

Carmen showed no emotion on her face. "And were they buried?"

Nagar shook his head. "Vizier Arbaim wanted to bury them, but Enheduanna suggested burning them to ashes since their bodies might be cursed by whatever had attacked them."

"Destroying proof of what happened." I clicked my talons together in an impressive and thoughtful manner. "That's convenient."

"What do you mean?" Nagar's eyes were suddenly lit by suspicion. Ah, the poor boy was going to turn into a collection of fears.

"Ignore that comment," I said. "I was thinking out loud. Please continue as long as your mortal constitution allows."

He leaned forward and absentmindedly grabbed the dragon playpiece. It was both comforting and odd to see an emperor move me around the board. "I don't understand what's happening," he said. "The other attack was on my dear uncle, the emperor. But this one was on servants. Why would servants matter to a goddess?"

"Goddesses can work very mysteriously," I said. "Sometimes even send toads to attack where it's clear a bigger attack is needed."

He nodded as if I'd said something very wise, then continued, "Enheduanna said she believed it was a goddess and was researching her. Something about the lotus scent left in the room and the symbol of snakes encircling a sun on the bathing chamber floor. It was the same as the one in the . . . you know, the arrival room."

"She would know all about goddess smells," I said.

"The attack may have been intended for you, Nagar," Carmen said. "It was, after all, your bathing chamber."

He stared at her in shock. Even though he was a reader, he might not be the brightest burning torch out there. "Truly? Arbaim would have suggested that to me."

Not if he was in on it, I sent.

You are a bundle of suspicions, Brax, Carmen sent back. *You would have made a good assassin.*

"The entity went after your uncle," Carmen explained. "But it might have accidentally missed killing you at the same time. So, it returned to finish its task."

He looked around the room, clearly expecting the smoke to appear.

"It may also be a warning," I said.

"Warning me of what?" He leaned back, pulling his legs against his chest. He was small enough to do so and place his feet on the chair. Nagar looked younger by the moment.

"I don't know," I admitted. "Goddesses and toads with tentacles and such aren't always clear about their warnings. Maybe you were doing something that angered her."

"I have done nothing official," he squeaked. "I only let the ravens fly with messages for all town criers to cry out that I am now emperor. Until I, um, get my feet under me, Vizier Arbaim and the council make the key decisions. They have even made a room of safety deep in the palace to protect me when the next attack comes."

"That is wise of them," Carmen said. "Maybe the warning was for Arbaim. Then again, any state decisions may not matter to such powerful entities. I know this goddess has a long reach, for she also attacked my brother."

"Your brother?" Nagar asked. "He lives here in Akkadium?"

She shook her head. "No. He dwells in a fief in Azadiq.

He is a wizard assassin, though I'm sure your spies know all of that."

"She—she can strike that far away?" He said this quietly. "There is nowhere to run to?"

"You won't need to run," I said with confidence. It is necessary to say things with confidence, even if you don't believe them. That way, other people will. "We're here."

He gave me a grateful look. "And your brother?" the boy emperor asked. "How did he fare?"

"He's dead," Carmen said. She even sniffed in a little sniff of sadness with a convincing amount of nasal goo.

Liar! I sent. *Did they have a "how to lie to innocents" class at the Red Keep?*

We don't need to share all our information with Nagar, she sent. *He does not seem good at keeping secrets.*

"My sorrow is deep," he said. "I . . . I feel responsible."

"How could you be responsible?" I asked.

"Well, if I could have done something when the attacks on my uncle happened, or my servants, then this would have stopped the creature. I am an emperor now. I should be able to stop these things from happening."

"Now." I put up a paw. "I don't want to belittle your powers since you are now one of the most powerful mortals in all of Ellos, but stopping that evil goddess was beyond you." I touched my nose. "I mean, I tangled with her, and she scratched my nose. And at that point, she wasn't much more than an animated pile of ashes. Feel no guilt, my young friend."

Nagar pulled his knees tighter. "Enheduanna gave me the same advice. She knows most of these entities and goddesses and is familiar with this goddess. She has spoken directly to her own Cowled Goddess to try to discover more about this invader."

More likely, she is talking directly to the Nameless Goddess, I sent.

We don't know that, Carmen sent back.

Nagar sniffed. "Enheduanna told me this is a power far beyond the ability of most mortals to face. Even though I am the Emperor Who Rules All That He Sees. Why give me these titles if they mean nothing?"

"We need to converse with Enheduanna," Carmen said. "To discover what she knows about these attacks. May we have your permission to visit her?"

"You have my permission," he said. "Alas, even the emperor can't demand to enter the Temple of Iktara, the Cowled Goddess. Only women are allowed inside, though I don't know if they make exceptions for male dragons."

"Everyone makes exceptions for me," I said.

"They should," the boy said. "But go see her and come right back since you no longer have your secret assassin friend watching me. I feel . . . well, I feel unsafe."

"We will return," I said. "I promise."

I didn't know if I should salute him, so I bowed slightly. This made him smile with pleasure.

We left the room, and since they didn't want a dragon and an assassin walking around the palace alone, a Golden Guard led us toward the ambassador tower. He kept his distance, which allowed us to talk.

"It's curious," I said. "When she first appeared to him, the goddess said, 'This is the first visitation; there will be three.' But she appeared to me, then later to him in the murder room, then in the library, and at Corwin's, and finally in the bathing room of the emperor. That's five visitations."

"I'm sure she doesn't count the first time she met you."

"That hurts," I replied loudly enough that our guard looked back. "But even so, that leaves four. Can't goddesses count?"

"What we don't know is what a goddess considers a visitation. We didn't see her in the library, remember."

"I still find it odd," I said. Then another topic came to mind. "You must really miss your friend Margery."

"It is Megan," she said. "And you know that. And you clearly know she wasn't killed in that bathing chamber."

"Yes, well, she brought food to us. I wouldn't forget that."

"Did you recognize her scent?" she asked.

"I don't give out my secrets."

"She will want to know," Carmen said. "We assassins need to perfect our techniques."

"I saw you pick up the piece of paper," I said.

Carmen sighed. "Oh, so it is *my* fault—twelve demerit points for me. I should have been more careful. Then again, you are keenly observant."

"Your compliment is keenly appreciated," I said. "What did the note say?"

"Well, that's the interesting thing. She wrote, in code, *Go visit Enheduanna*. Clearly, all paths lead to the Temple of the Cowled Goddess."

So that's exactly where we went.

CHAPTER 31
IT'S ALL RED INSIDE

The Temple of Iktara scowled down over the Akkadian market. I say "scowled" because the huge crimson building was in the shape of a woman's head, made of blood-red stone with a thousand arrow-slit eyes and thirteen narrow doors for teeth. A multi-pronged snake crown adorned her head—twisty spikes protruded from every part of the roof, preventing both pigeons and dragons from landing. A set of long, winding stairs in the shape of a cowl led up to her mouth. It was an impressive building insofar as mortal buildings can be impressive. Iktara, in this form, did not look like a goddess to be tangled with.

This religious head loomed over every Akkadium citizen who was out bargaining for their daily food and wares—the arrow-slit eyes suggested the priestesses were watching all the time. I bet that affected the prices in the market.

Iktara, the Cowled Goddess, is one of the oldest Akkadian religions, an annoyingly educational voice said inside my head. *At one time, it was more powerful than the church of the Bear God, but that was back when there were only empresses ruling Akkad.*

"Akkad was once ruled by women?" I said this aloud. We dragons, wise creatures that we are, let whichever dragon was the most powerful lead us—male or female. That's why my sister was queen right now and all Drachia was called a queendom. "I would like to think the empresses weren't as cruel, stupid, and power-hungry as the emperors."

"They were equally cruel, smart, and power-hungry," Carmen answered. "That's what my lessons taught me. The final empress, Xiantonia, was deposed and murdered. But she rose from her tomb and formed this church to cultivate a new power."

"She came back from the dead?"

"According to the histories," Carmen said, continuing her best lecturing voice. "Whether that truly happened, we can't know. But she said the goddess Iktara brought her back from the netherworlds, and that led many to worship the Cowled Goddess."

"So, High Priestess Enheduanna is spiritually descended from a line of empresses?" I said. "That explains why she hovers around the throne so much."

"You are an excellent student," Carmen said. The compliment made me glow—I would never admit to her I was proud of getting the highest marks at the Royal Dragon Academy for my years of study.

"It also explains why she is so haughty," I said.

I landed at the bottom of the steps, my back to a market stuffed with staring mortals. We could not easily hide our movements, so I thought it better to be out in the open. A gaggle of priestesses was likely eyeing us from the slit windows. Carmen launched herself into the air, her cloak flapping majestically behind her. She had jumped much higher than she needed to and landed expertly, with a bit of a pose at the end.

"How sad—you want to impress everyone watching you," I said.

"It's intimidation," she replied.

"Or showing off." She ignored my wit as she did her weapons check for the hundred-thousandth time. I looked up the narrow steps at Iktara's temple.

"Do you think they made the doors that small so dragons couldn't go inside?" I asked. The thirteen doors were at least twelve feet high but only wide enough for a woman or a smaller man to walk through easily. The few worshippers who entered, all female, looked as if they were willingly entering a grinning mouth.

"My guess is they wanted to control the movement of any enemies," Carmen said. "Dragons were probably low on their list of worries. Right after ammits and giant toads."

"I am offended by the very idea we are seen as lower than ammits and toads."

"The construction took place a millennium ago, back when dragons were mostly seen as myths by the people in Ellos." She motioned with her dagger, then resheathed it.

"If only we could have stayed mythical." I drew in a breath, preparing for a long soliloquy about how much better dragons would be without mortals, but caught myself: it was the kind of soliloquy that deserved a warm fire and a warm goat. "And your plan?" I asked. "I assume you have one."

"Why do I have to have the plan?" she said. "You are the one who constantly brags about your intelligence."

"Stating the truth is not bragging." My magnificent chest puffed out on its own. "But I take your point. I have the better, bigger, smarter brain, so I should come up with a plan. How about you go inside, and I'll wait out here. That seems the safest and smartest of all options."

"Safe for whom?" she asked.

"Well, for me. You'll be in danger. But I'll keep an eye on you." I tapped my dragon eye. "Besides, I have a feeling the priestesses dislike having men or dragons—especially male dragons—inside their temple." The entrance was the only visible way in, but there were likely tunnels underneath. Other things I did not like to squeeze myself into were mortal tunnels—that was a quick path to suffocation.

"Well, this is what I will do," she said. "I will enter that head and humbly ask for Enheduanna, pointing out that I have permission from the emperor. Then I'm certain I'll be taken directly to her."

That wasn't a half-bad plan since the priestess would want to obey her emperor, but I decided not to compliment Carmen. I find mortal egos, given even the slightest bit of encouragement, grow like mushrooms.

"That might work," I said. I waved a talon around like a lecturer. "Might. But don't forget to accuse her of attempting to murder us and your brother. That's where you should start your conversation."

"Leave the accusations to me," Carmen said, and without so much as a tap on the shoulder, she started up the steps toward the building.

In all honesty, a part of me wanted to pull her back. For all my blustering, I preferred to have by her side when there was danger. But she was a fully grown assassin, and there wasn't any obvious way for me to enter the temple. She was also protected by the fact she was a messenger from Drachia. One does not want to kill the dragon queen's messengers. A harsher message would be sent back.

I stood there, chest out slightly, muscles tight, looking my most royal. I knew there were many eyes watching us: the ones behind the slit windows were likely plotting how to rid the world—or at least the stairs—of my presence. The people in the market stared with a mixture of wonder and fear. Any nearby mortals made a wide berth around me, and even a few marketeers moved their wagons away from my intimidating presence.

Carmen approached the building's mouth. A door opened, and she slipped inside.

I expected her to be spat right back out, but the doors remained closed, and the temple quiet. I waited a full heartbeat before blessing her with a question.

What's it like inside? I sent.

There was no reply. She was still alive, for I could feel her mind. But she sent nothing back.

Carmen? Carmen? What's it like?

It's all blood, she sent back.

CHAPTER 32

A GREAT INSPIRATION

It took impressive self-control not to rush up those stairs and attempt to bash my way through Iktara's teeth.

Blood, I sent. *Is there a sacrifice? Are you the sacrifice?*

No, no, she replied. *I am safe. There is blood on every statue of Iktara, running from her eyes. And blood at her feet, too, from the daily sacrifices. There are also fountains spewing blood—though I am certain most of it is coloured water. On top of that, the Iktarian worshippers, the cowlers, as I'm sure you know they are called, really, really like red. It's everywhere. Crimson crystals embedded in the ceiling diffuse the light. It's all quite nauseating.*

I sat back on my haunches and let my muscles relax. Blood fountains weren't dangerous, just tacky. No need to charge in yet.

Well, don't throw up, I replied. *That's a sign of weakness. Your maestrus would be ashamed.*

I won't, she sent back. *Oh, here's an update: I am being approached by a woman with horns on her head. Ornamental horns, I should add. Her dress is that of a higher priestess. And she is smil-*

ing, which is disconcerting. She has begun to speak to me. I think it's best if you don't talk to me right now.

I will take great pleasure in not talking to you, I sent.

Then I sat and tapped my talon on the bottom step, chipping away at the stone. Since Carmen wasn't tossed out the front door by that horned princess, she must have been allowed farther into the temple.

In time, I grew bored with the waiting and glanced at the marketplace. The Akkadians had returned to their usual buying and selling as if there wasn't an amazing dragon standing on the steps of a temple. They were pretending it was a normal day now.

The only abnormal thing was that one bearded, crazy-haired man several yards away was concentrating his stare on me. An easel stood before him, and he was working madly at the attached canvas, pausing only to measure me with his madness-fouled eyes. I had inspired an artist! A perfect title for the painting would be *The Great Brax Suffers No Fools or Goddesses.* I sat a bit more stoically for a time, then my curiosity got the better of me, and I wandered over there as surreptitiously as a dragon could, careful not to step on any children or livestock. The artist didn't show the slightest fear at my approach; in fact, he projected disdain and consternation.

"Your inspiration has arrived," I said, which I thought was clever. He didn't smile.

I came around the other side of the canvas to discover a full-colour oil painting. He was clearly a master, for he had captured my dragon-god-like properties with the perfect amount of muscle definition and the exact handsomeness of my snout. My tail was at least two feet longer.

"You are a gifted artist," I said.

"Yes, yes, yes." He waved at me as if I were a pesky bug.

I settled myself down. "I rarely compliment mortals. You should take it with great aplomb."

"Yes, yes, yes." He continued to wave, this time sending a bit of paint to land at my feet. He had one more glorious wing to attach and the temple background to fill in.

"You would like me to return to my perch?" I asked.

"Yes, yes, yes," he said.

"Well, first, answer me this." I put a talon to my lip, which was a very famous thinking pose for dragons that he could memorize for a later painting. "I know you artists have themes. What is the theme of this? A great and powerful dragon deigns to visit the marketplace of mortals and doesn't show the slightest fear of gods or goddesses?"

He forcefully shook his head, making his wild hair slap the sides of his cheeks. "No. No. No. Its theme is how even the worm dragon looked in awe upon Iktara, the Cowled Goddess."

A very tiny snake tattoo was running along his neck. He was a cowler! "Your theme needs work," I hissed. "Oh, and your personality—like most artists. The dragon is not feeling awe. It is the goddess cringing before me."

"Iktara does not cringe," he said. And now that I looked closer, he had, in a few brush strokes, captured how the temple loomed over the square and me. He had added no other mortals. It was just me and the intimidatingly painted temple.

A realization hit me like a stone: I hated artists. Mortal or dragon creative types were all the same. Insufferable! I shuffled elegantly toward the steps again, deciding I would change my pose to make his final touches more difficult.

Maybe a better plan would be to kill him. That way, I

could title the painting whatever I wanted. And furthermore, I could—

Brax!

A wave of confusion hit me, for it was not Carmen's voice in my head.

Brax, she will need your help! Of course, it was Corwin cawing in my skull. His voice echoed from a great distance. *Time is of the essence. Don't look in its eyes.*

What are you babbling about? I sent. *And don't pop into my head whenever you want. Please set up a time beforehand to appear.*

Carmen will need your help, he repeated. *Or maybe it has already happened. And she needed your help.*

Could you be any more confusing? I sent back.

Time. Here. Drifting oddly. But use your eye. Your dragon eye. See.

Use my dragon eye? I asked. *How do you know about that ability?*

Know this: she is in great danger, but don't worry about her death.

I sucked in a breath. *Death from what? Are you certain? She just went into the temple and won't like me poking around.*

It's—oh, I have to go; the slithering ones have smelled me.

Who smelled you? I sent. But he didn't reply. Winged gods, that was a confusing visitation.

Carmen! I sent. *Carmen, how are things? Your brother is nagging me to check on you.*

She didn't answer immediately. And it was as if she had vanished from the connection we always had. Then her faint voice rang in my head. *Brax, it's—*

She went silent.

The only sane thing Corwin had said was *use your dragon eye.* I turned toward the temple and looked at the doors.

Then I closed my eyes and found that part of my mind that was still connected to her.

And to my old eye.

The dragon eye that was in her skull.

The one she'd stolen from me. Yes, I bring that up overly often.

At first, there was darkness, then a grey fog, and finally images that made sense—I was looking through my eye in Carmen's head.

Curse him, Corwin was right. Snakes surrounded Carmen. They hung from the walls and the ceilings, hissing and slithering and doing other snake things.

Carmen, I sent. *Carmen, what is happening?*

She didn't reply. Instead, she stared straight ahead, appearing frozen.

Enheduanna was a few feet away, her lips moving. It looked very much like one of those speeches that enemies give when they are about to kill you. As the recipient of many of those dramatic speeches, I recognized the particular look of gloating that comes over one's enemy.

Red smoke surrounded the priestess, and snakes entwined her arms and were coming out of her hair. Well, to be honest, the view was a little blurry. They could have also been tentacles, which was worse.

Carmen blinked several times to clear her dragon eye, then said something. Enheduanna laughed a fake laugh.

Carmen! I sent. *Reply to me. Let me know what is happening!*

She didn't reply. I had raced part way up the stairs without knowing it, which would wreck the painter's painting. But the higher I climbed, the faster I went. *Carmen!* I stumbled a few times because I was still looking in that room through her eye while running up the stairs.

As I hit the top stair, all the doors in the temple slammed shut, and I skidded to a stop.

Enheduanna pointed at Carmen's left eye.

Which meant she was pointing at me.

"You are not alone here," she said, her voice somehow appearing clear in my head. "Which means you'll have a witness to your death."

Then everything in that room turned red.

CHAPTER 33
ONE HURT HAIR!

At first, I thought the overwhelming redness was blood. Carmen continued blinking madly. The image of Enheduanna also went all wobbly and in and out of focus, and then she came back, but all the world around her was red.

She is saying that I must die, Carmen's voice came through, all ragged, even though it was speaking in my mind. *And I agree with her. It is right for me to die.*

Stop this mad talk, I sent. *Do you hear me, Carmen? I'm coming to get you.* She gave no reply, and the vision grew more and more blurry.

No, she sent, one last time, as if throwing her voice from across the room. *No!* And I didn't know if that was her telling me not to rush to her or that something horrible was about to happen.

Then Enheduanna became clearer. She held a very large axe that she may have stolen from an executioner. Her mouth continued to move, though I could no longer hear her. She swung.

My dragon eye's sight went black.

I strained my mental eye, but the room wouldn't return. My mind reached out to find no sign of Carmen. Not even the faintest lecturing tone.

Carmen! I charged up the remaining steps—fully expecting arrows or lightning or whatever priestesses threw at dragons to hit me, but the few worshippers scattered at my approach. I did not want to be a dragon who'd lost his mortal. Who cares if she's trained to be an assassin? She was still only a mortal and needed my protection.

As I reached the top, all the doors slammed as one, and the patrons trapped outside fled down the other narrow set of steps. One female worshipper even let out a scream and jumped over the ledge to land in a heap of straw and dung.

"Closed doors will not stop me," I warned. And with a paw that was angry—well, I was the angry one—I battered the nearest door, and it flew inward, revealing a giant crimson-coloured chamber. Blood really was flowing from a fountain against the far wall. And several small statues of Iktara bled from the eyes.

Other than that, the entrance room was empty. The priestess and followers had fled into their hidey-holes. The door was barely wide enough for my snout and part of my head, so I jammed it in there as far as I could, pressing with my forelegs on both sides, hoping to crack the foundations of the whole temple. The stone columns refused to budge.

"Give my Carmen to me, and I won't bring your temple down," I shouted, pushing harder, nearly getting my shoulder to squeeze in, but a logical thought niggled its way into my brain: *Don't get your head stuck in the doorway. You'll be trapped, and they'll behead you or, worse, paint your tail some garish colour.*

"Do you hear me?" I shouted. "I know you are in here. Tell Enheduanna that if she harms one tiny little hair on Carmen's head, she will be destroyed." My voice echoed impressively, but there was no answer. The temple could very well have been deserted.

I attempted to pull my head back and discovered I was stuck. I let out a roar and a blast of flame that melted a goddess statue several feet away, the blood in her eyes boiling. With another roar, this time flameless, I twisted hard and popped my head out. The overwhelming need to let blast after blast of flame at these doors, at the temple walls, everywhere, nearly took control. The smarter part of my mind realized the stone wouldn't melt. I've impressive heat, but it's not that hot.

I flew up toward the slit windows and hovered there, a giant angry burning bee. The windows slammed shut before I could see anything inside, and when I banged on them, they didn't budge. I could slam my snout against the shutters, but if I knocked myself unconscious, I'd fall to the stone below. I banged again, to no effect.

There were spells woven in there, I realized, made back when the wizards and witches worked with the emperors and empresses to construct their buildings. Clearly, a powerful witch was behind this, or a whole gaggle of them.

"Carmen!" I shouted as I circled the temple. "I am coming!" I flew over the top of the building with its many thousands of spikes. There was no opening that I could spot. How they got their statues and furniture inside, I did not know.

But I was seething. How stupid I was to lose my mortal. I was ready to start a war and break every single bone in this empire.

"I will return," I promised the Temple of the Cowled Goddess. "And reduce you to ashes."

CHAPTER 34

MORE PROOF THAT MORTALS ARE ANNOYING

A return to Drachia was not in the cards for me, though I was aching to bring back ten quant dragons and crush Iktara's temple to dust. No, my queenly sister would never allow that. It would start a war. And our other allies, the Zareks, those annoyingly polite mage giants, would refuse to enter a holy temple without weeks of discussion with the priestesses. They would be no help.

Instead, I flew to my nearest and largest ally.

If anyone had the power to force Enheduanna to release Carmen, it was the emperor, and he adored me. Well, most mortals did, when they weren't trembling in fear or getting up enough gumption to spear me, but Nagar looked up to me as a god-like father figure dragon. Plus, we were both readers, so he would listen to me. He could send his royal guards into the nest of the Cowled Goddess and her collection of horrid priestesses. Or maybe Nagar would command his vizier to float inside and bore Enheduanna to death by quoting Akkadian rules and regulations. The little emperor might even have a key to a secret door of Iktara's temple, which I'd open and be allowed to wreak havoc on my own. No one touched or insulted my mortal but me. No one!

I landed with a thump at the ambassador tower. Then, gathering all my anger, I charged at the door into the murder room, not waiting for an escort. I gave it a shove.

Someone had locked the door from the inside, so it didn't budge. I pulled back my foreleg to smash a paw through the wood, but before I could release a mighty blow, the door swung open.

A female servant cowered there, staring down as if she didn't dare look directly into my eyes.

"You . . . you should not . . . go inside." She could barely get the words out, she was so frightened.

"A servant?" I said. "All they send to greet Braxus Andorium is a servant? This is an affront! I demand to see the emperor this very moment so that he can explain this affront."

"Brax," the servant said, "the emperor cannot see you at this moment."

"What!" The continued effrontery set my anger to boiling. They didn't even send Vizier Arbaim! Instead, only a waif, trembling before my greatness. "You aren't even important enough to turn away a mongrel dog." I pointed at her, even though she wasn't looking. "Wait—" I pulled back my pointing paw and my anger. "You spoke my name as if you know me."

She chuckled, and in a heartbeat, her waifishness vanished, her shoulders widened, her back straightened, and she raised her head to look me directly in the eyes with a confidence no servant had ever displayed. Her eyes, which were a dark brown, changed to green. And even though she'd had no scent a moment ago, she now had a very familiar smell—of almonds. "I know you far too well, Brax," she said.

"Oh, it's you, Megan," I replied. "I knew it. Really, I did. And you're the only assassin I half respect."

"I take that as a full compliment." Her smile widened.

"So, some royal personages saw me coming in a magnificent arc toward the palace, and they sent you to greet me?"

"Not exactly," she said. "There have been reports about, well, let us say, a disturbance involving a dragon at the temple of the Cowled Goddess. Then the Danger Dragon Approaching bell rang—"

"There's a Danger Dragon Approaching bell? I have my own bell?"

"Yes, it rings every time you or another dragon gets near." She was patting her side and her back—a weapons check. One of the annoying habits these assassins had. "I glanced out, and since you had no rider, I drew several conclusions. A group of Golden Guards were dispatched to greet you, but they are sleeping in the stairwell now."

She said this all matter-of-factly, even though it was rather impressive that she had somehow incapacitated the guards without getting wounded or even having a lock of hair fall out of place.

"And what about the soldiers who watch us now from the towers?" I asked.

"As far as they are concerned, I was supposed to greet you."

"Great," I replied. "I need to see the emperor right now!"

"You can't," she said. "He's beyond reach."

"Last I saw him, he was playing with his toys. Where did he go?"

"The Astral Warning Bell rang before your bell, and Arbaim and the Golden Guards fled with Nagar to the deepest, safest room in the temple. It has a painted sun and desert scene on the ceiling and is protected by magical wards intended to keep the great emperor safe from any enemy, especially those from the spirit world."

"How many bells do they have?"

"Many! That bell was installed after the attack in the emperor's bathing room. It detects whether a visit from the nether realms is imminent."

"Another visit where?" Then I tapped my head. "At Itkara's temple." So that was what Carmen was facing. "I need to rescue Carmen."

"Why is Carmen in need of rescuing?" Megan asked.

"She's in the clutches of Enheduanna and likely facing whatever that horribly rhyming priestess has summoned."

"Oh, that foolish assassin," Megan said. "When I slipped her that note, I did not expect her to march directly in to see that viper. She didn't read between the lines that she should wait for me."

"I commanded her not to enter," I said. "But she didn't listen to me." I paused. "Well, it might have been a more nuanced conversation where we decided I couldn't join her because the doors to the temple were too small."

"I don't know how you put up with her. She believes she can survive anything." This was a true bonding moment between Megan and me—she understood the pain of dealing with Carmen.

"Yes, yes, tell me more about how horrible she is to work with," I said.

"I think it's that dragon eye," she said. "The dragon

blood gives her an air of invulnerability, and she makes irrational choices."

"Well, dragon blood also saves her," I pointed out. "But as much as I am enjoying pointing out her faults, I need to go to the emperor and have him burn down that temple for me."

"Assuming you can get through the many magical wards, do you think the vizier and the council will respond well to a dragon telling him what to do?" Megan was right, of course, and sounded far too much like my sister Brenna, who was always using logic in these situations. "There are already several rumours that a serpent has his ear."

"Serpent?" I said. "One should never call a dragon a serpent. Snakes don't have legs! I could make it a formal request."

"You know as well as I that he cannot attack the source of one of their Akkad religions. The only deity they worship on an equal footing to the Great God Bear is the Cowled Goddess. He might get every woman in the empire angry at him."

That sounded heart-stompingly horrifying. "Yes, yes, I suppose," I said. "I guess I'll go back there and tear the temple apart stone by stone."

"No," she said. "That is not what you'll do."

There was something in her tone that reminded me of how imperious Carmen could be. I missed the old days when these mortals saw me as a giant creature with murderous, flaming breath. Instead, they were used to my greatness and treated me as . . . well, as one of them.

"Please." I tried not to sound too angry. "Tell me what I am to do. You know I love that."

The sarcasm went over her head. "What you'll do

instead is you'll roar loudly, smack me with your paw, then carry me away in your talons. Without ripping me open, if possible."

"Will I? That seems an unfriendly thing to do."

She shrugged. "Well, it would look wrong if I rode out of here on your back."

"Who said I'm giving you a ride?" I asked. "I am not a flying wagon."

"I know that, Brax," Megan said. "It'll look like you're dragging me off to your cave to eat. It will be quite the scandal. But I won't be the first servant stolen by a messenger."

"And why am I stealing you?" I asked.

"I'll sneak into the temple and get Carmen," she said. "My work is mostly finished in the palace, so this is a clever exit. My fellow servants will talk about it for ages to come — I'm going out with a bang."

"You're going to march into that temple and rescue her from the clutches of that horribly rhyming priestess, and I'm going to wait outside again? I don't want to lose two mortals in one day."

"I have more of a plan than that." She pulled out a small square of red cloth from one of her pockets. "Recognize this?"

"No," I said. Then, "Wait, that's fabric from the priestesses' dresses."

"I'll become one of them and get you inside," she promised. "I can find a way."

"Fine, then," I said. "I'll do it."

Without another word, I roared, swatted her with my paw, snatched her up in my talons, and carried her off toward the temple.

CHAPTER 35
A BOLT OUT OF THE RED

I t wasn't a hard swat; I should point that out. And
Megan must have studied acting because she made the
fall look so very dramatic and followed up by screaming like
a female banshee as I flew away. Nearly every eye and ear in
the palace would be turned in our direction. There was no
flurry of crossbow bolts from the guard towers in response.
They clearly didn't care about her distress.

Megan stopped her theatrics the moment we were past
the palace walls.

"See," she said. "Not a single challenge. This sort of
thing happens all the time."

"Dragons drag away servants every day?" I asked.

"Most days. Traders drop royal slaves from cliffs when
they bring unwanted news; barbarian kings get angry
during negotiations with the emperor and stab a few
servants. It's a precarious life."

"I'm sure the new emperor will put a stop to it," I said.

"Well, he might," she said. "That boy has an annoying

streak of kindness. But some traditions are hard to change. Plus, trade partners will often feel regretful for killing a prize servant, so a deal is struck, and all is well with the people involved. Except for the dead servant, of course."

I sniffed. "Well, even I think that is rather monstrous."

Megan seemed perfectly calm, hanging above the city. One slip of my talons and she'd be splattered across the paving stones. "Monstrous is what happened to the three servants who drew a bath for the emperor."

"Nagar mentioned that. It seems odd that the goddess would first attack the previous emperor, then attack us and Corwin, but later lower herself to attack two servants."

Carmen yawned, again proving she was completely comfortable flying upside down above the city. And this was the nice part: she trusted me. "Though this will sound pompous," she said, "it could have been an attempt to get me. I drew his bath most other mornings but was called away to linen duty that day. Otherwise, we might not be having this pleasant chat."

"Why would someone want to kill you?" I asked.

"Arbaim has become suspicious that there is a spy among the servants—well, he's always suspicious. Though I am careful, I might have set off a magic ward. The vizier looks harmless, but he is dangerously observant."

"Are you suggesting he is connected to the goddess's visitation?" I said.

"He worships the Bear God, as do most in the palace. But he is an enigma to me."

"Yes, he walks like he has caterpillars on his feet."

Megan laughed. Her laugh didn't have the same innocent tinkle as Carmen—she sounded more bitter. "That's an apt description of his walking patterns. You are dangerously observant, too."

"I am gifted," I said, pleased by her compliment.

"As I said, Arbaim is an enigma. He spends some time in his room humming."

"Humming?" I said. "That doesn't seem like him."

"Well, it may be a meditation noise and . . . uh, not to switch topics suddenly, but I want to point out that there is something dark on the horizon."

"Oh, now you are making up dramatic portents." I had been looking down to speak with her but lifted my head. We were nearing Iktara's temple, close enough to see the goddess's giant head. Red smoke was billowing from every window and the open doors.

"The temple of the Cowled Goddess is on fire," I said.

"I am assuming you didn't leave it that way."

"No, I would remember." I thought back to my righteous rampage. I had burned down a statue. But there was nothing flammable inside that would cause this conflagration.

"Well then, it's a good and bad thing," Megan said. "Good, because they will be even more distracted than I had expected them to be. Distraction is power."

"Oh, wonderful, more maestru quotes," I said. "And what about the bad thing?"

"We will have to work quickly before Carmen is burned to death," Megan added with no emotion. "Drop me off over there." She pointed at an alley between two tall buildings. There wasn't anyone in the alley or looking toward it, partly because the fire was attracting all the eyeballs. Well, and the people with the eyeballs.

I arced down and dropped her. Because I sometimes forget how small mortals are, I released her slightly higher than she might have expected, but she landed like a large cat. Even without dragon blood, like Carmen, she was an impressive assassin. Impressive as far as creatures who don't breathe fire can be, that is.

She waved me away. "Now, scurry off and make a nuisance of yourself."

"Scurry? Dragons don't scurry." But I could see what she was getting at. There would have to be some bigger commotion to get her into the temple unnoticed.

My mother often told me I was gifted at being a nuisance. And for the thousandth time, I proved her correct. Since the temple was already on fire, I circled it, letting out a brief blast of dramatic flame here and there. The Akkadians were going to blame the whole burning of the temple on me anyway, but dragons have big shoulders. There was the occasional scream of petrified fear from the crowds below. Ugh! Mortals.

Meanwhile, being high above, I could see a long way down the streets. Architects had designed Akkadium so that the royal palace was visible to the population from every vantage point in the city. No guards came pouring from the palace gates, nor were there any other soldiers approaching from nearby barracks. I doubted my presence frightened them so much that they would cower behind their walls. Their lack of concern suggested that they didn't care about the fire. The emperors worshipped the Bear God and barely tolerated the Cowled Goddess.

Yes, I know that the Bear God barely tolerating is a pun, but I am too proud to point it out. The fact the emperors hadn't burned the temple down a long time ago was a surprise. History doesn't repeat itself, but the songs about it do.

A priestess with a lopsided gait entered the temple—the limp made me think it wasn't Megan. But then I realized she had likely changed her gait so she wouldn't be recognizable. These assassins were rather clever.

Flying around being dramatic was fun, but I have a complex mind and can do at least two things at once.

Carmen, are you there? I sent.

There wasn't an answer. I tried to look through my dragon eye in her head. Yes, I know it's mostly her eye now, but I was right to use it occasionally. Was that too much to ask? And so, I waited and concentrated while flying around in circles.

A moment later, I was looking through my eye that was in her head. And I saw a tentacle through a thick red smoke. Clearly, this was the source of the conflagration. And another, and everything was shadow, and the sky was very dark and solid. No, wait, I was turned upside down. That is, Carmen was hanging from the ceiling.

Carmen! Why are you upside down?

Again, she didn't reply, though I sensed her presence.

In a blur, her sword cut off the tip of a tentacle, and it fell, wriggling, to the floor.

I'll be there as soon as I can, I sent. She didn't reply, but I could feel what she was feeling. I tried to parse the sensation to understand what was happening. Oh, mortal feelings! They are so much weaker than my own. Resignation is what she felt, I realized, sensing the emotion through my eye in her head. And I know that is a strange sentence, but even stranger was the sensation.

Carmen was preparing herself to die.

Carmen! I am on my way!

A crossbow bolt hit my left flank and bounced off, getting my attention. I broke the connection with Carmen and looked down. Smoke continued to pour out, obscuring the roof, but I spotted a red flicker of movement.

A priestess had popped through some trapdoor on the top of the building and was pointing a crossbow at me. How dare she! I didn't think any of them would be trained for battle—partially because I didn't know what kind of battles priestesses would get into. But it was time to send her to meet her cowled maker. I spread my wings and dived, though in the back of my head, I was wondering why she was facing me on her own. That was rather brave.

And stupid. Often, those two things go hand in hand.

She waved her crossbow at me. And as I dived, she pulled back her cowl.

It was Megan.

In an impressive display of controlling both my emotions and my speed, I spread my wings and hovered in front of her. I flapped hard enough to make her hood fall off, showing her red hair.

"You hit me with a bolt," I said.

"It was blunted. I knew it would never break through your impressively impervious royal scales."

Oh, she knew how to compliment me. "You wanted my attention?" I said. "You have it."

"I have found a way in for you. Go down to the front doors, wait for a few moments, and we can rescue your little princess of an assassin."

"Fine," I said. "But once we're inside, you follow my commands. I take no orders from mortals."

"I wouldn't have it any other way," she replied. Then she popped down into the trapdoor, leaving me looking at the spikes.

I made my impressive way down to land in front of the doors.

CHAPTER 36
THE DOORS SWING OPEN TO A GREAT WINGED HERO

My landing was impressive. Not that it was much different from many of my other landings, but I had an audience, so I kept my wings wide, my muscles flexed, and my jaw, full of lovely teeth, open. This was both for any of the priestesses glaring at me from inside and for the mortals cowering in the marketplace.

And for the artist, too, who, like many artists, didn't know when to leave a party. He was the only one out in the open, still dabbing away at another canvas. There was no way he could interpret this burning building with a dragon as his goddess defeating me.

Brax! The voice blazed through my head so quickly and fervently that I nearly didn't recognize it. *Where are you?*

I am waiting to be let in to save you, I sent. *I have a better assassin than you aiding me in that endeavour.*

You got Megan? Good. Wait, who says I needed to be saved?

Oh, so you have everything under control, do you?

Well, I did for a while. But now it's all pear-shaped.

There was another illogical mortal saying. *Why would you bring up fruit?*

Well, I'm mostly fine. Though I'm upside down —

Your brother told me you're in danger, I said.

How would he know?

I assume he's in some sort of special mystical spying place that only allows idiots.

What were his exact words?

That you needed help. Or that you will need help.

That's different from being in danger. Did he sound urgent?

Now that I thought about it, he sounded distant. *That doesn't matter. He also said you would die. I need to know what is going on.*

I was having a simple conversation with Enheduanna, she sent.

That is not what I saw! She was swinging an axe.

You were looking through my eye again?

Our eye, I replied.

That's why it was itching and blurry. Listen, I don't need you mothering me.

But you still haven't told me what is happening. Ugh, it was frustrating, and I wanted to bang my way in.

Fine! Carmen sent. *But you will have problems comprehending it. Enheduanna tried to kill me, then I killed her, and we had a discussion after that, and now I'm hanging upside down.*

You're talking nonsense.

It makes perfect sense, she sent. *Here in this room. And Enheduanna doesn't want you to come in. The temple doesn't like you.*

The temple doesn't like me? What does that mean?

Carmen didn't reply. Who would ascribe emotions to a building? I slapped the stone wall in front of me, and it didn't respond with even the slightest bit of shaking. Well, it made a ticking sound. And a low grinding rumble followed.

Maybe it didn't like me so much it was going to fall on me. I took a brave step back.

The columns between the slit doors, immovable a moment before, rolled to one side in an impressive engineering feat. Maybe these priestesses were smarter than their silly cowls suggested. A wider doorway was now open for me. Megan came around the corner and leaned against one of the columns, exuding pride. She had a small crossbow resting in the crook of her arm. It was a dramatic pose if I'd ever seen one.

"Well, it's about time," I said.

"Now I see why Carmen likes you," she said. "You're consistently unthankful, and she thinks she can somehow change that side of you. What a fool."

"You did well with the doors," I said, showing that I could be magnanimous with a compliment. "For a mortal."

"Well, opening the doors this wide is how they get their overbosomed statues in," Carmen said. She motioned, which looked a bit like a command to me. "Welcome to the temple of Iktara, the Cowled Goddess."

I hesitated, not out of fear, but because, like the maestrus, I have a saying: "Don't stick your nose into a goddess-inspired temple you can't get out of." I made it up right then, but there was every chance those doors could slam shut on my tail, and I would be trapped in there and used in some holy sacrifice that would end with me being perforated. I gave a nonchalant glance behind me. Again, there were no Akkadian soldiers—so the emperor's forces did not care one wit about this conflict; their only task was to keep the emperor safe. And most of the people in the courtyard and the trading yard were hiding behind their carts or stones, watching, but from a great distance. The painter continued splashing his paint on his canvas, his face held in a serious-artist expression. He'd probably be creating a scene in which I was being swallowed by the goddess's head. Great, more posters all around the villainous land of Akkad showing dragons being defeated by their deities. Did anyone make a poster of me saving the bear at the library? No!

I strode in, still having to duck my head because there was no priestess as tall as a dragon.

Brax, Carmen sent, *I may have misspoken the amount to which I have control of this situation.*

That is a very complicated way of saying you are in trouble, I sent back.

Please hurry. I will need your help soon.

As you wish, Princess. Judging by her lack of reply, she did not enjoy my flippancy. I followed Megan into the maw of the temple of the Cowled Goddess.

CHAPTER 37
CHEATERS OFTEN WIN

The marble below my talons was smooth and very red. Glowing gems in the ceiling served as the only light source; they, too, were (obviously) red and cast a light that bedazzled my eyes and gave my beautiful brain a monstrous headache.

"They have a passion for crimson," Megan said. "Thankfully, it's my colour."

I was about to say something clever and cutting, but the light made her red hair glow and even I, who have little interest in how mortals look, recognized that the colour complemented her appearance. She glowed, too.

Winged gods! I was becoming as vacuous as mortals! Time to concentrate on my task: saving Carmen. Again.

To my left were several empty praying stations with burning incense. Over each, a live snake hung like a living decoration. Beyond them was a very long set of descending red stairs. "This way," I said. Oddly, Megan said the same words at exactly the same time.

"Great minds command alike," I said. Then, because I was the better creature, I led the way.

The stairway had also been noticeable because it was where all the colourful smoke was swirling up from. I sauntered over to the top of the stairs. Looking down, one got the impression that something horrible had happened to the interior of the building. At the bottom of the steps, someone had knocked over several snake statues.

"There's no smell of burning," I said. "It's not smoke from a fire. I'd guess this is more of a sacrament smoke—it's designed to look impressive."

"Exactly the conclusion I'd come to," Megan said. "Like many religions, it's all for show." I worried she was about to give me some sort of lecture about mortal religions, but she gestured. "Glorious prince before ragged rabble."

"Oh, you want me to go first?" I said. "Well then, let us charge forth."

The moment I placed my foot on the stairs, a chill raced from my paw to the tip of my tail. The problem with temples is that priestesses have had a thousand years to invest them with magic spells. My foot, which was not a mortal or bovine foot, had set off a trap that sensed my otherness. And likely my greatness, too.

A grinding came from the thick smoke below. A moment later, a very large cowled face appeared, floating in the smoke—it had angry red eyes, of course.

"Oh," Megan said. "Since you're the leader, you should get first smack at our new friend."

Great. As if this day hadn't been bad enough, a representation of the Cowled Goddess had just appeared in the bottom well of her temple. Just for me.

The face floating in the smoke didn't move, and a bit of

hope grew in my heart that this, like the smoke, was all for show.

My next step didn't set off any more noticeable traps, though the glowing red eyes in the head tracked me. Perhaps that was done with some clever mechanical device. So I took another step. And another. The giant eyes failed to follow my movement. It was a fake; that much was glaringly clear. All the smoke hid what it was attached to.

"Why are you going so slow?" Megan asked.

"I'm sure there's a maestro saying about being careful and living to fight another day—no, no, don't quote it." I took my fifth step. My sixth. And my seventh.

Sadly, I had forgotten that religious types liked the number seven. The moment my foot touched the seventh step, the head gave out an ear-splitting musical note that was both beautiful and frightening.

Hey Carmen! I sent, *I might be awhile because something in the stairwell is about to kill me.*

I'm busy right now, she sent, which was very typical. I mean, I could have my innards on the outside, and she'd be busy reading a book while saying, "Pick up your own innards."

"Fine!" I charged ahead, hoping I would find the floating head suspended by a chain. Alas, the blow that hammered me to the floor was all too real. The head had arms, and the arms were made of stone.

"It's a golem," Megan shouted from behind me. "They're invulnerable."

My knowledge of tactics against golems was small. One of my ancestors had defeated a gaggle of golems by luring them into a big, molten-metal pit. But here, there were only the stairs in front of me and retreat behind me—no sign of a molten-metal pit.

Retreat not being an option, I prepared to test the golem's invulnerability with my flames.

I opened my mouth, but the golem moved faster than legends. The next blow knocked me several feet back up the steps.

"Is your tactic to tire it out?" Megan asked.

"I notice you are not helping," I replied.

In response, she sent a bolt into one of its glowing eyes, but the bolt snapped.

"Perhaps face-on attacks will get your face ripped off," she said.

"Yet another saying?" I asked, this time dodging a swing.

"No, an observation. Do you mind leading it farther up the stairs?"

That was not a hard request to fulfill since the thing was now rumbling after me, moving on massive stone feet. "Come on, be a good goddess and follow me," I told it.

The stone goddess lurched up the stairs. A moment later, a blur bounced up to its head—Megan. At once, the golem goddess reached toward its neck, where Megan had ensconced herself.

"Hey," I said, jumping up and down like a jester with talons. "I'm right here."

The movement attracted the golem's attention: it stepped toward me with surprising speed and swung down. I literally slipped as my foot broke part of the stairs, but that meant the blow went over my head. "Any time now, Megan!" I shouted, avoiding a second blow. "Do whatever you plan to do."

Megan let out a cry that I thought was pain, but then I saw she was proudly holding a large, glowing red ruby. The golem stood still halfway up the stairs; its hand pointed at me, the other reaching for her—frozen in that awkward back-scratching position.

"Cheating pays off!" Megan said. She jumped from the golem's neck, caught its stone arm, and swung herself to the ground. "I read about this gem trick on one of Carmen's tests." She pocketed the gem in her robes. "Maybe don't mention that to Carmen."

"Which? The cheating or the fact her knowledge saved us?"

"Either," she said. "She will lord it over us, and it is best to never be lorded over by her."

"You and I have so much more in common than I ever understood," I said.

At the bottom of the stairs was a long hallway that went in two directions. Through my contact with my eye, I sensed Carmen was to the left, so I led us that way. The odd light from the red glowing gems on the walls and ceiling hurt my eyes.

"Their sense of decorating is an offence to all living things," I said.

Megan let out a low chuckle, which made me glow a little inside. There were smart mortals out there who understood my humour!

Megan walked by my side, which I thought was brave of her. If I were a scaleless mortal, I would have followed so the dragon could soak up any crossbow bolts, spears, snake attacks or other horrid things the priestesses had dreamed up.

"We're getting closer," I said.

"How do you know?" she asked.

"I can smell her," I said. That was what we dragons call a baldsnout lie: the truth was, I continued to be in contact with my eye. Also, smoke was rushing out from under a large, bejewelled door at the end of the hallway—crimson jewels, of course. And crimson smoke. "She's in that room right there."

We stopped in front of the door. It was an impressive entryway: the jewels were worth at least half the treasury of one of the smaller realms. And this was not a small door, for I would fit easily through it. What gave me pause was that every jewel on the door was marked with runes and pulsing with magical light.

Again, though I feel I am repeating myself, it was a red light.

"This is a door of great magic," Megan said. "Those runes indicate it is designed to both cross worlds and to keep something from those worlds inside."

"I supposed you cheated on Carmen's magic rune exam to learn that."

"I wouldn't have passed several classes without her unwitting help. She didn't cover her answers with her hand like all the other assassins."

"Well," I said, "I've never let a rune ruin my day."

She didn't laugh. Which made me question my friendship with her.

"I'm not a fan of puns," she said simply. "I'm sure that one was clever."

"It was," I replied. And, with no further to-do, I swung open the door.

Halfway across an enormous room, hanging upside down and held there by a collection of snakes, was Carmen.

She had her sword in her hand and was swinging wildly. There was a blurriness to the scene that made it difficult to make sense of what she was fighting against.

The sight of Carmen in distress motivated me to throw caution to the four winds, and I launched myself into the room with a popping sound. No, I didn't make the popping sound. Instead, I had unknowingly gone through what I could only call a spirit membrane. There was a sensation of spiderwebs dragging across me and my vision went momentarily blurry, then cleared. Megan followed me, making her own popping sound.

We both blinked. The room was now far too clear. Carmen's foe was Enheduanna, and she had changed for the worse. Her head was the same, but her torso was now that of a giant snake.

"Oh, great," I said. "I hate snakes. Even more than bad poetry."

The final change for the worse took a moment to register, for it made no sense. Enheduanna's arms were two long, sharp mandibles that would have been at home on a giant ant. It was an odd and extremely unattractive mixture.

"My foe!" Enheduanna shouted. "To the deep dark darkness, you go." Which I thought was a bit overdramatic and, to be honest, grandstanding.

Then she swung those sharpened arms.

And cut Carmen in half.

CHAPTER 38

A HORRIBLE GAME CALLED MURDER

"Arrrrgh-Arrgh!" was all I could get out as the two pieces of Carmen separated. One stayed attached to the ceiling, snakes twirling around it, and the other dropped with a thud. There wasn't a spray of blood, but I assumed that was because my mind was not showing me any of the details. Disbelief froze me in place, and all I could do was continue to go: "Arrrrgh-Arrgh!"

"By Belaz, goddess of assassins," Megan whispered beside me. She wiped at her eyes as if she couldn't believe what she'd seen.

The room itself was yet another shade of crimson, but there was something off about it as if the light were a colour that eyes couldn't quite make sense of. Trying to focus made me feel a little seasick, which is not a common feeling for a dragon since we rarely spend time on boats.

Enheduanna glanced toward us, satisfaction stamped across her face, which was underlined by a very, very horrid smile. "To the darkness, the assassin falls, to the Cowled Goddess, the one who sees all. She is standing in her hall."

"Listen, priestess demon," I said. "Enjoy the last few seconds of your life. We will let your followers know that a horrid poem was the final thing you said before I turned your entrails into long, entrail-coloured ropes." As a taunt, it was too terrible and long, but there was nothing I could do about that now. I drew myself up with impressive speed, and the darkness and anger in my heart propelled me forward, my belly full of hate. I would have her in my talons in a heartbeat.

Or I would have had her, but she retreated without moving. No, the room had elongated, making the priestess slip farther away, and again came that seasick feeling. This distance wouldn't stop me from getting absolute and unending revenge.

To cross the space with even greater speed, I leaped into the air, glad the ceiling was tall. The curious thing is Megan was leaping, too, as if we were the same avenging creature. She loosed a bolt from her crossbow and let out a vengeance yell unlike any I'd ever heard.

I will give Enheduanna this: she stood her ground. Well, she had no legs, so that description doesn't quite work, but she stayed in place and watched us without even the slightest bit of fear, her odd mandible arms held up in triumph. Megan's bolt flew through the air, and it looked like she would be the first to get vengeance, which I was mildly chagrined about, but the bolt slowed as it travelled until it stopped right before Enheduanna, who pursed her lips and let out a puff of air.

The crossbow bolt vanished.

I will admit to being happy about that because it meant that revenge would fall to me as I fell on the priestess. I spread my forelegs, talons out, mouth open, flames working their way up from the furnace of my belly.

Brax! A voice said inside my head. I could not tell if it was Corwin or, and this was the very odd part since I'd recently witnessed her death, Carmen. While one side of my massive brainpan struggled with this conundrum, the other side continued on with the idea of the complete removal of this priestess from existence. Whatever was going on, it would be best if she were dead. And so, I continued my attack.

Just as I was about to strike Enheduanna, she was not there. It was very curious, for she was only an inch from my gleaming talons. And then she was several feet away, continuing to grin.

I only had a moment to turn my head before my whole body struck an unforgiving wall, bouncing off it onto the floor. Megan twisted so she hit it with her feet, twirled over through the air, and landed beside me.

"Did Carmen say something?" she asked. "I thought I heard her in my head."

"It was a trick." I rubbed at my shoulder and gathered myself for another attack, turning to face Enheduanna. "This priestess is full of them."

The angle brought the death scene back into my vision. The part of the room where Carmen had died was fuzzy. Perhaps my mind still couldn't comprehend her death.

Enheduanna chuckled. "The winged serpent is confused as his beastly mind breaks. Faced with the Cowled Goddess, he quakes."

Something wasn't right here, and I'm not referring to her horrid habit of speaking in couplets. I decided, wisely, since all my decisions are wise, to hold back on my vengeance. "Do you feel a little odd?" I asked Megan.

"Yes," she said. "Since the moment we passed through the door."

Enheduanna spoke clearly. "Into the eye of the Goddess Cowled. The Nameless One scowled and welcomed you fowled things into her world."

"Do you also find the priestess's utterings confusing?" I asked.

"Yes. And aggravating," Megan said. "I failed poetry class. She would, too."

"I don't think even the kindest tutor would classify her nonsense as poetry." I shook my head to clear my vision.

"Behold," Enheduanna said and raised those odd, sharpened arms. "She who was sacrificed and broken like bread opens her mouth and speaks, for the flesh is no longer dead."

And, as she said that, the bottom part of Carmen that rested on the floor rose into the air, again all fuzzy. It then connected with her top part, which was hanging from the ceiling.

A moment passed, and my sight cleared. Carmen hung there dead, but her body was back together. It was an image I'd only ever seen in my worst nightmares.

"This trick angers me," I said. "Priestess, I will tear you from—"

Carmen opened her eyes, blinked twice, and shook her head. She then flipped out of the hold the snakes had on her and landed on her feet. I drew in a breath, perhaps my first since I'd seen her death.

She was alive! Alive! And angry, clearly, for her brow had furrowed in that cute way it does when she has been vexed by a puzzle. She didn't even check with us to see if we were feeling good about her recovery.

"Carmen," Megan and I said at the same time. We kept doing that! Why did I bond with these humans?

"The price is paid for sacrifice," Enheduanna said to Carmen. "Now pay it I shall and thank you thrice."

More nonsensical poetry! I might as well have been in one of those dragon pubs where overly artistic dragons created poetry on the fly . . . before fighting. A blanket would muffle her. Or a blast of flames.

But Carmen's brow had furrowed even more furrowy, and, without thanking us for trying to revenge her death, she pulled out her sword and rushed at great speed toward Enheduanna. I reached out to stop her, feeling she had gone mad, but she twisted out of my grip and leaped into the air, letting out a scream of absolute and somewhat terrifying anger.

Enheduanna didn't flinch. And that stupid sarcastic smarmy smile on the priestesses's face didn't flinch either.

The smile remained as the priestess's head flew through the air, and her odd snake body collapsed to the floor. Again, there was no blood, and she had become blurry.

I would have felt satisfied, except Enheduanna didn't look surprised. Instead, she let out a last chuckle before her eyes closed.

And as if all that coming back to life and beheading hadn't happened, Carmen turned toward us and said, "You almost wrecked everything!"

"First off," I said, "I don't like your tone. And second, how is it that you are still alive? And third, what in the seven Hades of the burning land of winged gods is happening?"

She let out a sigh like she was preparing to explain to a child why the sky was blue. "This is the Endless Room of Ritual Sacrifice," she said as if saying that somehow explained everything. "Enheduanna and I made a trust vow to each other in our souls and sacrificed each other to the Cowled Goddess. You remember, Megan, we took a class on the theology of the power of ritual sacrifice, right?"

"Yes, yes, I remember," Megan said in a tone that showed she clearly didn't. "Did you not learn about that at dragon, uh, academy, Brax?"

"I didn't take any classes on Cowled Goddesses," I said. "Mortal gods and goddesses are below dragon study. They are too weak."

At that moment, Enheduanna's head floated into the air, and her body rose toward it. Her head was laughing as it floated. Then it landed on her neck, and she stared directly at me pompously. "It is beyond your animal dragon mind," she said. "But this is the room we go to the goddess and find."

"My dragon mind is perfect," I said. "It's yours that is stuck on couplets."

"Technically, they aren't couplets," Carmen explained. "Because she doesn't use the same metre or rhyming structure. It's more free-form."

"Please don't torture us with poetry lessons." The words were in my head, but Megan had spoken them.

"Anyway." Carmen waved a hand to show she was finished with her lecture. "This is a ritual sacrifice. She convinced me to allow her to slay me here."

"I'm very curious how that conversation went," I said. "But please continue on and speak in a demeaning manner, as if I understand nothing."

"Yes, speak slowly," Megan said. "For Brax's sake."

"Three horned priestesses brought me down to this sacrificial room," Carmen said. "Enheduanna and I reached an agreement about sacrificing each other. And we have been slaying each other ever since. The spectral mist that you walked through as you entered means you were walking into another realm."

"We are no longer in the temple?" Megan asked.

"You are correct," Enheduanna answered. "For this is the room that is between realms when they intersect."

"When one of us gives up her life to the other in this room," Carmen explained, "it allows us to travel to the realm of the Cowled Goddess and become one with her."

"Well, I think even if you spoke slowly, that wouldn't make sense to me," I said. "But I have a more important question: who killed whom first?"

"She killed me," Enheduanna said. "She needed to have her own eyes see."

"You die in a not-real way, though it looks very, very real," I said. "You go to the Cowled Goddess's realm . . .why? If I wanted to take a trip somewhere else, I'd fly."

"We were looking for something," Carmen said.

"And what is that something?" Megan said. "Stop being so mysterious."

"That's not on purpose," she said. "I don't feel quite real yet."

I jabbed her with a talon.

"Ow!" Carmen squeaked.

"Now you feel real, I bet," I said.

"Yes, yes. I'm real now. Each time I die, I walk closer to the source of the attacks on Corwin and the emperor. In fact, this time, I saw Corwin. He is waiting at the entrance to another nether realm to guide us further."

"If he's there, why did he tell me to help you?" I asked.

"What were his words exact?" Enheduanna asked. "Please tell us, don't retract."

"He told me Carmen would need my help."

"So, you will have to help me in the future," Carmen said. "He sees something ahead that we don't see."

"I always have to help you, so it's not much of a prediction," I said. People who have arcane knowledge are endlessly pretending they know what this world is about. "I'm curious why you didn't mention that you're also tracing the attack on you and me in the library."

"Oh, that was me," Enheduanna said, her voice prideful. "I sent my own Gutian toad, you see."

"Yes," Carmen continued, likely because she saw the anger on my face. "Since the attack on the emperor happened at the same time we arrived, Enheduanna assumed we had somehow brought the goddess here."

"I should have known you did not have enough power to wave," the priestess said, "and send the emperor to his grave." There wasn't even the slightest hint of an apology in her tone. I filed that in the *Take Revenge When They Least Expect It* section of my mind.

"So, all of this ritual killing set off the Astral Warning Bell at the palace," I said.

"Oh, good," Enheduanna asked. "He is as safe there as in a cowled hood."

Megan gestured around. "I know my knowledge of such astral matters is limited. But what happened in this room shouldn't be strong enough to ring that bell, right?"

Enheduanna looked around the room as if there were an

answer in the hanging snakes and odd crimson light. "My power is a taller tower than I believed."

"A tower of madness?" I said. "I assume it set off that bell and so the emperor is safe. What now, do you keep killing each other?"

"Yes," Carmen and Enheduanna said at the same time.

And they began doing exactly that.

CHAPTER 39

TINY THINGS FULL OF TERROR

I did not think I could get bored with seeing Enheduanna die, but as the next few minutes turned into hours, a brainpan-numbing apathy crawled into my skull. I turned away when it was Carmen's turn to sacrifice herself. Even though this was a ritual, and she wasn't really dying, these were not memories I wanted.

Megan didn't take her gaze from the show. "So," she said. "Each time they die, they go a little further into this Cowled spirit world—and yes, I don't know the terms because I didn't spend time in class learning about it: my job was to send mortals to the spirit world. Each death gets them closer to discovering the name of the Nameless Goddess. Do I have that right?"

"Yes," I said. "Except you should have mentioned that the Nameless Goddess also has hairy legs." I am not obsessed with that observation; I only wanted to include every fact. "They are getting closer to the place from which she launches her attacks. And each death means they learn more about her. Corwin, who has been on the edge of death for some time, is guiding them." I thought about his body being guarded right now by Black Tooth. I so hoped she'd dressed him in a jester's outfit.

"Why can't Corwin stay dead?" Megan asked.

"You and I think alike in so many ways." I yawned as Enheduanna's head flew through the air again. "He's the crow who keeps coming back no matter how many times you shoo it away. Very aggravating."

"You didn't have to go to school with him. But I am curious about one other thing: can any of us die an actual death in this room?"

I considered this for several moments. She was being an assassin, setting up her tactics in case something untoward happened. "I'm uncertain," I said. "They have sworn an oath to each other. If you don't swear the oath, maybe you can really die."

"I'll tuck that in my mental quiver," she said.

"Hey, I like that saying," I said. "I may use it in—"

BRAX! Carmen shouted inside my head, loud enough to make me shudder.

"Are you all right?" Megan asked. "You went a little pale. Can I get you—"

I held up a talon. For the first time, I noticed that Enheduanna and Carmen had struck death blows at the same time, so neither was in this room.

Yes, Carmen, I sent. *I wish you'd knock gently first before shouting in my head. How may this humble dragon help you?*

Look through my dragon eye, she said.

We've been through this before; it's my eye.

Will you stop complaining, my friend, and look? Look!

I did not want to look at whatever she was seeing. I had

a terrible relationship with the netherworld. It always bit me in the tail.

Now! she said.

Hold your horses, I am coming, I sent. Then I closed my eyes and searched around in the darkness for my other eye. There was first a drifting, shadowy feeling that went from my own mental eye through my body—as if I wasn't only looking, but a part of me, my soul, if I believed in such things, was flying with speed to where Carmen stood. The cold was unnatural. The netherworld is an ancient place, and ancient things happened there. It was where all childhood terrors hid.

I was seeing what Carmen was seeing.

Enheduanna was a glowing form beside me. In the spirit world, she looked bright and had two legs, and the rest of her spirit body had a mortal shape. She pointed ahead. Over to my right—Carmen's right, really—was another glowing mortal, but much dimmer: Corwin. He was so insubstantial that a little cosmic breeze might blow him away.

Welcome, Brax, he sent. His voice was flat, but I still found it irritating to have in my head. Only my voice belonged there. And Carmen's. *We are stronger with your presence.*

You speak the truth, I sent. *Now, why was I brought to this little piece of desolation?*

Carmen will explain, he sent. *It is best if we all concentrate on not being annihilated.*

Annihilated? I sent.

Enheduanna moved out of my vision, and a sense of fear and revulsion swept over me. She had purposely been blocking my sightline.

The goddess is here, Carmen said. It sounded like Carmen was all around me, which, in a way, she was.

Mists cloaked the thing in front of us. A hissing grew in my head. But my eyes couldn't quite focus on the large black shape. It looked like it might be a stone.

Carmen waved her arm, and that made the mists clear. Corwin took a step back as if he might flee. Even Enheduanna retreated farther. It was Carmen, being brave or stupid, who was getting closer and closer to the thing. It was now so dark only the dim outlines of our companions were visible.

What am I looking at? I sent.

My head throbbed with pain. But we took another step, and then Carmen froze and looked down at something else in the mist. There was a long, powerful snout there. And dark red eyes, but thankfully, the creature was frozen. Here was an intelligent, powerful version of an ammit. A thousand times more deadly. *Corwin, using an ancient spell from Boqin to freeze time,* Carmen explains. *But the spell is already fraying.*

Then let us hurry, I sent. *I don't trust spells stolen from a dead wizard.*

If we awaken the guardians, she added, *they will tear us to pieces.* For there were other odd netherworld creatures with snouts, scales, and long teeth slumbering at our feet. Their eyes also burned red as the sun.

Then walk carefully!

She did, going around the spirit ammit and another mongrel creature. Their malevolence leaked into the mist itself.

We will only be able to glance at the thing, she said. *Long enough to retain the sight but not so long as to turn us to ashes.*

Turn us to ashes? What— She had to move as a snake spirit slithered over her feet. *I thought things were frozen here,* I added.

That serpent guardian lives out of time, she replied. The snake carried on as if we were not worth bothering about. But the place I was looking at, which was in my head, was getting closer and closer, and I wondered if outside my body, back in the real world—well, if that room I was in was even real—was freezing.

We are looking for the goddess's name, she explained.

Each step she took brought a fresh fear I had never felt before. Was it because I was looking through her spirit body that I was feeling a mortal's fear? I didn't think that dragons could feel such fear. But every tiny part of me, every thought, everything was screaming out to flee. That this was forbidden. This was wrong. This was doom.

Ah, she sent. As if she had discovered a new flower or a missing sock. *There it is.* For the fog of darkness had shifted, and we were looking down at what I could only guess was a sacrificial stone, hidden far back in the netherworld, stained by blood. The stone itself bespoke of a truly terrible history. It was the same shape and size as the one in the Empire Garden at the palace. The snake circling a sun was carved on the side.

On it, hands curled tight, hairless and frightening, was the worst thing I had ever seen.

It was a mortal baby.

CHAPTER 40

TO BE CLEAR, THIS WAS NOT A CUTE BABY

When I say mortal baby, I do not mean that it was all pink and nauseatingly cute and gurgling. No, this feminine child-thing had the tiniest silver-black scales all over its body and was curled up asleep with one clawed thumb in its mouth. The shading of its skin was as if an artist had mixed darkness, foreboding, and horror into a colour. Every broken thing in existence lurked inside that child, waiting to be loosed upon the world.

Mortal infants are ugly, I sent. *But this is beyond ugly.*

Carmen didn't reply, couldn't reply, because she was standing as still as a statue surrounded by ice. My deepest, darkest guts were telling me we did not want that infant to wake up. She would be the death of us, the death of those I loved, maybe all the worlds at once. And when I said ugly, in my natural sarcasm, I was not being entirely truthful, for it was also completely beautiful and perfect. As beautiful as a sharpened talon, a newly forged sword, or a well-planned murder. It was that kind of dangerous beauty slumbering right below our noses.

That child is the physical embodiment of the Nameless Goddess's name, Carmen sent. She sounded as if she were a continent away, which was odd since I was inside her head, looking at the baby. *This corner of the nether world is where she hides her secret self. Her title. If we have her name, then we will know what and who she is. We can battle her.*

All I see is this infant, I sent. *Even now, she hides her name from us. I don't think this brat will tell it to us.*

The name is written on the child's forehead. Carmen's voice had shifted even farther away. *We need the child to open her eyes and look directly at one of us. Then we will know her name.*

Oh, wonderful, I replied. *In order for that to happen, she will have to wake up and turn our way, right? And everything else in this room of horrors will come to life.*

Yes, Carmen sent. *She seems powerful now, but this is the Nameless Goddess slumbering. Awake, she will be too bright and too dark to look at.*

Leaving the oddness of that sentence aside, I sent, *which one of us will read this name?* But the answer to this question was already clear in my mind.

It's why I asked you here, my friend, Carmen sent.

This is the help Corwin told me I would give, I replied.

Yes. Only you, looking through my eye, safe in the Room of Eternal Sacrifice, will be strong enough to read and retain her name. You are a dragon, and you have an inner strength and ancient power that we mortals lack.

You're only saying nice things to me to get me to do this horrible task.

She chuckled inside my head. *Partially, but it is also true. Dragons have a closer connection to the original stuff that the worlds are made of.*

We are great stuff, I agreed.

But she continued, *If you can hold the child's gaze, read the name, and it will become a part of you. Enheduanna and Corwin and I will be here to protect you, spirits for you to lean on. And maybe, just maybe, we will all survive the sight.*

Those two maybes are doing a lot of work in that sentence.

It is all I can offer you, she sent. *You don't have to do this.*

As if I'd abandon her here. *Dragons never retreat!* I replied. *But are you certain about how all this baby-waking and name-reading works? I mean, did you learn this in a class?*

Enheduanna explained it to me.

Oh, great, I sent. *And did she ask you to ask me to come here?*

No, inviting you was my idea.

Good thinking on your part. And you trust her?

Yes, she sent. *I killed her. And she killed me. So, I trust her.*

Well, I haven't killed her, I sent back. *Yet.*

But you trust me. So, I ask you to look, Brax. Then, we will have the sacred knowledge of the Nameless Goddess's name and be able to act. We might even save an emperor.

I usually kill them, I sent. Every part of my being, of who I was, said *no. Don't look!* That warning voice screamed inside my head like a banshee. Gazing upon that infant's name meant I would be forever scarred.

I did not know what would happen when the infant looked at me with all its waking might. But I thought of the other people in this room—well, of Carmen, that is. And Megan, behind me (and yet right beside me at the same time). Briefly of Corwin. And finally, of Nagar. He was a book reader. The world needed more of those. Especially if they were emperors.

Plus, this Nameless Goddess had scratched my snout on our first meeting. I did not forgive easily.

Fine, I sent. *But you'll owe me one.*

I owe you many. Her voice was a whisper in my head. *Now prepare, for it will all unfold rather quickly once I do this.*

Do what? I asked.

Without answering, she reached out and tapped the infant's shoulder. I held my breath, both back in the sacrifice room and in this horrid netherworld. I fully expected Carmen to turn to ashes the moment she touched that girl's flesh. But she pulled her spirit hand back and stood incredibly still. There was one movement I noticed: Enheduanna came a little closer as if drawn by the danger before us. And then Corwin, off to the side, also edged slowly in as if he was very, very afraid but still had to look. Even in the spirit world, his one wizard eye glowed. He had someone else inside him, too—what an odd crew we were. Each of them put a hand on Carmen's shoulders, and a connection grew between us. I was made stronger.

And what seemed a decade later, the infant slowly moved those scaly arms and turned its perfectly evil head toward us, eyes closed.

Its forehead was blank. *There's no name!* I sent. *This is a trap.*

Patience, Carmen replied.

Then the child, who was a symbol of the most basic form of the goddess here in this hidden place, raised its eyelids, revealing eyes that could have been carved from obsidian. In the centre of them burned two pinpricks of flame from the deepest bowels of destruction.

The infant stared right at Carmen's dragon eye, which meant she was staring at me, perhaps attracted by its glowing. I felt like I might turn to ashes, but at the same moment, a word blazed across the child's forehead. It was in letters so old I couldn't recognize them, but they burned themselves into my eye, my soul, into who I was.

The Nameless One's name. Written right there. The very source of the goddess. It was the type of power that could pull down mountains, make lava burst from the skin of the earth, and drain oceans, leaving all the fishies dead.

The letters became a name in my head. I didn't dare think about it. Or say it.

Then the infant's eyes flashed red.

Flee! Corwin sent to us. *Flee with great speed, my companions.*

The infant opened her mouth and screamed. It was the wailing of all infants ever in all the worlds, wailing as if a great toy had been stolen from them. The scream hit Corwin like a fist and his spirit tumbled, seemed to come partly apart, then flew with speed. *Flee!* he sent one last time before disappearing altogether.

He didn't have to tell me twice.

I was still shaking and still inside Carmen's head. She retreated, her eyes on the baby infant as she ran backwards. She dodged the snakes and the gory ammits that were coming out of shadows and biting, hissing, and spitting acid at us.

Enheduanna, though, did not run. She was frozen in place, staring at the child.

Enheduanna! Carmen sent her voice throughout the room. *Enheduanna, come!* That infant now was turning its eyes toward the priestess, and it was clear the child's destructive force would crush her in a heartbeat.

Run, you foolish, stupid priestess, I sent, and something about being in this other realm meant my thought reached her, for Enheduanna jerked upright and began running desperately backward.

When we had some distance, we, including Enheduanna, were yanked out of this horrid part of the netherworld.

I was quite shockingly and suddenly made of flesh and in my body.

And I was blind.

CHAPTER 41
THE POWER OF NAMES

The darkness meant I might not be in the place I'd left. But I was in my body because my heart was beating. There was air coming into my nostrils. And the smell, the smell of that room, was familiar.

It was the room of Endless . . .

Of Endless . . .

Ah! Names had left me. Had been scattered by one name inside my head. I tried to think of my name, but it was gone. Only a few moments ago, I'd known it. But now I didn't even know what I was anymore.

I had a certainty that I was something powerful and interesting. But what was it? A star in the sky? A mountain? No, it was an amazing creature of flesh. I squeezed a paw, and something sharp poked into my palm.

"Ow," I said.

A talon had poked me. I had talons. Even though all was darkness, I now knew that fact. An image of worlds coming apart entered my mind, of stars in the sky winking out. Of names being forgotten.

Something great and unimaginable had been seen by me. What was it?

Something so powerful and unforgiving that the sight of it had destroyed who I was.

I tried to move my legs and the rest of my body.

"Watch your tail!" a voice said.

I had a tail? *What is a tail?* Something behind me that was attached to me swung around and hit a solid shape.

"Ouch!" the voice said again, but I was too amazed by the part of me that swerved and curled behind me to pay much attention. "I said watch your tail!"

Yes, there was an extension out behind me. It was called a tail. How wondrous! I swung it a third time.

"Hey! Hey!" That voice was a woman's voice. Was woman a name? All the names of things were coming unglued. Concepts and understanding of how things work were disassembling like shredded wefts in a basket.

Then I tried to take a step, and apparently, all that amazing corporeal substance that made me up was too much for my spirit because I fell over. "Brahhhhhhz," the woman said. "Brahhhhhz."

She was yelling a name, the name of someone, but I was not that name.

I had read another name that obliterated all the names I knew, all the names of all the things in existence. A name of power and destruction that was eating away at me.

I blinked and light came into my eyes; they had been squeezed shut as if I were looking at the sun, but now all I saw was a dimly lit room.

A young woman was holding a crossbow and staring at me with wide eyes. I remembered her name. "Megan!" I said. "You, Megan."

"Did your brainpan melt?" she asked. "You look confused."

"Am I a you?" I asked. "You said I am a you."

"You *are* confused." She snapped her fingers near the holes in my head. Ears! They were ears! And I heard the snaps. "Snap out of it, Brax."

An important vital part of me recognized that sound. That name. For that title had been given to me, in dragon tradition, by my mother. I had been named after my great-granduncle, Brax the Destroyer. That name that had been called and cursed so many times in my lifetime.

I managed to stand up and announce: "Me, Brax. I am Brax. Brax I am. Me Brax, Brax, Braxi, Braxorus, Braxer, Braxiekins, Brax." I put a paw to my chest. "I, Brax."

There was a soft thud several feet away, and Megan turned toward the sound. "Great, you know who you are. Now tell me, what happened to Carmen?"

We both looked for this person called Carmen, who had recently fallen to the floor. She let out a soft sound that could be a final breath. Megan got to her first, for I had to remind myself that I had paws and a tail and that movement was possible. I dragged myself over to them.

"Carmen, wake up," Megan said. The young woman did not respond other than taking a guttural inhalation of air. "Carmen, it's time for our potions exam," Megan said. "The maestrus are waiting."

"Good thinking," I said. At first, there wasn't a response, then something horrible happened: Carmen opened her eyes. They were obsidian black with little red pinpricks.

"Dear winged gods!" I shouted. "The infant has infected her!"

"What infant?" Megan asked. "What are you talking

about? Do I have to slap you to snap you out of whatever is going on?"

"You're Carmen," I shouted, grabbing the front of Carmen's cloak and perhaps getting a bit of royal dragon spittle on her face. "You Carmen! You Carmen!"

Carmen blinked and whispered, "Carmen?"

Those ungodly eyes looked back at me. I could barely bear to look at them. "Yes," I said. "Carmen Dore, sister of Corwin. Assassin and professional whiner."

Carmen put a hand to her head. "Where, who?"

"Say your name," I said. "Mine brought me back."

"My . . . name?" She looked around as if for something she lost. "What was it again?"

"It's Carmen. Say 'I, Carmen,' it will help," I said. "Trust me. All you have to do is say it. Say it!" I resisted the temptation to shake her again. Mortals are so easy to break.

"I, Carmen," she whispered, closing her eyes. When she opened them a heartbeat later, I was glad to see they were the same blue and grey as before. It was her.

"I may have been imagining those obsidian eyes," I said. "I really hope I was."

"No." Megan's face had gone pale as snow. "She had something else in her eyes, maybe even looking through them. But let's hope we never see that again."

Carmen shook her head. "We survived. I didn't think we would."

"Yes, we survived." Enheduanna stood a few feet away, holding her head. I should point out that it was still on her shoulders. Her body had changed back into a typical priestess body: two legs, two hands, two normal, angry eyes. "I, Enheduanna, say we thrived." Enheduanna rubbed her eyes.

"I see your annoying habit of rhyming survived, too," I said.

She ignored my jibe. "You carry the name in your head —it is malleable when it can be read."

"Half the time, I don't know what you're saying," I said. "The other half, I don't care."

She grabbed my foreleg. "A name can change the named; a name can change the game."

"I am not the kind to get foreboding sensations," Megan said, "but for some reason, I sense a horrible danger. Usually, if I stab things, I feel better."

"The Endless Room of Ritual Sacrifice is a waystation," Enheduanna said, gesturing around. "And our doom, it may hasten."

"Are you suggesting we are not safe in this room?" I asked.

"As I mentioned before, this room is not truly part of the temple," Enheduanna said. "It's between worlds, which should make you tremble."

"Then why are we standing around in here swapping names and listening to bad poetry?" Megan said, taking the words right out of my mouth. "Let's leave with speed."

"Let us go then and not stay," Enheduanna said. "We should leave this room and pray."

"I never want to hear another of your poems," I said, perhaps with more vehemence than I intended. These snappy, snarky words were keeping me together, reminding me who I was. Because I was Brax.

That other horrid name was digging around my brain-pan, wanting to blot me out.

"Depart the Room of Eternal Sacrifice and back into the world we start." The priestess took a step, stumbled, and caught herself from planting her face on the floor. "Oh, my thoughts are in the dregs; I seem to have almost forgotten how to use my legs."

"Well, not your mouth," I said. "Which is good," I added after she gave me a withering glare. "Otherwise, how would we receive your poetic wisdom?"

"Brax," Carmen said. "Could you help me? My legs don't seem to work properly."

"Well, if you hadn't let her kill you so many times," I said, for those memories were coming back to me, "you might not have this problem." I grabbed her by the shoulder and dragged her in a stumbling gait forward. "I could eat about a hundred and one goats right now."

Megan took Carmen's other shoulder. Truth be told, I'm not sure I was strong enough to hold her up. Together, we took a step toward the door. And another. But with each step, I was getting a little heavier. Weaker.

The name I'd seen emblazoned on the infant's forehead burned like lava in my mind, looming over every thought. It was growing brighter.

And with sudden intuition, I knew what that meant. "The name," I whispered. "The owner of the name is getting near."

"What do you mean?" Carmen asked.

I didn't need to answer because purple smoke began rising between us and the door to the inner temple.

"Oh, dear," I said. "I, Brax, have a particularly horrible feeling right now."

To accent that feeling, something horrible rose out of that smoke.

The Nameless Goddess herself.

Hairy legs and all.

CHAPTER 42

THE PROBLEM WITH GODDESSES

When I had seen her earlier in the desert lands, the Nameless Goddess had been made of ashes, and so I felt as if I could literally puff her away. But now, emerging from the purple smoke, the Nameless Goddess was solid flesh and bone and jarringly real. I do not want to dwell on her legs and their hairiness, but they were impressive golden hairs like that of the jaguar—except thicker and longer. Her skirt was bright green and layered with copper metal scales that went to her shoulders—a vest of armour—an armour that no mortal blade, dragon talon, or bolt would ever pierce. And she had powerful hairy arms that could, well, lift mountains, I assume.

And there were only two arms, which was important to note because who knows with these goddesses how many arms they might have? Both were orange and powerful, with claws at the end of the seven fingers on each hand. My gaze was drawn to her face: a long, fierce snout. It was very unattractive—and this is coming from someone who has a snout (though mine is angular and perfect). You would think a goddess could work on improving her looks, but clearly that ugliness was a part of her entire presentation to the world.

And behind that snout rested dark, yet burning, eyes: black as black, with flickers of flame in the middle. They beamed out the most important aspect of her that was now filling the room: anger. Oh, so very much immortal anger. She was thinking about turning us all into shredded meat.

Another difference from the ash version of this goddess was how horribly full of colour she was. One leg was a bright red that glowed, and her other leg was a bright purple. Her scales were a green that went all over her torso.

She pointed a clawed finger at me. "You have seen my name, and my name has seen you, and so your insides must come out."

I mentally grasped for something sarcastic and brave to reply in order to show that this dragon was not frightened of a desert goddess. But there was nothing in my mind other than more fear.

No, that wasn't quite true because her name was turning like a poisonous worm in my mind. It wanted out. It wanted me to shout that name aloud. It wanted to join her again, so I clamped my teeth together. I could hardly get a breath out.

An overpowering need to fall to my knees before her absolute power came over me. I wanted to beg for forgiveness. Beg for my very existence. Or beg to be obliterated. Even Megan and Carmen struggled to stop themselves from falling down before her. Carmen placed the tip of her sword on the floor, leaning on it.

But Enheduanna, in a surprising move, stepped in front of us, her robes rustling. It was a very brave thing to do—I could not have taken that step.

"Hear, hear," Enheduanna said without even the slightest waver in her voice. "Iktara doesn't fear, fear you." At these words, the Nameless Goddess drew back her finger. There might even have been a brief flicker of consternation in her eyes. "Iktara hears your voice, the message you send, and she whispers her life-giving powers and secrets to defend." Enheduanna grew a little taller. Perhaps it was because she was standing with her back mostly straight. Her poetry, now that it was turned against the goddess, sounded like music to my ears. Good music. Well, mostly good. "No lie. The Cowled Goddess doesn't wither. She doesn't die."

"Iktara died a long time ago," the Nameless Goddess said. And this time, her voice shook the very room. "I choked her to death. Not a ritual death, a real one. You worship nothing but dust now. Begone, insect!"

"Not truth," Enheduanna said, though her voice was weaker. "Not real. The Cowled Goddess lives in every worshipping heart. Inside me, the truth is sealed."

"She is unsealed and broken!" The snout-faced goddess appeared to be enjoying these words. "I will make you choke on your beliefs and your own entrails." Again, I was impressed by her threats. They pummelled Enheduanna, and she shrank.

"The—the—the . . ."

Someone began to say someone. Then I realized it was me speaking because Enheduanna needed my support. Once I recognized my voice, I continued. "The winged gods of the dragons, the gods of fire and vengeance, don't fear you either," I said, though my voice came out as a whisper. "They don't."

"Neither does Belaz, goddess of assassins," Carmen spat out. *Good girl!* I sent.

"Yeah," Megan added, which wasn't as impressive, but speaking in the presence of this goddess was a feat in itself.

"Winged gods! Assassin gods!" The Nameless Goddess looked at me, and it was as horrid as seeing the infant's gaze. Well, it *was* the infant's gaze, all grown up. Her name inside my head turned over again, threatening to blot all my thoughts at once. "You speak names of weak entities that passed long into the eons of time. Their names are all broken, their wings cut from their serpent bodies, their cowls ripped, their hoods torn asunder. I am the survivor. I am the one whose name could never be discovered. And you will die with my name in your head."

Well, this discussion is all fine and well, I sent to Carmen. *But we must get past her.*

She is a goddess, she sent, and there was some finality in her words. *And thus impassable. She —*

"She hears you speak to each other in your tiny minds," the goddess said. "You are right; you will not pass, and I will be birthed upon the world. Then I will eat your minds."

"That sounds horrible and messy," I said and was proud to get out a somewhat snappy reply. I was still me. I still had it.

Her eyes hadn't stopped glaring. I smiled, finding a new strength in my snarkiness.

"And furthermore," I began, working up to an epic insult that my ancestors would be proud of. "You are a —"

The Nameless Goddess snapped her fingers, and a thick bone in my foreleg broke, making me collapse. Great-winged gods! It had taken nothing for her to do that. She was toying with us.

"Your barking annoys me," she said. "I will eat you like a roasted insect in the sun." I wanted to say something about how that wasn't up to her usual quality of insult, but I was in too much pain to reply. The good thing about having four legs was that I could stand on three of them, and I slowly and carefully brought myself to my feet. After all, I should be some sort of example for Carmen and Megan. And that priestess.

"Fie! Fie! About the death of the Cowled Goddess, you lie!" Enheduanna was awaking from a daze. "And I, I can prove she didn't die, die."

"Oh, this should be interesting," Ol' Snout face replied. "Explain to me how my sister isn't dead when I watched the light go out of her eyes for the rest of time. Show me, mortal. Prove it."

"In all believers is the power of the cowled mask," Enheduanna said. "All you have to do is ask."

Even though it was like walking through burning tar, the priestess took another step toward the goddess. I fully expected a snapping of fingers resulting in Enheduanna's head likewise snapping off, but perhaps the goddess was slightly entertained, for she allowed the priestess to take three steps. Then Enheduanna glanced over her shoulder at us. "These are not my friends; they should flee before they meet their ends."

"Hey!" I shouted. "We're on your side. No sense abandoning us when we are facing someone this powerful and ugly."

Enheduanna winked at me. It was flattering and a little odd that she would use her energy to entertain me with a wink. Then I understood what she was signalling.

The priestess wrapped a heretofore hidden cowl around her face and pulled her hood up as if preparing for a storm. With her next steps, she grew. From one head taller to two heads, then five, then ten, so that she soon dominated the room with her size and was looking down on the Nameless Goddess.

It was a trick, I was certain. But it still gave me chills.

"Cowled Goddess, I let you into my spirit blessed," Enheduanna's voice no longer sounded mortal at all. It echoed with power. "I grant Iktara my heart, my blood, my nest of flesh."

I stepped back a half-step, for there was something powerful emanating from the priestess. She had become something else. "Sister Nameless," Enheduanna, or whatever was inside her, said. "So good to hear your voice again. Let me finally rip you from the heavens and cast your broken body on the bones of the worlds." It was the most beautiful taunt to hear. And it didn't rhyme.

The Nameless Goddess narrowed her eyes. Though her snouty face was mostly unreadable, I thought perhaps it contained a look of fear.

"Enheduanna is taking on the aspect of the Cowled Goddess," Carmen said. "She is letting her goddess into herself."

"Oh, great," I said. "Another one of your assassin lectures coming to life. I should point out she winked at me. Which means she intends us to take advantage of this distraction."

"And well we should," Megan said. "Right now."

Enheduanna reached back into the misty darkness, and suddenly, there was a giant venom-slavering snake in each hand. She whipped them toward our enemy, their mouths open.

The Nameless Goddess stood unconcerned as if even a flea would have been less frightening. The first snake missed, but the second one bit into the goddess's cheek, and black blood ran down.

"What is this?" the Nameless Goddess shouted, her hand on the wound. "You punctured my flesh!"

"I, Iktara, the Cowled Goddess, never dies," Enheduanna shouted. "I live within my worshippers. Within their strength. I am born again in every chant and sacrifice."

The Nameless Goddess swung her claws toward her sister, and somehow, whatever was possessing Enheduanna caught the goddess's arm, stopping the blow. It was as if she had halted a flying mountain, but this newly enlarged Enheduanna hadn't even staggered. She pushed, and the Nameless Goddess was knocked back several steps. This was quickly followed by the whipping out of another snake that bit her sister's other cheek, giving her matching wounds. This was an epic battle any dragon would pay to see.

"We need to flee now," Carmen said, for a space had been opened, and we had a straight line to the only door into the real world.

"I've told you a thousand times." I pushed Megan and Carmen forward. "Don't use the word flee. I gallantly charge away." My plan worked until I accidentally used my broken leg and fell, nearly rolling over my two mortal friends, which would have been messy. I struggled back up, and the tail of the Nameless Goddess struck out and smashed me down.

Seeing this, Enheduanna gave her another mighty swipe of a snake, and it was a horrible and wonderful sound to hear the goddess scream in anger.

With heroic concentration and Carmen's help, I found my feet. And this time, I swept my companions up, using my wings as extra limbs to push us toward the door. All three working legs made the leap for me, getting us a few feet into the air. We were going to hit the barrier at full speed, and I hoped the door wasn't barred on the other side. I aimed my forehead at the portal.

I struck the spirit webbing first, tearing through it, my eyes clearing a little before we smashed into the door. It flew open, and we landed in the hallway.

I managed not to squish either of my friends with my marvellous muscled body and turned to look back.

The room was a miasma of fighting, of blasts going off hither and yon. Viewing it through the spirit web gave it a distant, grainy look. But the two goddesses traded glorious blows back and forth that shook the very bowels of the temple.

A movement to my left made me look away from the glory of their battle. A line of priestesses stood there, still as statues, their faces cowled and their eyes closed.

"They're praying," Carmen said. "Each of them has a part of the goddess inside her and is sending it to Enheduanna."

It was very creepy to see, but I was a full believer in this religion now. "Pray hard!" I said. "Pray as if our lives depend on it—which they do."

They didn't respond. So, I turned back to the battle. The praying was working, for Enheduanna looked even larger. She had lifted the Nameless Goddess in both arms while her snakes bit each shoulder of her enemy.

"To the bones you go," she shouted. It was a victory cry, and I briefly wondered if this battle was done. In my heart, I would be quite happy to have Enheduanna crow about defeating that evil goddess on her own.

"Yes!" I said.

I was even more excited to see the Nameless Goddess throw back her head as if her spine were breaking.

Victory for our side was here. I could smell it.

To add to that winning feeling was the horrid sound of pain that the Nameless Goddess made. It penetrated the veil, echoing like a song in my ears. It was glorious to hear.

Then, the noise shifted. It was still muffled but clear enough to make sense of: the Nameless Goddess was laughing. For when she twisted her head forward again, she opened her mouth, and though it was a very ungoddess-like thing to do, she spat.

Her children, the ammits had a spit that stank so much it made one delusional. But she being their mother, and a goddess, her spit was different.

It was acid.

Enheduanna screamed, dropping the goddess and putting her hands to her face. Her snakes fell to the floor and slithered off.

"Goodbye again, sister," the Nameless Goddess said.

And before Enheduanna could react, the goddess swung her arm.

The screaming ended. It was clear that Enheduanna was dead. Mostly because her head was no longer a part of her body. She shrank down to a normal mortal size.

All the worshippers beside us fell unconscious to the floor.

The Nameless Goddess dropped the shrinking body and pointed in our direction. Then, with goddess-like speed, she ran toward us across that long room.

"Slam the door!" Megan shouted. She charged at the

doors as the goddesses, arms out, claws at the ready, reached through the spider webs.

And grabbed onto my shoulder.

The name in my head leaped and bounced like it would knock a hole in my head.

"Yes, close the door," I shouted, grabbing at the floor with my good legs and talons to stop from being dragged back into that room. The goddess's claws tore into my shoulder.

Megan and Carmen pushed at the door.

I don't understand all the rules of the netherworld, but the Nameless Goddess was not as powerful outside that room. Our world did not yet allow her presence.

Once I realized that, the name in my head stopped banging at me long enough for me to bite down on her arm. A distant yell of pain sounded, and she pulled back the arm.

And Carmen and Megan, good mortals that they were, slammed the door in her holy face.

CHAPTER 43

OUT OF THE FRYING PAN INTO HADES...

There was banging on the door and a screaming that rattled around inside my head—made louder by the fact her name was screaming right back at the Nameless Goddess. How did I allow those mortals to talk me into carrying a goddess's name around in my skull? I stumbled backward, using my wings to wrap up the two assassins and pull them close and maybe protect them if the doors burst open. The thudding and holy swearing continued, but the door held. The goddess was trapped in the other realm inside the Room of Endless Sacrifice and, seemingly, could not enter here.

Then the thudding stopped.

A glorious silence followed. Even the voice in my head slept like an infant.

"Is she gone?" Megan asked.

"I pray to all the deities that she is," Carmen said. "And that she has gone back to whatever realm she crawled out of. Never to return."

"Can we be that lucky?" I unwrapped my wings from

around them, happy to see that neither was harmed. Now that the fight was over, the pain of a broken bone was niggling at me. Well, niggling in an insistently horrible way.

"I am not gone," a surprisingly gentle voice whispered on the other side of the door. "You meatbags should know I am coiling myself."

"That sounds painful," I replied. "Maybe get a goddess physician to look at that."

"I shall strip your wit from your tongue." Again, this came as a gentle whisper under the door. And I felt the sudden fear that she could somehow become smoke and drift through the crack. "But first, I'll lacerate, eviscerate, and obliterate your friend, the one who resides in your heart. Right before your eyes."

She was clearly threatening Carmen. "Over my dead body," I said.

"That is the eventual plan," the goddess whispered. "Say my name and stop me—you will save the friend of your heart. This is your chance. Open the door and say my name."

"Brax." Carmen put her hand on my chest. "You know she is goading you. She can't visit this plane without your help. She wants you to say her name aloud, which would open our world to her."

My mouth had opened of its own accord. Her name was eager to be spoken. But the curious thing is that I don't believe I could have said it, for it was in a language so old I couldn't speak it. Which maybe made us safe. "I won't be speaking it, don't worry."

"She seems to think she will dine on all of us soon," Megan said.

"She is grasping for a way in," Carmen said, though her

voice was ragged. "But the Room of Endless Sacrifice is only a waystation. Here we are safe. I am certain of it."

"You don't sound certain," I pointed out

"Well, she is a goddess," Carmen replied. "And the rules don't always apply to those with power."

"I guess I won't be opening that door," I said to the door. "And I won't say your name. As much as I would like to." Considering she had broken my leg with a snap of her fingers, I had no desire to face her ever again.

The goddess laughed lightly and the fact it was so much more controlled made it even more frightening. "A door closes. Another door opens. There is soon to be a doorway where the child emperor waits for my teeth. I will see you all soon."

The door rattled, and then her laughter retreated.

"Is she gone this time?" Megan pointed her crossbow at the door. "Or was that a feint?"

"The only way to know for certain is to open the door," Carmen said. "And we're not doing that. Let us leave here."

"But what did she say about the boy emperor?" I asked.

"My hope is that was another taunt. I didn't memorize the book of how goddesses cross into our realm. Not that there is one."

"We should go," I said. "We'll check on the boy. I don't like the idea of his only protection being Arbaim."

We walked past the collection of priestesses. They were pale and deathly looking, but not dead, confirmed when Carmen touched one of their necks.

"They live," she said. "Whether their minds will survive that battle is anyone's guess."

"Let ours survive, then," I said, leading them down the hall. The goddess's name continued to turn inside my head.

To distract myself from that particular pain, I asked, "Do we owe Enheduanna for our lives?"

"She certainly was valiant and impressive," Megan replied. "I didn't know priestesses had that in them. I may be a little more careful around them now and less derogatory."

I hobbled up the stairs. "Is something wrong?" Carmen asked. "You seem to limp."

"It's nothing," I said. "A bone broken by a goddess. Barely worth mentioning. Of course, it takes a goddess to break one of my bones. I'll be better by morning." In truth, though we dragons have magnificent healing capabilities, I knew it would not heal easily. Without some sort of intervention, I would need a dragon healer—or any competent healer, for that matter. Carmen gave me her look of *I know better, but I won't say anything for now.*

We went past the golem version of Iktara, who was still reaching for the top of her head, and we slowly worked our way up the stairs. Well, if I must admit it, I was the one working slowly.

I looked up because a familiar figure now stood at the top of the stairs.

Enheduanna.

CHAPTER 44

THE PROBLEM WITH DEAD PRIESTESSES

I nearly tripped over the next step and narrowly missed planting my snout on the hard stone. It took a moment for my eyes to make sense of what I was seeing.

It was a tall female figure in a cowled robe, looking powerful and confident. She raised one hand to point at us, perhaps intending to throw some especially horrible spell or bring the heavens down upon us.

Enheduanna.

Then she let out a little screech, and her eyes grew wide. I assume that was the moment the smoke cleared enough to reveal my true size.

The screech let me know that this wasn't Enheduanna. And her words proved it.

"Who are you?" she asked. "What are you?"

Because she hadn't made a rhyme, I was doubly certain this was another priestess who had the same shape as the high priestess and a similar robe. Enheduanna was dead, and the dead rarely walk again unless spells or demons are involved.

Another priestess joined her at the top of the steps, soon followed by three more. All of them looked very similar to Enheduanna, which made me think they were grown in a boiling, murky pot somewhere in the back of the temple. "Follow me, sisters," the first priestess said. She lurched over to the far side of the wide staircase, and the others followed. I found it impressive that they didn't flee.

"Don't open the door into the room of endless murdering," I said. "Please." I added the please in honour of Enheduanna of the last stand. "Hey, I think I'll call her Enheduanna of the last stand," I added. And maybe I said it too loud, for the priestesses stared at me, either shocked that a dragon could speak or frightened because I had passed along the knowledge that their high priestess was dead. I guess hearing it from a dragon wasn't the best way to learn they no longer had a leader. "She was a brave woman. Write that down in your scripture. She allowed the goddess into her heart." The priestesses each made a warding sign and kept moving along, hugging against the far wall.

"They will close off the Room of Endless Sacrifice," Megan said as we reached the top of the stairs, which made me feel as if I'd summited a mountain.

"How do you know that?" I asked.

"Because I spent several months as a priestess. They were clad in the sacred robes of the Ritual Room."

"Oh," I said. And I briefly—briefly, because I had other important matters on my mind—thought about Megan's life of always pretending to be someone else in order to kill people. It likely affected how she saw the world. But the bigger thoughts took over as we reached the front door. We stopped as if frightened to enter the real world.

To break the spell, I said, "What now? I have this horrid

name rattling around in my head. It's rattling around yours, too, I assume, Carmen."

"I didn't read the name," she said. "Only you have it, Brax."

"But you, Corwin, and Enheduanna came closer to look at the horrid infant."

"That was curiosity. We wanted to see the infant more clearly and to understand the Nameless Goddess more deeply. But I didn't look directly into the infant's eyes. Being that close was nearly enough to destroy me. You are the vessel for her name."

"I'm an important vessel," I corrected. "Handsome, too." I would have patted myself on the back for being so clever, but my foreleg was broken. "Then what now? I mean, I can make plans, for I am an expert planner, but I would like to give you a chance to make some clever plans for all our behalves. This whole carrying a goddess's name around in your head thing was not what I had in mind today." I let out a low exhalation, for I couldn't help saying next, "Have in mind, get it? I have the name, and it is in my mind. It's a clever play on words."

Neither Carmen nor Megan laughed, which was insulting. Mortals!

"Can you fly with that broken leg?" Carmen asked.

"Of course," I replied bravely. Although landing would not be pleasant. Nor taking off. Nor the parts in between. "And my wings work perfectly fine." I unfurled them to check and see if they were both airworthy. Neither had a single new hole. I considered that a minor miracle.

"Is there anyone you can think of you can trust who can read the name from your mind?" Carmen asked. It was perhaps one of the oddest questions I'd ever had.

"Uh, how does this person do this reading?" I scratched at my skull. "Toss my brains around on the floor like pig entrails?"

"No," she said. "It would have to be someone who is close enough to look inside your mind and powerful and knowledgeable enough to read the name in the old tongue and erase it letter by letter. Once we do that, we will prevent the goddess from arriving in this world."

"Looking at the name was enough to nearly break me," I admitted. "But helping someone else destroy it . . . that may be a nasty task."

"But we have to do it. Perhaps Corwin —"

"I don't want him looking in my head with his wizard eye!"

"Well, it will have to be someone like him. Clearly, no one in Akkadium, so we will probably have to travel."

"I will admit that I do not know what you two are talking about," Megan said. "I slept through *What To Do With Powerful Names Stuck Inside My Head* class. All I saw was Brax fall asleep. Then, all three of you woke up. Then a goddess appeared, and things got downright ugly. So, I'm no help with that."

"Can you continue to keep an eye on Nagar?" Carmen asked.

"Yes," Megan replied. "I've been contracted to observe the emperor by someone else." She made a motion, and her robe fell away. She was fully clothed beneath — she was now in plain garb that any worker in the palace could be wearing. A breeze picked up the crimson robe, and it flew away as if it had never been there. It was an impressive move, and I wondered if she'd practised it.

I didn't want her to know that I was impressed, so I asked, "Who contracted you?"

She wagged a finger at me. "Tut-tut, my sharp-toothed and sharp-witted friend, my business is between me and my clients. I'm pleased my work dovetails with helping my friends. But I will be in touch—my plan is to show up when you least expect me."

She lowered her head and cricked her neck so she looked like someone who was used to bowing to power and tied her red hair back with a leather string. Then she took a dye from one of her pockets, and in a moment, her hair was black.

All rather impressive.

Without another word, we stepped into the world. The sun was shining brightly, making my eyes narrow, and I blinked several times. I breathed in and pretended that none of the previous events had happened.

The market was not roiling with business, but since there was no more smoke pouring from the Cowled Goddess's Temple, people had gathered at the bottom of the steps, watching the comings and goings. It aggravated me that the artist was still posed in front of his canvas, splashing, slashing, and smashing his brush against the canvas, clearly to create an image of the temple goddess disgorging a dragon after chewing it up and breaking its leg. "I bet he calls it *Broken Dragon Disgorged From Goddess.*"

Carmen shot me a worried glance. "What are you talking about?"

"Nothing, nothing." I had bigger things to be worried about. There still weren't any Akkadian soldiers waiting for us or even there to express concern about the happenings in the temple, and I wondered what relationship the Cowled

Goddesses' priestess had with the palace. Now that Enheduanna was dead, I guess the gaggle of priestesses would get together in their room of snakes and choose another leader. I might even miss her aggravating and off-metre poems. All the same, I hoped they'd pick a new high priestess who didn't have to spout rhyming lines.

We all seemed a little stunned by the sunlight and the real world before us.

When we were farther out onto the steps and away from the bulk of the temple, we had a clear view of the palace.

It was burning like mad, smoke filling the skies.

"Everything catches on fire in this city!" I said. "And I'm mostly certain that this time, it isn't my fault!"

CHAPTER 45

BAD LUCK RIDES ON MY BACK

I wondered if the painter was capturing me against the backdrop of the palace in flames, subtly implying I was the cause of all the destruction. Clearly, I was the focal point of his artwork and likely would be for the rest of his bitter life. "Once you've painted a dragon," I said, "there is no joy in rendering mere mortals prancing around."

"What in the seven Hades are you talking about?" Megan asked. "Is having that name in your head driving you mad?"

Yes, I thought. Though at this moment, the goddess's name slept. I turned my massive mind back toward the sight of the palace burning.

"Who is burning the palace now?" I asked.

"The Nameless Goddess had mentioned a door closing and another one opening," Carmen said. "And the emperor waiting for her teeth. But I assume she still can't cross over to our world."

"There is a small chance that another kingdom has chosen this time to invade," Megan said. "The best time to strike is when there is a new leader and chaos at the top. It may be a rebellion, though no one has mentioned a heightened level of anger amongst the populace."

"Rebellions! Attacks!" I waved a talon around, even though I had to lean against the temple to do so. "Something nefarious is afoot! Although actually, nefarious suggests it is beneath the surface and sneaky, and this is very much above the ground."

"But from your accounts," Megan said, "the Nameless Goddess can only appear briefly to, say, kill the current emperor's uncle or a few servants, attack Corwin, or even scratch Brax's nose. She can't be doing this."

Was she being sarcastic by including the nose-gouging in her list? Megan's face was as straight as an expert card player's. "It is kind of you to equate my nose with emperors and wizard assassins. You value my snout that highly?"

"It is a valuable snout," she said, again with no apparent sarcasm.

"Enough about your snout, Brax," Carmen said. "One thing is clear: we should investigate."

"If the boy is safe in turn," I countered. "Let the palace burn." Winged gods! I'd made an inadvertent rhyme. I hoped that Enheduanna's spirit wasn't haunting me.

As someone who always wanted to get her way, Carmen was gifted at coming up with additional reasons. "At the very least, your sister, the Queen of Drachia, will want to know who is burning the palace. We could fly very high and look down in order to make a royal report."

"I know my sister is the queen!" I spat. Carmen so often spoke to me as if I were an easily manipulated child. "A distant look at the conflagration—I bet! I know how your tiny brain works: you'll want to save any mortals in distress, and there are always mortals in distress."

"You know we have to go," she insisted. "Why are you arguing?"

Several reasons came to my amazing mind: I didn't like mortals or their battles. There was a fire, so I'd be blamed for it, even if I arrived after it had started. I also had a broken bone in my left foreleg, so any flying would be excruciating, and I didn't want to go through any amount of pain to save Akkadians from a fate they probably deserved. The cherry on top of this cow dung dessert was that a horrible goddess's name was echoing in my head, threatening to melt my brain. It whispered of dark deaths. Instead of bringing any of that up, I said, "I enjoy arguing. But let's go."

"I'll be in touch," Megan said. Without looking back, she descended the steps and began running toward the palace. The way I was feeling, she might beat us there.

"And how is your leg?" Carmen gave my shoulder a gentle nudge. "Tell me the truth, my friend."

"It is still broken. I heal fast, but I'm not a walking miracle." I drew in a breath as I tried to take a step. "Literally."

"Should we hunt down a healer in the market before taking to the air?" This question, coming from Carmen, who was usually the one rushing in to save the innocent, marked a significant compromise. It hinted at how much she cared for me. A tear nearly formed in my mortal eye. "There may be a powerful one in the market—amid all the fakers."

"Healers, pfft!" I waved my good arm. "I'm not missing this fight. Not that I want to join in, but maybe the vizier is on fire right now. I could cheer myself up by memorizing that image. Hop on." I lowered myself to make it easier for her. She climbed on carefully, but even with that slight bit of extra mortal weight, my bones shifted, and a minuscule groan escaped between gritted teeth.

"You are more hurt than you let on," she said.

"That was a hunger pang," I replied. Which wasn't too far from the truth, because under the pain, I did feel a great hunger. Though the idea of even swooping down to eat a goat with this hurt leg made me feel a little sick to the stomach. "Hang on."

It was difficult to get into the air, what with the inability to take a few steps to really launch into the sky. Oh, and all the buildings in the way didn't help. I had to rely on my powerful wings, lifting us up from the steps and shaking every bone in my body. More teeth grinding followed, along with hoping my slight bit of groaning would be mistaken by Carmen as grumbling. Once in the air, my leg hung loosely and ground the broken parts of the bone together, which was a rather horrid feeling. If I lost consciousness now, we'd be a pile on the ground.

But I bravely persevered. Poets will write poems about it. Balladeers will sing epic ballads about my great launch off the temple steps. There might even be a painting titled *The Great Dragon Rises*.

The city skidded by below us as we passed the homes and businesses of the Akkadian citizens. They already had their heads poked out of windows or were gathered on the streets to look toward the fire, though most were wise enough not to be walking toward it. They had seen enough of the struggles of empire and emperors to know getting close to conflict could very well mean death. Several of them looked up at us, amazed by the grandeur of a dragon.

As I winged my way toward the fire, a philosophical

thought came to mind: everything always gets messier. That is how life works. Bad luck seems to follow me around. Or . . .

"Bad luck rides on my back," I said aloud.

"I know you don't mean me," Carmen replied. "But that is a horrible conflagration before us. And we do seem to attract trouble."

"I won't take the blame for that," I said.

We came to the palace proper. It was, very improperly, burning to the ground.

CHAPTER 46

THE STUPID THINGS MORTALS MAKE US DO

Dragons invented the word conflagration. Most of the good words about fires, flames and burning came from us, of course, and conflagration is one of my favourite words of all time. It means a whole bunch of everything is burning.

The Emperor's Palace put the word conflagration to shame. In fact, it also put the words decimation and obliteration and chaos to shame. Green, red, and grey smoke poured out of the many palace windows, along with tongues of brilliant orange flame. None of the magic wards meant to keep large, powerful, winged god-like creatures like me away from the palace were going off. Which meant something larger had already triggered them, or the defensive magic was all being concentrated on whatever was happening around the palace. Each sweep of my wings made the destruction clearer.

Servants were fleeing across the well-manicured ground, dodging between fancy columns, broken statues, and demolished gazebos in the garden.

The reason there weren't any armies at our little dust-up at the cowled temple was they were all in the palace, doing the busy work that soldiers do with swords, bows, and spears. Both Golden Guards and regular Akkadian soldiers fought side by side across the courtyard, near the great white tower, beside the palace, and along the many paths.

It was hard to see exactly what they were fighting because their multitude of enemies moved with such speed. But the blurs looked stinkingly too familiar.

"They are under attack by an army of extremely fast ammits," Carmen said.

"I came to that conclusion several moments ago," I replied as I watched a captain recoil from being struck by ammit spit. The screaming and hallucinogenic-inspired dancing that followed would have been entertaining if a maelstrom of biting and slashing creatures had not suddenly surrounded him. I fully expected Carmen to ask me to rescue the poor soul, but she was looking in the other direction. His comrades were leaping in to help, anyway.

"How could so many of them be inside the city walls?" she asked. "They're almost unbreachable."

"The answer is there." I pointed with my good foreleg at several glowing portals in the ground. Ammits and strange jackal-like creatures were springing forth out of those magical doorways. Jackal men ran on two legs, holding giant tusks that they wielded with great accuracy. The ammit spit flying through the air didn't bother them a wit. The Akkadian soldiers, though, were getting the worst of it.

"We should close those portals," Carmen said.

"No," I replied. "Our mission is not to stop the battle. That is the army's concern. We would have to kill whoever opened the portals to stop this, uh, unholy visitation of spit-mongers. But we are only here to be certain the boy is safe."

"Then we should find him," she replied. "Quickly!"

It was always my task to keep her on task. She wanted to save everything she saw, which was a horrible way to live one's life. She clearly didn't pay enough attention to the heartless-murder classes in her assassin school. I will sheepishly admit that I had the desire to swoop in and take care of a few ammits myself but wasn't certain how that would help the overall battle, and fighting with my body in this shape was foolish. My hate for the creatures shouldn't overtake my logic.

"The inner courtyard is the source of all the smoke," she said.

We soon discovered that is where the largest, most impressive battle was happening. First, we flew high enough to go over the palace, crossing through the thick lines of smoke. It was mind-boggling how things had gone so far downhill in the short time I was inside the temple. My only hope was that the emperor still hid in that safe room deep below the palace.

Having recently visited the Empire Garden, I had fond memories of the food I'd eaten there. I also remembered the wonderful foliage, statues, and fountains.

The Empire Garden was not having a good day today.

No longer was anything green. The Banyan trees from the north were on fire, the grapevines from the south reduced to ashes. And in the middle of it all was a titanic battle.

On one side was Vizier Arbaim, who, to my surprise, wielded his bear-headed sceptre like a magic staff. It glowed with enchanted power as he used a series of light rays to hold back a host of extra-large ammits, Gutian toads, and more of those jackal men.

"He's a wizard!" I said. "No wonder he moves so weirdly."

Arbaim and his enemies looked tiny because rising out of a magic circle was the Nameless Goddess herself—snout and all. Seeing her this close and this large nearly made my heart stop. Her name inside my head screamed a horrible infant scream.

It wanted Mommy!

"She's not real," Carmen said. Which sounded a lot like wishful thinking. "She isn't."

"You mean the real version of her isn't down there, right?" I shouted. "Because we know she is real. I have her name screaming that fact to me!"

"That can't be her real self," Carmen replied. "Because she has no way to get into this world."

When I narrowed my dragon eye, I could see bolts and spears going through her as if she were made of smoke.

"You are correct, Carmen," I said. "She's an imitation of herself." And this realization made me feel a little better.

I circled thrice, searching for the young emperor.

My expert eyes spotted him at the very centre of the conflagration. And, because nothing could be easy in my life, poor little Nagar was dressed in a white robe, trussed up with ropes, and bound to the Sacrificial Stone of Slaughtering Kings.

Almost as if he were about to be sacrificed.

"Uh, I think the goddess might have found a way to get into this world," I said.

CHAPTER 47
WHAT IS IT WITH ALL THE SACRIFICES?

White was the official robe colour for any sacrificial victim in most mortal cultures. The reason was clear—the sick, depraved, horrible humans wanted to ensure that every observer saw exactly how much blood they spilled in honour of their gods and goddesses.

"Someone is trying to sacrifice him!" Carmen shouted because we were circling lower now, and the conflagration and chaos were very loud.

"Just another day at the Akkadian palace," I replied.

The Golden Guards had surrounded the sacrificial stone; their spears pointed out as they fought off the ammits and jackal men. Meanwhile, Creepy Toes, the vizier, shot more powerful beams out of his sceptre. First, he'd melt an ammit; next, bloodlessly skewer several of the jackal men, and occasionally, he'd aim his magic beams at the smoky goddess, which made parts of her vanish.

"Arbaim appears to be protecting the emperor from her and her minions," Carmen said.

"Maybe he's not as horrible as his greasy hair suggests," I said.

"My guess is that this is her final attack on the emperor," Carmen said. "And that somehow, killing him will bring her back to this realm, despite you having her name. We need to find the right angle to join the battle."

She, who didn't have any broken bones, seemed very excited about the idea of attacking. But now that I saw what was happening below, I decided she was correct. "Yes, yes," I said. "Leave it to me. I'll take out a horde of ammits and try to send her back to the shades so she can grumble in the afterworld. No problem."

The goddess's name turned over in my head like a poisonous worm as I said this.

But something else turned, too.

The vizier let a tremendous blast of power out of his sceptre that made his enemies make several steps backward. Then he reached into his robes and pulled out a very long, jagged knife.

"That's a God Bear knife!" Carmen shouted in my ear, nearly deafening me with her following lesson. "Akkadian priests have used them for thousands of years to perform sacrifices to the Bear God. Arbaim is going to sacrifice Nagar!"

I chose not to point out that she was stating the obvious. Nor did I mention that, even while we were in the middle of a battle, she felt the need once again to teach a lesson passed down from her annoying maestrus.

"I don't care if he has a God Bear knife," I shouted. "He's soon not going to have any arms."

I paused briefly to mentally pat myself on the back for that delightful combination of words, and then I dived, making a straight line toward the vizier, who was now raising that blade, its steel catching the few rays of sun penetrating the smoke. Arbaim wouldn't know what hit him.

He swung the blade downward toward the boy emperor.

He never finished that swing. Not because I sent him and his body parts to Hades. No, it was worse. At the last moment of the swing, maybe seeing my awesome reflection in the blade, he glanced in my direction and immediately gestured with his sceptre.

A ward spell, louder than a thousand banshees, exploded beneath me. Like a giant invisible fist, it gave me an uppercut in mid-air, jarring my bones. I spun, wings and legs all madly trying to remember how to fly. Thankfully, Carmen had a good grip. The spell pushed me so high I momentarily thought we might reach the sun, but once out of the garden, we were tossed onto the palace roof. I rolled along the tiles, knocking off the heads of stone gargoyles and jarring parts of my body that did not appreciate being jarred. Carmen managed to keep herself intact by slipping around to my stomach and riding me like a sled.

I let out a horrid and angry roar, and the slightest bit of fire came out of my nostrils. Carmen bounded back onto my back.

"I assume we're returning," she said.

"Like a fireball from Hades," I said. "Hold on."

Her dragon strength gave her a good grip. I spread my wings, caught the wind, and ignored any pains. Instead, I went up with the full intention of coming back down at speed.

"Why did he strike you? And why is he on the side of the demons? He must be possessed!" Carmen said.

"I don't care about his reasons," I said. "The boy is the

only one we've sworn to help. The goddess and that viper of a vizier can battle over the rest of the palace and empire."

"Then we will get the emperor," Carmen said.

"To be clear," I hissed as I began my dive. "I want to crush the vizier and all his internal organs. Like pastry. Or . . . or . . ." Ah, my body was hurting, and my thoughts were only anger. "Or other crushed things."

The Empire Garden was completely obscured by smoke now. The goddess still loomed there, pointing at the vizier, guiding her minions at him.

I followed her gesture and dived straight at him again. I thought Carmen was maybe shouting my name, but anger made my hearing dim. That vizier was going to see red. Or be red. Ha! Even in my fury, I was hilarious.

Like a bolt of handsome lightning, I shot through the smoke. And the winged goddess of luck was on my side. First, the smoke hid me from his sight until I broke through with my talons out and my mouth open, prepared to destroy him and end all of this. I hoped Carmen had her sword out —that would really add to the whole impressive aspect of us emerging right above Arbaim.

But the vizier looked at us with those sneaky eyes, and those feet, those stupid feet that made him float, darted him back several yards. The vizier raised his sceptre.

"Brax," Carmen shouted. "Our promise is to the boy!"

Oh, how I hated having a conscience riding on my back.

And so, I grunted in mid-air, turning so the ward he threw missed me, went past the hairy legs of the goddess, and slammed into the wall. That part of the palace shattered like a plate, bricks and columns crumbling down. He likely had more where that came from.

I turned. Ammit spit hit my back, and something jarred

my leg, but I swept down to the sacrificial stone —a stone that would not get the life of this emperor.

I scooped Nagar up, slamming my foreleg against the stone, which made me scream a most horrid yet royal scream.

And up, up, up I went despite the pain. The goddess herself swung at me, and I wondered if it would hurt, but she was only ashes this time and her fury passed through me.

Then we were out of the palace, the boy in the grip of my one good foreleg, Carmen on my back.

We aimed for the sun.

CHAPTER 48
AN ANNOYING VOICE FROM BEYOND

The emperor, the ruler of all of Akkad, the God Who Walks Among Us, the wearer of the Bear necklace and direct descendant of the Bear God, weighed about as much as a sack of potatoes. He was also so still that I wondered if he was even breathing. We winged over the walls of the palace and farther above Akkadium. I expected one of the magical wards to go off at any moment and swat me to the ground or for a ballista bolt to pierce my lovely scales, though either of those attacks would crush or skewer the emperor, Nagar. Maybe they were holding back.

Or the Nameless Goddess was keeping them busy.

Smoke continued to drift high above the palace. *Good, may it all fall apart*, I thought. This boy could rule from the seaside city of Eladium if he had to. Enough blood had been spilled to keep this city as the jewel of the empire.

"They may not be trying to knock us down because they're worried about hitting him," Carmen said. Again, she was thinking similar thoughts to my own, and I found that oddly comfortable. Yes, she was a mortal, and they had much smaller brains, but this was clearly a sign of my influence. I was making her a better thinker.

"The ammits are likely spitting madly at them all." My breath was getting laboured, my leg vibrated with horrid pain, my brain vibrated with dark whispers, and, well, a long list of other parts hurt.

We were soon past the city walls and over the countryside, where I took a deep gulp of fresh air. There continued to be no signs of any armed mortals or pursuing ammits. It may have been a coincidence or the guiding talons of the winged fates, but we came across the same hill where I'd released the bear and he had thanked me and told me his name, promising me help. I'd settle for a share of his kill that day.

Or had that part been my imagination? Still, the memory of helping him gave me strength. Taking that as a good sign and feeling that Carmen needed a rest, and maybe me a little, I lowered Nagar to the ground and then made to land beside him.

Carmen was off me and at his side before I could even touch a talon to earth. Which was good because she didn't see me collapse onto one side, then quickly push myself up and force a handsome grimace onto my face.

She had her fingers on his neck. "He lives," she said.

"Good, because I am completely against rescuing corpses." I coughed, and a bit of blood came up, which I spat away from her and the boy. Not out of kindness, but so she wouldn't start getting needlessly worried about what was happening to my internal organs.

I shouldn't have worried: her attention was all on the boy. The ward spell had slammed me hard, leaving jagged glass pain tickling my insides. There was always something broken in me, I thought, ever since I was first banished by my father years earlier.

That was a maudlin reflection! I shook my head. Why was I getting so muddled? Was it seeing the boy, an unwanted prince in his own way, below me?

Carmen pressed a hand against his chest, not because his breathing was weak, but for some other assassin reason. "He will not come out of this daze," she said. "I've tried to activate his nerve cluster. But he is in a spell state."

"The vizier cast a spell on him?"

"It is a logical assumption that it was Arbaim who placed him in this partial coma." She sniffed above Nagar's half-open mouth. "Oh, and they dosed him with lotus honey to be certain he'd stay asleep. He won't be explaining anything to us for at least a day." She glanced over at me, and I held myself still to look strong. "So, we have to solve this on our own. From what we were seeing, though it was a bit of a maelstrom of activity, Arbaim was attempting to perform a royal sacrifice. For centuries, as I'm certain you know, they have used that knife and the black stone for the Bear God sacrifices."

"And that sacrificial knife sends these souls to the Bear God? So, the vizier was going to sacrifice Nagar to prevent the goddess from bringing her full self into our world?"

"That's a logical interpretation," she said. Big words always sound funny coming out of mortal mouths. "She may have been trying to prevent the sacrifice. It is possible she needed Nagar to bring herself into this world. I will admit my knowledge of gods returning to this plane is only what I've read in novels."

"Your maestrus did the best with the unworkable clay they had," I said. "But even my great dragon brain is a little confused at what we were witnessing. Only that the boy was in the middle of their conflict. And didn't Arbaim swear to protect the child?"

"He did, yes," she said. "Though he is also sworn to protect the realm and perhaps believed slaying the boy would save the empire—which may be true. I was impressed by the extent of the power the vizier had hidden from us. Maybe from the entire court. I wouldn't have thought he had that much magical ability."

"He has his creepy surprises," I said, glancing back toward Akkad. I expected something dark and horrible to rise from those spires to attack us.

Carmen shook her finger, which meant she'd had a thought or possibly an itch. "We don't know if the Nameless Goddess has another way of succeeding. She certainly wants to gather in this realm as soon as possible because she knows you know her name. She fears you'll destroy it."

"Then how do we do that?" I said. As if it knew what our topic was, the name was now twisting behind my thoughts like a worm. With teeth.

"Have you thought of anyone who could get the name out of your head?" she asked.

"Me?" I gestured innocently. "Did I ask for this name? No, I did not. I had it thrust upon me. And now *I* must figure out how to expel it?"

My leg was numb now and the numbness was working its way up my long, capable neck into my brain, so I no longer wanted to think at all. I needed some pain salve, even though dragons didn't normally use such things because attempting to ease one's pain is a sign of weakness.

"Yes, yes," she said, continuing to hold the boy. Clearly, she wasn't giving my grievance the attention it deserved.

"We have to fly by the seat of our pants, so to speak. Maybe the mage giants can help us."

"They would have too many questions. And I don't trust them seeing inside my head."

"Concentrate, Brax," she said. "Is there anyone else?"

I thought seriously about it. Having someone poke around in my head to read a name did not make me feel comfortable. Who knew what else they would find? And I would likely have to stand still while it was done. A mage dragon might have the knowledge to destroy the name, but I wouldn't trust my sister's mage. They are bound to the throne and might see this goddess's name as a powerful weapon to keep the throne safe. "Maybe we can cut it out of my head," I said, uncertain if I was joking, for the name had become so heavy. "Your sword, Lilith, could do it."

"Don't even jest about that," she said, though she put a hand on her sword pommel. Yeah, that sword would do it on its own. "I could send a sparrow to Maestru Beatrix — she has much more arcane knowledge than I."

"A librarian?" I said. At that point, I searched for something derogatory to say about librarians but failed. Then, a memory came to me of someone who had died and come back again.

Here, Corwin said inside of my head. *Come here. Bring the boy, too.*

Carmen looked at me. "Did my brother talk in your head at the same time as he did in mine?" she asked.

I didn't want to admit it. Because I know what his request, his demand, meant.

"Yes," I said.

I have the answer, Corwin sent. *Come here.*

"Stop telling me what to do," I said, but I don't know if the words made it back to where he was.

"You don't want to go," Carmen said.

"I don't want to travel," I replied. "Not that I have any plan to stay on this hillside until I become a head to mount in the Empire Garden. But I assume we don't have a choice. I guess we're going to see your brother again."

There was a flash above Akkad that shot upwards, then spread in all directions. Ravens made of light flew like comets through the air.

"The vizier is looking for us," she said. "He's won."

A glowing raven shot past us, then circled back, slowed and looked down. "I'm not one to run from ravens," I said. "But we should be leaving. Can he travel?"

"His heart should be strong enough." She knelt on one knee and lifted him easily. The image of her doing that gave me pause. This was who Carmen was . . . always carrying, saving, caring. I was lucky to know her. Despite the pain, I knelt to make her climb onto my back easier. She took her place, holding the boy in her arms, one hand on the horn sticking out of my back; clearly, she was more hurt from our battle than she was letting on.

"Hold on to our little mortal," I commanded in a royal tone. "It will be a rough ride. I guarantee it."

CHAPTER 49

LIFE IS A HORRID, AWFUL CIRCLE...

I had undersold the experience by predicting a "rough" ride.

Instead, it was horrid: the equivalent of a trip through Hades and the burning netherworlds upside down and backwards, with winds battering me the whole way and my wings on fire. And the worst thing of all was that I had an empty stomach.

I don't know what it was like for Carmen and her charge, for I found the less I communicated with her, the better. I needed to concentrate on getting into the powerful airstream in the heights to rattle us at great speed toward an island nation stuffed with wizards and witches.

Speaking of rattling, the broken bone in my leg rattled inside my flesh. And the name, the cursed horrid name, rose higher and screamed louder inside my head—as if the farther we went from the goddess, the more her infant wailed inside me. It was growing tendrils and reaching out into my mind, poking me with sharp baby fingers. Between all that and the bones vibrating in the airstream, I was a wreck.

The one smart thing Corwin had done, perhaps in his whole life, was to guide us toward the quickest route—when we climbed high enough, a glittering line appeared in my mind. Which I followed like it was a glowing goat.

Brax, talk to me, Carmen sent.

I'm flying.

But it's never been this rough.

It's a bad airstream. We'll have to deal with it. Plus, I'm carrying two mortals. And parts of my body and mind feel as if they might fly off. Also, I realized I haven't finished the latest novel about King Croke and I don't want to die before I'm done. Now let me concentrate on us not crashing and burning.

Normally, there is so much speed in the airstream that time spins quickly. But with the name of the goddess burning in my head, time was molasses-slow. Also, though this may have been my imagination, I felt as if the goddess was searching for the name—and if she found me, she could swat poor Brax like a fly out of the heavens, and Carmen and I and the boy emperor would be dead.

It wasn't the most pleasant of feelings.

For the second time in a short period, we were going to Azadiq. All for a boy and a destructive, ego-driven goddess who, since her appearance, seemed to want to destroy me particularly. Though I am aware of how incredibly important I am to history and the well-being of the worlds, it seemed odd that she'd chosen me. Perhaps I should take it as a compliment.

When we reached the end of the glowing line that Corwin had sent, popping out of the airstream, it was all I could do to ignore the jarring of muscle and bones as we slowed down. I barely kept my consciousness in my skull. Everything threatened to go black.

The path had taken us to the very centre of Azadiq.

I got a sickening feeling when I looked down. Below us was a familiar round chasm that descended into darkness — the Gorzed Circle. In the middle of that chasm, which might lead to the very bottom of the world, was a flat, circular floor of rock that appeared to be levitating. There were obelisks around the perimeter of the circle, so it looked a lot like a dinner plate with several rock saltshakers set in place by a giant. In my reading about magic, I had learned that circles were the most powerful symbols in spell casting. This platform was a place where magic could be amplified.

"Why would he bring us to the Gorzed Circle?" Carmen asked.

"I will never try to understand Corwin's mind," I said, staring at the circle where wizards and witches held their monthly meetings to decide what horrible law they would enact or which dark spell to create. "I don't have fond memories of this bad-luck place. Too many wizards and witches have stood on these stones." We had once been set upon by those very wizards and witches in this very place — a long story. Now that I thought about it, I realized that was the first time Blacktooth had attempted to murder me.

My skin tingled, along with my bones, and I wished for numbness. And to be honest, I wanted that numbness inside my head, too — the Gorzed Circle made me feel small. "The circle is empty." I said this with a pinch of relief.

I landed in the centre of the stone platform. Well, landed is a strong word — more like impacted gracefully — but Carmen, clever girl that she was, jumped off and skidded to a stop at the edge of the circle, holding little sleeping Nagar in her arms. She stared down into the abyss, then backed away.

"Ugh," I said. "That will not go down in history as a great landing."

"You should be commended for getting us here in one piece," she replied.

"My back is aching," I replied. "Have you been eating too many desserts? And adding the boy's weight didn't help."

"Well, now you're lashing out. You do that when you're embarrassed."

"No, I do that when I carry too much on my back and a name around in my head that could soon suffocate me." And that was the truth, for the moment I touched the stone, there were whispers in my head as if this place was pulling the goddess's name out of my head. Her name was sending spikes of pain here and there through my thoughts to convince me to leave.

"Where is that brat, Corwin?" I asked.

"You mean, where is his body?" she said. "Corwin himself could be anywhere in the netherworld. The between worlds. The—"

"Yes, yes, I get it. He's floating somewhere." I had little patience concerning netherworlds. They were untrustworthy and sneaky and not real and never enjoyable to visit. Give me sunshine and goats instead of web-laced netherworlds.

"There doesn't seem to be anyone here," she said.

"Then why would he bring us to the circle?" I looked up. "Oh." And, instead of saying anything else, I pointed a talon to the west.

A black shadow in the distance crossed over the horizon

and raced closer; it also crossed over my heart. This was not good news.

For the shadow was made of a thousand wings, and it smelled like death. Yes, the smell preceded the horror that approached. "Blacktooth is coming," I said. "I should have known this would get worse."

CHAPTER 50
A DISTURBING DISPLAY OF POWER

A murder of ravens crossed the distance in about three eye blinks and then circled around in such a mass that they hid whatever they were carrying. Dusty feathers and the occasional small bone drifted down on us in a mockery of a pleasant snowfall. I had a great desire to let out a blast of flame but knew that would be unhelpful to our purpose.

"I hate ravens," I said to Carmen and the sleeping boy. "And I hate dead ravens twice as much."

The ravens, as if hearing this with their dead ears, flew lower, and both Carmen and I stepped back a few steps, clearing out the centre of the Gorzed Circle. Like a slow, evil tornado, they descended, spinning enough to toss up dust and expel more feathers and flakes, which made me cough. The coughing jarred my broken bone, and that jarred my anger.

The ravens lifted slowly, leaving more feathers and flakes to settle on the stone.

Corwin, still frozen and near death, lay on the ground — his pale face made him look like a tiny human-shaped glacier. Well, a colourful glacier since Blacktooth had stayed true to her threat and had him dressed in a jester's outfit. There were even bells on his toes.

Standing over him, grinning blackly, was Blacktooth herself. "You have returned to my realm," she said. "It is sad how much you miss me."

"Like a man misses an excised goitre," I said. This amazingly clever reply got her to frown, which meant she covered up her teeth. That was a blessing. Her presence made my insides ache. And that goddess's name inside my head recoiled at each word she spoke. I seemed to have something in common with the name.

"Well, I fulfilled my task," she said, now addressing Carmen. "I protected your brother by retreating deep into the deepest cave on Azadiq. Sipping teas and memorizing death spells." She looked down at what Carmen was carrying. "Oh, and I see you brought a child with you. Was the dragon hungry?"

"You can go now," I said.

She cannot go. At first, I thought it was Carmen who was speaking inside my head, but it was too masculine.

"Your brother is annoying me with his thoughts again," I said. "Tell him to stop."

"I can hear him, too," Carmen answered. "He sounds closer."

Blacktooth will aid us. And help me come to life.

Blacktooth looked down at Corwin's icy body. "This is one of the most powerful places in all of Ellos," she said. "It is here that we will bring your brother back from his distant journey to the ends of the netherworlds." As if these words were a summons, a sixth creature joined us, its wings spread.

Carnda, the swan, landed at the far end of the circle and nodded in my direction. Clearly, the swan knew whom to respect. "You see," Blacktooth said. "Even his swan, simple as she is, knows what is coming now. As the head of the council of Azadiq, I have the right to awaken the sleeping power here."

"Bringing people back from the nearly dead doesn't seem the kind of thing you'd be good at," I said.

"I may surprise you." With that, she used her staff to gesture toward the heavens very dramatically. Nothing happened. I nearly giggled, but dragons never giggle, so I made a tiny grin and laughed gutturally. She gestured again. Nothing continued to happen. To rub in her failure, I hummed a jaunty tune as if I were finding this all very entertaining. The snarkiness helped to keep my mind off the name now writhing around in my skull.

A white glow flashed a great distance away, then raced across the sky. I thought it might be a burning comet aimed at me, which would not be the first time she'd struck at me from the sky, so I stepped back and stopped humming.

The comet arced down toward us at an incredible speed and, just as incredibly, stopped in mid-air, blowing bright enough to make me partially cover my eyes with a paw.

The glowing thing landed next to Corwin.

It was another raven, but white and pure-looking, its blue, glowing eyes measuring us. Those eyes showed intelligence and emotions I did not expect from any bird, let alone a raven that was connected to Blacktooth. This creature had compassion. Love. Trust. It placed a foot on Corwin's chest and looked over at Blacktooth as if for guidance. She nodded, and the raven opened her mouth and sucked in a breath. At first, I thought it was gathering breath to spray Corwin with some poison, but it soon became clear the white raven was drawing out the cold from within him. The more it breathed in, the more the frost covering him dimmed and melted.

The surrounding stones moaned and leaned in with each breath, too, as if the bird were drawing strength from the Gorzed Circle. The platform we were on trembled, and I remembered we were above a chasm. If the stone fell, well, I might have to choose which of these mortals I'd save.

Clearly, Carmen would be first.

Then, to my surprise, we had another visitor. A white mortal shape stepped out of one obelisk and strode across the platform—a glowing version of Corwin. He stared at his body as if it were something he had not seen for a thousand years. He approached and settled down into his own flesh, becoming one with himself.

Even the name inside me had stilled for a moment as I watched. And then, with one last breath, the raven drew in the last layer of ice covering Corwin's body.

"It's like watching meat thaw," I said. Carmen didn't respond.

Corwin grew pinker as the blood in his veins flowed again.

The white raven tapped on his chest three times and the endlessly suspicious part of my mind wondered if it was about to rip out an organ and fly away, but Corwin's chest expanded and contracted. Pleased with that reaction, the raven then landed on his forehead, and, again fearing the worst, I expected it to peck out his eyes and flee with them like jewels. Yes, I needed to work on my ability to trust . . . but despite being all white and glowy, this thing was a raven. And I was again disappointed. It blew out a breath of whatever it had inside it, and the last of the frost melted from Corwin's face.

The raven then looked up at Blacktooth, and the witch did the oddest thing: she touched her heart and gave the very slightest head bow. The raven nodded to her as if there were some deep bond between them and then flew away.

I will say, and perhaps it's been displayed over the last while, I have cynicism about ravens, but I felt a longing sadness—because I had seen a winged beauty, and now it was gone.

"What was that?" I asked.

"My good self," Blacktooth whispered.

These words hit me hard. I didn't exactly know what she meant but guessed she had put all her goodness into one bird that she kept some distance away from herself and that it had come to do good things because it could. The warps and wefts of the mortal mind were something beyond my ken. Especially the wefts of a witch's mind.

"Thank you for allowing us to see that," Carmen said.

"Yes, thank you," I echoed. And there was no sarcasm in my voice.

Blacktooth, who may have looked like she had an emotion other than anger, opened her mouth to respond. But she was interrupted, for Corwin drew in a deep, rasping breath and opened an eye.

One eye. It was his normal eye—if I can call it that. Not the wizard eye that had begun glowing behind its lid. Its presence reminded me of how he was always competing with his sister. She had a dragon eye, so he went out and got a wizard eye. Which is, as wise people know, nowhere near as valuable as the eye of a dragon.

Corwin looked around.

"The real world," he whispered, barely moving his still blueish lips. "It is so."

"Absolutely," I said.

He opened the eye that a half-dead wizard had given to him as his last act. And that eye looked right through me as if trying to figure out if I existed. Boqin's eye was always a little disconcerting. For was it Corwin looking at me now? Or the wizard spirit of Boqin?

Either way, it made me shudder. Mortals are gross.

Carmen handed Nagar to me. The boy was small enough I could hold him with one leg and rely on the other unbroken ones to keep me standing. She knelt beside her brother, brushed off the last of the snowflakes, and took his hand. "You are alive," she said. "This is the real world. You are on Azadiq in the Gorzed Circle."

"Yes." His voice sounded very distant. "That was too long in the netherworlds. I stood too close to the goddess, and she screamed me a great distance away. Almost into pieces." The rocks were vibrating around us as if happy at his arrival.

"Well, you're back," I said. "And looking . . ." I eyed him up and down. ". . . marginally healthy. Now you can tear this name out of my head, and I will never have to think of it again." The name was beating against my thoughts again like a battering ram. "Let us start at this very moment."

Corwin shook his head slowly. "No. I won't be able to do that. Not ever."

"Then why did you bring us all the way here?" I asked.

"Because," he said, turning to look at me with both his eyes, "Blacktooth will be the one to look inside your mind and destroy the name."

You could nearly hear my jaw drop.

CHAPTER 51

ADD ONE MORE INSANITY TO THE PILE

"You have gone totally insane." I said this with such calmness and sincerity that Corwin had a somewhat surprised look in those glazed, still partially frozen eyes. "You forgot to bring your brain back with you from the netherworlds."

"I, for the very first time, agree with Goat Breath," Blacktooth said. "This witch will not be aiding that dragon in anything other than his winged carcass departing quickly from our lands."

Corwin sighed like a father wearisomely explaining the way of the world to his children. "You both know in your hearts that is not how this will unfold." His confidence was aggravating. "Blacktooth has, over time, seen the glint of goodness in you, Brax."

"There is no goodness," I said. "None. Not even a glint."

"Not true, Brax." Carmen pointed at me like I was a display in a gallery. "You are holding a young man that you have rescued from certain sacrifice. What other dragon would even bother with fighting a congregation of ammits and jackal men to rescue a mortal?"

"I am only saving him to eat later," I said. Saying that made me feel a little nauseous. "Anyway, clearly, me rescuing this youth is a sign of madness, not a sign of goodness."

Corwin slowly raised one of his fingers. "You have seen Blacktooth's soul," Corwin added.

That bird. The mention of it. The beauty of the creature. The idea that something so perfect and . . . and *good* . . . was a part of Blacktooth made me feel unsteady.

"It's not enough to mention whatever goodness we may or may not have." Blacktooth stabbed her staff against the rock, and the sound echoed. "I can sense that . . . that *thing* in his head. Even the Gorzed obelisks fear the latent power he carries. I do not know how he's strong enough to hold that monstrous name—I will admit that I fear it greatly."

Her eyes were steady, but being afraid was a condition most witches or wizards would never admit to. Especially the leader of all Azadiq. I toyed with taunting her by saying she was the worst of all winged creatures: a chicken. But some aspect of her speaking her own truth moved me. And maybe knowing that the perfect white raven was part of her soul added to that feeling. On top of that, she'd said I was strong because I held the name in my head. It was a compliment from a woman who had only sent verbal barbs my way.

I mean, she could have said amazingly strong or impressively strong, but I shouldn't hold that against her.

"The goddess's name is heavy," I admitted. "And it must be removed from my mind and destroyed. Here's the truth of it: we are never meant to be friends, Blacktooth, but allies are often not friends. We both know the destruction that will happen if we allow this goddess to be birthed into our world. All joy and light in our world will be dimmed. She might even eat all the light, for all I know. Would . . ." This was the hardest part to say. "Would you, Blacktooth . . .who can be rather annoying, but who is also the strongest of your kind . . . would you aid me in destroying this name?"

Blacktooth glared silently at me for several moments as if she were searching for a stinging insult. She opened her mouth as if to speak, then clamped those teeth shut, making a snapping sound. She followed by gargling up a rather horrendous collection of phlegm, turning her head, and spitting it an impressive distance. I imagined the globule would burn right through the stone platform.

"What is required of me?" She addressed this question to the annoying wizard assassin in the garish outfit.

"It is nothing and everything," Corwin said in a very vexing manner. If I wasn't holding a mortal child in my only good foreleg, I would have boxed his ears for his typical wizard obfuscation. Couldn't they say anything clearly? "But I will guide you both. Set that child down."

I did so, gently lowering Nagar next to Carmen so she could guard him. She removed her cloak and swaddled the youth as best she could to keep him warm from the cold stone of Gorzed. Nagar stirred slightly but never opened his eyes. If he was lucky, he was dreaming a dream set inside one of the many novels he'd read. Maybe he was chowing down beside Xadia of Fluffle, who lived on an island of sugar canes and chocolate.

Then Corwin stood up with the help of his sister, leaning against her. They looked even more like twins in this position—well, except for how brightly he was dressed. For the first time, Corwin looked down at himself. "Oh," he moaned. "You really dressed me up as a jester."

Blacktooth let out a little chuckle. "The gods of humour told me to. Who am I to disobey them?"

He shuddered, then got control of himself. "Well," he said, "I will set my fear of jesters aside. We need to get to work destroying this name."

The brother and sister, one with a dragon eye, the other with a wizard eye, looked at us.

It was disconcerting.

"Get to it," I said. "I have books to read and goats to eat."

Corwin put one hand on Blacktooth's shoulder—she looked as if she wanted to bite him but held back. He nudged the witch closer to me. I expected her to smell as bad as her birds, but—and this was a shock—she exuded a baked bread smell. Bread was never my favourite food unless it had meat inside that I could rip out, but the smell was soothing. (That said, I'm more of a mutton-smell type of dragon.) And unlike her dreadful birds, she didn't shed.

Soon, we were shoulder to shoulder and not scratching at each other. She leaned on her staff and I, well, did my very best to stand straight and tall on three good legs.

Corwin set a palm on my forehead and the other on Blacktooth's. His hand was cold and clammy and uncomfortable—well, it was always uncomfortable to suffer a mortal's touch.

Well, not all mortals. For Carmen placed a hand on my shoulder, too. "You have this, Brax." I could have hugged her despite all the troublesome situations she got me into. "You have this," she repeated.

"I know," I said. She responded with a chuckle. I nearly

chuckled back because clearly, that reply was pure ego. I did not want to look at that horrible goddess's name and unfold it into this world.

Corwin cleared his throat, closed his mortal eye, and gazed into my eyes with his wizard eye. And somehow, he looked with that same eye at Blacktooth, another magical trick.

His wizard eye flashed.

The shade of the wizard Boqin, who I think may always dwell in Corwin's magic eye, appeared. He who had walked a thousand dead worlds walked around us—building a bridge between me and Blacktooth. Then, as the bridge finished, he vanished.

But the connection he had made did not vanish. For now, I was a part of Blacktooth, and she was a part of me, through that bridge between our minds. I saw inside her the spirit of the white raven, there to support me and strengthen me as we began this horrid task.

"The name," a voice said, and it didn't sound like Corwin, but it came from his mouth. "The two of you must bring forth the name and lift it up, understand it, and then we will destroy it. But do not say it aloud."

And, without asking exactly how any of this would be done, a part of me searched through that section of my mind where the name was hiding. Blacktooth was there beside me, and as if we had, well—and this is a stupid description —mental hands and mental paws, we were both lifting the name up and wiping off the darkness surrounding it. The name was heavy as a mountain, and we strained, but Corwin lent us his own strength.

The name wriggled and fought like a black worm with spikes that threatened to go right through my mind. But together, Blacktooth and I lifted it from where it had driven itself into my head. We looked at it, and the language it was in was now readable by me.

"Read it," Blacktooth said. "Only you are strong enough to read it."

"Yes," Corwin added. "You are the strong one, Brax. You can hold the knowledge in your head. You must make it your name. A name you can understand."

It was a destroyer of worlds, so powerful that when I looked at it, I shuddered. But they had both complimented me, rightfully so. And their belief in my strength strengthened me. This time, the name was not in the ancient tongue of the gods and goddesses but in Old Tongue, a language I had studied in dragon school.

And I read it. It became even more a part of me, a name I now owned because I knew it and could speak it.

"I know her name now," I said, even though it was still wrestling against me. "It's—"

"Don't say it aloud," Corwin hissed. "We need to make it into a form we can destroy."

"Oh, like a vase?" I said. "And smash it on the stone?"

"Something like that," Corwin said. "It will come clear as we work together. We have only surmounted the first step."

Oh, but now that the name was something I could read and say, I wanted to speak it so badly. It, of course, had been designed that way. Her name, which had been written on the infant's forehead, began promising me so much. Images and whispers flew into my head. It told me I could have wings a hundred yards wide, which wouldn't be helpful in a smaller space but would look impressive from a distance. A crown upon my head, and all of Drachia, Ellos, Azadiq, and even Gnagnia at my feet.

Speak my name aloud, the goddess's voice said inside my head. She sounded friendly and caring. *All those treasures will be yours. And all you need to do is speak my name. You will become a god, Brax.*

It was so very tempting. "Not interested," I said. Sadly, if the name had suggested I would live in a world of roasted goats, it would have done better.

"Not interested in what?" Carmen asked.

"Nothing," I said. "Nothing. Ignore me."

"We will destroy it now," Corwin said. Because I knew the name, Blacktooth and her spirit hands and my spirit paws began folding back its layers, making it into a word that could be torn apart. "And she will never be allowed on our world again."

You cannot destroy me, the name hissed inside my head. The spikes coming out into my mind were bringing up memories. I saw my father die again. My brother. Then Carmen appeared, the greatest grief on her face. *I will burn down all you love.*

"This may be late in the stage to ask this," I said, ignoring the screaming voice. "But how do we destroy a goddess's name?" My voice echoed as if it were a hundred leagues away. "It seems a big ask."

"Here in the centre of Azadiq's power," Corwin said, "in the centre of the Gorzed Circle, with all the power of the past wizards and witches buried in those stones, we can render it unspeakable."

"There are wizards and witches in those stones?" I asked. "No wonder I hate this place. Err, I mean, let's get to erasing this name."

"Yes," Blacktooth said. "I don't want to ever be near that name again. Destroy it—send it away, never to be read or remembered."

"Then I will wake the stones." Corwin stepped back, taking his hand from our foreheads, and we were left alone with the name between us, holding it there in the open.

Speak it. Speak it! The name commanded. Blacktooth had her mouth pursed in an angrier look than ever. But she was holding me up now. I bit down on my tongue.

Let me destroy the worlds. It is what I am made for!

Blacktooth and I held the name in place on that bridge between us. But it was taking every part of my will to keep it there.

Corwin sang. It was not in any language I understood, but the surrounding stones vibrated and shook, making a high-pitched note that joined his song. The spirits of the wizards and witches inside the stones were waking up and singing a song so powerful it could make green crops grow or tear down mountains. That singing came toward the name we were holding and, bit by bit, with our guiding help, chipped away at it. It was as if the notes were water flowing around a stone, wearing it to nothing.

The power of the goddess was invested in that name.

No! No! The goddess screamed, and both Blacktooth and I shuddered at her pure strength, but we stood our ground and kept our traps shut.

The song Corwin and the obelisks sang was getting louder. Whether I could hold myself there long enough to hold the name in place was another question. I couldn't do it without Blacktooth.

No! The goddess shouted again, but this time, it was not as loud. As we chipped away at the Nameless Goddess's power, it became clear we were winning. We would wipe it out, and the goddess would never step foot in our world

My leg was burning. I had to be unaware of my body and it was no easy feat to ignore it so that only my spirit, I, Brax, was shining on the name. Destroying it. Wiping it out with Blacktooth, her own brightness shining down, too.

We would win.

Which is when I felt Carmen's hand leave my side, making me a little weaker. Why had she stepped away *now*? Because she no longer held me up, my foreleg hit the stone, and the broken bone jarred me. She let out a distant cry that could have been pain.

And then I got the sense someone else stood next to me. It took enormous concentration to turn my mortal eye toward the small shadow.

Nagar was at my shoulder. The young man smiled, showing both his dimples.

"We're doing this for you," I whispered.

"I know," he said. "Oh, how I know."

He kicked my leg, striking the break in the bone.

I collapsed. The bridge of strength between Blacktooth and me crashed down into a thousand glowing shards. In that moment, I caught a fleeting glance of Carmen on the ground, face down, her own dagger in her back.

Then I hit the hard stone, and the pain of the name was all-consuming.

"Speak the name," Nagar hissed into my ear, his voice powerful. It was more than an emperor's power. As if the goddess herself were lending him power.

Without the bridge to Blacktooth, I was alone. The stones had stopped singing. My tongue burned to say the name. My mind ached to speak it.

Speak my name, the goddess said.

"Speak it," Nagar said, a thousand spikes of pain going through my head.

And I couldn't control myself. I wasn't even me anymore. I wasn't anything at all unless I spoke the name.

So I opened my mouth.

I, Brax, spoke the name of the Nameless Goddess.

CHAPTER 52

SPEAKING THE NAME

Blacktooth let out a shout of betrayal and anger. "You imbecilic dragon!" She clutched her ears and collapsed. Carmen also made a noise, which could have been a cry of pain, but I took heart because this meant she was still alive. Corwin had been knocked several feet by the power of the spoken name and was now lying with one arm dangling over the edge of the chasm.

And Nagar, sweet child-like Nagar, whom I had been protecting all this time, looked down at me with a full, leering grin. I couldn't even raise a paw to knock him away.

"That is the most perfect name I have ever heard," he said. "The name I couldn't find in any books in all the libraries of Akkad. Only you could find the name of the Nameless Goddess, dear dragon. Only you were strong enough to bring it into this world inside that lovely mind of yours." The youth loomed over me as if he had grown. He was the only one who could stand after hearing her name. "I arranged for the goddess to find you. And, eventually, for you to find her."

My tongue still burned from having spoken her name. The funny thing was the name still lingered in my head, too. Speaking it hadn't completely released that abomination. Every thought in my head was surrounded by pain. My bones were vibrating. The name, even here in this circle of powerful magic, began whispering itself over and over as if it were becoming something real—rising and taking solid form. The symbol of a snake encircling a sun burned itself into the platform, the molten rock bubbling. And from that place, purple smoke poured out.

"H—how," I said, "do you have this power?"

"Because I read books," he replied. "I didn't want to live forever in an Eladium hovel, staring out at the world with my half-mad mother. I consumed all the knowledge of the world through books. The greatest of all stories. The deepest of all sciences and magics. I read so much and with such depth that the words became spells themselves. They became me, and I became their master: I am the one who, with a single powerful magical utterance from a hundred leagues away, convinced my uncle to make me his heir. Then I devoured all the spy papers, which led me to the feats of you, Carmen, and Corwin. I suggested the vizier raven a message asking your sister to send you on a delegation to accept me as the inheritor. Akkad's spies saw you coming across the sky, and I sent the Nameless Goddess as ashes to challenge you. All part of my plan to bring her into the world. It was I, Nagar, who led my uncle into the greeting room and wrote the beautiful symbol that summoned the goddess to kill him—"

"Th-that is why he cried out, 'It's . . . it's you . . .' before his death," I whispered.

"Yes, so delicious to have him understand at the last

moment. As delicious as this moment of revelation is with you."

"You and I have different definitions of delicious." It took all my strength to get this comment out. The purple smoke was getting thicker and, though this will sound inadequate, it looked eviller.

"Ha!" The boy lifted a fist. "It was soul-fillingly delicious. The goddesses and her servants killed him and his most loyal Golden Guards. I, in fake fear, covered my eyes as they tore him apart. But I watched the whole show through the cracks. I had her attack Corwin, knowing he would be driven to the spirit world to find her name. Then you would retrieve the name of the goddess, for, despite all my knowledge, I was not strong enough to carry her name to our world."

"Why?" I still could not speak in more than a whisper. "Why did you do all this?" My words were garbled and didn't sound real. They were not the strong words of a dragon.

"Because I will be the emperor who rules all the mortal lands under the power of the Named Goddess," Nagar said. "Finally, all of our world—from Ellos to Azadiq to Drachia to Gnagnia—will properly belong to the Akkad Empire. Dragons, giants, and mortals will all be trodden beneath my feet—Nagar the Great, the God Emperor whom they will worship. That is what I learned from my reading. That is what books have taught me. True and absolute power."

"You chose the wrong sections of the library to visit," another voice said.

It was so ragged it took me a moment to realize Carmen had spoken, and I so hoped this was a clever line before she slid a blade into the boy. Alas, she remained on the ground, though she was now seated and clearly in great pain. She pulled the dagger from her back and dropped the bloodied blade next to her. She then found a powder in one of her many pockets to staunch the wound. She was in no shape to launch an attack. Or even to stand.

"I am the library now," Nagar said. Which might have been the most insane thing he'd said so far.

But I guess with the power behind him, he could be whatever he wanted. Purple smoke continued to hiss up on the stone platform. The goddess was closer to arriving with each moment that passed.

A movement drew my attention, and I squinted one eye to focus. Corwin had dragged himself to lean against an obelisk, perhaps intending to use it to protect himself from what was unfolding. He placed both his hands against it as if he were trying to give the giant rock a hug.

"Why use me?" I asked, even though I knew the answer. It was a good time to provide a distraction.

"Because only your mind would be strong enough. A witch alone? Not enough mental fortitude. A half-dead wizard and his assassin? No. But with Andorium royal dragon blood in your veins—a bloodline that leads back to the dragon gods themselves—you could carry her name. And then unleash it.

"The good news is you will be the first to be consumed. The first sacrifice to the goddess, which will fully release her name unto the world."

"She'll get to lacerate me from liver to limb," I said darkly. "Wonderful."

"Oh, it will be much worse than that," Nagar promised.

"But . . . but you read books," I said as if that was the greatest betrayal of all.

He giggled madly, gesturing around him. "How else would I become the most beloved child of the most powerful of goddesses? How else would I bring her into the world?"

"No goddess will be born today," a voice said. It was hard to turn away from the boy, but I managed it. Corwin was now standing, one hand against an obelisk. The stone glowed an impressive red. The spirit of a wizard was waking inside. The wind had whipped up, making Corwin's assassin cloak flap impressively. If it was a pose, it was a good one.

Another ragged voice spoke. "We will stop her from breathing her first goddess breath." Blacktooth had her hand on another obelisk across the way while raising her staff with her left hand. She stood even straighter. And here I was in the centre of the platform, so small, beside this boy and what was forming in the smoke. The name, which was still partially in my head, echoed with glee.

"We will wake our own gods," Corwin promised. He did sound rather impressive, though I didn't think the wizards or witches worshipped gods. For them, it would be hard to bow down to anything other than their own huge egos. "We will bring forth the greatest powers of the universe."

The stones began singing, a beautiful tone that made my ears ring and caused the name in my head to scream with anger. The sound swept against the unravelling smoke, trying to force it down.

Nagar's chuckle started out deep; then his voice hit the caterwauling, crackling pitch of a mortal's teen years. "You are nothing to the Nameless Goddess."

And this time, he spoke her name as if he'd known it all his life, knocking me down further. One of the nearby obelisks cracked.

Out of the gathering purple smoke came a large hand

with claws on the end of the fingers. It tapped an obelisk, and there was a scream from inside the stone as if someone were dying as it broke apart and fell over the edge of the platform into oblivion.

But the other stones held, and the strange power of the goddess was being pushed back as if all the wizards and witches of Azadiq were leaning against her.

Nagar opened his mouth to say her name again, but Blacktooth gestured with the staff and a wind hit Nagar, drying his throat. "Be silent, child!" she shouted.

Nagar again tried to speak, but nothing came out. Then he coughed. Maybe he'd pass out.

A tentacle sliced out of the purple smoke and struck Blacktooth, breaking her staff and maybe her body, too. And speaking of her body, it was thrown over the edge of the platform. Her neck looked to be at an improper angle.

If I had the strength, I could dive after her into that abyss. But I couldn't even lift a talon.

There was a flash of light as something bright followed her. Before I could figure out what it was, Corwin, who was now standing alone, made to lift his white willow staff. Another tentacle smacked into him, smashing him against the obelisk and knocking him to the ground. There was blood on the stone. He didn't move. In the distance, his swan let out a cry of anger.

"That is all you have?" Nagar said, his voice clear. "You truly are nothing before us."

I tried to find the fire inside me to burn Nagar to ashes. But I had spoken the name, and I was weak. Her name still grew its own tentacles of fear inside my head.

A glint of light—the white raven was coming toward us in the distance. Maybe it would join the fight.

But in that moment, Nagar said, "Enough. This is not where the goddess wants to emerge—not in the middle of a collection of dead wizards and witches embedded in stone. She chooses life where she was meant to be born."

He put his little hand on me and spoke her name again. At that same moment, something stabbed into my under-belly, perhaps the start of that whole liver-to-limb evisceration.

Then, as if the boy were all powerful—which he kind of was—we were no longer there in the darkness of the Gorzed Circle.

No, now a bright sun was shining down, heating my bones.

I was looking up at the sky from the centre of the Empire Garden, the Akkadian palace all around us.

And I was lying on the Sacrificial Stone of Slaughtering Kings.

I don't think it cared that I was only a prince.

CHAPTER 53
FINAL MOMENTS ARE NEVER FUN

Clearly, there had been some cleaning up done, for there were no longer ammits and jackal men running around creating havoc. They had also tidily disposed of any torn-up bodies of mortals or monsters—that's the thing about empires, they do like keeping everything, even battle-fields, nice and neat. Perhaps Vizier Arbaim and the rest of the council were pretending Nagar had not been taken away and wanted the palace to look completely normal for any guests. I assumed the smoky version of the Nameless Goddess who had been hovering over the Empire Garden had vanished the moment we stole away Nagar.

A shame, really. When Nagar was last here, he had only been seconds away from being sent to the shades by Arbaim. It had looked like a horrible and evil act at the time, but now it was clear the vizier had come to the logical conclusion that killing the boy would stop the goddess. Looking back at it now, it seemed I maybe should have asked a few questions before snatching up the young emperor. Oh, well!

The servants who were cleaning up the broken branches and blood were, to put it mildly, in a pantaloon-soaking state of surprise when we appeared. It was as if we had come out of nowhere—a dragon, a boy, and a swirling cloud of purple smoke from which a goddess was about to be born.

Or reborn. I do get these divine appearances confused.

The ugly, black sacrificial stone dug into my side as I sprawled across it, unable to move. It whispered for my blood. It would have to get in line. My stomach still hurt, but I didn't glance down to check the source of the pain, fearing I might see my entrails. Instead, a look around showed me Nagar standing beside the sacrificial stone, proudly presenting his very own creation: the gathering cloud of purple smoke. From this cloud, an occasional snout or tentacle would protrude as if the goddess were trying to figure out which form or part of her body would emerge first into the world.

If I were her, I'd start with a hairy leg. The scariest part of all.

I know; I do go on about them. Having scales, I naturally find hair on legs disturbing.

For my part, huddling against the sacrificial stone was the only reaction I could have. The coldness of that delightful garden feature suggested that, although it had sucked up the blood of many, many sacrifices, it was still quite eager to taste mine. Now that I was touching it, I sensed several types of deep, dark, evil magic inside that rock. But I didn't have the strength to move again, so I did my best to not completely collapse, holding myself steady with my one good foreleg.

I noticed a small etching on the stone, barely visible: a snake encircling the sun. At one time, this stone had belonged to the Nameless Goddess. The emperors likely stole it from her temple millennia ago—they were always borrowing from other religions. She was going to claim it back. Along with everything else.

There came that painful poke in my stomach again. My entrails were rather important to me, so I cricked my neck to look down at my underbelly.

An eyeball was looking back at me.

My eyeball!

Somehow, Carmen had attached herself to my gorgeous stomach when we were back at the Gorzed Circle. She was now holding tight to my scales, clinging like a brilliant parasite, out of Nagar's sight. Another sharp jolt of pain made her method of sticking to me clear—she'd used her dagger to pry one of my scales up enough to grip, hoping it didn't tear right off. She'd manage not to be squished.

I didn't have the strength to send her a *good girl*. But what a clever little assassin! She was a card up my sleeve—a human saying that made little sense as a dragon, but I had always enjoyed it.

Lure him closer, she sent.

"Your goddess is only using you," I said as a hairy arm tested the boundaries of the purple smoke cloud, tapping a statue of an emperor and shattering it. The arm retreated into the smoke.

Nagar continued to grow taller, looking down at me. There was a deeper power filling him, and I will admit to wanting to get away from it. Not that my body was responding to any of my commands at that moment.

Ah, but my mouth, my dear, clever mouth—no one could ever shut *me* up. "She's promised you everything, but goddesses don't share power: she'll tear you into shreds, like one tears up the pages in a book. "

"Don't ever say that!" he hissed.

I, too, was shocked that I could even mention a page in a book being torn. But Carmen had wanted me to get his attention, so I had chosen the most disturbing thing I could imagine. Nagar took a step nearer to look right down at me.

"I am the son of the Nameless Goddess who is now named. Her doorway. Her fulcrum."

"Fulcrum? Soon you'll be *full* of *crummy* bleeding holes," I said with some confidence. "I know how power works."

The smoke was growing higher and getting more solid and smelling like a rotten mountain of lotus flowers. The servants continued to do their best screaming and running. I assumed if one of them had wits about them, they would tell the vizier, and he could rush here to . . . well, to do what, I didn't know. Die valiantly? Endings never were much fun.

Nagar took another step to be right beside me to deliver his look of disdain much more effectively.

"She will not betray me," he said. "Her name is a word, and I am the reader of words."

"I spoke her name first," I said.

"You are not the genesis: it is through my will that she is coming here. I have seen my promised future, dragon." Nagar's skin was growing more tanned like he was becoming the colour of a desert storm. His eyes glowed with a red-coal light. "The power you feel when you read a book, when you ride along with your hero—I will feel that for real. I *am* feeling it."

"I read to escape," I said. "I find the real world far too full of annoying children."

You can strike him at any time, I sent to Carmen. But my

little hanger-on didn't reply. *Carmen? Carmen?* I didn't dare look at her. Maybe she'd passed out.

A crackling thunder came from the purple cloud. It was with some fear that I saw the smoke rising even higher and twisted figures popping out—ammits and jackal men, who immediately began running after the few remaining servants.

"A new army is born, too!" Nagar said, laughing.

"There is far too much birthing going on here," I shouted, but my voice was drowned out by more thunder. The name, which was still there in my head, was vibrating with each crackle and roar. The goddess had nearly arrived.

"You hear her, don't you?" Nagar said. "The goddess whispers to you and to me. I will take the last of her name out of your head. It's time for you to be her first royal sacrifice."

"No, I won't," I said. Admittedly a weak reply, but a part of me would be so pleased to have her name out of my head. No matter what the price.

Please rid the world of him, Carmen, I sent. *Today. Not next week.*

But it wasn't Carmen who struck. An Akkadian spear hit Nagar in the chest and went right through him. He looked down at it, surprised because it was stuck in the stone behind him, the shaft vibrating—clearly a sign that the point was well-forged. Alas, there wasn't any of the stuff coming out from inside him that usually comes out when mortals are pierced clean through by a weapon. He was just incredulous that it had happened.

"She promised me invulnerability," he said. "It is here." He touched the shaft of the spear, and it disintegrated.

Nagar slowly looked toward the highest balcony on the walls of the palace.

There were seven Golden Guards up there, six with spears. One without. Nagar pointed at the spearless guard, and he turned to ashes without even letting out a peep. Then the others drew back their arms to throw their own spears and, with a flick of his fingers, became ash statues holding spears. The wind caught them, and they drifted away.

"I am become a god!" he shouted. I wasn't certain of his grammar but didn't correct it because he let out a mad chuckle that only a god-boy would make.

"Gods often fall," I said, which I thought would be a good time for Carmen to skewer him, but she didn't make a dramatic appearance. Her timing was not impeccable!

Instead, there was other drama, for the large double doors at the opposite end of the courtyard blasted open from inside, and the vizier float-walked his way out with another collection of Golden Guards around him. The few ammits that had been released from the cloud set upon them and were, in a blink, dispatched by the soldiers. All in all, it was a very impressive arrival. I did not think the vizier had that kind of style in him.

He also had a bit of bitterness in him, too, for he ignored Nagar and pointed at me with his staff. "I tried to end this, you foolish dragon," he shouted. He had done something to his voice to make it echo. "But you, in your idiocy, prevented me."

It seemed very much like he was accusing me of perhaps being too rash in stealing Nagar from him.

"Your caterpillar feet crept me out too much to let me trust you," I said.

"Caterpillar feet?" His voice echoed around us. "What in the hallowed Bear God's name are you talking about?"

"Why are you speaking to the dragon as if I don't exist?" Nagar shouted. His glowing eyes had dimmed a little. "I am here, Arbaim. The purest form of power. The beginning of a new age is on the threshold, and I usher it in. This is the place where the Named Goddess will arrive, and the entire world will shudder."

"I don't worship any goddesses," the vizier said. "I am a cub of the God Bear. And the Akkad Empire is his child. Forever."

"You will worship my goddess," Nagar replied. "Believe me, you will."

The vizier said, "Not while I am breathing." He held his staff high, and it sent out a red ray of energy that struck Nagar in the head. The blast turned bright and created so much heat that even my own scales couldn't deflect it. Surely, this had to rid the world of the youth's head!

But, when the light beam had faded, Nagar still stood smiling that annoying, two-dimpled youthful smile. He gestured, and the vizier's staff snapped in two. Then the boy shook his fist, and Arbaim banged against the ground, flew up, knocked over several of the Golden Guards, and, with a final flick of the boy's finger, floated in the air like a puppet.

A sandal had fallen off, and I was disappointed to see that his foot didn't look like a caterpillar.

"You will watch, Vizier Arbaim," Nagar promised. "And she will devour you, and that is how it will be."

"Do you remember Emperor Engon from the tale of Zantch?" I said to Nagar. For now, the ground was cracking, and it was hard to look toward whatever was going to emerge. The goddess's name had become a hot coal in my head. "He never betrayed his country."

"I am giving Akkad the grandest of all destinies. I am the hero here. Engon died in the end."

"He sacrificed his life to save all," I replied.

"He was foolish," he said. "And badly written."

This literary argument had brought him closer again, and Carmen, who had finally crept around the stone, threw herself into the air at the youth. I didn't know what to expect, whether she would go right through him or lop off his head. But she held her sword, Lilith, out front.

It was the oldest sword in all of Ellos. A cursed killer of a sword. It slid into him, and he shouted, arching his back.

"What! What? My invulnerability!" For the blade had emerged from the other side.

Carmen then slammed into him, but it was as if she'd struck a statue, for she bounced off and fell at his feet.

He looked down at the sword stuck in his chest. He grimaced, and I prayed there would be blood coming out.

Instead, laughter came out. The blade was crackling with energy, trying its very best to kill this half-god, its runes on fire. But like he was pulling out a sliver, he pulled out Lilith, and the sword clattered to the stony path.

That was your plan? I sent.

I was hoping it would come to me as I flew through the air.

You failed, I sent. *But I'm still proud of you.*

"You will die, too," Nagar said, pointing at Carmen. "You'll watch your dragon friend be sacrificed, and then you will die." He kicked her so that she landed beside me, seeming to only find the strength to raise her head.

I expected Nagar to make another threat, but he was

silent. A moment later, I saw why: the goddess's head was rising from the purple smoke, and it was very hard to look at. First, the snout came out, mouth open to reveal the glint of her world-eating teeth. Above them, her eyes were as red as a spouting volcano. *This is the name made flesh*, I thought. She had spent thousands of years being ignored and getting angrier. It was all there in her eyes.

"MY CHILD," she said to Nagar, her voice so loud that it shook the ground and threatened to shatter my eardrums and the stone I lay across. Carmen covered her ears. "YOU HAVE FULFILLED YOUR PROMISE. YOU WILL BE REWARDED WITH FULL GLORIES."

Nagar was looking up at his goddess with the purest of pure joy on his face. Tears poured down his cheeks. "The words are coming true," he whispered. "The name is becoming real."

"I AM ALMOST HERE, ALMOST ONE WITH YOUR WORLD. BUT YOU MUST SEND THE VESSEL TO THE SHADES."

Again, her words were so loud it was hard to make sense of them. Something about sending a vessel —a ship? —to the shades? No, that didn't make any sense.

Then Nagar jumped down to the ground and lifted my head. I could barely move or fight back.

"Oh," I whispered. "I am the vessel."

He lifted my head further, revealing my long, slender, handsome neck.

"SEND HIM TO THE SHADES. COMPLETELY RELEASE MY NAME."

And Nagar reached behind him, pulling out the God Bear sacrificial knife. I didn't know the rules of these things because that knife belonged to the bear. But maybe the knife and the sacrificial stone didn't care.

Her name was screaming like a child again in giddy joy, about to be released from my head and to be fully hers.

It was a name. And a name is a word. I have read thousands of them; written, spoken, and even, usually away from prying ears, sung them. I knew the power of words. The power of her name.

Nagar lifted the dreaded knife to send me to the shades.

And two names came to me. The Bear God knife reminded me of another bear I had once met and who had spoken to me. A bear trapped outside a library.

"Ursus in thanks," he had said to me. "Ursus in need. Ursus is here for you when you need. Just call."

And I now knew who Ursus was. That bear had given me a one-time gift. The name of the father of all bears. The father of all Akkad. The God Bear. Ursus.

"Ursus," I said. "Ursus, I am in need."

And, without a moment's hesitation, there was a roar behind me and a bear, white and powerful, rose out of the ground, towering over the boy and the smoke. I was uncertain if he was an apparition or reality, but my eyes believed in him. Perhaps this was my last hallucination.

The bear let out another roar, so loud that the goddess turned her glowing eyes upward to look upon the actual ruler of this land.

And so did little Nagar, the knife becoming loose in his hand.

With no fuss, Ursus attacked the Nameless Goddess. His paw went through her, but she screamed.

"No," Nagar shouted. "No." And I will give the little boy

credit, for he was brave in his religious zeal. He charged at the Bear God with the knife held high.

Ursus swung again, giving out another roar. Arbaim, still hanging in the air in the distance, stared at his god in awe. The goddess tried to staunch the blood that had appeared on her face.

Though it was an impressive battle, it was not for me to watch, for I still had the goddess's name in my head, screaming along with her. Perhaps I grew too enthralled, thinking Ursus would destroy her—this was his land he was fighting for.

But then the boy reached him and raised that knife that had taken the souls and blood of so many kings.

He struck the bear in the leg, for that was as high as he could reach, and the blade sunk into flesh as if Ursus was really there.

And Ursus turned to look at me, let out one more roar, and vanished.

"Ha!" Nagar shouted. "I am become a god killer!"

He had one line he wasn't afraid to use twice. The evil youth looked toward me, the knife in his hand.

"SACRIFICE HIM," his goddess commanded. *"RETURN MY NAME TO ME."*

Nagar began walking in my direction, the knife raised, the gleam of zealotry and power in his eyes.

But she was right! I had her name. And she wanted it.

A calmness came over me. I remembered Enheduanna's wink. Her sacrifice. Her sacrifice would not be for nothing. Then I thought of Blacktooth and how her name no longer made me angry. Not since seeing the white raven that was her good self. The way her name affected me had changed.

And a third name came to me.

Corwin.

Yes, of all people, I thought of him.

Corwin, who had called himself by several names, had taught me something.

A name could be spoken. It was not made of stone. It could be changed—and come to mean something else. Once, Corwin had been the enemy of his sister; now, his name meant her loyal brother.

Names mattered. And their meaning could be changed.

And so I sucked in a breath and said the goddess's name aloud, and my lungs, my lips, my mouth burned.

But I said it again and again, each time thinking that the name meant less. It was smaller. Less frightening. She glared at me with her pitiless eyes as I said her name a third time. It bounced like a fish caught in the open air inside my mind.

I wasn't changing her name for her, for she knew her name. I was changing it for *us* so it no longer inspired awe or fear. It would not bring her power to this land. It was just a name. Like Carmen. Or Nagar. Or . . . even Brax. A name.

I, Brax, believed that.

Each time I spoke, I pictured her getting smaller, and she became smaller, for her name didn't mean as much as it had before. I said it again and again.

"No!" Nagar said.

The goddess let out a scream that tore at my ears. But not as loudly as before.

"No," Nagar said. "No. Stop."

And Nagar leaped with that knife in his hand, his eyes still holding some of that godlike power. His aim and his name were true.

I would die with her name on my lips.

But inches before he hit me, a blur struck him, and he was thrown to the ground to bounce along the greenery and pavement stones.

Carmen had thrown herself into him. He stabbed at her, but she was an assassin, trained by the greatest of maestrus. His blows didn't land. Without any further fuss, she punched him full in the face, and he fell.

Speak her name, Carmen sent. *Speak it until she's nothing.*

I spoke it again.

"No," Nagar whispered from the ground. Belief had given him power. But he no longer believed he was invulnerable, so he wasn't.

The goddess looked at me. She opened her mouth to say something, perhaps a final curse that would haunt me or destroy all of my kin.

But I found the strength to stand, staring right back. Ignoring my leg, hobbled as I was, I went to her.

She was much smaller now. Shorter than me. I stepped on the Nameless Goddess's head, forcing her further and further down into the purple smoke. "There will be no lacerating of livers today," I said. She moved her mouth, but her voice was too tiny to hear.

The goddess sank back into the ground until she was gone, and the smoke dissipated as if she had never been there.

All that remained was the weeping moan of a boy child and the smell of lotus flowers.

I wiped my paw on the ground.

"Good work," I said to Carmen. "Have I ever told you how much I like your name?"

"Don't go getting maudlin on me," she said.

Vizier Arbaim float-walked up to us. A mean-looking Golden Guard had Nagar by the scruff like he'd caught a rascal stealing in the market.

I turned to the vizier. "I am sorry about the mess," I said.

Then I fell to the ground.

CHAPTER 54
AN ENDING OF SORTS

"Braxus Andorium, you have been a hero to the great empire of Akkad," the vizier said. He did not announce this in front of a crowd of adoring Akkadians, nor were there any servants present, though I saw one lurking by the stairwell who may have been Megan. Instead, these words were spoken in the receiving room where the previous emperor had gurgled his last gurgles.

Arbaim's compliment echoed around us. The only other thing in the room was a sack with some object hidden inside. "And you also were a hero, Carmen of the Red Assassins. You have stopped the unholy destruction of our land."

"It was our duty and our pleasure," Carmen said.

"Pleasure is the wrong word," I added, motioning with my wounded foreleg. A female Akkad physician had wrapped a healing poultice around my leg and used a small mending spell, but the bones still ached. "It was more of a horridly unforgettable pain. That said, I accept your accolades as being justly deserved, though I will mention that they seem to come without a glorious feast."

He ignored my culinary comment and said, "The people outside these doors cannot know how close their empire was to being destroyed by the Nameless Goddess. It would shake those citizens and slaves to their very cores. Our next emperor will not delve into the dark arts. Or read fiction."

"It is a wise idea to be a bit choosier about your emperors," I said. "Even the innocent-looking ones can be nasty."

"On that topic, how will you choose your next ruler?" Carmen asked. She always loved discussing politics and political systems.

"There has been some movement for finding the closest relative to our previous emperor, but . . ." He glanced at the no-longer-bloody floor. "That holy line is perhaps not the best stock to select from. With Enheduanna's sacrifice, there are some who whisper about nominating a woman."

"That would be an interesting change," I said. "Enheduanna, in whatever poetic afterlife she inhabits, would glow and spout poetry at learning that."

"We will see," he said. "Others say it should be a vote. Among the viziers and consuls, of course. Not the common citizens."

"That way, you can blame each other when things go wrong," I said.

"These are hard choices," Carmen said. "The Akkadians used to vote for their king in the age of the great flood, which I read of in the annals of—"

"The annals of 'let's not give a lecture,'" I interrupted. "We can hear that later, Carmen. For now, I am certain that the great and wise vizier wants to reward us. Taking every goat in Akkad is far too much, and I don't have enough lifetimes to eat them, but a good portion of your goats. along with a meal, and some of that endless meat, and . . ."

"In the future, there will be a feast of great wonders prepared for you." The vizier smiled, which was an awkward thing for his face to do. "A meal you will be proud of, much better than the emperor's meal. It will take weeks to plan, so an invitation will be sent."

"I await with salivated breath," I said.

"But you are not to leave empty-handed," Arbaim added. "Or with empty paw, so to speak. We have an important gift for you." He went to the wall, picked up the sack, and brought it over.

"A sack?" I said. "What a wonderful surprise. One can never have enough sacks."

Clearly, Vizier Arbaim now knew me well enough to ignore my clever comment. Instead, with a touch of flourish, he pulled a rectangular piece of glory out of the sack: a painting. And what a wonderful painting it was—an expert rendition of me above the city, the temple of the Iktara, the Cowled Goddess, below. The rendering made me look a little heavy but still strong and mighty, with an intelligent gleam in my eyes. Even my mortal one. There was also a small rendering of Carmen in the painting's corner, looking subservient.

"It is wonderful," Carmen said. "It captures your essence, Brax."

"We call it *The Protector of Akkad*," the vizier said. "*And His Rider*," he added as if he'd just thought of it.

I searched for something sarcastic to say, but the artist was talented for a human. And, though this rarely happened, I fell a little in love with a piece of mortal artwork.

"Oh, wrap it up and take it with us," I said, handing it to Carmen in an attempt to hide my joy. "I thank you, and the wall of my room in the royal palace of Drachia thanks you."

Carmen wrapped it carefully and placed it in her haversack. Once that was done, she turned to Arbaim. "What will happen to Nagar?" she asked.

"That boy nearly brought down the empire." Arbaim's voice was icy. "Horses should pull him apart. But that would be messy, and we don't want the world to know of our little trouble with the goddess. We will spread the story that he fell too sick to rule."

"A truthful lie is the best kind," I said.

"Yes, it is. He'll be kept from books. And power. And for the rest of his life, he'll work on a pig farm near the tar pits."

"That sounds fair," Carmen said.

"And he may fall down a well one day," the vizier added. "These things happen." He shrugged. "If you don't mind, I have business to attend to. You may show yourself out." He floated away on his caterpillar feet without a backward glance.

We walked out into the open air. There were soldiers waiting behind the windows in towers, watching us. I wondered if they looked at me with new respect and admiration.

"I think they admire me," I said because most of my thoughts deserve to be said aloud. "Those soldiers in the towers. And the people of Akkad, in general. I can feel it radiating right up to the top of this tower."

"Everyone admires you, Brax," Carmen said. "If not for your kindness, for your brazenness and your ability to be completely humble."

"Well, they'll have to admire me in the air," I said, and she got on my back. I would choose a slow, pleasant route to

Drachia, my sister's queendom. No sense in spraining anything.

Of course, not all plans unfold according to their intended design. We travelled past the city and over a few small hills, and as we reached the small mountains, something horrible appeared.

"Oh, no," I said. "Not again."

It was a spellbird. And if my eyes didn't deceive me, it was familiar—the same one we'd seen earlier in our travels.

The tiny demonic creature landed on my snout before I could snatch it out of the air and swallow it. "Are you Braxus Andorium of Drachia?" she asked.

"You know I am," I said.

"You must reply to the question, dear, semi-intelligent dragon," she said. "Are you Braxus Andorium of Drachia?"

I contemplated flipping my snout and chomping down, but Carmen would decry that move. Her admonishments would make the rest of the trip uncomfortable. "Yes, I am," I sighed.

"Brax," the spellbird said in a raspy, horrid voice. "It will pain you to know that I, Blacktooth, am not dead. My soul-spirit raven saved me, though it cost me one of my lives." The idea that she had more than one life was very unsettling. "And if you mention to anyone that she exists, I will eviscerate you from lamb to liver. That is from the lamb inside your stomach to . . . well, I am certain you understand."

"It is a great threat," I said. And I meant it.

"We have heard, in our own ways, that you and your rider were successful. I would thank you, but it is likely your fault that the Nameless Goddess nearly came to this world, so instead, I will say congratulations on living, too. Someday, perhaps over tea, you could tell me the story."

For reasons I did not fully understand, the idea of having tea with her did not sound so horrible. Was it seeing her white raven? Ah, sometimes even I cannot penetrate the mystery of my amazing mind.

"As your rider, what's her name, is likely wondering about the fate of her brother, well, let me say this." There was a long pause, and the bird nodded several times, to the point I wondered if he was having a fit. Then it dawned on me what she was doing. She was mimicking the witch drinking tea. "Yes, he lives," Blacktooth said. "Not all of us are pleased, but at least I have memories of him in a jester's outfit. Anyway, my tea is cooling, and I have other tasks to do. Goodbye."

"I believe her ending without an insult is a good thing," Carmen said.

"Is there something I can do for you?" the bird asked. "Do you have a reply?"

I was going a little cross-eyed, looking at the bird. "I have no reply."

"Is there something I can do for you?" the bird insisted.

I knew this was part of the spell that motivated it. "Yes, go to her and steal one of her teeth."

"I cannot cause physical harm to other beings, as pleasing as I would be to see Blacktooth with a gap in that smile."

"Well, then, I have no further—"

"Brax," Carmen said. "I have an idea." She then leaned ahead and whispered in my ear.

"I can't do that," I said. "It's—it's very undragonlike."

"Do it. Please."

I rolled my eyes. "Fine. There is something you can do for me. Go to a grove in the warmest part of Ellos, near Avenus. There, you will live your life, eating worms or seeds or mice, whatever it is you do, and thinking your own thoughts for the time of twenty years. You can read books if that is possible. After that, return to me and tell me of your time away from being a servant to messages."

The spellbird's eyes widened. "Truly, you would free me of this slavery for twenty years?"

"It is a command," I said. And somewhere in the tiniest part of the inner chambers of my heart, I felt glad, knowing this was right. "Perhaps by then, this will be a kinder world for spellbirds."

"Thank you, thank you, thank you," she whispered.

"Begone," I said. "Before I change my mind."

And she was gone in an eyeblink.

"You are not all bad, Brax," Carmen said.

"You will tell no one of this. And twenty years from now, when that birdbrain bores me to death with her tales of birdseed, I will remind you it was your fault."

She didn't reply. Instead, she patted my back as if I'd done a good job.

I picked up speed, aiming for Drachia. It was not home, exactly, for I am most at home in the sky when I am with Carmen.

But a rest at the palace would be a wonderful thing. There would be time to read a novel.

I'd be sure to choose one that didn't have any mortals in it.

ABOUT THE AUTHOR

Arthur Slade was raised in the Cypress Hills of southwest Saskatchewan (on a ranch). He wasn't raised by wolves. It was elves. And one grumpy dwarf. He began writing at an early age. It took a few years but he is now the author of more than thirty novels, including *Dust* (which won the Governor General's award), *Dragon Assassin*, and The Hunchback Assignments. He currently lives in the mythical city of Saskatoon and does all of his writing on a treadmill desk while he listens to heavy metal. Really. It's true.

Find him online at arthurslade.com, on Facebook @arthursladefan, or on X @arthurslade.

ABOUT SHADOWPAW PRESS

Shadowpaw Press, a traditional publishing company located in Regina, Saskatchewan, Canada, was founded in 2018 by Edward Willett, an award-winning author of science fiction, fantasy, and non-fiction for readers of all ages. A member of Literary Press Group (Canada) and the Association of Canadian Publishers, Shadowpaw Press publishes an eclectic selection of books, including adult fiction, young adult fiction, children's books, non-fiction, and anthologies.

You can find Shadowpaw Press online at shadowpaw press.com or on Facebook, Instagram, or X @shadowpaw-press. Email: publisher@shadowpawpress.com.

MORE BOOKS FOR YOUNG READERS

Also by Arthur Slade

The Canadian Chills Series

Return of the Grudstone Ghosts

Ghost Hotel

Invasion of the IQ Snatchers

Picture Books

The Wind and Amanda's Cello

by Alison Lohans, illustrated by Sarah Shortliffe

Middle-Grade Books

Stay by Katherine Lawrence

Young Adult Books

The Headmasters by Mark Morton

The Sun Runners by James Bow

The Emir's Falcon by Matt Hughes

Blue Fire by E. C. Blake

The Ghosts of Spiritwood by Martine Noël-Maw

Spirit Singer, From the Street to the Stars,

The Shards of Excalibur Series, *Soulworm*

by Edward Willett

www.ingramcontent.com/pod-product-compliance
Lightning Source LLC
Chambersburg PA
CBHW031841310726

48972CB00005B/1356